D1797769

THE SKULL CHRONICLES
Book IV

KHALIA'S TOMB

D K Henderson

Published by Lyra Publishing, 2016

Lyra Publishing
Wiltshire, England

Cover design by EBook Launch
www.ebooklaunch.com

ISBN 978-0-9934125-2-3

www.dkhenderson.com

This book is dedicated to my family of crystal skulls, who have accompanied me on every step of my journey into their fascinating world

THE SKULL CHRONICLES
Book IV

KHALIA'S TOMB

KHALIA: The Jade Skull

Part I

THE GRAND COUNCIL OF GALACTIC ALLIANCES
(around 100,000 BCE)

1.

'No.' Ashar's powerful utterance echoed through the Council Chamber, cutting across the clamour of voices raised in argument and objection. Immediately the room fell silent. The tall, charismatic First Officer of the Grand Council of Galactic Alliances fixed a steely gaze on his fellow councillor, Ka'ark.

'No.' More quietly this time, the full weight of his authority carried in that one short word. 'It must not be, and it will not be. What you propose contravenes our mandate completely and is in violation of everything this Council stands for.' Although he spoke courteously and respectfully, no-one who listened was in any doubt over his resolve.

Ka'ark returned the stare, his yellow-green snake-like eyes unblinking. He was not in the least intimidated by the Council's elected leader.

'The Plan is not working. They are a primitive and unintelligent species who will never be capable of ruling themselves. Councillor, for their own good, and to ensure their survival, they must be controlled. We must hold them to our will.'

'We must not. That was not what was intended when our ancestors set out on this path so long ago. Humankind must be free to develop as it will. Though primitive now, it holds the potential for greatness and the highest expression of love and compassion. It is our belief, as it was our ancestors that, watched over and guided by the Skulls of Light, it will achieve this potential.'

'You are wrong, Ashar. Humans are violent and warlike. It is their inherent nature. They will not change. If we allow them to advance to the level where they can create the necessary technology, they will one day destroy their world. I do not need to remind you of the devastating consequences of such an eventuality, not only for their own solar system. The energetic fallout will reach far beyond this galaxy to threaten the stability of the entire universe.'

'The Council does not share your fears, Councillor Ka'ark. The Skulls have been in place for eons, and we see clear evidence that the people of Earth have benefitted greatly from their presence. The time is fast approaching when the Skulls will be brought from hiding to live among the humans as friends and allies. Anything less than that would be unacceptable.'

'It would be a grave mistake. If the Skulls are to be brought forth, let it be as gods and masters, feared by the humans. Their power is so great that it will not be difficult. Use them for control. Keep the humans in fear and they will never come to realise their own power and potential. They will never progress to the point where they are able to self-destruct.'

'That is not the purpose of the Skulls nor their nature, as you know well.' Ashar could not prevent anger colouring his words.

'Then take them away. Stop the evolution. Let the humans be governed by higher beings.'

'Evolution can never be halted, only guided. Tell me, Ka'ark, who do you propose would rule the Earth people?'

'We of the De'aku would be willing to take on the role. Earth has an abundance of natural resources. We will employ the humans as our workforce – they are a strong species – and in return we will clothe and feed them and heal their physical bodies when necessary. They will be well cared for.'

'They would be your slaves!' The Council's First Officer slammed his fist onto the table top in a rare display of fury. He fought to regain control of his anger. 'No, Ka'ark, that will never be. Humans are not slaves. They must, and will, remain free to find their own destiny. Yes, they have made mistakes and they will make many more. But they are still as children, and children must be allowed to find their own way. Would you deny that alongside those mistakes they have made great progress? Their consciousness is deepening with every generation that passes and their thirst for knowledge surpasses anything we could have anticipated. Give them time, Councillor. Give them time.'

The other members of the Galactic Council watched this exchange closely. Tension between the factions had been simmering for centuries as those who wished to modify the original agenda looked for an opportunity to overthrow the majority's consensus. It appeared that this conflict was reaching its climax.

'How much more time, Councillor Ashar? For how much longer is the Council prepared to endanger the integrity of the universe? Are you ready to wear the blood of the inhabitants of millions of worlds on your hands?'

The Councillor looked across at his opponent, standing belligerently on the petitioner's dais. Sorrow had replaced his anger.

'It is you who are wrong, my friend. The human essence is love, and that love will prevail. It may be that the people of Earth have a long and difficult road to travel first but in time they will awaken to their true nature.

When they do, the Skulls will be there to guide them forward.'

'We shall see, Councillor, we shall see. We have all seen it happen too many times. Civilisations that cannot or will not evolve beyond the need to destroy themselves and their worlds. And we have seen the consequences – planets blown apart, sending the balance of their solar systems into chaos causing the annihilation of countless other innocent life forms. Are you willing to take that risk?' Scowling, Ka'ark turned on his heels and stalked out of the Council chamber, his few allies following in his wake. Ka'ark's camp was very much a minority amongst the thousand or so Council delegates. Nonetheless, they were strong and zealous; it would be foolish to underestimate them.

Ashar turned to address the chamber. 'My friends, I do not believe we have heard the final word from our brother Councillor Ka'ark and his supporters. We must be vigilant. His race is headstrong and often intransigent, and he will not readily accept defeat. I fear he will attempt to influence others to his point of view. He may also work to actively sabotage this project. This cannot be allowed to happen. The stakes are too high.'

A chorus of assent rippled through the Chamber. Ka'ark was well known for his obstinacy. He would not back down, nor give up without a fight.

Ashar drew his hand through a slender beam of violet light emanating from the console in front of him. All those present turned their attention to the centre of the room where a large three dimensional image was gradually forming. A beautiful blue and green sphere flickered and shimmered in and out of focus until the emerging hologram settled into the perfect representation of planet Earth.

Ashar smiled softly to himself as his gaze rested on the image, which never ceased to move him. A hush had settled over the audience; it always did when this special world came into view. Special because it was by far the most beautiful planet in the entire galaxy. Special because of the virtually infinite variety of plants, insects and other animals that lived on its surface. Special too because of the human life form that was evolving in its unique, oxygen-rich atmosphere.

Tens of millennia earlier, the Council's forefathers had seen the potential of this world and its infant race, and had sworn an oath to protect and nurture it. It was they who had created the Skulls of Light and placed them across her continents. As the current elected First Officer of the Council, it was Ashar's responsibility to ensure that this legacy remained intact and that the original objective was held firm. A fleeting doubt fluttered in his chest. What if Ka'ark was right? What if humankind was incapable of moving beyond its primal destructive instincts and fears into full consciousness? What if it did destroy its unique and exquisite home?

No, he would not give Ka'ark's fear-mongering space in his heart. It would not happen. Not here. Not this time. Earth was different. Earth had everything necessary for humankind to develop to its fullest potential. Few other planets in the entire galaxy were as well equipped to do so. The Elders had chosen carefully, making their decision only after lengthy consideration. They had read the future timeline of the human energy field and seen its potential and its evolution. They had also seen its darkness and dangers. And, in the end, they had seen that the consciousness and energetic influence of the Skulls would mitigate the worst excesses of the dark times and protect both the Earth and her people from the ultimate harm.

GEMMA, 1

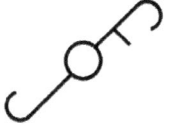

2.

I lay without moving for a few moments, shaking and dripping with sweat. Waiting for my mind to catch up with my body. It was back again. The dream. The one I'd had for the last four nights. Each time it came it was more real, more urgent, yet always the same: Callum, beaten and bloodied, bound to a hard wooden chair in a dirty, empty room.

What was it telling me? Was it a warning of events yet to come, or was he even now a prisoner in some dingy basement? Or was I being shown what had already taken place, and Callum was already dead? Because that was to be the final outcome, I was certain of it.

Why was I being shown this? Joe and I were powerless to help him. We had no idea where he was and we'd had no word from him in over a month. OK, so communication with Callum had always been sporadic, even at the best of times. Since he had gone on the run after being framed for the murder in his hotel room, it had dwindled to practically nothing. Just an occasional cryptic text or email, or a few hurried words on the phone.

He had been lying low, that much he had told us, moving from town to town, never staying in any one place for more than a few days. It wasn't only the police who wanted to find him; Callum was in no doubt that whoever had set him up would be hunting for him too. He was desperately looking for some evidence that would clear his name, and all the while he continued to poke around in a cesspool of secrets that it would perhaps be wiser to leave well alone. Only he wouldn't. He couldn't. His freedom, and more likely than not his life, were at stake. The skulls,

Jack, the murder – it was all tangled up in an impenetrable web. Callum had got too close for comfort and was paying the price. Who was behind it all, and where did the skulls fit in? So many questions, to which I had no answers at all.

I shivered under the cosy warmth of the duvet. Bubbling up in my thoughts, unwelcome and alarming, came Joe's firm conviction that, if Callum ever fell into the clutches of his enemies, sooner or later he would tell them everything they wanted to know. If he hadn't already. Having heard about their previous handiwork in Callum's hotel bedroom it was a terrifying thought, and one on which I couldn't let myself dwell. I had been burgled once. Despite the police view that it was an opportunistic thief targeting an isolated home, I believed differently. As did Joe, which is why I was still sleeping in his friend Duncan's spare room more than a week after the break-in.

I wriggled and fidgeted, still disturbed by the dream that flashed back in random fragments every time I closed my eyes. For heaven's sake! I was so tired. All I wanted was to go back to sleep. Grumpy and restless, I flicked on the light and stared at the patterns the shade threw on to the ceiling. After a long while, my body grew heavy and I started to drift off…

In a flash the entire vision returned in all its original clarity. That was it… That's what was bothering me. Tonight it had been different. Only a little, but enough to have played on my mind. Whereas previously I had been looking down on Callum from high above, as if from the ceiling, tonight I had been standing right in front of him. And he had known I was there. With a monumental effort he had raised his head and looked straight at me, pleading, crushed, his eyes dull and defeated, all hope gone. My eyes filled with tears as I took in his swollen, lacerated face and the utter despair there.

'Help me,' he had whispered, barely able to form the words through his bruised and bleeding lips. 'Help me.'

'Oh Callum.' My heart went out to this broken man, unrecognisable from the confident – no, let's be honest, arrogant – archaeologist who had led his team across the arid deserts of Arizona and who had made love to me on the same warm sands under the stars.

His steel grey gaze locked onto me. 'Help me.'

I sat up, wide awake now, understanding at last. Somehow Callum was reaching out to me, begging for help. Which had to mean he was still alive, if barely. From the state he was in, he wouldn't be for much longer. I – we – had to do something. What though? Neither Joe nor I had any idea at all where he was, which could be anywhere from Aberdeen to Penzance, and that was assuming his kidnappers hadn't smuggled him out of the country. Even so, we had to try. His life depended on it. I fell out of bed, bundled on my dressing gown and ran to Joe's room.

His sleep-heavy voice eventually answered my persistent knocking. 'W…what is it? Whaddya want?'

'Joe, we have to find Callum.'

His tousled head appeared behind the opening door, yawning. 'Gemma, it's three o'clock in the morning. Can't it wait?'

'No. That dream – the one with Callum tied to a chair? I know what it means. He's asking us to help him, Joe.'

He opened the door wider to let me in and clambered back into bed.

'He's in trouble. Real trouble.' I explained the latest developments.

Joe slumped back against his pillows, grumbling. 'Callum, you can be a right royal pain in the arse!' He caught my frown. 'Sorry. I'm not very friendly when I'm woken up in the middle of the night.' He yawned. 'Tell me again.'

I repeated my story. This time he listened properly.

'So Callum is in deep shit and needs our help. Only... what can we do? Where the hell do we even begin to look for him? He could be anywhere. It'll be like looking for the proverbial needle in a haystack.'

'I know.' I slumped down beside him and snuggled against his shoulder, looking for reassurance. I was at a total loss and deeply frustrated.

'Cathy!' The idea came out of the blue, so obvious now that I wondered why we hadn't thought of it before. 'Cathy,' I repeated to Joe's blank expression. 'She's as psychic as it gets. We can ask her to have a go at tuning in to him.'

Joe brightened. 'It's worth a shot. If anyone has a chance of locating him, she does. Where are you going?' I had jumped up and was heading for the door.

'To call her.'

He caught my arm. 'I know this is urgent, Gemma, but it's the middle of the night. Wait until the morning. We're shooting in the dark anyway. A few more hours won't make that much difference.'

He was right, of course. I looked at the clock – three twenty-four. 'I don't know about you but I doubt I'll get any more sleep tonight. I'm going to make some tea. D'you want some?'

So we spent the remaining hours until morning nursing cup after cup of hot tea and speculating wildly over what might have happened to Callum.

3.

By eleven o'clock Joe and I were settled in Cathy's living room with yet more tea.

'Now, tell me what's come up,' she ordered, plonking the biscuit tin down on the side table with a no-nonsense clatter. So I did. Cathy and I have been best friends since we were ten years old and she had been a huge support throughout every twist and turn of this crazy adventure I'd been living over the past couple of years. She was also powerfully psychic with a gift for seeing things that others could not. That's why we were here.

I trusted Cathy implicitly. I had already spoken to her about the recurring Callum dream so I only had to update her on the previous night's developments. It took no more than a couple of minutes. When I finished she sat quietly, tuning in to the bigger scene.

'Have you called on Tim to help?' she asked. Tim was my little obsidian skull.

'I've tried but I don't get anything. I'm not psychic like you, Cathy. I'm given the information I need to know, not what I want. Can you help?'

'Maybe...' Again she took on that faraway look, as if she'd gone off to some distant place leaving her body behind. 'Yes. Yes, I think so. Is Callum still in the UK?'

'As far as we know, yes,' Joe put in. 'He's still wanted by the police so every port and airport will be on high alert for him. He'd find it hard to leave even if he has his passport. Which I don't think he does.'

'Hmmm. Do you have a photo?' I'd forgotten that Cathy had never met Callum.

'I don't. Do you, Joe?'

'No. I can pull one up online though. It might be a bit old, that's all. Can I use your laptop, Cathy? The screen on my phone will be a bit too small to see clearly.'

A couple of minutes later he passed the screen across. 'There. It's not particularly good but that's him. Callum is obsessively camera shy and likes to keep a low profile. He doesn't always succeed. Doing what he does and stirring up controversy the way he does, he can't completely avoid publicity.' We were looking at a group of men and women standing in the artificial pose that is habitual of conference photographs. Callum was in the back row, his features clearly visible over the head of the much shorter woman in front.

'Will that do?' he asked.

Cathy nodded. 'Give me a bit of time.' She concentrated on Callum's photo for a few moments before closing her eyes and relaxing back into the sofa cushions. She was tuning in to Callum's energy.

'OK, I think I've got something, although it's all a bit vague and bitty. I'm picking up dark streets. Meetings in pubs and coffee bars and car parks. A strong feeling I don't want to be seen.' Well, that all made perfect sense. 'It all looks and feels very film noir. The theme to The Third Man is playing in my head.' Cathy's forehead wrinkled into a frown. 'I see Callum. Walking down a street. It's not dark. Late afternoon, I'd say. Two men are coming towards him.' She drew in a sharp breath. 'They're attacking him. One is punching him in the stomach. He's collapsing. They're catching him. Bundling him into a car...No, a van. A white van that's drawn up alongside.'

She opened her eyes, letting out a long, shaky breath. 'That was pretty damn slick and professional. Whoever has Callum knows exactly what they're doing. There were several other people on the street and none of them noticed anything.'

'Can you tell us where he is?' Now that we knew what had happened, Cathy's next challenge would be to locate him. She closed her eyes again.

'I'm in a street of back-to-back terraced houses. Really grotty and run-down.' She let the images form. 'Most of them are empty, boarded up with planks. Some with metal grills and shutters. Lots of graffiti. Abandoned. Desolate.'

'Where is it, Cathy? Can you tell?' My frustration was growing.

'I don't know.' She sounded as exasperated as I felt. 'Wait. There's a street sign. Paradise Terrace.' She snorted derisively. 'Some paradise!' She fell silent. Eventually she opened her eyes again. 'Sorry, Gemma. That's it.'

'Are you sure? You didn't get any clue as to where this Paradise Terrace is?'

'No, nothing. My feeling is that it's an industrial area. Maybe the Midlands, or somewhere further north? Nothing specific though.' She slumped back dejectedly. 'It doesn't help much, does it?'

I glanced across at Joe. What could we do next?

'Wait a minute…' Cathy had jumped to her feet. 'Why didn't I think of it before? What a numpty!'

Joe shrugged, as much at a loss as me.

'Pendulum,' she threw over her shoulder as she dashed out of the door. In no time she was back, dangling a teardrop shaped brass weight on a crimson cord. 'I'll ask the pendulum to show us where he is.'

Cathy curled up in the chair and let the weight hang loosely from her hand. 'Show me *Yes* pendulum, please,' she commanded. Immediately it started to circle clockwise until it was spinning out at a clear angle from the vertical.

'Now show me *No*.' Within a second or two the movement has switched to a very obvious back and forward swing. She asked a couple more simple questions to verify the movements then nodded, satisfied.

'Excellent. It's behaving itself. Grab that Road Atlas off the bookshelf will you Joe, and open it at the page that shows the southern half of the UK?'

With the atlas spread open on the floor Cathy slowly moved the pendulum over every inch of the page. 'Show me where Callum is,' she instructed. Nothing. She turned the page and repeated the procedure with the north of England and Scotland. Still the pendulum resolutely refused to move.

'Is Callum still in the UK?' she asked, puzzled. This time the pendulum circled strongly. That was a Yes. When she held it over the map again, it came quickly to a standstill, hanging inert on its cord.

'Why isn't it working?' I was baffled. I'd seen Cathy use her pendulum plenty of times before, always with astonishingly accurate results.

'I haven't the faintest idea. Usually it's spot on. Whatever the reason, we aren't going to get any answers from it today.' She turned to us crestfallen. 'I'm sorry. I haven't been much help.'

'Are you kidding?' Joe refused to be downhearted. 'Thanks to you we have a street name and at least a rough idea of what the area looks like. That's a huge step forward from where we were two hours ago.' He grimaced. 'We've a lot of hard work ahead of us though.'

'What are you thinking?' He'd lost me completely.

'We search the street indexes of all towns and cities north of – oh, I don't know, Warwick say – for Paradise Terrace. Then we use Google Earth and street view to see if any match what Cathy saw. We can...' Joe halted mid-sentence. He had caught sight of our expressions. 'OK, so it's still a needle in a haystack,' he conceded, 'but it's a much smaller haystack. Look,' he continued, 'Callum's got himself stuck up to his neck in the brown stuff, yes? So we have to help him. If you can come up with a better idea, fine. If not...'

Of course there had to be an easier way. The only drawback was, as Joe had pointed out, we hadn't worked out what it was.

I sighed and stretched. 'We'd better get started then. We could be in for a very long day. Was there anything else at all that could help us, Cathy?'

'No, sorry... Yes.' Memory flooded back. 'The actual house. I saw it. Red brick, dark green front door and window frames, boarded up with what looked like old floorboards.' She squeezed her eyes shut to hold on to the picture. 'And a house number. Seven. I think there was another number in front of it at one time that's fallen off.' She blinked in delight.

'Seven, seventeen, twenty seven, and so on. The haystack has shrunk a little bit more,' Joe grinned.

Cathy walked us to the door. 'I wish I could help but I've got clients booked in for the rest of the day. Let me know if you come up with anything though. I can sneak a look between appointments to see if it matches the image I've seen. I'll be able to help out tomorrow if you need me.'

Walking to the car with Joe my spirits were in my boots. I could tell that behind his confident facade he was feeling much the same. Realistically, our chances of finding Callum in time were slim to none. Nevertheless we had to try, for our sakes as well as his.

24

4.

After more than four straight hours peering at a computer screen, I was losing the will to live. In that time our efforts had revealed nothing other than the knowledge that virtually every town and city in England had at least one Paradise Terrace. None had yet matched Cathy's description. Across the table Joe was looking equally downhearted. Eventually he voiced the doubts that were niggling at both of us.

'We're putting all our trust and energy on to Cathy. I know how good she is but... could she be wrong?'

'I know.' My eyes ached, my back ached, and I was sick to death of Google Earth. 'But you said it yourself, we have to start somewhere, and Cathy is as good a place as any. If anyone can find him remotely, she can. Let's face it, what else have we got to go on? Besides,' I groaned inside as I spoke, 'we still have an awful lot of Paradise Terraces to look at.' So we carried on.

* * * * *

It was no good. My eyes felt like sandpits and I was seeing double. We had been searching for hours. Enough was enough. Stiff and lethargic from sitting for so long, I headed to the kitchen. We needed food. We had been on the trail of Paradise Terrace since two and it was now nearly eight in the evening. So far we had come up with nothing that even remotely matched Cathy's description.

Joe's excited yell brought me running back. 'Got it. I've bloody well found it! Look.'

His screen was filled with the image of a decaying terrace of derelict red brick houses. 'No wonder we couldn't find it. It's Paradise Avenue, not Paradise Terrace. That's where he is.'

'Are you sure?' While the road certainly matched Cathy's description, I wasn't convinced yet. 'There must be hundreds of streets like that. And Cathy was really clear that the street sign said Paradise Terrace.'

'Yes, I know. But look. There.' He tweaked the cursor and a road sign appeared – Paradise Avenue – then disappeared as Joe moved down the street. He stopped in front of one of the houses and zoomed in. 'Take a look at the door.'

Sure enough, a number seven in once-white plastic hung forlornly from its paintwork. To its left, two screw holes marked where another number had once been. My pulse quickened. Had Joe really found where Callum was being held?

'Where is it?'

'Leeds.'

'Leeds? What the hell was Callum looking for in Leeds?'

'Maybe he wasn't. He could have been taken there.' His fingers flew over the keyboard. 'OK. I've just emailed the link to Cathy. Keep everything crossed that she confirms we've found the right place.'

Less than a minute later the phone rang. 'That's it,' Cathy bubbled with excitement. 'That's the house I saw. Heaven knows why I saw Terrace instead of Avenue but that's definitely it. What are you going to do now?'

Joe was already grabbing his car keys.

'We go and look.' I was on his heels. 'I'll call you when we find Callum. Nice work, Cathy.' Her grin of satisfaction reached me through the phone. Deservedly so. She was good, was my friend Cathy.

KHALIA: The Jade Skull

Part II

TAHR

5.

The dull ache in Tahr's back throbbed from his shoulders right down to his hips. He stood up stiffly, slowly straightening his kinked spine, grunting in pleasure as he felt the muscles and ligaments loosen. It had been a good day's work. He had been testing the health of the rich, dark soil and lush crops that filled the shallow bowl of the open valley to the south of the Golden City, and had found it as good as ever. His gaze settled on towering stone walls that at this hour were drenched in the warm, golden glow of the evening sunshine. Affection filled his heart and a contented smile played on his lips. This was his home and he was happy here.

* * * * *

The City was a vast sprawling metropolis of sparkling grey stone, a magnificent man-made jewel in the heart of an ocean of jungle. It was home to over a million men, women and children who, thanks to the wise rule of its successive governing councils, all enjoyed comfortable and contented lives.

It was ancient. Millennia old. None who lived there now knew who had built it or why they had chosen this particular spot; by the time the first ancestors arrived, those original inhabitants had long since departed. The newcomers had stared in awe at its splendour, so far removed from the simple wooden huts and earth track-ways they had left behind, and wandered open-mouthed through the paved streets and elegant architecture of the buildings, constructed of faultlessly carved stone blocks so closely bonded that a hair would not have fitted between the joints. It was like nothing they had encountered before. Many of them believed it must have been transported here from another, far-off world. Supernatural or not, the City soon cast its spell on them, and they stayed.

In the years that followed, as the ancestors explored their new home, it began to share its secrets. While those who had originally built it and lived within its walls had long since gone, their legacy remained. Some was in clear view. More would only be revealed much, much later. At first, stumbling upon the technology the Ancients had left behind, the ancestors came to the conclusion that it to be some form of highly advanced magic. Surely there could be no other explanation for the miracles they found? As time and generations passed, however, and discovery after discovery was made, understanding increased. Resourceful and intelligent minds grew curious. Recognising connections and patterns, these minds sought a more rational, down-to-earth explanation. In tiny steps the ancestors embarked upon the long and painstaking process of unravelling the technology behind the magic.

Such research was a dangerous undertaking for those brave early pioneers. They worked in complete ignorance of the level of power in their hands and of the grave consequences of its misuse. Spontaneous disappearances, serious injuries and frequent deaths were the inevitable result of their inexperienced trial and error approach, which was all they had available. But they were dedicated and tenacious, and with an astonishing degree of determination, perseverance and sheer blind luck, little by little their knowledge expanded.

Over the generations that followed, the ancestors' understanding of this technology reached a point where they were able to harness at least some of its benefits for themselves. They revived and replicated the strange flying platforms that had been discovered at various locations throughout the City. They brought back to life ancient computers that relayed their data through images drawn in the air with multi-coloured light rays. And they created an inexhaustible power supply after deciphering data in the information library that taught them how to harness the sun's energy and convert it into electricity, which they stored in the natural crystal reservoirs that honeycombed the bedrock beneath the City's foundations.

Yet still they knew nothing of the people who had created this technology so long ago. The Ancient Ones remained a mystery. Who were they? Did they hope that others would come and settle here far in the future, and if so, did they deliberately leave their secrets to be found by those who followed? Or was there instead a far more sinister explanation for their disappearance? It was a mystery that remained unsolved.

*   *   *   *   *

At the centre point of the City, a colossal dome of glistening white limestone rose up, dazzling in the sunlight. It was this glowing beacon that had shone out across the landscape, drawing the ancestors irresistibly to the City. And it had been this beacon, gleaming like gold in the rays of the setting sun, that had given the Golden City its name.

From the Dome's summit, a spire of pure gold thrust skyward, piercing a massive, faceted sphere of ice-clear crystal that rotated constantly in the thermal currents spiralling up from below. Above this sphere, at the very pinnacle of the spire, sat a pyramid, also of pure gold. Sunlight poured down the sides of this pyramid, reflected off the sphere's textured surface and spilled down to the ground, bathing the paved avenues and squares in a never-ending, constantly moving kaleidoscope of rainbow colour and light.

Inside the Dome a magnificent entrance hall greeted visitors, from which a maze of passageways ran off into ante-chambers, smaller halls and corridors that wound their way through the huge structure. To those early ancestors the Dome had been the most awe-inspiring as well as the most intimidating building in the entire City, and it was still a place of reverence and hushed voices. In those first days, even half-buried in vegetation, it was immediately obvious to those who stood outside and craned their necks to the sky that this was the most important and sacred of places, a monument unlike any other in the City.

When at last, digging through the debris of thousands of years, they had found their way inside, they had come face to face with wall after wall after wall etched in figures and symbols drawn in glowing, flowing white gold, like liquid light. Over time, a small number of these writings had been deciphered, bringing quantum leaps in the knowledge and understanding of those who studied them, and as a consequence great benefit to the people of the City. Yet the sections decoded formed only a tiny fraction of what was there, most of which remained incomprehensible to even the most intelligent and dedicated of the scholars and researchers. The sequences and structure of symbols and images changed from room to room, as if a complex combination of different languages had been used. Progress was painfully slow, many times grinding to a complete halt for years on end. A few of those involved in the process, more fanciful perhaps than their colleagues, had even suggested that they were only being allowed to decipher certain information, the rest being deliberately withheld from them, although they could not suggest why. And in the bowels of this magnificent edifice they had discovered the greatest treasure of all. It was one that that had remained a closely guarded secret since the time of her discovery for, although Khalia was known to everyone, and was honoured by the people as the goddess protector of the City, her true identity was only ever known by a handful of the most senior members of the High Council. It had always been so.

In the hearts and minds of the City's population, Khalia was a constant, if unseen, protector who bestowed her blessings and grace on the City and its people without limitation. She was Goddess of the Rains, the life source of the land. Without her, the crops would fail, bringing famine and misery. Legend, embellished more with each passing generation, told how Khalia had been the most beautiful of maidens, blessed by the Great Spirit, who lost her beloved betrothed, Kairh, before they had been able to consummate their love. The life-giving rains that poured onto the land each summer were the tears she shed every year on the anniversary of his death, flowing freely until she was spent. Khalia was the gentlest and kindest of goddesses, it was said, whose eternal grief filled her with deep compassion for the humans she watched over, and the enduring desire to see that no-one else should suffer, for no matter what reason, as she had suffered.

6.

Tahr blinked, drawn from his thoughts by the low late afternoon sun which was now burning right into his eyes as it continued its journey down towards the horizon. He turned to look at the City where the first lamps were twinkling in the dusk. Soon it would be ablaze with light. It was time to return home.

The Golden City had been his home for all of his twenty two years. He had never felt a desire to leave, as many of his peers had done, to explore other lands beyond the green ocean of the jungle whose tall leaf-heavy trees grew right up to the field boundaries, surrounding the City on all sides. As a boy he and his friends had played and explored and had adventures within its dark, humid interior, and he still knew it well for perhaps a day's trek in any direction, but beyond its outer fringes the clutching vegetation closed in tightly and travelling any distance through the dense, unbearably stifling and virtually impenetrable undergrowth was not a choice anyone would make willingly.

So there was nowhere to go and no way to get there unless he took one of the flying craft, those floating circular platforms that even at this hour were hovering like a swarm of mosquitos over the rooftops. The smaller of the craft carried people around the City; the streets and avenues below were reserved for those who preferred to travel on foot. Larger platforms, up to fifty paces in diameter and covered with a clear dome, ventured further afield, transporting merchants to trade with other lands and travellers seeking adventure and new horizons. Every visitor to the City arrived on these platforms.

Tahr refused to set foot on them, choosing to keep his feet firmly on the ground. Watching them, suspended in the evening air, grief-filled memories rose up unbidden to tug at his heart. Even now, so many years later, they were achingly clear. Grandmother's face, white and tear-stained, her voice cracking as she told him that there had been an accident. Telling him that the platform carrying his mother and father had crashed to the ground, killing everyone on board. He had been only five years old. He hadn't understood what she was saying. The sob that she had been unable to hold back when she explained that they were dead, and that they would never come home. It was a loss from which he had never fully recovered. 'And I don't think I ever will,' he acknowledged silently as his eyelashes grew moist. 'If it hadn't been for Grandmother…' He no longer saw the City's walls, now falling into shadow as the sun sank lower. The past had reclaimed him.

Grandmother. Despite the painful memories, he smiled fondly. She wasn't his real grandmother; all his real grandparents had died long before his birth. But he had always called her that and he adored her as if she was. Although many, many years older than his parents, she had been their closest and dearest friend and, childless herself, she had loved little Tahr with all her heart. When his mother and father had died, she had taken him in and cared for him as her own, nursing him gently and patiently through his grief, all the while dealing with her own heartbreak. He could not have asked for a better guardian. Over the intervening years the bond between them had forged iron-strong.

A throaty roar pulled his attention back to the fields. The sun was low enough now to caress the horizon and the beasts of the jungle were waking, preparing for their nightly hunt. Very soon they would venture into these fields, prowling their shadow-filled boundaries in search of prey. It was time to go home.

* * * * *

Two imposing towers, four storeys high, flanked the City gates – steadfast sentinels standing watch over their domain. Tahr had always found them a little incongruous. There had never been a threat to the City in all the years his people had lived here, and it was unlikely there ever would be. The City was isolated, self-contained and harmless. Moreover, if an ambitious ruler in some far-off kingdom should by any chance decide he wanted to take the City for himself, the jungle created a natural and extremely effective defensive barrier. Nonetheless, the towers' presence was reassuringly solid and unassailable.

Walking through the streets, his thoughts returned to Grandmother. He adored her. When he was not working in the fields he spent most of his time with her, caring for her needs as lovingly and devotedly as she had once cared for him. She had been an old woman when she had taken him in. Over a decade and a half later, the years had taken their toll. These days she was desperately frail, physically, and becoming more so by the day. Not so her mind, which was still sharper and more agile than that of anyone he knew. In her younger years she had been a highly respected and influential member of the governing council. Even now her tiny bent body carried an authority that defied challenge. Though retired from public office for many years, the council still sought out her opinion on important matters.

Grandmother. He laughed out loud. Despite her advanced years, she was still a force to be reckoned with.

7.

'Tahr? Is that you? You're late. Where have you been?' It worried Tahr to see Grandmother so agitated and anxious. She was by nature a calm, unflappable woman. This wasn't like her at all. What had caused her distress?

'Grandmother? What can I do? What's wrong?' No matter how much he pressed and cajoled, she would not give him a reason. 'Why won't you tell me?'

'Because it is not clear.' The old woman spoke more sharply than she had intended, her words honed by frustration and worry. Her tone softened. 'I cannot speak until I am certain, Tahr. Darkness. That is all I see. Darkness.'

'Grandmother,' he asked gently, 'are you sure your mind isn't playing games?' As her steely gaze fixed on him, he immediately regretted asking. It was a look that still made grown men quake in their shoes.

'My mind is perfectly clear. It is the vision that is uncertain.'

He wondered. After all, she was well into her one hundred and fiftieth year. Could not her mental faculties be fading, just a little? It had happened to too many at a far younger age than she was.

'My mind is clear,' she repeated. Her tone was cold, allowing no argument. She had been reading his thoughts. Well, that ability was obviously still as sharp as ever, he thought, wincing at the reprimand. 'Bring me my supper, if you will, and then leave me. I must consider this more deeply. I must find out.'

Gently her hand settled on his, light as a feather and cool as marble. 'I know you doubt me, Tahr, but I have not lost my reason. Something is wrong and I must find out what it is.' She squeezed his hand; it felt like a butterfly resting on his skin. 'Trust me, Tahr. I am right in this.'

* * * * *

Early the next morning, so early the sun was only just cresting the farthest treetops, Grandmother summoned him to her room with an urgent call.

'There is something we must do. Please, don't refuse or question me. Just do as I ask. We have to go to the Dome, now. Help me.'

Tahr just stood there. What was Grandmother thinking? Why did Grandmother want to go to the Dome today, and so early? This minute, in fact. She hadn't set foot there in a very long time, not since her body had started to fail. What was so special and urgent about today?

'Tahr, please. There is no time to waste and I need you with me. Now, help me.'

'Why are we going to the Dome?'

'I will tell you when we get there. Hurry now.' Although she clearly had a great deal on her mind, she would say no more.

Only a few minutes later Tahr, pushing Grandmother in the cushioned wheeled chair she used whenever she had to walk more than a few short paces, was hurrying down the wide thoroughfare that led to the Dome's main entrance. At this hour the streets were deserted. The majestic form of the Dome rose up ahead, its glistening white limestone standing out in vivid contrast to the clear blue of the morning sky. High above the streets, the crystal sphere was already scattering its rainbow cascade down onto the ground, and the golden pyramid shone like frozen sunshine.

Tahr paused. They had reached the square that lay in front of the Dome. A graceful flight of wide, shallow steps led from the street to the ornate arches of the main entrance.

'Not that way.' A wave of Grandmother's skeletal wrist emphasised her words. 'Go to the right. There's a small wooden door half way along that hardly anyone ever uses. We'll go in that way. I'd prefer it if we aren't seen. I have no desire to get caught up in trite conversation or to answer anyone's curiosity today.'

Stranger and stranger. Why all the secrecy? What was Grandmother up to? With some considerable effort of will, Tahr pushed down his doubts. Although he could see that Grandmother's anxiety was still gnawing at her under the surface, she appeared to have got it under control. Her speech was clear and composed. By contrast, a storm of questions churned and boiled in Tahr's mind. He forced them down to join his doubts. Grandmother would tell him when she was ready and not before. Only then would he discover what was troubling her and why she had brought him here to the Dome this morning.

8.

The door wasn't locked. Of course it wasn't. Grandmother would have known that. With a gentle push it swung open to reveal a gloomy corridor lit only by the sunshine that filtered in through a row of narrow slits set high into the top of each wall. At the far end was another door. This one was sealed tightly shut, with no trace of a handle or a lock.

'What now, Grandm...?' He stopped mid-sentence, staring at the slim wafer of quartz crystal she had produced from beneath the folds of her skirt. It was roughly as long and as wide as his thumb and only a fraction thicker than his fingernail. At its mid-point gleamed a strange symbol, delicately cast out of what looked to be pure gold, bonded to the crystal's surface. Never in his life had he seen anything like it, though the City was filled with symbols. Two straight arms, one of which was crossed by a second smaller line and each of which curved back on itself at the tip, led in opposite directions off a small centre circle. Its delicacy captivated Tahr.

'To the right of the doorway, about half way up,' Grandmother's matter-of-fact tone dragged him from the crystal's spell. 'There's a slight indentation in the wall.' He stared at her in astonishment.

'An advantage of serving on the High Council,' she winked, amused despite her impatience by his bewilderment. 'You get to learn the secrets of the Dome. There are many.'

She fell silent for a moment and when she spoke again sadness weighed heavy in her words. 'Today, before you leave here, I will have revealed to you the greatest of those secrets. It will be one you will wish you had not been shown, given the circumstances.'

Brisk and business like once more, the old woman turned her attention back to the door. 'Feel for the dip with your fingertips. It's easier to feel than see. When you find it, press the key into it.'

There! Tahr's fingers brushed the slightest of irregularities in the otherwise smooth surface. Taking the delicate sliver of crystal he pressed it gently into the depression. For the briefest of moments the quartz glowed golden, and with a soft click the door slid ajar. Another empty corridor stretched out ahead of them. Unlike the first, however, this one was brightly lit by a series of circular lights fixed to the ceiling.

'Quickly now.' Grandmother's impatience was breaking through. 'We have no time to lose.'

Although it had been decades since she had last visited these halls, her memory was faultless. She guided him confidently through a maze of corridors and rooms, up and down, and down, and down again, until they came face to face with a huge archway that towered high above their heads. On either side the wall curved out of sight, the corridor sweeping around to follow it. With a weary wave Grandmother gestured him to stop. They had reached their destination.

He stared, squinted, and peered more closely at the opening. No, he hadn't been mistaken; a curtain of a strange, mist-like substance filled the space. It was opaque, white with an amber tinge, and it swirled slowly like heavy fog in a breeze. Only more substantial. It had a fluid solidity that challenged his senses and made him feel slightly nauseous.

'W – what is it?' Tahr stumbled over his words as he attempted to put his thoughts in order and failed utterly. He had long since lost all sense of direction. He feared he was now losing most of his grip on reality.

Despite her visibly rising tension, Grandmother laughed out loud. 'The technology of the Ancient Ones,' she chuckled. 'Some form of plasma shield. It's quite impressive, isn't it?'

The shifting fog was making him dizzy. He tried to focus elsewhere. 'Where are we?'

'At the very heart of the Dome, far below ground level. The room on the other side of this doorway lies directly beneath the great sphere and golden pyramid. You will see smaller versions of them in the room.'

'We're going in here?'

'Of course we are. Why else would we have come?'

'So how do we get in? Just walk straight through this misty stuff?' He stretched a hand out towards it.

'No!' He froze at the sharp warning. 'Don't touch it. That room has been well protected against curious eyes and uninvited visitors. It looks like it would be easy enough to walk straight through the mist but you can't. If you try it, you will disappear.'

Reality slipped even further away from Tahr. 'Disappear? Where?'

'No-one knows. Those foolish enough to attempt it are never seen again. I've watched it happen.' Her eyes grew damp as she drifted back to her memories.

'It was a long time ago. One of the newest council members didn't believe what he was told. He thought it was simply a rumour put about to stop unauthorised people entering the chamber.' Her voice wobbled for a moment, taut with remembering, and a heavy sigh escaped her slight frame.

'He was young and rash and he thought he knew better, so he decided to prove he was right. I was here. Twelve of us were. We thought it was just empty words. We didn't realise he would be so foolhardy. He had moved before anyone could stop him. Walked through the doorway into that mist and vanished. No sound, nothing. He simply vanished. When the guardian eventually arrived and opened the way for us to enter, the room was empty. The boy had disappeared, and we never found out where.' Her body slumped, weighed down by the reawakened sadness of a distant tragedy.

'It was a long time ago, Tahr, a very long time ago, and yet it haunts me still. While we have learned so many of this City's secrets, that one continues to elude us. Where *did* he go?' Another deep sigh. 'Such a waste of a young life. He would have become a great man.' Teardrops sparkled in Grandmother's age-reddened eyes for just a brief moment. In the next, she had clawed her way out of the grip of her emotions to focus on the task that lay ahead of them.

'Enough of that. Such things do not serve our purpose here. We must hurry, Tahr. We must hurry. There is so little time left.'

'You keep saying that, Grandmother. What do you mean, so little time?'

Grandmother didn't answer. She had struggled to her feet and was leaning against the wall, unsteady but determined. In her hand was a second crystal wafer identical, as far as Tahr could see, to the first. Shakily, she pressed it to the wall. Within seconds the dense amber-tinged mist lightened, glowed brilliantly for an instant, and dissolved completely. Grandmother collapsed back into her chair, her strength spent, indicating with a faint nod that it was safe for them to enter.

9.

It was magnificent. It was beautiful. It was… nothing like he had been expecting. Tahr made it barely three paces into the room before he came to a standstill, gaping.

Beneath his feet, a floor of polished, inky black marble studded with glittering gemstones mirrored the night sky. In them he recognised the patterns he saw in the heavens after the sun went down: constellations and galaxies, planets and moons. Glassy translucent panels in every shade of amethyst from the palest mauve to the deepest purple clad the curved walls. And in the centre, high above his head, hung a silvery crystalline sphere, identical in all but size to the one that sat at the apex of the Dome. This one was a lot smaller, though even through his stunned bewilderment Tahr estimated it would take at least two men to encircle it with their outstretched arms. As far above again, a golden pyramid, also much smaller, hung directly in the path of an intense beam of light that streamed down through the ceiling. The light hit the pyramid's tip and poured down its sides onto the sphere, which in turn sent out countless splinters of light that filled the chamber.

'Sunlight,' Grandmother told him, seeing his puzzlement. 'A highly reflective conduit that reaches to the roof of the Dome, coming out directly beneath the sphere. It collects the sunlight and funnels it down to this room. But come over here. There is no time to marvel, though by the heavens it is worthy of marvel. This is where our purpose lies.'

She pointed to a clear, glass-like column that rose up in the centre of the floor directly beneath the spheres. It had six even, flat sides and stood as high as his waist. So many other incredible sights had captured his attention that Tahr had not noticed it until now. Curious, he drew closer and bent to see more clearly.

What the...? He jerked back with surprise and considerable alarm. A face was staring back at him. Only... it wasn't a face. It was a death's head – a skull, carved from some kind of deep green stone. Cold fingers of unease traced up and down his spine – not from the object itself, though in the moving light of the sphere it looked eerie enough. No, this was something more. While common sense was telling him this was merely cold, inert stone, he couldn't shake off the stubborn impression that it was alive. Watching him. Weighing him up.

He tore his gaze away. Grandmother was speaking again. If she had noticed his discomfort, she was ignoring it.

'This is Khalia, sacred goddess and guardian of our City.'

Khalia? It couldn't be. Grandmother was wrong. Khalia was a beautiful young goddess in flowing blue robes. Not this...thing.

'This is Khalia.' Grandmother was firm. 'She was found by the first ancestors in the exact place you see her now and kept here in safety all this time, holding our City in peace and prosperity, She is the reason I brought you here today.' Her hand was cold and trembling as she took his. Tears glistened on her lashes.

'Look on her, Tahr, and see her goodness. Look past her form to the spirit within. Then you will know why I ask you to carry out my wishes.' She sank back into her chair, exhausted by her emotions.

'Death comes upon us. Soon. Very soon. Perhaps even today. No-one in the City will survive. You must take Khalia and leave. Now. Save her, Tahr. Take her to safety. She must not be destroyed. The future of the world depends on it.'

'Grandmother, you are mistaken. We are safe here. Nothing threatens our home.' Yet he could not deny the urgency and bitter sorrow in the old woman's plea.

'I wish I was, my beloved grandson, but I am not. Death comes, and it will not be stopped.'

Still he hesitated. How could such a catastrophe come upon them? The City had no enemies, and the ground beneath their feet had never once posed a threat to their safety.

'Death, Tahr,' his grandmother repeated. 'I have seen it. It will come. Fire and destruction pouring from the skies. Do not doubt me, my child. I have seen it, I tell you. It is upon us.'

'Then we should warn the people...' If Grandmother *was* right, surely she should let the Council know so that it could take action?

'They would not listen. Why would they when even you doubt me?' She shook off his denial. 'I see it in your eyes. You don't believe me. You are worried that your Grandmother is losing her reason.' She gripped his hand, desperation giving her strength. 'I am not.'

She bowed her head sorrowfully. 'They would not listen,' she repeated. 'There is nothing I can do to save the City or its people. But I can save Khalia, and I can save you. Because, even though you believe I have gone mad, you will do as I ask, if only to humour me.'

She slid open the three front panels of the plinth. 'Give her to me, Tahr.'

He lifted the skull and placed it into Grandmother's lap. With hands trembling from anguish more than age, she wrapped it in her shawl and handed it back to him, weeping as she said farewell to the secret she had kept for so long.

He held the skull as cautiously as if it were a cobra about to strike. This was Khalia? His mind was in a whirl. So much had happened in such a short time. Only yesterday he had been working contentedly in the fields and now, just a few short hours later…

'Take Khalia and go. Take her and run as fast and as far as you can. I would entrust her to no-one else. Do as I say, Tahr, please. Go. Now.'

In the midst of the maelstrom of his confusion and doubts, Tahr was still certain that Grandmother was wrong. What she had told him was simply not possible. Nevertheless, she had been right on one matter – he would do it because she had asked him to, as she had known he would. He had seen the fear real and raw in her eyes, the tension in her fragile bones so taut he feared they would snap, and she was becoming more agitated with each moment that passed. Yes, he would do as she asked. He would take Khalia and leave the City. And in a few days' time, when nothing untoward had occurred and Grandmother had accepted she had been mistaken, he would come home. Together they would return Khalia to the Dome and place her back in the crystal column.

'Go!' She had slapped him as hard as she was able on his shoulder. 'What are you waiting for?'

'What about you? I need to take you home.'

'You need to leave. Didn't you understand a word I said? There is no time. I will stay here until it is over.

There is nothing more I need to do. Nowhere else I need to be. Now, for the love of Khalia, GO!'

He bent and kissed the agitated old lady. 'I will do as you ask, Grandmother. And when I return, you will see that your fears were for nothing.'

She looked at him sadly, her thin, crooked fingers gentle on his cheek. 'You have been the greatest blessing in my life, and I leave it content that it was so. Goodbye, Tahr.'

He turned and retraced his steps out into the sunlit streets. In a very short time, he was certain, he would return and Grandmother would see that her fears had been unfounded.

10.

Tahr picked his path with care. The City with its sunlit streets and carefully tended fields was behind him, and he was bathed in the dim otherworldly green light of the jungle. It was difficult to find a way through the tangled web of creepers, vines and snagging undergrowth that crisscrossed between the trees like gigantic spider webs waiting to capture an unwary wanderer in their snare. Under his feet the ground was uneven and treacherous, littered with fallen branches and pitted with animal burrows that would punish any careless step.

He was in no rush; he had no wish to twist an ankle, or worse. Nor could he see a reason to hurry. Despite the very real fear that Grandmother had shown, he could not accept that there was any reason for her fears. As he had walked through the streets from the Dome, the City had been going about its business as usual, the cheerful atmosphere mirroring that of the weather that blessed them. Dear Grandmother. No disaster would come upon them. She was growing fanciful in her old age. Seeing ghosts in the shadows. Nevertheless he had hated seeing her in such distress. For that reason, and that reason only, he had agreed to do what she asked of him. He would not stay away for long.

Tahr was paying little attention to where he was heading. He knew this part of the jungle well and had no worry that he would get lost. He would find a pleasant spot to camp out – perhaps on one of the rocky ledges below the falls – and spend a lazy day or two swimming in the river and dozing in the sunshine. It would be an enjoyable interlude in the easy, familiar rhythm of his life. So why then was a nagging anxiety twisting in his gut? Slight at first, so faint it taken a while to recognise that it was there, it had grown stronger as the day passed. He was doing his best to ignore the feeling, but it would not be silenced.

'Thank you, Grandmother,' he muttered. 'Now you've got me seeing ghosts too.'

He had just crested a bare rocky ridge from where he could look back over the dark green canopy to the City. The Dome was sparkling like a jewel in the sun's low rays and his home looked tranquil and lovely in the evening light. Everything was as it always was.

'You see,' he spoke aloud, 'there is no cause for fear, Grandmother.'

Barely were the words out of Tahr's mouth than hell descended on his world. The ground buckled and shook beneath him and a booming crash, a hundred times louder than thunder, threw him to his knees. . He couldn't breathe. Panic, unbearable, heart-strangling panic, gripped him. His gaze was still locked onto the panorama stretching out in front of him – first the treetops and beyond, the glittering walls and sun-gilded rooftops of the City. Moments later he was knocked flat by a blast of air that hit him with all the force of a charging elephant, sucking the air from his lungs.

Fighting to draw breath, he eventually struggled to his knees and looked back towards the City, from where the blast had come. No! No, it couldn't be! Above the distant rooftops, a plume of fiery smoke was rising up high into the sky, which had turned a ghastly shade of red. Flashes sparked and blinded as the sun and fire caught on unfamiliar craft that swooped and dove out of the sky like giant winged hawks, flames spitting from their wings.

Another thunderclap. And another. Flames and smoke belched and bellowed across the skyline.

Lost in the horror unfolding before him Tahr stood and stared, unable to move. This wasn't happening. It couldn't be. It wasn't real; it was nothing but a nightmare. He would wake up soon. Except – grim comprehension slowly penetrated his numbed senses – this wasn't a nightmare. It *was* real. The realisation jerked him out of his trance. With no idea of what was happening or why, only one thought filled his head. His City, his home, was being destroyed. He had to go back. He had to help.

'Run, Tahr. Run. Take Khalia to safety.' Grandmother's voice echoed through his mind.

Grandmother? Tahr's eyes filled with tears. What had happened to Grandmother? Why could he hear her? He had to go back. He had to find her.

'Don't worry about me.' It was as if she had heard his thoughts. 'I am safe. Nothing can harm me now. But you must go, or you will die. Go, Tahr. Now. Run. There is no time to lose.' Always the same phrase: *There is no time to lose.*

'Go!'

Still he hesitated, unwilling to leave his home to its fate.

'GO!'

At last he obeyed. With a final aching glance at the City, he blundered down the far side of the ridge and back into the trees. He was running as fast as he could now, stumbling and tripping, no longer caring about the invisible obstacles beneath his feet. All his focus was on obeying Grandmother. He had to get as far from the City as he could, as quickly as he could. Her warning, so recently merely empty words to him, had suddenly acquired an urgent and terrifying truth.

His lungs were ready to burst. With every step it was harder and harder to breathe, as if the oxygen was being sucked out of the thick, heavy air. The constant roar behind him swallowed up every other sound.

* * * * *

At the top of the falls Tahr slowed, panting, his chest heaving and his legs burning with the effort of his flight up the steep cliffs. This morning he had intended to come here to sleep and swim and while away the time until he returned to the City. That all now seemed a very long time ago.

Needing to catch his breath and rest his aching legs, he turned and looked back the way he had come. Listening. Something was different. What was it? It took a moment or two to come to him, the blood thudding in his temples masking the change. Of course. That was it. The thunder had stopped. The world around him had fallen eerily quiet and still. The birds were silent. The insects were silent. In the undergrowth, only a short time ago so busy and filled with life, not one creature scurried or scampered or slithered. Tahr stood frozen with foreboding. It was an ominous menacing silence. The world was waiting, holding its breath. For what?

A thousand thunderbolts assaulted him, their crashing roar blasting his eardrums and hurling him to the ground once more. He clutched at his head in pain, blood trickling from his shredded eardrums and down his neck. Through it all, Tahr saw a sight so majestic, so appalling, so monstrous, that nothing else registered in his mind. High above the far-off, ravaged City, an enormous mushroom of smoke and flame was rolling up into the sky. Higher and higher, expanding even as it rolled back in on itself. Rising up into the dark storm clouds that had appeared out of nowhere to blanket the sky.

It was the end of the world. He had to get out of here, away from the demons that were devouring everything he had ever known. Filled with blind panic, Tahr fled. He was deaf from the blast that had shattered his eardrums, hearing only a high-pitched whine that emphasised the rhythmic thumping of the blood in his temples. Stumbling, tripping, running as fast as he could through the unforgiving vegetation and uneven ground of the jungle. Somehow, he still had the skull clasped in his hands.

All manner of birds and beasts raced along beside him, terror driving them to escape the hell had unfolded behind them and the worse one that their instincts were telling them would follow. Surefooted, fleet of wing and paw, they overtook him in crowds and disappeared into the gloom.

Tahr's blood ran cold. Through his deafness, he became aware of a dull roar, chilling in its steady, relentless menace. The air rushed past him, hot and getting hotter. It was no use. He could not outrun this. It would catch him and he would die here. He would fail Grandmother and betray her trust in him.

'I'm sorry, Grandmother, I'm sorry,' he gasped, bitter tears hot on his cheeks. He should have believed her.

11.

Tahr's foot caught in the burrow of some small rodent and he tripped, his free arm flailing, grabbing at anything that might break his fall. There was nothing. He tumbled heavily off the river bank into the shallow water and lay there, winded, while the ghosts of a thousand hungry tigers roared around him, their scorching breath raking his skin. Shelter. He had to find shelter. Shaking his head to clear the fog, he desperately searched for somewhere to hide.

The fall had perhaps been his salvation. The bank here overhung the water by some way, its remaining thin crust held in place only by the tangled root system of a group of young trees. The underside was hollow, scoured out by one of the frequent flash floods that washed down through this valley. On hands and knees, clumsy through carrying Khalia, he scrabbled across to the flimsy shelter and burrowed as far back as he could into the dark soil that formed the rear wall. Above his head, a myriad of pale roots dangled like the hideous tentacles of some nightmare creature. It was a poor refuge, but it was all he had.

The tigers were upon him, snarling and roaring with a ferocity that froze the soul. Their scalding breath ripped the skin from his back and limbs in a wall of superheated wind that emptied the air of its last traces of oxygen as it swept by. Even under the protection of the bank, its touch was searing. Excruciating. Tahr's skin bubbled and flaked as it tore past. He screamed in agony; the air roasted his lungs as he drew it in. And then it was gone. His body lay blackened and twisted. No-one, no thing, could have survived that fiery onslaught. The hush of death settled in a shroud over the ravaged land. But by some miracle, he was still alive, denied the sweet release of death by forces he would never understand. Mercifully unconscious, the torment of his charred flesh would wait.

* * * * *

Tahr's eyelids flickered. Flickered again, and opened, his vision blurred with pain. In front of his face he saw what had to be his hand, although he scarcely recognised it. Charred and raw, it resembled more a rotted branch than a living limb.

Inch by agonising inch he crawled out from beneath the bank. Every breath was torture, every movement agony. The lush green jungle was gone, in its place a ravaged wasteland of blackened, smouldering tree stumps. Not a bird sang, not an insect hummed. The stench of destruction filled the air. He was the only creature left alive. Here and there lay the twisted, charred corpses of those creatures who had been caught in the inferno. Soon his battered corpse would join them, of that he was certain. Comforting, soothing blackness was already returning, settling around him, embracing him. Taking away his pain. He let his eyelids fall. He saw that Death had come for him, and he welcomed Death gladly.

Tahr had no idea of the extent of Khalia's power, however. From beneath the bank where she lay embedded in the soft, rich soil, her energy was reaching out to him. Healing him. He should not have survived the conflagration at all. Had it not been for Khalia, he would have perished instantly. The skin had been seared from over eighty per cent of his body, leaving him a mass of raw, weeping flesh. His lungs had been roasted, virtually destroyed. Even if, in some impossible way, he had survived that initial fiery onslaught, he should have succumbed to his injuries within a few, torment-filled hours.

Instead, wrapped in the anaesthetic of unconsciousness, his body was healing. Tender new skin was already growing over and sealing his wounds, both external and internal. With every hour that passed, his breathing eased a fraction. Three days after the holocaust, Tahr woke up. He hurt all over, but the pain was just about bearable. Not like…. In an instant he was wide awake, memory flooding back. He should be dead, and he wasn't. Unless… Had he really lived through that flaming, burning nightmare, or had he only dreamed it all?

With some effort, he raised his hand in front of his face. Saw the delicate fresh skin, as pink and tender as a baby's, that covered his hand and arm. Saw too the devastation that surrounded him. It had been real. Even in his confused and weakened state, he could recognise a miracle when he encountered one. Khalia! Grandmother had told him she had powers beyond his comprehension. The skull had have saved him from certain death.

Where was she? Panic fluttered as he searched the ground around where he lay. She wasn't there. Her green stone would stand out like a brilliant beacon in this blackened world. Of course. The bank where he had huddled in a vain attempt to protect himself. The skull must still be there. Wobbling and dizzy, he tottered weakly to the river. There she was, pushed back deep into the soil. Reaching in, his fingers found the smoothly curving cranium and pulled her free. He examined her carefully. She too had come through the devastation unscathed. Another miracle.

'What now?' he asked to no-one in particular, holding Khalia up to the light. 'What in the name of all that is sacred do I do now?'

'Nothing has changed.'

'Grandmother?' How was she speaking to him? She was surely dead, had perished alongside every man, woman and child in the fiery hell of the City. The harsh jaws of grief gripped him.

'Do not concern yourself with me, Tahr. I am safe. Hear me. Nothing has changed.'

'No!' How could she tell him that nothing had changed? In the space of a few short cruel hours, all he had ever known had been taken from him. The future was a frightening void. Everything had changed.

'Those who tried to destroy Khalia by laying waste to our home will not give up. As soon as you are well enough, you must take her and leave.' She paused, as if listening. 'I must go now. I am being called. I love you, Tahr.'

His head dropped and the tears fell, hot and stinging on his tender new skin. Wherever Grandmother was now, she would never return to speak with him again. This was their last goodbye.

'So be it, Grandmother,' he whispered. 'I love you too. Goodbye.'

He wept for a long time – for the loss of the City and its people, for Grandmother, and for himself and a future that he could not dwell on. When at last the tears dried and his courage returned, Tahr's heart was heavy but his resolve was firm. He would give his life if necessary to keep Khalia safe. He would not let Grandmother down again.

*   *   *   *   *

Khalia's healing energy was indeed powerful. Within another two days, he was strong enough to move on. In truth, he had little choice. He needed food. While the river water was once again clear and sweet, its constant flow having cleansed it of the fall-out from the recent cataclysm, there was nothing to eat. Everything had been destroyed. While he could quench his thirst as much as he wanted, water alone would not ease the gnawing hunger that tormented his belly.

Every movement was painful. Tahr's fresh tender skin was still not strong enough to withstand more than the slightest knock without breaking open, his breathing still harsh and laboured as his lungs continued to heal. But if he stayed, he would soon die of starvation. After the miracle of his recovery, he would not give up so easily. With slow, measured steps he set out, his heart as heavy as his legs. All around him, for as far as he could see, were nothing but ravaged wastelands. His home was gone, its streets and homes, the fields and the Dome, vaporised in an explosion with a force that was beyond his comprehension. A million people had been wiped out in a heartbeat. He was filled with a crushing sadness that would never ease.

Questions multiplied as he hobbled on. How *had* he survived? Come through the injuries he had sustained? He understood now why Grandmother had been so insistent in her demands that he take Khalia to safety; he was in no doubt that it had been the skull that had saved his life and brought him back from the brink of death. But how? Who… what was she? Where had she come from? When? And why? Who had created her? Question after question, whirling endlessly. Questions to which he doubted he would ever find answers.

* * * * *

Tahr's world had been turned to ashes. It was another two difficult days before the first splash of colour entered the drab monochrome of his surroundings, a tiny flash of vibrant green breaking into the dreary monotony, pushing out from the blackened twig of an otherwise naked shrub. Soon after he spotted another, and then another. Green leaves budding here and there on a few plucky branches. They were withered and battered yes, but they were alive and growing.

The patches of green grew more frequent. Tahr's hopes rose, and with them his spirits. Perhaps there was still somewhere in this world that had not been touched by the massacre he had so recently survived.

It was none too soon. He was desperately weak, barely able to place one foot in front of the other. His only focus was the hunger that clutched and twisted at his stomach. He had to find food soon or he would fall in his tracks. Khalia had been his saviour so far, would she save him again?

'Help me,' he pleaded silently. 'Help me.'

No sooner had Tahr made his plea than his right foot sank into a patch of soft soil, pitching him headlong to the ground. This time he did lose his hold on the skull. She bounced across the soft spongy earth and came to rest unharmed against the sprawling, tangled branches of a low-growing shrub.

'For all that's sacred...' Tahr lay where he had fallen, winded, exhausted and in pain. The tumble had scoured the still-fragile new skin from his palms and knees, which were now raw and bloody. So much for Khalia's help. It was a long moment before he could pull himself to his elbows to look for her.

There she was. And there was… He immediately forgot his grazed body and physical discomfort, for hanging from the branches of the bush, barely above ground level, were scores of plump purple berries. Had he not fallen, he would have missed them completely. They were too well hidden, invisible from above. He crawled across and grabbed at them, shovelling them into his mouth as fast as he could pick them, eating all he could find. They were delicious, tart yet sweet at the same time and although by many standards it was a meagre meal, to his empty, cramping belly, it was a banquet.

12.

With each step now the scars of that terrible day lessened and the landscape grew greener, returning to its natural, healthy vigour. First came the hum of insects, then birdsong and the rustling of all kinds of creatures going about their daily business under the cover of the vegetation. They crossed his path ever more frequently – mammals, birds, reptiles and insects, large and small. An ample supply of berries, fruit, nuts and shoots appeared and, for the first time, Tahr allowed himself to believe that he might survive.

For the first time too, now that the pressing needs for his survival were being met, he felt the full weight of the events that had overtaken his land. The loss of the City, his beloved home, of his friends and so many other innocent men, women and children. Of Grandmother. Released from its bonds, the grief was overwhelming. He stumbled on blinded by bitter tears that stung his eyes and washed down his cheeks. Tears of loss, of grief, of fear. Tears of rage. And tears of loneliness. Such loneliness. An inconsolable recognition that, for the first time in his life, he had no-one. He had never felt so utterly and wretchedly alone, not even in those dark, tear-filled days after his mother and father had died. Because then he had still had Grandmother. Now she was gone too. There was no-one left.

Heavy with heartache, he went on. There was little alternative, unless he simply stopped where he was and waited for death to claim him in this stifling green world. He could not go back; there was nothing to go back to. With her last words Grandmother had asked him to take

Khalia to safety. Where safety was, Tahr did not know, but it was not here. Yes, he would go on, for as long as it took. He had let Grandmother down once. He would not do so again.

Where he would go, what he would do next, were beyond his ability to consider. Too much had happened too quickly. In the briefest of time spans, he had experienced both the worst of nightmares and an impossible miracle, and he was travelling blind in an unknown world. This deep jungle was alien to him. He had spent his life in the City and the neat, carefully tended fields and familiar jungle fringes that surrounded it. Now that was gone forever, obliterated from the face of the Earth, in a few short, horrifying hours. This was his new world.

If anything the vegetation was getting thicker. He hadn't thought it possible but it was. Over the past few days, progress had changed from extremely difficult to virtually impossible. With every step he had to force his way through a tangled web of creepers and vines, some as thick as his thigh, that swept down from the canopy high above. Everywhere he looked a dense green wall stretched upwards and out of sight. With no tools to help, his hands were raw and blistered.

It was claustrophobic. The dank, still air hung like a shroud, heavy with the cloying perfume of exotic blooms, the earthy scent of damp leaf mould and the pungent aroma of rotting vegetation that was alive with the scurrying, slithering creatures that scavenged there. No sunlight reached down to the jungle floor. It was dark and gloomy, a cauldron of stifling heat and suffocating humidity where the air was trapped and stagnant, without the slightest movement to cool Tahr's skin. Swarms of mosquitos settled on his face and arms to drink his sweat and his blood. No sooner had he batted them away than they returned with even greater determination to torment his still tender skin.

* * * * *

Had he lost track of time? No. It had to still be early in the day. He had set out at sunrise and had only been walking for a little while. So why did the low light of the jungle floor seem even gloomier than usual? Tahr pushed the thought away. He was imagining it, his mind playing tricks in this monotonous endless green world.

He yelped in pain. His right foot had stubbed painfully against a hard, unyielding bump in the ground, crunching his toes. Nursing his injured foot, he looked to see what had snagged him. The ground rose a little here, by roughly the width of his hand, the change in level hidden under a camouflage of soil and fallen leaves. That was why he hadn't seen it. He cursed colourfully. These tree roots were a constant hazard that lay in wait to trip him at any careless step.

Except…He peered more closely, damaged toes forgotten as his curiosity was aroused. That couldn't be a root. The ridge in the ground ran in a straight, even line across his path, too regular to be natural. He brushed away the soil that covered it, revealing the sharp edge of a stone. A worked stone. Tahr sat back in amazement. If this stone had been worked by hand – and he was certain that it had been – someone had deliberately put it here. But who? And why?

He stepped back a pace and studied the area intently. Above the ridge a flat area, perhaps thirty five paces deep and the same from side to side, sloped gently up towards a towering rock wall whose lower reaches were swathed in vegetation. It had only become visible once he had emerged from the cover of the trees. Watching the ground carefully, Tahr stepped forward. Two paces from the first small ridge, the one that had crumpled his toes, he found a second. Two more paces, and another. He counted thirteen in all. Thirteen steps, leading up to a level platform behind which a jagged cliff face of dark grey rock stretched up into the deep blue sky. It was so high it surely had to have pierced the heavens. On the terrace its shadow turned midday to twilight.

Intrigued, Tahr's fingertips scrabbled in the soil of the platform. Only a little way below the surface they scraped unpleasantly on hard stone. Quickly he scooped earth aside until he had uncovered a patch roughly the length of his forearm in diameter. It was paved. He could make out a distinct joint between two flagstones. It looked identical to those which formed – had formed, he reminded himself sadly – the City's streets. Was it possible that this platform was also the work of the Ancient Ones?

For the first time since he had watched helplessly while the City was razed to the ground, Tahr felt a spark of life ignite in his belly. Curiosity mingled with the growing certainty that he had not stumbled on this place by mere chance. He stared at the skull. A tug in his guts confirmed that this was indeed Khalia's doing. Why had she brought him here?

He sat back on his heels, and the cliff loomed up before him, a writhing mass of roots, vines and creepers slithering and coiling over its surface like giant serpents. The jungle was mistress here. And yet… He stared intently. Surely there was something not quite natural about the two trunks, covered in thick vegetation, that pressed tight up against the rock face about ten paces apart. Everywhere else the stems kinked and twisted as they moulded to the irregularity of the rock that supported them. Only these two stood completely straight and vertical to perhaps three times his height.

Using his bare hands, the only tools he had, Tahr grabbed and hauled at the stiff, unforgiving stems, pulling with the full weight of his body. They held fast. He tugged and tore until his hands were raw and bleeding. A force, far stronger than his reasoning mind, was driving him on, pushing him to find out and he continued to attack them long after he had no strength left to give. A sudden loud crack shuddered up his arms; the thickest of the coils had given up its hold.

With the main anchor gone, clearing the remaining cover was a much easier task and Tahr found a renewed impetus. At last he stepped back, his breath taken away by what his efforts had revealed: a massive column of silver-grey stone, etched with intricate and beautiful carvings. Snakes, butterflies, and cascades of full-blown flowers and heart-shaped leaves wound their way around its circumference, between which strange symbols and figures danced. The second trunk had to be another column, the twin of this one. He sank to the ground, trying to make sense of his discovery. This had to be the Ancients' work. It was too similar to the City to be anything else. But what did it mean?

Of course. Now that he had seen it, the answer was glaringly obvious. His gaze had been drawn over and over to a spot at the base of the cliff between the two pillars. He had looked, but he had been so busy thinking that he hadn't seen. At last he grasped the significance. A flight of steps, a wide open terrace, two identical columns, flanking… Leaping to his feet, his tiredness forgotten, Tahr ran to the rock face. There had to be an entrance behind the heavy wall of vegetation. And beyond that…? He had no idea, but he intended to find out.

Wary, his heart thumping with excitement, Tahr reached the dripping green curtain. Anything – both earthly and unearthly – could be lurking in it. Or behind it. Remembering the ordeals he had already survived, he reminded himself that whatever lay beyond could not be worse than the hell he had so recently lived through. He pulled and tore at the mat of thick stems until there was a gap wide enough to wriggle through. Caution took over and he pushed an arm through the gap. It met with empty space.

Twisting and turning his torso, Tahr forced his way through and into the void beyond, sprawling on all fours as his foot caught in the steel-strong stem of a bramble. He stayed on his knees for a long, long time, staring at the sight that greeted him. Barely a glimmer of daylight penetrated the dense living curtain at the entrance; even so, he could see clearly. A low yellow luminescence, its source unseen, rose up from floor level to illuminate in a soft, warm glow the immense vaulted space that opened out before him and disappeared into its furthermost recesses.

13.

It wasn't the size of the chamber that had the greatest impact on Tahr, nor the mysterious light source. It was the procession of giant stone statues on either side of the centre aisle that stretched away into the distant shadows. They stood four, maybe even five, times his height, each one different and each one exquisitely carved and painted. In the pale glow that shone up on them from below, casting strange, sharply contrasting shadows on their forms, they seemed alive; sleeping, resting, waiting. So much so that he was afraid that they might suddenly speak to him or climb down from their pedestals to wander the vault.

They carried an air of the unreal and other-worldly, gods from the heavens come to Earth, their size emphasising their power and the insignificance of those mortals who entered this, their temple. Not one of them was fully human in appearance. Some bore the heads of animals or birds. One, of a man, with his loins and upper legs wrapped in a cloth skirt, stood bare-chested, his head that of an eagle, or perhaps it was a falcon, that looked out into the vault from on top of broad, very human shoulders. Others were of even stranger forms, with skin of blue or red or yellow; or with too many limbs, or heads, or with the feet of a leopard or a stork. On and on they stretched, spookily lifelike and at the same time so impossibly formed.

They were watching him, taking measure of him. No, he told himself sternly, it was only his mind playing tricks. They were nothing but carved stone figures. Magnificent yes, but inanimate and cold. There was nothing supernatural about them. He forced his rampaging imagination back under control and almost succeeded. The sensation that he was being observed refused to die completely however.

With faltering steps he walked deeper into the void, following the rows of towering figures. He counted thirty, forty, and still they flanked his route. The faint glimmer of daylight had long since vanished behind him, his way now lit solely by the unwavering golden glow of the unseen light source. A pebble, caught by his foot as he walked, rattled against a statue's plinth in a hollow echo that reverberated over and over and over, until it faded to nothing, swallowed up by the vast, empty vault above his head.

Tahr had taken some several hundred paces before he reached the final figures. They came to an end in front of a deep stone dais on which rested a huge chair of glistening white marble; each ear of the backrest was surmounted by a sphere of the same stone. It was huge. The seat alone was level with Tahr's head and as wide as his outstretched arms. It had to be a throne of some kind, created for a giant. Or a god. Maybe one whose likeness stood guard in this hall?

He turned to look back the way he had come. The two rows of statues formed a colossal guard of honour that flanked the straight path from the entrance to the dais. Honouring who? Tahr breathed deeply. Wonder, awe, more questions – so many questions – flooded through him. But he wasn't afraid, not any more. With each step he had taken into the belly of this temple, a sense of reassurance and security had wrapped itself around him, dissolving his fears. He would be safe here, and so would Khalia. This place would protect them both.

'Welcome home, Tahr.' Her soft whisper enfolded him in its embrace. 'Welcome home.'

* * * * *

No-one else came. There was no-one left to come. Not one man, woman or child had survived the fiery hell that had devoured the City and laid waste to the once-fertile jungle to far beyond the horizon in every direction. Outsiders no longer ventured near. Although the land where the City had once stood had grown back as lush and thick as ever in the decades after the inferno, the region was feared. It was considered cursed, destroyed by the gods for having incurred their fury. In the far-off kingdoms where Tahr's people had once traded their goods and swapped stories over tiny cups of potent liquor, it was said that the City had brought its fate upon itself for playing with the toys of demons. Those few brave, or foolhardy, souls who from time to time sought glory and strode head high, chest out – and palms sweating – into that place, without exception lost their reason and crawled out wild-eyed, jabbering manically about two-headed, six-limbed and other hideous creatures. If they ever came out at all.

So Tahr remained alone. He didn't mind, not if he didn't think about it. Khalia was with him, a constant comforting presence, and soon the statues became his friends. It didn't matter that they didn't talk back; he would sit and chatter to one or the other of them every day, sharing his hopes and fears, telling them what he had been doing or how he planned to spend his day. He took a simple though profound pleasure in the green cathedral of the jungle that surrounded him, so different from the vibrant, bustling atmosphere of the starkly beautiful stone City. If he was lonely, he did not allow himself to think of it. Doing so would not change anything, unless it was to plunge him into a dark dungeon of despair, a state of mind completely unwarranted by his surroundings. And in time, there was Chiachi, the small brown monkey that never left his side. The little creature was funny, intelligent and full of mischief – the perfect companion.

In all the years he lived in the temple, however, Tahr was never able to discover who had built it, or why.

14.

They arrived one morning many years after that terrible day when Tahr had stood on the ridge and watched his home burn. He was by then perhaps well into his ninth decade, although he had long ago given up counting the days and years. What was the point? It had long ago lost any meaning.

It was just after dawn, and he was sitting at the foot of one of the great statues delighting in the sunlight that bathed him in its gentle warmth. He loved this time of day when the waking rays of the sun spilled onto the great stone terrace and in through the entrance of the temple chamber. Pollen danced in the sunlight that filtered down through the gaps in the canopy in slender golden shafts through which jewelled birds and butterflies of every size and species danced and flickered.

He had closed his eyes to listen to the sounds of the jungle waking, as he so often did, and soon he was daydreaming. He was fully lost in his reverie when a shadow fell over him. He opened his eyes hastily, fearful that a tiger or some other large predator was considering him for its next meal. Blinked, and blinked again, not believing what he was seeing. Three strangers – two women and a man – stood on the terrace watching him. He was so shocked that for some time he was unable to move, or even to speak. No-one had come to this place in… well, forever. When at last he scrambled to his feet, he grabbed the statue's base in alarm. These people were giants. His head barely reached the bottom of their ribcages.

'Greetings, Tahr.' He stared at the woman. She had addressed him in his own language. Even so, it had been so long since anyone had spoken to him that it took a full minute before the meaning of her words registered.

'G-Greetings.' He hadn't seen another human face for almost as long as he could remember. Who were they, these giants, and how did they know his language? And his name? He backed away hesitantly, suspicion growing. Perhaps these strangers were the same merciless enemy who had annihilated the City and slaughtered every one of its inhabitants. He retreated further into the temple. Had they now come now to murder him too? But for what reason? So many years had passed.

'Peace.' Khalia's lilting reassurance whispered through his body. 'These are friends, Tahr. My friends.' His mouth fell open.

'Yes.' The woman was speaking again. 'It was our ancestors who built the City. It was a good place to live. A happy place. We were pleased when your people found it and made it their home.' Sorrow mingled with a considerable anger swept across her face. 'Its destruction was cruel and unwarranted. It saddened and horrified us.'

She glanced up at the stone figures that towered above them. 'We built this too. You are the only one who has ever found it.'

'Who are you?' Tahr was staring openly at his visitors now. All three had blond, almost white hair that fell to their shoulders in a glossy silken sheet, and eyes the colour of the afternoon sky. Aside from their height, they looked as normal as anyone he had ever met. Except… no, not quite normal. Not quite solid. He was sure that if he touched them, it would only take a slight effort to push his hand right through their bodies.

'I am Pilar. These are my companions, Luja and Minak. We have come a long way to find you.'

73

'From across the ocean?' As a child, the merchants' stories of a vast expanse of water, saltier than tears and that stretched on forever, had fascinated him. It still did, when he allowed himself to think of it.

'Further. We come from a place that in the future your people will know as Alcyone.' She bowed so low that her white gold hair brushed the stone of the floor. Her companions followed. 'We have come to offer you our gratitude for saving our beloved Khalia. Her importance to your world is beyond anything you can imagine. Her loss would have been more than a tragedy. It would have destroyed a process that still has so much to accomplish.'

Tahr was no longer listening. One phrase alone filled his mind – 'your world'. Were these visitors then not of this Earth? He had heard such things as a child but had never believed them.

'It is true, Tahr. We are not of your world. Our home lies far away, deep amongst the stars. You know of her. When you look up to the sacred family, clustered together beyond the outstretched hand of the hunter, it is our beloved Alcyone that shines more brightly than any of her sisters who surround her.

'In the earliest of days – days long passed by and forgotten – we came to Earth, drawn by a desire to learn about this beautiful and unique world that glows like a precious jewel in the black cloak of space. We fell in love with it and we stayed for a little while. We have returned many times since.

'We built the City as our home, and we built this temple to guide and teach those who would come after us. No-one did, not until you. Maybe, one day, others will come who can truly see, and learn, and understand.' Her words carried a soulful wistfulness.

'Learn what? Understand what?' Tahr had been poring over the temple's mysteries since he had discovered it, and in all that time hadn't found even one clue as to its purpose or its origins. The latter question had now been answered; the former remained unresolved.

'It is of no matter. Not now.' Pilar's tone left no room for further discussion.

'Why have you come back?' A cold trickle of apprehension seeped into Tahr's veins. He already knew why, didn't he?

'For Khalia.' Tahr's heart thudded to his groin and the trickle turned to ice. No. They couldn't. He wouldn't let them. She was his strength and his comfort in this lonely place. In that moment, and perhaps for the first time, he fully felt the crushing solitude of his existence. It threatened to overwhelm him completely.

'We must.' The man, whom Pilar had introduced as Minak, spoke gently, feeling Tahr's dismay and pain as if it was his own. His voice was mellow and deep. 'Khalia is no longer safe here. Others are looking for her. Others who will use her power to increase their own. Once they have her in their hands, they will have no conscience at destroying other cities as they did ours. Yours.'

Tahr wasn't listening. His only thought, blasting through his mind with the fury of a hurricane, was that these people wanted to take Khalia away. Khalia, who had healed him from injuries that should have killed him instantly. Who had led him to this place and to safety. Whose constant companionship ever since was the only thing that had held him back from losing his mind. Yes, there would still be Chiachi and his statue friends, but without her warm, all-encompassing presence, he wasn't sure he would survive for long. He was even less sure that he would want to.

'I can watch out for her. I can protect her,' he gabbled desperately, recognising the folly of his words even as he uttered them. How could he protect Khalia against an enemy with the firepower and inhumanity to wipe out the City and all its people?

'You know you cannot, Tahr. Though you still have a strength and courage than many of far younger years would wish to possess, you are an old man now. You have no way of defending yourself or Khalia. You would be as an ant beneath the heel of those who will come for her.'

With a sudden flush of painful perception and a tortured sob of inevitability, Tahr recognised that this glowing man was speaking the truth. The words sank into his consciousness, bringing with them a vision of a nightmare future: cities ablaze, forests charred and smouldering. Screams, such dreadful screams. Bodies piled up carelessly in the streets for the vultures to feast on. No, no matter what the cost to himself, he would not let that happen. Not again. Never again. He must relinquish Khalia to Pilar and her companions. He must live the rest of his life without her. All at once, he felt very, very old and very, very tired.

Taking in a deep and somewhat wavering breath, he drew himself up to his full height, clutching tightly on to his resolution in case it attempted to escape.

'I will fetch her for you.' Tears were already streaming down his age-parchment cheeks. Praying that his courage would not fail, Tahr turned and walked slowly past the silent sentinels to the dais at the far end.

* * * * *

The skull was heavy and warm in his hands. He wished Khalia would speak to him one last time. She did not, for really, there was nothing to say.

At the temple entrance his three visitors were huddled together talking. Tahr waited in the shadows, grief-filled, shaking but resolute until Pilar left the group and approached him.

'We have been considering your situation. It is not usual… However, on this occasion…' She broke off and threw a questioning glance at her companions who nodded their assent.

'Tahr,' she began again, with renewed confidence, 'we have already told you how important Khalia is, and we have expressed our deepest gratitude for your courage in rescuing her and keeping her safe all these years. Without you, she would have been destroyed and the future of humankind would be much less certain. We see clearly how difficult it is for you to give her up to us, and yet you are willing to do so despite your fears for your future. That in itself is an act of supreme bravery and sacrifice. Mere words seem poor recompense for your actions.'

She paused for a brief moment, watching him closely. 'Will you come with us, Tahr? Live with us, and remain as Khalia's guardian for the rest of your years?'

Tahr's heart was pounding so hard he feared it would burst from his chest, the blood surging through his veins roaring so loudly that it blocked out all other sound. Go with them? Never in a million lifetimes could he have expected this.

His first thought was to refuse. After all, he was old. Too old. Too entrenched in his peaceful, uneventful existence. He could not make such a huge change in his life. Immediately on the heels of that first reaction came the realisation that his peaceful, uneventful existence had already been changed forever. From this morning Khalia would no longer be here with him. He reconsidered the possibility. He may be an old man but he was still fit and healthy. What did he have to lose? A tingle of excitement sparked into life and rippled through his bones, growing stronger with each heartbeat. It would be an adventure, and what an adventure! He had always dreamed of seeing the ocean. Now he had the chance to see... well, he had no idea, other than whatever it was, it would be astonishing.

'Yes,' he told Pilar, his voice trembling ever so slightly. 'Yes. I would very much like to come with you.'

She smiled and beckoned him forward. Clutching tightly onto Khalia with both hands, and with Chiachi scrambling up onto his shoulder, Tahr left everything and walked down the shallow stone steps into a new and unknown future.

* * * * *

With Tahr and Khalia gone, the jungle rapidly reclaimed its territory. In a few short years it had again swallowed all trace of the elegant terrace, sweeping steps and massive pillars in its lush, clinging grasp. Vines, roots and branches once more concealed the magnificent entrance in a leafy living curtain, so dense that no indication remained of the marvels that lay behind it.

Centuries, millennia, tens of millennia passed. All evidence of the holocaust and its aftermath were buried ever deeper under the vegetation that built up, layer upon layer over the ruins. In time, new peoples came and settled along the banks of the river, blissfully ignorant of the tragedy that had once unfolded there. Nonetheless, from the earliest days a vast expanse of jungle, from where the

City had once stood to the massive wall of rock with its green curtain, was shunned. A series of deaths gave birth to a powerful conviction that the place was cursed, haunted by demons and other evil spirits who would seize and slaughter in the most horrible ways anyone foolhardy enough to venture too close. Though unfounded, the belief spread and strengthened throughout the generations until the day when, by common consent, the area was declared taboo, and abandoned.

Much later still, when the outside world had become a very different place, outsiders – explorers, scientists and adventurers from distant continents and unsympathetic cultures – ventured into these unforgiving lands, drawn by legends of lost cities and fabulous temples, immortality and priceless treasure. This virtually inaccessible region could only be reached after months of gruelling trekking through hostile, unforgiving jungle, and almost all of those who journeyed here from foreign cultures came unprepared for its rigours. Only a handful of the hardiest and luckiest ever reached their destination.

None of them found their treasure or their immortality. Most didn't live to return home. They were not stricken by curses, or slaughtered by evil spirits taking their revenge, as the local population believed. Their fate had nothing to do with the ghoulish activities of demons, and everything to do with the environment. Venomous reptiles and insects, poisonous plants, disease that ran rampant in the humid furnace heat, and the fiercest of predators – among them leopard and tiger – were the enemies here. For anyone not born and raised in the jungle, survival was the exception. Getting out alive depended more than anything else on sheer good fortune.

And so the temple remained undiscovered and untouched, as it does to this day.

KHALIA: The Jade Skull

Part III

THE GRAND COUNCIL OF GALACTIC ALLIANCES

15.

'How many?' The curt question reflected Ashar's sombre mood.

'Nearly a million, Councillor. The City was obliterated. They didn't stand a chance.' His advisor's voice cracked. Like the rest of the Council, he was struggling to come to terms with what had happened.

'Survivors?'

'None. No-one could have lived through that.'

'And Khalia? Was she destroyed too?'

'No, Councillor. The Skull is safe, although her guardian is mortally injured. He had already fled the City when the attack came and was far enough away to survive the initial explosions, but he couldn't escape the wave of super-heated air that followed.'

'The Skull will do what is necessary to heal him.' Ashar stared out of the full-height curved window that wrapped around the full circumference of the craft's observation deck. Far below, the thin blue arc of Earth's atmosphere appeared too fragile to support the life that scurried about on the planet's surface. Tears streamed down his face as he gazed on this breath-taking blue and green world. From up here it all looked so peaceful. There was no sign of the fiery hell that had unfolded on its surface only hours earlier. A million lives extinguished in a few short minutes. How had he not foreseen this? Hadn't he known not to underestimate Ka'ark? And yet how could anyone have anticipated that such carnage would unfold? He and his colleagues had badly misjudged how far Ka'ark would go in his opposition, none of them able to conceive that Ka'ark would carry out such a murderous attack on a defenceless population.

He turned to his companion. 'Do we know where Ka'ark is now?'

'He is being brought back here under escort by our patrol craft. His command vessel has been boarded and neutralised, and is also under our control.' The advisor was thoughtful. 'Councillor, I do not believe that the majority of his crew knew of his intentions. They appear as horrified as we are at what happened.'

Ashar nodded his agreement. 'I believe you are right, my friend. This was the work of a very small group of rebels. But as we see, it did not need great numbers to create such slaughter.'

'What did they hope to achieve? They must have known they could never escape punishment.'

'They are convinced that the human race will destroy the Earth. Because the Council refused to remove the Skulls, Ka'ark decided to ensure it would never be possible for the thirteen to ever be reunited. Destroying even one would serve his purpose – his own fate was irrelevant. Thankfully, he failed, though at a dreadful cost to the people of the City. Now we must ensure that a tragedy like this can never happen again.'

* * * * *

Ashar stood before a subdued and still shocked assembly. The recent events on Earth had shaken everyone out of their complacency.

'Brothers and sisters of the Grand Council, the tragedy we have so recently witnessed has affected us all. We were all in some way to blame, myself as much as anyone. I was naïve. I did not want to believe that Ka'ark could act in such a way. I was wrong, and the people of the City suffered. That is a burden I will carry for the rest of my life. Rest assured that Ka'ark and his friends will pay the penalty for their actions.

'We cannot undo what has been done but we can and must ensure that it will not happen again. Earth, and the humans who live on her, must be protected from those who would control or destroy their lives. Let Ka'ark's actions be the warning we cannot ignore.'

For the second time in only a few days, Ashar drew his hand across the monitor in his desk. Once more the blue and green sphere slowly materialised in the centre of the chamber – Earth's hologram. As the audience watched, a glittering web of gold lines spread around the globe, settling at the edges of Earth's atmosphere in an intricate web of light.

'The energy grid that you see in the hologram has already been set in place around the outer edge of Earth's atmosphere,' he explained to the silent members in the Council Chamber. 'It has been designed to fully protect the planet against any future attack.'

'How?' The query came from a short, squat Metulian councillor in the third row.

'Firstly, no craft from any star system will be able to pass through it into Earth's atmosphere without authorisation. That authorisation has to be granted by one of the thirteen members of the Senior Council Forum, who will then have to enter an access code into the programme to allow the craft to proceed.

'Access will be closely monitored, although it will only be denied under extreme circumstances. This is because the shield has been programmed to detect all known weapons and will automatically block the passage of any vessel suspected of carrying them, even after authorisation has been granted. In addition, the light web will deflect any longer range attack.

'Secondly, from now on it will be impossible for the Skulls of Light to be taken off the Earth. Any craft attempting to do so will find it is unable to pass out through the grid. This element cannot be overridden. Should it prove necessary in the future for us to intervene to rescue the Skulls, we will have to remain within the atmosphere and work with that limitation.'

A hand went up at the back of the chamber and a tall, regal woman with intense violet eyes rose to her feet.

'Councillor Sharika.'

'Councillor Ashar. Can you explain more about this net?'

'Of course. The grid is formed from a web of light that is linked to, and anchored by, the crystalline light grid that lies deep beneath the planet's crust. The Earth grid draws energy from the core crystal and transmits this power to the Sky grid. This light is of an extremely high vibration, more so than we have ever employed before. It must be, in order to be effective against the ever-advancing technology of those who challenge our objectives.'

'Will it work?'

'We must pray that it does, Councillor Sharika. We must pray that it does.'

* * * * *

The First Officer of the Grand Council of the Galactic Alliances stared out of the bubble window of his cabin. Around him stretched the inky infinity of the universe in all its splendour. Stars filled the sky; millions of pinpricks of light glittered on a cloak of obsidian satin, each one of them a sun shining out like a rainbow-coloured beacon. Towering nebulas of brilliant-hued stardust light years high pulsed and dazzled. A comet swept past, its flaming tail cutting a swathe of light through the darkness.

Ashar saw none of it. Responsibility weighed heavily on his shoulders, yet it was as nothing compared to the grief for a million meaningless deaths that filled his soul. Never before had he faced a situation that came even close to what had just taken place on Earth's surface. He had been First Officer for two hundred and fifty revolutions, roughly five hundred Earth years, and it would be another two hundred and fifty before his term of office came to an end. He suspected it would be a long tenure.

Ever since the devastating attack on the City, he had been stalked by the unwelcome premonition that this was only the beginning. Ka'ark was not the only opponent to the Plan; before long, others would step forward and take his place. The Council's critics could afford to be patient and take their time laying their plans and garnering support and allies. Humankind was still a long way from being technologically advanced enough to pose a threat to its world. But Ka'ark had sown the seeds of dissension and at some point those seeds would germinate. There were plenty of worlds whose inhabitants did not share the Council's principles of peace and self-determination, and who would be only too delighted to have access to the treasure chest of natural resources that was the planet Earth. The Council would have to stay constantly vigilant.

Ashar drew a tired hand across his eyes. He hoped he was wrong; he feared he was right. Only time would tell.

GEMMA, 2

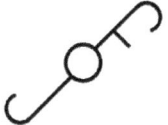

16.

Joe put his foot down, defying the speed limits and traffic patrols. Duncan's big Mercedes ate up the miles in comfort and in well under three hours we were entering the outskirts of Leeds and heading towards, then through, the city centre. A couple of miles further on, we turned off the main thoroughfare into a maze of quieter back streets. The further in we went, the more neglected the buildings became, until we were driving through a ghost town, uncomfortably aware that the big luxury car was totally and conspicuously out of place amongst the dirty, derelict buildings.

A bit of additional internet research had revealed that the former residents of these homes had been relocated years before, the site earmarked for a redevelopment that had not yet progressed beyond the planning stage. It was a sad and lonely place, the once busy streets now decaying and desolate. I half expected a tumble-weed to come rolling down the middle of the road. Overcast skies and thick drizzle did little to lighten the mood and I shivered as I got out of the car. Life had abandoned this place long ago.

We pulled up outside the house Joe had pinpointed. Like all its neighbours it was boarded up and neglected with no sign that anyone had been here in a very long time. I glanced at him, discouragement taking hold. Cathy was so good at what she did, and had been so sure, but even she couldn't get it right every time. Had we come all this way on a wild goose chase? Joe's gloomy expression gave away that he was thinking the same. Well, we were here now. We would lose nothing by nosing around a bit.

The house was roughly a third of the way down a long line of terraced houses, all of them identical. To the left of what had to be the living room window, the front door opened straight onto the pavement. A picture of a tired, work-worn woman scrubbing the doorstep fluttered through my thoughts. 'We may have been poor but that was no excuse for a dirty doorstep,' she seemed to be telling me. What would she think if she could see it now, chipped and smeared with grime, and half-hidden under old crisp packets, cigarette stubs and chip wrappers that the wind had piled up against it? Heavy planks had been nailed across the front door and windows, including the two on the first floor. No-one had been in or out of here in months, if not years. And yet… There on the door was the number seven with two empty screw holes in front of it where another number had once been, just as Cathy had described.

We looked at each other, unsure what to do next. I blinked. Out of the corner of my vision I could have sworn I saw the woman with the scrubbing brush beckoning at me to go in.

'Cathy was certain,' I offered. 'If she's right and Callum is here… We have to take a look.'

Joe tugged hard at one of the planks. He staggered backwards, only just keeping his balance as it came away easily. Too easily.

'Gemma, look.' He pointed at the door frame. 'The boards aren't fixed. The screws are just resting in their holes.' With a new sense of urgency he grabbed the second plank.

I put a warning hand on his shoulder to stop him. 'What if they're inside?'

Joe paused and considered. 'No, I don't think so. They wouldn't go through the rigmarole of setting up the planks after themselves. There's no need. There's no-one here to take any notice. In any case, if anyone did walk in while they were there, you can bet he wouldn't walk out again. My guess is that they board the place up when they leave to stop anyone poking around. Squatters wanting to take up residence or what have you.'

I glanced over my shoulder at the car. 'Shouldn't we at least move that? It's a bit of a giveaway.'

Joe looked at me solemnly. 'If they come back while we're in there, we're stuffed anyway. Hiding the car won't make any difference. We won't be able to get out without being seen.' He put down the plank and took hold of my shoulders, deadly serious. 'Are you sure you want to do this?'

The stark truth was that no, I didn't want to do it. Neither Joe nor I had even half an idea of what we might find inside, only that what we were about to do was going to carry us deeper into the rabbit hole. But I was going to do it anyway. If Callum was here I wasn't going to abandon him and run away, any more than Joe was.

I stared back at him steadily. 'Let's do this, Joe. Get in, rescue Callum, and get out again.'

'If he's there.'

'If he's there,' I echoed, praying that he would be. Joe took my hand and we stepped inside.

17.

The inside of the house was in an even worse state than the exterior. It was dank, dark and damp, and smelled like the less savoury type of public lavatory. A heap of junk mail and newspapers had been kicked aside from behind the front door and lay sprawled up against the wall. If anyone was holding Callum in this house they clearly didn't spend any more time than necessary here. A quick glance showed that the living room was empty except for a collapsed sofa covered in a thick layer of dust and wide swathes of yellowing wallpaper peeling from the walls. The kitchen contained only a filthy sink, its pipes pulled from the wall, and a broken cupboard. Beyond that, an open door to an equally squalid bathroom indicated the source of the stench. If Callum was here, he had to be in one of the upstairs rooms.

At the top of the stairs two doors led off a yard-square landing. One was hanging crookedly from its hinges, the other was shut. It had to be that one. Joe gripped the handle, turned and pushed. The creak the door gave as it opened was probably nowhere near as loud as it sounded in the silent house; still, my heart missed a beat. We froze, waiting. Nothing.

I breathed again and followed Joe into the dingy, unlit room. He was already on his knees beside a motionless figure lying on the floor. Callum. He was tied firmly to the chair just as I had seen him in the dreams, only now he was lying on his side. He must have toppled sideways and been unable to get himself upright again.

'Is he...?' I could hardly get the words out.

'He's alive. He's not in a good way, though.' Joe had his fingers at Callum's neck, feeling for the pulse. 'We have to get him to a hospital, fast.'

I had my phone in my hand when Joe stopped me. 'No. We'll take him in the car. If the kidnappers are anywhere near and an ambulance turns up, sirens and lights blazing, they'll know he's been found. They could easily find out which hospital he's been taken to and find a way to get to him later. More worryingly for us, they'd probably spot us too, which would put us firmly in their sights. Not a good place for us to be! The longer we can stay out of their spotlight, the better.'

The possibility that Callum's captors might be nearby did little to reassure my already taut nerves. I swallowed down my anxieties. There was no time to dwell on that now. We had to get him out of here, and do it as quickly as possible. Together we fumbled with the tight knots that bound him to the chair. He was tied wrists and ankles with a thick nylon cord that had cut deep into his skin, creating angry raw weals. He groaned in pain every time we moved him – which was, I think, a good sign. I spoke to him as we worked, hoping he could hear me.

'Callum, it's Gemma and Joe. We're going to get you out of here and to a hospital, but you'll have to help us.'

His eyes flickered open – well, as open as they could through the bruises – stared blankly for a moment and then closed. He had slipped away from us again. Which left us with one huge problem – how were we going to get the unconscious Callum down the stairs and into the car?

I still don't know how we did it. Although Callum wasn't heavily built, he was a good six feet tall and, unconscious, he was a dead weight. I gave silent thanks that over the last few months Joe had taken to going to the gym several times a week; even so, it took a Herculean effort from both of us to haul him up, out of the room and down the stairs. Every muscle in my body screamed in protest as we pulled and pushed and staggered along with him, supporting him as much as we could. It was nothing to what Callum's body had to be going through. Although we were being as careful as we could, we had to be aggravating his injuries with every clumsy step.

We made it to the street, exhausted but, miraculously, without serious mishap and dragged Callum into the back of the Mercedes where I sat cradling his head in my lap while Joe closed the front door and replaced the boards. He fired up the engine and we raced off to the nearest hospital at well over twice the legal speed limit.

Thirty minutes later Joe and I were sitting in the A & E department waiting for news. One look at Callum's unconscious form sprawled ashen-faced in the back of the car, and a team of medics had wheeled him away with a haste that was far from reassuring, leaving us staring in his wake.

18.

'Mrs Mason?' A stocky man in a grey suit was standing in front of me. I hadn't noticed him walk up; I'd been too lost in my thoughts and my worry about Callum. I nodded, glancing around. Joe was nowhere in sight.

'D.I. Chamberlain.' His warrant card was in his hand. 'I'd like a few words.'

I nodded again and he sat down next to me. 'I understand you and your friend, Mr Cunningham, brought Mr Davis here. Tell me what happened.'

I took a deep breath. Not for the first time since the whole skull business had started, I was about to lie to the police.

'I, we, got a call from Callum earlier this evening. He sounded scared. Terrified, actually. He said he was in Leeds and that some people were after him. That they'd already caught him and beaten him up once but he'd escaped. He didn't say how and I didn't ask. There wasn't really enough time.' I hoped fervently that Joe, wherever he had got to, was sticking to the story we'd agreed on.

'Anyway, he told us where he was, and asked us to go and pick him up. He said he wanted to give himself up to the police, that he'd be safer in custody, and that he wanted Joe and I to go with him as moral support.'

'Then what?'

'We jumped in the car and came up to Leeds, to where he said we should meet him. Only he wasn't there. At least, we didn't think he was. We waited for a while, but there was no sign of him. It was only when Joe got out of the car to look around that he heard groaning. He discovered Callum on the ground under some trees a little way away. Whoever had been after him had obviously found him. We didn't want to hang around in case they were still near or came back to finish the job, so we put him in the car and brought him here.'

'That's all?'

'All? It feels a lot to me.'

'I mean, there isn't anything else you want to add?'

'No. That's it.' Over the last few months I had discovered to my dismay that I was a damn good liar. While I wasn't proud of it, right now I was praying that my dubious new-found talent wasn't going to let me down. Thankfully, it seemed to be holding up. D.I. Chamberlain had got to his feet.

'You are aware that Mr Davis is wanted on suspicion of murder?'

'Yes.'

'Is this the first time he's been in touch with you since he disappeared after that murder?'

'Yes.' More lies.

'And you have no idea where he has been since then?'

'None at all.' That, at least, was the truth. More or less.

'We'll want to speak to you again, Mrs Mason. There are still a lot of points we need to clear up. But that's all for tonight. I want to see you at the station at ten o'clock tomorrow morning to give your statement.' He pushed a business card into my hand. 'The address is on my card along with my phone number. Call me if you remember anything else that might help our enquiries.'

'Yes, OK.' All at once, I was bone-weary. The events of the day had just hit me like a hefty blow in the stomach. All I wanted to do was sleep.

'Goodnight, Mrs Mason. We'll see you in the morning. Ah, Mr Cunningham.' Joe had appeared with a uniformed sergeant. 'I want to see you at the station in the morning too. Goodnight.'

Joe sagged into the newly vacated seat. He reached over and squeezed my hand. 'He'll be OK.'

I let my head fall back against the wall, my eyes closing. 'I hope so. Right now, I'm more concerned about us. I have a feeling D.I. Chamberlain has an awful lot of questions that we aren't going to be able to answer.'

I forced my unwilling eyelids back open; Joe had nudged me in the ribs. At the end of the corridor, DI Chamberlain was speaking with a doctor

'She's just come out of Callum's room,' Joe whispered. Chamberlain and the doctor disappeared back inside the room, still talking. The clock in the wall said three thirty two. In the morning. We had been sitting here for nearly four hours.

Despite the discomfort of the waiting room chair, I was slipping in and out of a half-sleep and next to me Joe was dozing restlessly when footsteps roused us both. It was the doctor we had seen talking to the D.I.

'How is he?' I searched her face, looking for clues.

'Holding his own and lucky to be alive.' Her calm expression reassured me.

'Can we see him?'

'Are you family?'

'Friends,' Joe put in. 'We brought him in. I don't think he's got any family. He never talked about them if he has.'

'I see. Well, not tonight. He's heavily sedated and needs to rest. Come back tomorrow. You can look in on him then, though I have to warn you, it's unlikely he'll be conscious. He's got a pretty nasty concussion and we may well decide to keep him under sedation for a couple of days.'

'Will he be OK?' I couldn't leave without knowing that much at least.

'He's been badly beaten and has multiple abrasions and extensive serious bruising, both internal and external. Severe concussion, some broken bones and cracked ribs. The most serious injuries are the internal bruising caused by heavy blows to his body, and a punctured lung. He wouldn't have survived very long with that.' I winced, remembering the clumsy way we had manhandled Callum down the stairs and into the car.

The doctor was still speaking. 'It's a miracle that there was no serious damage to any other major organ.' She paused. 'He's been badly hurt, but given time he should make a full recovery.'

19.

The following morning Joe and I reported to the police station to give our statements as D.I Chamberlain had directed, where we were taken to separate interview rooms. Over the next hour and a half or so I faced a barrage of questions. It was the same for Joe, so he told me afterwards. This time the questions weren't just about the assault on Callum; we were also asked about the murder for which he was still the prime suspect. For the first, we stuck to our story unwaveringly. For the second we had no answers to give. We could only repeat over and over again our conviction that Callum was innocent.

I was puzzled. I could see that Chamberlain wasn't completely buying what I was telling him – to put it bluntly, he knew I was lying. So why wasn't he digging more deeply into the more questionable parts of my statement, or challenging me at all? It was as if he was simply going through the motions to tick the necessary boxes on the paperwork and it all seemed a bit odd. Not that I wasn't grateful, only… why? I couldn't work it out.

He was also more than a little concerned for our wellbeing, much more than the situation, as I had related it to him, warranted. That concern was confirmed when, eventually, he accompanied me back to the entrance lobby. I had turned to leave when he put out a hand to delay me.

'Whoever did this to Mr Davis knew exactly what they were doing. It was a very skilful job. They knew where the line was between keeping him alive while inflicting maximum pain and damage, and killing him. The punctured lung was a mistake. Maybe one of the hired thugs got a little over-enthusiastic.'

He stared at me intently. 'I don't believe you or Mr Cunningham had anything to do with this, but I do know that there's a lot you aren't telling me. Take my advice. Stay out of whatever Callum Davis got himself mixed up in. Make no mistake, whoever was responsible won't hesitate to come after anyone else they believe is involved.' As if I wasn't uncomfortably aware of that already!

'You've got my card. Call me if you're worried or if you remember anything else, no matter how trivial you think it is.' He was still staring at me, reinforcing my conviction that he hadn't believed anything I had told him.

'Go home and keep your head down. And don't disappear off anywhere without telling me first. We'll be interviewing Mr Davis as soon as he is well enough to answer our questions.'

'Can we see him before we leave?'

Chamberlain hesitated. 'OK. Not alone, though. One of my officers will accompany you.'

While that was the last thing we wanted, it was obviously the only way we would get to see Callum. I nodded my agreement.

* * * * *

Joe joined me at the car a few minutes later. 'Do you think they believed us?' he frowned.

'Do you?' He shook his head. 'So why did they let us go?'

'I haven't a clue, Gemma, and to be honest, right at this moment I'm too tired to care.'

I sank into the passenger seat, letting the luxurious soft leather enfold me. I was bone-tired too, more than a little scared, and I had had enough. On top of all that, I was furious with Callum for dragging us into his mess. Which really wasn't fair. Hadn't I been the start of it all? I leaned back, letting my head fall against the headrest and my eyes close as my mind raced.

'Chamberlain is no fool. We both agree that he knows we aren't telling him the truth but, for whatever reason, he's letting us get away with it, at least for now. It could be that he let us go to see what we do next. Maybe he's simply playing his hunches. Or perhaps there's something bigger going on here, something we don't know about and he does. Or… Oh, I don't know, Joe. It could simply be that despite our dodgy statements he really doesn't believe we have anything to do with it all. What do you think?'

'Same as you. I haven't got a clue.' He hesitated. 'One thing though. I'm pretty certain that he's on our side – whatever side that is. He believes Callum is innocent.'

'What makes you say that?'

'Gut feeling? Nothing I can pin down. A couple of throwaway comments he tossed into the interview. Mostly just a feeling.' The engine roared into life.

'Come on, let's go and find out how Callum is today. I hope he's awake. I've got one or two questions I'd like answered.' Joe's expression was set. He may have been concerned for Callum. He was also as angry with him as I was.

Joe's quest for an explanation was to be thwarted. We arrived on the ward to be told that Callum was still under sedation and had been pumped full of painkillers. According to the ward sister it was extremely unlikely he would realise we were there and even if he did, we wouldn't get any sense out of him.

'Can we look in on him anyway? We're heading back home this morning and would like to at least see him before we go. Please. Just for five minutes?'

She gave in. 'Two. No more.' She led us to a door off the main ward where a uniformed policeman sat on guard. He stood up as we approached.

'Gemma Mason and Joe Cunningham. D.I. Chamberlain said we could come and see Callum and that he would phone the authorisation across.' I spoke with all the confidence I could muster, hoping the message had got through. It had. The officer opened the door and led us into the room.

'Two minutes.' The sister's order followed us.

I was shocked at the sight that greeted us. I had known Callum was badly hurt, but hadn't expected that. In the light of day he looked so much worse than he had done, masked in the darkness of the previous night. I suppose I had been so concerned then that he might die that I hadn't focussed so much on his appearance. This morning the damage was all too visible. He was hooked up to an array of drips and monitors, his body bristling with wires and tubes. The only sounds were the beep of the machines and his rasping, painful breathing. One eye was puffy and closed, the colour of thunderclouds, edged with the sickly green and yellow of older beatings. His whole face was swollen and livid, a mass of cuts and grazes, his lips split and weeping. Between the bruises, his skin was the colour of the sheets he lay on. His right wrist was in plaster. Callum looked dead, despite the reassurance of the doctor that in time he would heal.

'Oh Callum,' I breathed, pity and compassion for this battered, broken body flooding through me and washing away my anger. 'What in God's name have you got yourself mixed up in?'

Joe was already moving to the bedside. 'Hey, Callum.' His voice trembled as he gazed down at his friend. 'Well, we found you, mate. Now it's up to you.'

I stifled a squeak of surprise. Callum's eyelids had flickered and his good eye had blinked open. Only for an instant; nonetheless I was certain I hadn't been mistaken. I shot a quick look at Joe. He had seen it too. Callum wasn't yet out cold, and the urgency in that split-second one-eyed gaze had revealed that he was still completely lucid. He wanted to tell us something. Only he couldn't, not with his police guard in the room. Or could he?

Time was of the essence. We had barely a minute. Luckily, Joe and I were on the same wavelength. Joe moved casually to his left as if to take a closer look at the monitors, a move which shielded Callum from the direct view of his police chaperon. At the same time, I moved to the bed and leaned in as if to drop a kiss on his forehead. One slate grey eye blinked open again, this time holding the glimmer of a smile, echoed in the faintest tremble in his lips – all that his damaged flesh would allow. No, Callum wasn't knocked out – yet.

My lips brushed his hair. 'Thanks.' The words came out barely a whisper, so faint that I struggled to hear them, even though my ear was only a couple of inches from his mouth. 'Seems you arrived… just in time.' He broke off, fighting for the strength to continue. That tiny effort had drained him. 'No time. Drugs kicking in.'

'Rest, Callum,' I murmured, 'we'll come back another time.'

A shake of his head, the faintest of movements. 'No. Now. Important,' he wheezed through his damaged lungs.

I leaned closer, hoping Joe was still shielding the guard. 'Envelope. King Street. Twenty five.' Thinking he had finished, I started to move away.

'Guildford. Find it first.' He stopped again, fighting the power of the sedatives as they flooded his system, stealing sensation from his limbs and numbing his brain. 'Don't look. Promise. Hide it. Keep it safe.' His words tailed off and his head lolled as the drugs claimed him.

'I promise,' I whispered, stroking his cheek.

'Hey, what are you doing?' The police constable stepped around Joe.

'Giving him a kiss goodbye.' I took Joe's arm. 'Come on, Joe, we've had our two minutes. Let's go home.'

KHALIA: The Jade Skull

Part IV

MAHLEENA

20.

The two great wooden doors loomed up in the half-light. Taller than two men, they separated the temple interior from the wide open courtyard beyond, and past that again, the streets and avenues of Yo'tlàn, capital City of Atlantis. This was the vast and ancient Pyramid Temple in the heart of which lay the Skull Chamber where the thirteen sacred Skulls of Light had been held in safety for thousands of years. During daylight hours, the doors to the temple were always left wide open so that those who sought guidance from the Priests and Priestesses of the Light could enter freely. At this time of night, however, they would normally be locked and barred.

Mahleena approached warily. What if some problem had arisen? No, all was well. Tonight the heavy bar had been removed and was leaning against the wall. Those who had set this plan in motion had prepared the way. She set her hand on the gleaming, wrought-gold handle and tugged gently. The heavy door opened without a sound, no reluctant hinge betraying her presence. She darted through the opening, pulling the door shut behind her, and skirted the walls keeping to the shadows until she slipped between the two massive stone pillars that stood sentinel at the courtyard's entrance, and out into the street. Her legs were shaking; there was no going back now. From this moment she was a fugitive facing an unknown and uncertain future filled with danger and hardship. For a single heartbeat she doubted the decision that had brought her to this point before she drew her courage around her like a cloak and crossed the street.

It was the middle of the night. No-one else would be out wandering the streets at this hour. Nevertheless, she couldn't take any chances. Not tonight. The precious bundle she carried reminded her just how perilous her life had become in the few short hours since dusk had fallen. At all costs, she had to avoid an encounter with the Dark Ones who had taken to carrying out random night time patrols, stopping and searching anyone they found in the streets after dusk. If she was caught, all would be lost.

Mahleena gasped in terror. An arm had snaked out of the darkness, pulling her into the black shadows of a doorway and a gentle hand covered her mouth, stifling her scream. The hand was immediately replaced by warm lips that pressed tenderly against her own, lips that she recognised and welcomed.

'Edric?' She pulled back from the familiar caress, relief and dismay filling her in equal measure. 'What are you doing here?'

'Coming with you.' He halted her objection with another kiss. 'No arguments, Mahleena. I don't know what's going on or what you're mixed up in, and it really doesn't matter. Wherever you're going, I'm coming with you.'

'But…'

'No buts.'

She snuggled against Edric's chest, breathing in his scent, letting it soothe her taut nerves. If only he could, but it was impossible. And even if it was possible, how could she ask it of him? Ask him to leave behind his whole life for… what? Danger, hardship and, very likely, death.

'No arguments,' he murmured into her hair. 'I will not let you go alone.'

In that moment, with those words, the future appeared a great deal less dark and terrifying to Mahleena. With Edric by her side, she could find the courage and strength to carry out the task she had been given.

'How did you know?' she asked.

'My darling, you are a poor liar and a worse actor. You have been behaving strangely for days, and even more so all day today. When you left for the Temple tonight, I knew in my gut that this was it. Whatever *it* is. When I discovered your bags, packed and ready to go in the back of a cupboard... There was no way I was going to let you leave without me, so I followed you.' He took her hands, cold as stone despite the warmth of the night, and gazed deep into her eyes, lifting her still trembling fingers to brush them with his lips.

Mahleena pressed even closer to her lover, hugging him tightly. Felt the strength of his arms as they encircled her shoulders, the warmth of his skin through his clothes. Felt his heart, beating in time with her own. She could do this alone. She was, after all, a Priestess of the Light and Guardian of the sacred Skulls of Light, but the truth was that she didn't want to. The knowledge that she would have to walk away from Edric forever had filled her with an almost unbearable grief, her heart breaking ever since she had been chosen for this task. It was a sacrifice that had caused her more pain than she had ever believed she could feel. In leaving him, she would be leaving part of her soul. Nevertheless, the question would not go away. Could she really ask him to give up all he had ever known to accompany her on a journey that would more than likely end in an early death for both of them?

'You aren't asking. I'm volunteering.' There it was again. That uncanny ability Edric had of picking up what she was thinking. Yet he had no idea of the mission she was undertaking. And he mustn't, she vowed. Not yet. Not until they were far away from here.

His hands cupped her chin and lifted her face so their eyes met. 'Why would I want to stay here without you, Mahleena? You are my life. I have no idea where you – we – are going, or why. You can tell me, or not tell me, it makes no difference. I am coming with you.'

She held him tightly, her heart drowning in love. No, she had not asked him. She could not. She had sworn an oath to the Elders that she would tell no-one that she was leaving. Now, out of nowhere, her prayers had been answered. The Elders would be furious if they knew. She was betraying their orders and her promise to them. Well, she no longer cared. It was too late. They would never find out unless – her nerves prickled painfully as she allowed the thought in – unless she was captured. And in that devastating scenario, Edric's presence would be the least of the Elders' problems. All at once, the task that lay ahead of her seemed a little less daunting. A little less impossible.

'It will be dangerous. You risk your life if you come with me. Before very long, the Shadow Chasers will be hunting us down.'

'Mahleena, *you* are life to me. I would rather die with you than live here without you. And if my life will be in danger, then yours must be too. Do you believe I would let you face that alone?' He winked. 'So, we have strength in numbers. We can watch out for each other.'

Mahleena locked her hands behind his neck, pulled him close and kissed him hard. 'Have I ever told you that I love you?' she murmured with a smile.

He kissed her back, and all the love he held for her was expressed in that kiss. 'Maybe once or twice,' he grinned. In truth, she told him every day. 'But I think I can cope with hearing it again.'

Her eyes told him just how deeply she did love him. 'I love you more than you will ever know,' she whispered softly. 'I'm so glad you are coming with me.' She grew serious. 'Come on. We need to get back to the house, pick up my belongings and pack a few things for you. We must hurry. We can't afford any delay.'

This time, Edric's grin almost split his face in two. 'Already done.' He indicated two large bundles lying on the ground behind her, virtually invisible in the shadows. 'I brought them with me.' Mahleena raised a questioning eyebrow.

'I packed earlier, as soon as I realised you were leaving tonight. So you see, I was always coming with you, whether you said yes or no.'

'Oh, were you...?'

Edric's finger pressed a warning against her lips. Now she heard it too – footsteps, approaching the doorway where they huddled. Mahleena and Edric shrank back further into the gloom, hardly daring to breathe. They were well hidden in the shadows and unless anyone peered closely, they were unlikely to be seen; nevertheless the risk was there. Within moments, scarcely beyond arms' reach, two Shadow Chasers strode by engrossed in conversation and disappeared around the corner.

Mahleena let out a long slow breath, a sigh echoed by Edric. That had been close. Too close. If the Shadow Chasers had come by only a few heartbeats later, the two groups would have run right into each other. It was a stark reminder of the perilous situation the now-fugitives would face from that moment on. They waited a few more seconds until they were certain the patrol was not returning, then shouldered their packs and, hand in hand, slipped out into the deserted street.

21.

Some hours later, when the sun was just beginning to lighten the eastern sky from below the horizon and they were far enough from the city gates to feel at least a little safer, they rested in the shelter of a small copse. Edric was sleeping peacefully, not so Mahleena. Exhausted as she was, she could not sleep. Nestled within the crook of Edric's arm she lay wide awake and restless with apprehension. Slowly, carefully, so as not to disturb him, she eased out of his embrace and moved to the small campfire they had set under the cover of the trees. There she sat, staring without seeing into the embers.

After the initial close call with the Shadow Chasers' patrol their escape from Yo'tlàn had been uneventful, and once outside its walls they had made swift progress across the moonlit countryside. Their objective was the coast where a small ship would be waiting to carry them away across the ocean to another land. Beyond that, nothing was certain. They would be walking an unknown path on an unknown continent where they would have to rely on their wits, strength and courage to survive. Their only ally was the priceless treasure Mahleena carried in her backpack: Khalia, the fifth of the thirteen sacred Skulls of Light.

Their safe escape would count for nothing, however, if they did not reach the ship in time. With the immediate danger of the Shadow Chasers was behind them – the patrols would be easier to avoid in the cover of the fields and woodlands – time was now the critical factor between success and failure. They had to be on board the ship when it sailed on the first tide after nightfall in six days' time. Omar had believed they had ten days at most before the

Dark Ones discovered the Skulls were missing from the Pyramid Temple, at which point all the ports and harbours would be locked down immediately. Ten days – *if* the fugitives were incredibly lucky. In reality, it was likely to be much sooner.

The constantly shifting crimsons, golds and ambers of the flames and their flickering warmth were gradually working their magic, soothing Mahleena's unease. Instead of worrying about what was to come, her thoughts drifted back to the events that had brought her and Edric to this darkened wood and the very different future to the one they had planned that lay ahead of them.

*   *   *   *   *

Life in Atlantis had been changing rapidly, and not for the better. The once open, easy-going society had closed down and withdrawn into itself. Whereas once, not so very long ago, the faces of those who lived there carried smiles and kind words, now they were darkened with suspicion and fear. The reason for this change? The rise in the power and oppression of the Shadow Chasers; the Dark Ones, the people of Atlantis called them, as much for the shroud of energy that imbued and surrounded them as for the dark cloaks and uniforms they wore. Even in her own, relatively short life – she had only just entered her thirtieth year – Mahleena had witnessed the cold fingers of this change pinching ever more harshly. Even so, she had not understood how close the Dark Ones were to taking complete control until that morning – had it really been only five days earlier? – when she had been summoned quietly, furtively even, before the Temple's Council of Elders with strict instructions to tell no-one about the summons or the subsequent meeting. During the course of that meeting it became brutally clear why such secrecy was essential.

Sitting in the sunlit room with the fragrance of ten thousand blossoms drifting in on the breeze through the open windows, and serenaded by the gentle splashing of the fountains and trilling birdsong in the gardens below, she found it hard to take in what she was being told. The story laid out before her was a harrowing scenario that struck an incongruous and monstrous note in the serene sanctuary of the Temple. Yet it *was* real. Horribly, frighteningly real. She stared at the sombre faces of the Elders who sat facing her. There were four of them. Omar was the most senior, the High Priest of the entire Pyramid Temple complex. On the far end sat Oolan, second only in authority and seniority to Omar. Between them, silent and grim-faced, were Haanu and Regus, High Priestess and Priest respectively and senior guardians of the Skull Chamber. In the usual course of affairs, only one or two of them would preside at meetings. If they were all here... Mahleena shivered as icy tentacles of foreboding plucked at her flesh.

Omar did most of the talking, the solemn expressions of the others giving weight to his words. The Shadow Chasers planned to seize the Pyramid Temple. More specifically, they wanted control of the Skull Chamber and the power of the thirteen skulls, crushing mercilessly anyone who stood in their way and, given their past record, many who didn't. The fall of Atlantis, Yo'tlàn and its Pyramid Temple was now set. The fate of the skulls, however, was not.

Mahleena was one of twelve priests and priestesses from the Temple who had been chosen by the skulls themselves to become their new guardians. Five days from that meeting, after night had fallen, these guardians would enter the Chamber one by one, take their skull and set a replica in its place. They would then leave the city unseen and flee Atlantis with their precious charge. They would all be travelling a dangerous, difficult and lonely road. No-one must know. They were to tell no-one that they were leaving. If the slightest hint of the plans reached the Dark Ones, they would storm the Temple immediately and seize the skulls before they could be spirited away.

When she asked who the other chosen guardians were there was no answer. She must not know, as none would know, the identity of the others.

'If you are captured, Mahleena, you will tell them everything they want to know. You will not be able to resist. They will show you no mercy.' Ice replaced the blood in her veins at Omar's words. 'If you do not know, then you cannot tell.'

'But you,' she interrupted, 'they will know you are involved. And you know who we are. Even if we do all escape, they will come for you.'

Sorrow darkened Omar's eyes. 'Do you believe we have not thought of that? Do not worry, child. We know the danger. They will not learn anything from us.'

The four familiar and dearly loved faces watched her sadly. Tears were welling at the corner of Haanu's eyes and moistening her lashes. Mahleena's heart lurched as the meaning of his words sunk in. She stared back at them wide-eyed and filled with grief, and her own tears fell.

'We are not afraid to do what must be done, child,' he continued. 'We, and the skulls, are asking you to risk your life. We can do no less. But that is not your concern. Go now, and return here to the Skull Chamber four hours after sunset, five days from now. As soon as you have the skull, you must leave. Immediately, do you understand? You must not remain here a moment longer than necessary.'

'Which skull has asked for me?' Mahleena was calling on every shred of her self-control to focus.

'Khalia.'

Khalia. Birthed among the stars of the Maidens, created from the purest deep moss-green jade. She should have guessed. She had always had a strong connection to Khalia, who emanated a strong yet gentle energy of peace and comfort. Like a coming home, Mahleena had always said. She was glad. Khalia was the skull she would have chosen for herself.

'One of us will bring the replica to you in the morning of that day. Keep it out of sight. I cannot repeat enough how vital it is that no-one else learns of our plans.'

'I understand.' Mahleena's mind was a churning maelstrom. Her world had just been turned upside down and would never be the right way up again. She was trying to make sense of everything she had heard and failing spectacularly. Fear, bewilderment and confusion were rapidly overshadowed by a growing understanding of what would mean for her. Edric. She would have to leave Edric. The pain hit her like a physical blow.

'Mahleena?' She did not answer. Numbly she rose and left the room, no longer seeing the sunlight streaming through the windows, no longer hearing the birdsong or the splashing of the fountains.

22.

Curled up next to the glowing warmth of the embers, Mahleena's thoughts wandered further back in time to the day she had first met Khalia. She had been only twelve years of age, still a child, and a recent initiate into the Temple's fold, and yet the day remained as clear as crystal in her memory. At that time Omar had been the senior Guardian of the Skulls as well as their tutor and one day, as part of their education, he had taken her, with three of her companions, to the Skull Chamber. It had been a pivotal moment for Mahleena. She had stared wide-eyed and lost for words at the rich amethyst lining the curving walls and the massive crystal cluster that dominated the circular room. Mostly though it had been the thirteen skulls that had captured her attention. Twelve rested on clear crystal plinths, the thirteenth crowned a massive cluster of ice-clear quartz points in the centre of the room. They had gazed back at her, silent and unmoving, nothing more in appearance than inert lumps of carved rock. Yet even then, inexperienced and young as she was, Mahleena had sensed the life and intelligence held within them.

The small group had gathered around the Priest, enthralled and eager to learn, as he related the story of these thirteen Skulls of Light. He had told them how each skull had been created by a different race of highly evolved beings on worlds scattered throughout the star systems of Earth's galaxy and beyond. How, since their arrival on earth, they had been cared for and protected by groups of men, women and children carefully chosen for their qualities of courage, compassion and selflessness. How it was only here, many millennia earlier, in the

Pyramid Temple of a young Atlantis, that all thirteen had been brought together for the first time.

Omar was a master storyteller and his tales were filled with adventure, bravery and danger. Mahleena had listened spellbound, oblivious to everything but his words, in her imagination living the stories of each of the skulls as he told it.

'Throughout their history,' Omar had become serious as he reached the end of his narrative, 'there have been those who have sought the skulls' power for their own profit. Whenever their threat has become too great, the descendants of those who created the skulls have done what was necessary to keep the skulls safe. Though they have rested peacefully here in the Pyramid Temple for lifetimes, we cannot become complacent. There will always be those for whom greed outweighs humanity. The threat has not gone away, and it will not. We must always remain watchful.'

* * * * *

His prophecy had proven right. It was happening again, Mahleena thought sorrowfully, becoming aware of the dying embers and the pre-dawn chill that was seeping through her cloak.

Had it really been only five days ago that she had been summoned? It felt much longer. Now here she was, fleeing Yo'tlàn and the Temple forever. She was under no illusion that she would ever return. Tears prickled her eyelids and trickled down her cheeks from the grief that weighed heavy in her heart. She was already missing her home.

Well, she had made her choice; this was her life now. There was no use in regrets. In that moment Edric's hand enveloped hers, the simple touch a reassurance that she wasn't alone. Mahleena smiled at him through her tears. Difficult though it was to leave, she felt a deep comfort that Edric would travel by her side. How much more impossible would it have been to have walked away leaving him behind? Would she really have found the strength to do so? He smiled down at her, his eyes filled with love and encouragement. Well, it didn't matter any longer. It was a choice she hadn't had to make. He was here and they would face this adventure – and the perils of their future – together.

23.

It was a long time before Mahleena revealed to Edric the secret she was holding. Countless moons had waxed and waned, many seasons passed, since they had fled the night-dark streets of Atlantis. They had travelled far from their home, had crossed oceans and plains, rivers and deserts, mountains and forests. Time had long ago ceased to have any meaning for them. What did it matter? Counting the days or the seasons would serve no purpose. She had no idea of their destination and at times wondered if there was one, yet with Edric by her side, she carried on, ever faithful to Omar's promise – that she would know when she had arrived. She travelled blindly, trusting completely in Khalia to guide her footsteps.

Edric was true to his promise. He had never pressed her for an explanation, despite his curiosity. No, that wasn't right. It was far stronger than curiosity, this burning desire to know that she saw growing ever more strongly within him by the day. He had given up his former life, everything he had ever known, to accompany her on an unknown quest for an unknown reason. Nevertheless, he kept his word, occasionally asking, never insisting even if, at times, she could see the frustration boiling within him. Always, however reluctantly, he would accept Mahleena's quiet reply that it was not time for him to know.

That time must come soon, however. Edric's questions were coming more frequently, and although he continued to accept her answer without argument, she could sense his growing impatience. She, and Khalia, owed him an explanation. He deserved no less. She doubted she would have made it this far on her own. He was her warmth on cold nights, her strength when fear threatened to rise and overwhelm her. Every day she loved him more for his patience, acceptance and love.

Khalia had remained dormant since they had left the Temple, as Omar had told her it would be. The Dark Ones were highly trained in sophisticated mental and super-mental skills that would allow them to tune into the skull's energy from a considerable distance, so Khalia would not awaken until she could communicate in safety. Nevertheless, in such close and constant proximity to her – Mahleena carried the skull always in a bundle slung over her shoulder and slept beside her at night – the travellers absorbed her energy. It was like a warm, comfortable blanket that soothed weary legs and troubled hearts. Mahleena knew that Edric felt it too, soaking into his cells and his soul, encouraging and inspiring him to go on.

Edric was sensitive. Mahleena suspected that he had guessed that the bundle she carried contained an object of great power and importance, and it was likely that he suspected its nature. She trusted him implicitly, completely confident that he would not betray that trust. She would tell him, when the time came. She prayed often that that time would come soon.

* * * * *

They had taken shelter in a small cave. Outside, the rain fell in torrents, running in brown, muddy rivers down the hillside and cascading over the entrance in a small waterfall. Inside, however, it was warm, snug and dry. Fire danced happily in the centre of the floor – warned by the ominous bank of approaching thunderclouds, they had found shelter and gathered firewood in readiness – and they were well fed. Earlier that day, Edric had successfully lifted several fish from one of the small chuckling rivers that criss-crossed the landscape here and the sweet roasted flesh had been complemented by roots, greens and juicy, tart berries that grew in abundance on these scrubby hillsides.

He was sitting with his back against the smooth wall of the cave. Contented and sleepy, Mahleena nestled up against him, snuggling into the hollow between his shoulder and his chin, taking pleasure in the warmth and comfort of his arms around her and his breath tickling her hair. If it was possible, she had grown to love him even more in the time that had passed since they had left Yo'tlàn. He was strong, emotionally and mentally as well as physically, and he adored her, which would have been more than enough without any of his other qualities. Their lovemaking had warmed many a cold night, kisses and passion stoking a fire within them both and reviving their weary commitment to whatever lay ahead. How lonely she would have been without him, how much harder this path she had been thrown upon. Moreover, Edric had, to the surprise of both of them, proven his skills as a hunter. She was certain Khalia would have led them to sufficient food but she doubted they would have eaten half as well. Her own hunting abilities were limited to trapping the occasional dozily unsuspecting fish.

Then there was the companionship and the conversation. They never fell short of something to talk about, whether reminiscing about their previous life in the bustling city of Yo'tlàn, discussing the day's adventures or speculating on the future. They would make up stories of how they would live once they reached their destination, and when neither felt like talking, the silence was easy. Today, comfortable in that silence, they dozed in front of flickering orange-gold flames that cast dancing phantoms of light on the roof and walls of their tiny refuge. Recently the terrain had become difficult. Progress had been slow and draining. It was good to rest for a while.

'Mahleena.' A gentle call, whispering in the slumber of her mind, trickled into her consciousness. 'Mahleena.' The young woman's eyes fluttered open. After so long, it took a few moments for recognition to awaken.

It called her again. 'It is time, Mahleena. Time to tell him.' The skull had awoken.

'Khalia?' No sound crossed Mahleena's lips. There was no need. She would speak with Khalia through her thoughts.

'He has waited long enough. Tell him now, Little One.' Mahleena felt a great weight lift. For so long she had carried this secret, wanting to share it but unable to do so. Now, at last, she could tell her beloved companion, who had waited with such patience for this moment. She glanced at Edric, snoring softly beside her.

'Edric.' She shook him gently. 'Edric, wake up.' She felt him stir, rising slowly from the depths of his sleep.

'What is it? Is something wrong? Is it time to leave?' he mumbled sleepily.

'No, my love. It is time for you to know. Khalia has spoken.'

He was wide awake now, looking at her in surprise. 'Here? Now?'

She gave him a wide smile. 'Yes. Why not? It's as good as anywhere.'

'Khalia…' The name finally registered. 'But she's…'

'One of the Skulls of Light. Yes. She's the secret I couldn't share.'

Edric nodded slowly, his suspicions finally confirmed. 'I thought as much. That it had to be one of the skulls, though which one, I couldn't guess. I couldn't find any other reason so important that you would be prepared to leave the Temple or your home. Leave me. But why? Why do you have her? Why have we taken her from the Temple?'

'Let me show him.' The words, as warm and comforting as the fire that lit the cave, drifted through Mahleena's mind. 'Give me to him.'

Mahleena unwrapped the soft woollen shawl that protected Khalia. As the skull emerged from its folds, Edric's heartbeat quickened. Although he had known of the skulls all his life – everyone in Atlantis did – he had never set eyes on one. They were fiercely protected by the Priests and accessible only to them. Now he was about to look upon the one who had been his hidden travelling companion for so many moons.

Revealed in the firelight, Khalia appeared unearthly. Magical. Sinister even. The dark hollows of the eye sockets, which in a living being gleamed and shone with life, were impenetrable black pits. The lines of the skull plate sutures, etched into the cranial dome, stood in dark contrast to the deep green stone. More was to come.

'Give me to him.' Khalia repeated.

'Take her. She has asked it.' A momentary flicker of apprehension washed over Edric's face. His heart racing in anticipation and not a little nervousness, he offered his cupped hands.

'There is a story she wishes to show you,' Mahleena explained. 'Just close your eyes, relax and watch. There is nothing else you need to do.'

The skull was unexpectedly warm on his palms, and heavier than he had anticipated. He let his eyelids fall and began to breathe slowly and rhythmically to calm his fluttering pulse. As he focussed his attention on the heavy object resting in his hands, a tingle ran though his fingers, across his palms and up his arms, eventually filling his entire body as if every cell was vibrating in unison.

'Come with us.' Khalia's command was for Mahleena. Obediently, the priestess closed her eyes so that she could link with the vision Khalia was transmitting to Edric.

24.

They were looking up at a clear night sky. She and Edric.
It was dark, so dark. A backdrop of the blackest black,
studded with countless stars so thickly clustered they
looked like diamond dust on an obsidian plate. More stars
than she had seen on even the darkest, clearest moonless
night. Colours. So many colours, sparkling like jewels
caught in the light. Blue and silver. Red and green. Pink
and gold and so many more. Precious, twinkling
gemstones in the sky. Glancing around, totally immersed
in this world Khalia was creating, she saw Edric standing a
little distance away, lost in wonder at the awe-inspiring
beauty of the cosmos that was being revealed to them.

One cluster in particular was drawing Mahleena's
attention, a constellation of seven... eight... nine stars.
Pulsing. Calling to them. The Maidens. She recognised it,
and yet... Something wasn't quite right. Of course. That
was what had confused her. The Maidens were only seven
stars, here there were nine. Two were much fainter than
their sisters, certainly, but they were unmistakeably there.
She was certain she had correctly identified the Maidens,
with two additional stars that were not visible from
Atlantis. In which case, how could she see them now?
Where was she?

A shaft of light, shimmering silver blue, appeared in
the distance and travelled rapidly towards them, growing
larger as it approached until it was big enough for her to fit
comfortably in size. At that point, its momentum paused
and it divided into two. One shaft sped towards Edric,
surrounding and capturing him, the other headed towards
Mahleena to envelop her in a dazzling luminous cocoon.

Smoothly, although she had the sensation they were moving extremely quickly, they were lifted and carried to the left of the cluster, towards one specific star that was shining more brightly than any of its companions.

The star was surrounded by satellites. Instinctively she knew what they were – other worlds, just like the one she and Edric lived on. Edric. Where was he? Secure in the silver blue beam, he was utterly lost in his experience, the wonderstruck expression on his face matching her own feelings of ecstasy as they flew through the vastness of space.

They were hovering over one of these worlds now, flying so low that they could see clearly the features of the surface, though never landing. Mountain peaks of silver stone, like highly polished knife blades, thrust miles up into a violet sky. Thick forests of emerald green were dotted with gleaming golden lakes that reflected the light of an immense orange sun, and between the trees rose up a city of slender towers – one hundred, two hundred storeys high, their walls of some transparent glass-like material.

The silver blue beam took them lower, skimming above a clearing in the forest, so wide that a thousand paces wouldn't have crossed it. A vessel, unlike anything she had ever seen, filled the centre of this clearing. It was a massive disc whose outer skin was a dull blue-grey like the sea in a storm. Men and women – or were they? They looked very different to the men and women she knew – bustled about. They all looked alike, tall, with long white-gold hair and sapphire blue eyes, and every one of them dressed in long blue and gold robes. As if at a signal, the activity suddenly stopped. Five people – two men and three women – were moving through the crowd. One of the females led the group, followed by a male who carried

127

a square box with no visible hinge or clasp. It was made of a dull, dark metal and its sides were etched with strange symbols. The remaining male and two females brought up the rear.

Mahleena caught her breath. She recognised the symbols on the box. There were identical ones in the Pyramid Temple, carved sharply into the stone frame and lintel at the entrance to the Skull Chamber. Instinctively she knew that this box held Khalia. What was this place? Where had the skull brought them?

The five walked up the sloping gangway into the vessel. No sooner had they disappeared from view than the ramp slid closed, sealing the entrance. The crowd had vanished from the clearing. Without a sound, the huge craft rose silently from the ground, and in the blink of an eye, it was gone.

For a split second Mahleena was plunged into darkness. When the light returned, the scene had changed. Edric was still to her left, a little further away now, his face a mask of confusion. Far ahead of them in the distance, to the horizon, ghastly flashes lit up the sky, the ground burned and, even at such a distance, crashes, roars and explosions assaulted her ears. Dense jungle spread out below them. They were descending again, down to the canopy and beneath it, lowering through the tangle of branches and creepers until the thick leafy soil of the jungle floor became visible. Something was crashing through the undergrowth. No, not something. Someone. A man, small, dark-skinned, wiry, stumbled panic-stricken towards where she watched, invisible to him. He was dressed in an ornately embroidered tunic and leggings, now ripped and stained from his headlong flight. He wore a mask of terror, more terror than Mahleena could have ever imagined anyone could feel, and blood trickled down his face and limbs from deep scratches where thorns and branches had snagged his skin. In his hands, holding on to it as if his life depended on it, was a carved, moss green skull. Khalia!

The darkness enveloped Mahleena once more. When it lifted, she was looking down on the Skull Chamber. Edric was much closer now; if she reached out her hand, she would touch him. Mahleena blinked in surprise. She was looking down on herself. Mesmerised, she witnessed the scene unfold exactly as she remembered, watching herself lift Khalia from the quartz pedestal, set the replica skull in her place and slip through the temple gates to flee through the streets of Yo'tlàn with Edric at her side.

The scene shifted back to the Temple. It was daylight and the entrance courtyard was swarming with Shadow Chasers, bludgeoning their way into the main buildings, arresting – brutally – everyone unfortunate enough to be in their path. Xy-Barian, supreme commander of the Shadow Chasers, swaggered arrogantly and triumphantly through the corridors of the complex, strutting into its most sacred area, the Skull Chamber, with the air of one who believes he has achieved his greatest ambition.

His expression morphed from triumph through disbelief to blind fury with the bitter realisation that he had been cheated of his prize. He was too late. The skulls he had for so long coveted were gone, those around him nothing but worthless copies. Tears poured down Mahleena's face as she watched him wreak his devastating vengeance on the chamber, smashing to splinters the replica skulls, their crystal plinths and the amethyst lined walls, and ordering his men to turn to dust the massive central plinth and the equally massive cluster of ice clear quartz points that sat upon it. She sobbed heartbroken at the destruction of her beloved Temple.

Her shattered heart contracted further in grief as Khalia showed them the misery that had fallen upon Atlantis since that day, a misery born of fear and tyranny. Xy-Barian had severely and mercilessly punished its innocent citizens for his thwarted ambitions. The people huddled in their homes, beaten and afraid, all freedom lost, and the vicelike grip of the Dark Ones crushed ever tighter.

The scene vanished. It was done. Mahleena opened her eyes. Beside her, Edric was staring at the skull he still held. He looked shocked, bewildered and angry.

'I understand.' His tone was icy, his jaw clenched. 'I understand why the skulls had to be taken from the Temple. I understand why you could not tell me. What I don't understand,' his fist smashed violently into the floor, 'is why, if the skulls are so all-powerful, they couldn't stop the Dark Ones. Why they couldn't – or wouldn't – save Atlantis from the fate that has fallen upon it.' His eyes glittered angrily.

'Because they cannot go against our free will. They will not go against the choices we make.' Mahleena's voice was soft and soothing.

'No-one in Atlantis chose this.'

'Yes Edric, they did. Unwittingly. Unconsciously, it's true, but they did make that choice. If they had not, it could not have happened. The mass consciousness was ready and willing to submit to the tyranny of fear and all it entailed. Had it been otherwise, the skulls would have acted.'

Edric glared at Mahleena, angrier than she had ever seen him. 'That is total nonsense. I don't accept for one moment that the people of Atlantis wanted what has come upon them.'

'Wanted it? No, nor do I. But neither could they believe that they could change what was happening. They saw the rise of the Dark Ones as inevitable and felt powerless to do anything about it. In believing themselves to be powerless, they became powerless, and granted those events their tacit acceptance.'

'Maybe.' Edric's shoulders slumped and his expression softened. He pulled Mahleena to him and held her close. 'Is that really all it takes for evil to triumph?' he murmured softly to the night, his lips brushing her hair. He sighed wearily. 'What's done is done,' he acknowledged. 'We made our choice a long time ago, and must see it through. What now?'

'We go on. Until we reach our destination, wherever that might be. What else is there to do?'

'Nothing else, my beautiful, wise love. Nothing else.'

'Maybe one day soon, we'll find it. Then we can stop and make ourselves a home.'

'And a family?' Edric asked, his eyes twinkling.

'That would be nice,' Mahleena replied as his lips found hers and she melted into his embrace.

25.

They continued their journey, day after day, month after month, and still they did not reach their destination. They trudged across endless open plains where the sun beat mercilessly down on the scorched earth and grass burned brown by its heat, and when the summer's heat turned to winter's cold they lowered their heads and plodded on through those same plains, now scoured by bitter winds and driving hail that blasted down from the Arctic tundra. They scaled soaring mountain ranges and battled through forests so thick as to be virtually impenetrable.

Just as they believed that the world had thrown the worst it had at them, another mountain range rose up in their path. It was a sight more imposing, more frightening, more impossible, than anything they had previously encountered in all their long years of travel. The towering peaks went on, it seemed, forever, their upper heights lost in the clouds, snow blanketing the slopes, in places almost to their base even now, at mid-summer. Mahleena's heart sank. Was there no end to trials they were being asked to overcome? There was no doubt in her mind – this was their route onwards. She threw an apprehensive glance at her lover.

'You're sure that's the way?' Apprehension flooded Edric's face.

'I'm sure. But I'm not sure we'll make it.' Her voice trembled a little. They had been through so much, survived against all the odds. Never before, though, had they encountered a challenge such as this. Was the obstacle ahead the one that would finally beat them? Fear flirted with her courage and Mahleena felt her heartbeat quicken.

It would be all too easy to die amongst those peaks. She forced her thoughts away from the possibility and looked at Edric, needing his strength.

'Can we do it? Can we get through?' For once, her courage and determination were faltering.

Briefly, Edric looked as daunted as she felt, then he straightened his back and squared his shoulders. 'If we're going in there, our biggest challenge will be getting through it alive. It's going to be dangerous, bitterly cold, and we have no idea what other dangers we'll meet. Which means we need to consider the practicalities. If we aren't properly prepared, we'll die.

'Can we do it? I don't know. But we've survived other mountain ranges, so we have some idea of what to expect.' He smiled to reassure her. It was far from convincing; Edric was no more certain than she was. 'And we have Khalia. She hasn't let us down so far. She's protected and guided us to here. Maybe we just need to trust her now, more than ever before.'

Mahleena nodded, drawing on her dwindling reserves of strength and resolve. Impatient as she was to keep moving on, she recognised the wisdom in Edric's advice. 'You're right, my love. If we go charging in there now unprepared, we'll be dead within a couple of days. We need food supplies, furs, firewood. There will be precious few of any of those once we head into the higher passes. We can't take much time getting it all together either. If we haven't made it through to the other side before winter sets in we'll die up there, and we don't know how far we have to go or how long it will take us.'

They set up camp on the lee of a small hill where, for fifteen days, Mahleena gathered berries, roots and anything else edible she could find, and Edric put his

133

hunting skills to good use. In the searing summer heat Mahleena dried the meat on sun-baked stones until it was like leather. It was unappetising but would be nourishing. Edric was venturing daily into the highest crags of the nearest foothills searching out those animals whose coats would provide the insulation they needed – snow leopard, wolf and bear – and together they cured and fashioned the pelts from his kills into crude but effective clothing and boots. They hacked down the few straggling trees that grew in the vicinity, binding the longest branches into a crude litter with animal sinew. They would need more supplies than they could carry if they were to have any chance of survival. The remaining wood they chopped for firewood. It would be green, but better than nothing. Then they rolled their supplies into bundles which they fastened to their makeshift sled. It was a meagre reserve for such a perilous expedition.

* * * * *

It was time. They must wait no longer. The morning was clear and bright without a cloud in the sky and, even this early in the day, the sun's warmth played on their skin. In good spirits, refusing to be pessimistic in spite of a sense of trepidation at the formidable trek they were about to embark upon, Mahleena and Edric hoisted the remaining packs onto their backs, grabbed their sled and set out into the mountains.

Once off the flat lands of the plain, progress was difficult, even on the lower slopes. The ground was steep and was made up of loose shale that slithered and slid unpredictably under their feet so that they slipped and stumbled constantly, the clatter of dislodged stones tumbling behind them a stark reminder of the consequences of a misplaced step. The higher they climbed, the more likely the risk of a fall became and the more severe its outcome. Edric was now hauling the litter awkwardly over the rough ground single-handedly while Mahleena went ahead to pick the easiest and safest route for him to follow

* * * * *

Mahleena dropped to the ground, massaging her aching leg muscles. A moment later Edric sank down next to her, panting hard. It had been an exhausting struggle up the treacherous loose mountainside, but the scree beds were at last behind them and they had solid dark grey rock beneath their feet. From now on the terrain would be easier, at least for a while, less steep, and stable underfoot. They had stopped to rest at the entrance to a natural pass flanked by two jagged spires that stood like sentinels marking the boundary of the range and leading the way into its heart.

When they crested the saddle-shaped corridor a short while later, they stopped in their tracks, open-mouthed and struck silent with awe. Nothing had prepared them for the spectacle spread out before them. From here, half way up to the roof of the world, mountain after mountain after mountain spread out for as far as the eye could see in a display of unprecedented beauty, each peak reaching higher than the one before it. Virgin snow sparkled in the pure, clear sunlight as if it had been sprinkled with diamond powder, in vivid contrast to the deep grey rock and the bluest of cloudless blue skies. From the apex of each rocky spire, delicate veils of snow spray trailed across the sky, carried off by the fierce winds that swirled constantly around the crags and pinnacles. Mahleena and Edric had seen many wonders since they had left Atlantis.

Nothing though had matched the vista they now encountered. It was heart-achingly, breath-takingly beautiful. And it was utterly terrifying. How would they ever find their way through? Surely even Khalia would be unable to lead them safely to the other side of this.

Mahleena's teeth were chattering. In spite of the bright sunshine the wind was bitingly cold, cutting through her clothes like a knife to slice at her skin. They had already climbed high into the foothills and the temperature had dropped correspondingly. Even here, a long way from the high passes, dying of cold was a real possibility. She rummaged in one of the bundles, dragged out a roughly-fashioned cloak and wrapped it around her body. It was thick and heavy – and it stank – but, blessing of blessings, she felt warmer straight away. Next to her, Edric was binding his own cloak with some rough strips of leather.

She pulled a face. 'Phew, you smell even worse than I do. This stench is going to get some getting used to.'

He grinned back. 'I don't expect Khalia will mind.' Grabbing her hand in one of his, the other tugging on the litter, he led her into the mountains.

26.

Mahleena shuddered violently. She wasn't physically cold. The thick furs that bundled her from head to toe protected her well from the bitter winds and sub-zero temperatures. It was the howling, like crazed wolves, that echoed across the barren, boulder-littered valleys and around the stark jagged peaks of the mountains towering above her, that chilled her to the marrow. Mournful, lost, the unearthly wail rose and fell in time with the gusts that buffeted the two lone figures battling their way through this alien landscape.

There had been a brief respite as they had come down from the high pass into this wide, shallow valley in the lee of a sturdy shoulder of rock. No snow lay here, unlike in the higher passes where they had trudged thigh deep at times through clinging drifts that sucked the strength and life from their legs.

She paused, her chest heaving, sucking in painful lungfuls of the thin air, hungry for the scarce oxygen. Edric was already sprawled on his back, his breath rasping like a blunt saw. At this altitude, every exertion demanded a monumental effort and their progress had slowed to a snail's pace. They had to stop ever more frequently to rest, and it took longer to recover their strength each time they did.

Mahleena's gaze had been fixed to the ground all day, as she had concentrated on negotiating the uneven rock beneath her feet without falling. Now she lifted her eyes to look ahead, and immediately wished she hadn't. Another wall of mountains filled the horizon. Another perilous pass to cross. Beyond it would be another, and another. How many more? A heavy grey shroud of futility enveloped her. She dropped down beside Edric, not wanting to think about it. Not wanting to think about anything.

She was tired. They both were. No, tiredness was nothing compared to this bone-numbing fatigue that gripped her body. She could not now remember a time when she had not felt this exhaustion. On and on they walked, to where they did not know, holding on to nothing but the promise that she would recognise it when they arrived. The journey had been so long already, longer than she could ever have imagined. How much further would it be? A day? A year? Ten years? Khalia did not enlighten her. Did it really matter in any case? Mahleena was at her limits. She could not go on much further and she doubted that Edric could either. This latest obstacle, this endless series of impossible climbs and gut wrenching descents, in air too thin to feed them, was testing them in every moment. She had had enough. All she wanted to do was stop, lie down on the hard frozen ground, and sleep. And if she never woke up again? Well, in this moment, she really didn't care.

If she had known in the beginning, so long ago now, how it would be, would she still have accepted the task? Yes, of course she would have. She had had no real choice; Khalia had chosen her.And Omar and the other Elders had emphasised repeatedly that the future of humankind was at stake. What was her one small life in the face of such a threat? She *had* accepted, in full knowledge of dangers far greater and consequences far more brutal than any conditions she had yet endured. She had accepted, understanding clearly that if she was captured by the Dark Ones, she would face slow, agonising torture until death. Here, in the empty desolation of this frozen landscape, those dangers lay far behind in another world. The golden domes and wide tree-lined avenues of Yo'tlàn were a distant dream. Only the weight of Khalia, slung over her shoulder, served as a constant reminder that the dream was real.

Slowly, like automatons whose power source was running low, the two travellers struggled back to their feet and trudged across the valley floor, stumbling up the low rise on the far side. Beyond it would be another ridge, and another, and another, in an endless procession. A few steps in front, Edric turned and reached for Mahleena's hand, pulling her up the last few paces to the crest. For a split second she saw an expression of utter hopelessness and defeat in his eyes. Then it was gone, replaced by his usual smile of encouragement. It had been there though, and she had seen it. She wished fervently that she hadn't.

* * * * *

On the other side of the rise, a snowfield stretched out across the wide, shallow bowl of the valley, which lay between two jutting arms of the mountain that came together at the southern edge to rise up majestically in a vertical wall of dark grey, almost black, rock. Even the most reckless of mountain goats would have thought twice before attempting those cliffs. At the upper, northern edge, a good thousand or so paces from where she and Edric stood, the mountain – and the snow – fell away into empty space. There was no way around the snowfield. They would have to go across.

From their vantage point, not a mark, not a paw print, marred the smooth sparkling surface. Staring down on it, a chill of foreboding shivered through Mahleena, standing the hairs on the back of her neck on end. She had the strange if irrational sensation that the snowfield was mocking them with its white purity. Come on, it seemed to say, there is nothing to fear here. Over the years that they had been travelling, she had learned not to dismiss those instinctive nudges.

'Is something wrong?' Edric was watching her carefully.

'I've got a bad feeling about this. I can't explain it but I really don't like it. We should find another way.'

'There isn't any other way,' he told her gently. 'We would have to backtrack for days to find another route, with no guarantee that there is one. We're virtually out of supplies now. I'm not dismissing your intuition, my love, but hasn't Khalia been guiding us? If she has led us this way, don't we need to trust her now?'

'I know.' Mahleena looked up. The sky was turning gold and pink, already deepening to violet on the horizon. Night fell quickly here and darkness would very soon be upon them. They would be unable to set out until morning in any case. 'The sun's going down.'

Edric nodded. 'We'll stop here for the night. We can decide in the morning.'

They had been well above the tree line for days and their firewood was virtually exhausted. As their supplies had dwindled, they had no longer needed the litter and they had broken it down, the framework temporarily boosting their wood stock. Even so, the little they had left was unlikely to last the night. They ate sparingly of their remaining sparse rations and, cuddled together for warmth and reassurance, settled down for another cold and uncomfortable night. Mahleena's sense of impending disaster grew stronger by the hour and she slept fitfully, shivering and uncomfortable, waiting for daylight.

27.

Mahleena blinked her eyes open to a cold, grey dawn. The sky, which had been so clear and blue for days, was this morning overcast, the thickening clouds ominous with the yellowish hue that warned of snow. She was cold and stiff. As expected, the fire had not lasted and only a few faintly glowing embers survived as a memory of its previous cheery warmth.

Beside her Edric stirred, waking slowly. He shook himself and stretched painfully. His muscles protesting at their night on the hard, unyielding ground, he clambered awkwardly to his feet and hobbled to the ridge. Mahleena followed slowly. This morning, the white expanse taunted her even more, challenging them to take it on.

'Well?' He looked at her. 'It's your decision. If you've really got a bad feeling about crossing this, we'll retrace our steps and look for another way.'

Mahleena stared at the snow covered ground. The sense of foreboding was more compelling than ever, yet behind it she could feel Khalia's encouraging presence. 'All will be well,' the skull was whispering. 'All will be well.'

She made up her mind. Khalia had not let them down yet. She had to trust that this would not be the time that she did so, and that these feelings were simply the product of her own fears and imagination, magnified by hunger, cold and exhaustion.

'Khalia is telling me it will be alright.' She drew in a deep breath, apprehension still clutching at her chest, and made her decision. 'We'll go across.'

'You're sure?'

'Yes.' Anxious to move before she changed her mind, Mahleena grabbed her pack and slung Khalia's pouch over her shoulder. 'Let's go.' Nevertheless, they both paused as they scanned the snowfield.

Mahleena turned to squarely face Edric. 'Tell me the truth, my beloved. Do you really believe we can survive...this?' With a flick of her hand she indicated the peaks and crags around them.

'I don't know, my love. I really don't know. But what choice do we have?' This time, he did not even try to hide his doubt or his fears. 'The alternative is to stop – and die – here.' He cupped her face in his cold hands and kissed her gently. 'Do you want to turn back? It's not too late.'

'You know that it is,' she replied softly. 'What is there to turn back to? We have no food, no firewood. If we are going to die, we'll die going forwards rather than back.'

She shook herself irritably. 'Oh pay no attention to me. Of course we aren't going to turn back now. Not when we've come this far. I'm exhausted. I'm frozen. I'm unimaginably hungry and I'm feeling sorry for myself. I'll get over it. You said it yourself. Khalia has always guided us safely, why would that change? After all, she is depending on us to take her to where she needs to be.' Giving Edric a smile that wasn't in the least convincing, she started down the slope to where the snow began. 'Come on,' she called over her shoulder.

* * * * *

Situated to the north of the mountain and overshadowed by its bulk, the sun never reached this valley even in the height of summer. Shaded from the warmth of its rays, the snow lay thick and white all year round. Within a few paces, the cold, clinging white blanket was up to

Mahleena's knees. The field stretched perhaps two thousand paces across. Every one of those paces was going to require an extreme effort that would drain even more of their precious reserves of strength. Well, they were committed to it, and they would see it through.

Suddenly, she sank up to her waist. Cursing in frustration, she hoisted the pack holding Khalia more securely onto her shoulder, struggled out of the drift, and set her sights once more on the far side of the hollow. Never less than knee-deep, frequently more, all too often she found herself waist-deep again in wet, clutching snow, and having to dig herself out with frozen hands. Every step demanded energy-sapping effort. Edric was less than a dozen paces ahead of her and faring little better as he also sank deep into the white mire with every step. He continually stopped and waited for Mahleena, never letting her drop far behind.

About half way across, the underlying ground rose slightly so that a small platform of solid rock pierced through the softness. She collapsed onto it, gasping for breath in the thin air, leg and shoulder muscles burning. Edric was gulping in great lungfuls of air, too short of breath to speak. This was an eerie, forlorn place. The only sound was their laboured breathing, interrupted by the sporadic banshee wails of the wind as it howled around the crags. Mournful phantoms warning them off? The thought penetrated unbidden through Mahleena's exhaustion, icy fingers clutching at her spine, their chill freezing the blood in her veins.

'Courage, little one.' Khalia's gentle comfort broke the spell. 'Courage. It is not far now.' For the first time since they had embarked on this journey, the skull's words failed to reassure her guardian. A powerful unease, the

143

sense of foreboding that she had felt when she had first gazed down on this valley, had returned even more strongly than before. Mahleena was very afraid.

'Come on, let's go. I want to get out of here.' She surveyed the featureless white expanse that confronted her. It was deceptively smooth, giving no clue of what might lie beneath: the suddenly deep drifts, the invisible rocks that would turn an ankle at the first careless step. The sooner they were across and standing safely on the solid bedrock of the far side, the better.

With every second that passed, with every step they took, those snow-bare slopes drew a little bit closer. Beckoning them on. Tantalising in their promise of an easier passage ahead.

28.

Mahleena's terrified scream cut through the crystal-clear air and rolled around the cliffs and crags. Her hands scrabbled and clutched, desperate to grab hold of something – anything – solid as the ground gave way beneath her. Legs flailing in empty space. Ice-numb fingers clinging to the sharp edge of the crevasse that had opened up under her feet.

'Edric... Help me!'

'Mahleena!' She heard him scream her name, high-pitched with shock, and the rustle of his body as he fought his way back to her through the thick snow.

She couldn't hold on. She was falling. Somewhere far away a wild animal let out an unearthly wail that echoed through the depths of the crevasse. Only it wasn't an animal, it was her, screaming her death terror...

A split-second later a steely grip seized her and stopped her plunge with a jolt that felt like it had torn her arm from her shoulder joint. In the instant her fingers had slipped from the frozen edge of the crevasse, Edric had reached her and grabbed her wrist. It hadn't been a moment too soon.

He had saved her life, but for how long? How long could he hold her like this, by one hand? Though she was thin and malnourished, her weight was greatly increased by her heavy fur clothing and the pack on her back. In turn, Edric's strength, depleted by lack of food and oxygen, was a fraction of what it had been before they had set out into these wastelands. Her wrist slipped through his grasp by a fraction and his desperate fingers dug painfully into her flesh as he fought to retain his grip.

'Hold on to me, Mahleena. Grab my arm. I can't hold you like this much longer.' Blind terror was palpable in his voice.

'I can't.' She looked up at him, barely able to make out his features, his face a dark shadow silhouetted against the sky. 'My fingers won't work. They're too cold.'

'You must. I won't lose you. Not now. Not when we've come so far.'

She concentrated on her hand, willing strength and feeling into her nerves and muscles. It was no use. They would not obey her. It was as if they belonged to someone else. She gritted her teeth, renewing her efforts, and in doing so, glanced down. A black, yawning void waited there for her, gaping like the open jaws of hell hungry for their next victim. She screamed again, her free arm flailing the air, searching for the safety of Edric's grasp.

He was on his knees, both hands gripping her wrist, holding on to her for now but unable to do any more. He simply did not have the strength left to pull her up. 'Your other hand. Give me your other hand,' he yelled.

She couldn't. Her struggling had caused Khalia's pouch to slip from her shoulder to her upper arm, and now the weight of the skull was pulling her arm down. She wriggled, trying to move the bag back up to her shoulder but her efforts only succeeded in dropping it down further, to her elbow, and then to her forearm. The movement put an extra, unbearable strain on Edric's arms.

'Keep still,' he begged.

'Khalia…'

And then the skull was gone, sliding from the pouch at Mahleena's wrist, her frozen fingers unable to stop her plummeting into the black abyss below.

'NOOOOOOOOOOOO!' Mahleena's agonised wail filled the crevasse, reverberating around the void, returned and amplified until it filled her whole awareness. She stared blankly downwards, forgetting her own desperate situation, conscious of nothing but the loss of the jade skull.

'Mahleena. MAHLEENA!' Desperation and panic crackled in Edric's voice. 'For Sirius' sake, please. Give me your other hand. I'm losing you.'

'Khalia,' she sobbed. 'She's gone.'

'I know, but you can't think about that now. You have to help me to help you. I can't get you out of there otherwise.' With each word, the fear grew more pronounced. Eventually, his words registered in Mahleena's brain and she flung her free arm upwards so that Edric could seize it. 'Now, pull yourself up.'

'I can't.' It was true. She couldn't. It was all she could do to hang there, holding her weight. She had nothing left.

'You have to. I haven't got the strength left to do it by myself.' His grip slipped again. 'Please, Mahleena.'

She gazed up at him, a heart-wrenching look of resignation in her terrified eyes. This was it. This was the end. There was nothing more either of them could do.

'I love you, Edric. Always. More than life itself. Remember that.'

'No, Mahleena.' He understood what she was telling him. Refused to accept it. 'I won't let you die. Not after all we've been through. Not here. Not now.'

She looked up at him sadly, love overflowing from her heart for this brave, honest and wonderful man who had given up everything to be with her. She could barely make out his dark eyes, glistening with tears. She did not want to say goodbye, to leave him forever, but there was nothing she could do. She was resigned to following Khalia down into the void.

'No! Mahleena, no. I won't let you die. Help me. Pull yourself up. Please. Try.'

'I can't, my darling. Like you, I have nothing left.' She was slipping, in tiny fractions. Each fraction carried her closer to the dark drop. 'I love you, Edric.' This was it. This was the end.

She heard Edric's low whisper as he too recognised the inevitability. 'Mahleena…'

The pain in that simple word broke her heart. She locked her gaze on his in a desperate, heart-breaking farewell, drawing courage from his love in the face of her death.

She blinked in astonishment. A second dark shadow had appeared behind Edric, blocking the daylight. A second pair of hands, strong and confident, gripped her forearms. Helping Edric. Helping her. Dragging her upwards over the edge of the crevasse. Up into daylight. Shoulders, hips, knees, until she was lying safe, if spent, on the snow. Never had she been so glad of its cold embrace. Instantly, Edric's arms were around her, holding her, his lips pressed to her hair, her face, her hands. Oblivious to the pain of the tears that streamed down his face and froze on his skin in the icy air. He was shaking violently, as violently as she was, as their bodies succumbed completely in reaction to the near tragedy. For a very long time they clung to each other, unable to speak or move.

29.

Mahleena was still cradled in Edric's arms, unwilling to leave the security of his embrace. The trembling in her limbs had finally eased and her heart no longer fluttered like the wings of a captured sparrow. She was safe. Edric had saved her. She snuggled deeper against the warmth of his body... A second later her eyes flew open as she remembered.

No more than three paces from them a short, wiry man stood motionless in the snow. He was watching them closely, nodding and grinning to himself. Of course, it was he who had rescued her. Grabbed hold of her wrists and helped Edric to haul her from the crevasse at the very moment she had believed she was irretrievably lost. Without moving from Edric's arms, she studied her saviour. He noticed her interest and bowed his head in greeting.

The man was small in stature – he would barely come to Edric's shoulder. His sinewed frame must have been immensely strong to have hauled her up so easily. And virtually single-handed, for Edric had had no strength left. Mahleena guessed that he was in the prime years of his life for his shaggy mop of jet black hair didn't show a trace of white. His skin, however, burned nut brown by the sun, was wizened and wrinkled like an old man's. From beneath heavy lids, amber eyes twinkled with a combination of curiosity and warmth. Like Mahleena and Edric, he was warmly dressed in the thick furs of the animals that made their home in these high, stark valleys. Unlike them, his were skilfully made and well-fitting. She owed this man her life.

Mahleena struggled unsteadily to her feet, her legs still weak, pressed her hands to her heart and bowed deeply to him, trying to convey her gratitude.

'Thank you,' she told him, though he would not understand her words. 'Thank you for helping us. Thank you for saving my life.' Edric had also risen to offer his thanks.

The man grinned, flashing surprisingly white and even teeth, and returned their bow. 'Kenzak.' He patted his chest. 'Kenzak.'

'Mahleena,' she responded, pointing to herself, and then indicated her companion. 'Edric.'

Kenzak grinned and bowed again, nodding. As he straightened, his expression turned serious. Mahleena and Edric followed his gaze. Over the peaks to their right, the sky was darkening. Heavy, menacing clouds were rapidly sweeping across the already overcast skies. Gesturing wildly, Kenzak beckoned them to follow him across the remaining expanse of the snowfield. The urgency in his action was unmistakeable.

Mahleena felt her heart pounding as she took the first step. Panic threatened to overwhelm her. What if there was another yawning abyss hidden beneath the innocent white blanket? One that this time would not let her escape. The near tragedy was too recent in her memory.

A firm hand took hers. 'Come on. Let's go.'

Edric had seen her fear and was already at her side, giving her the encouragement she needed. Ahead, Kenzak looked back anxiously and beckoned again. They needed to hurry. Warily they followed his footsteps, far more slowly than their new guide wished. He fidgeted as he waited for them on the solid bedrock of the snow-free far ridge, hopping from one foot to another in his impatience.

Mahleena understood his anxiety. Nonetheless, once they reached him, she was compelled to stop and look back at the black gash, an open wound in the snow, that had so nearly claimed her life. And which had stolen Khalia from her forever. She felt a profound guilt at having failed to keep the skull safe and fulfil her mission and a powerful grief at her loss. Khalia had been a constant and reassuring presence. Already her absence was proving painful.

Edric's arm encircled her waist, comforting and tender. 'It wasn't your fault. There wasn't anything you could have done.'

'If only…'

'If only nothing. You did everything you could. You were asked to keep her safe and conceal her in a place where no-one would be able to find her.' He smiled ruefully. 'It seems to me that there probably isn't anywhere safer or more inaccessible than buried in the depths of a mountain. Maybe it was even planned that way. How can we know?'

'I could have died. Khalia wouldn't have sacrificed me for her own safety. Would she?' Mahleena stared at Edric, horrified at the possibility.

'I don't know, my love. This whole journey has been filled with unanswered questions. This is just one more. How can we know?' He became thoughtful. 'I wouldn't be surprised if I'm right. The more I consider it, the more possible it feels. Think about it. Wasn't it a massive coincidence that Kenzak appeared out of nowhere just in time to save your life? We haven't come across anyone for… well, I can't remember when. Certainly in a good many moons. And he turns up at exactly the moment we need him?'

'No.' Mahleena shook her head vigorously. 'It would have been too much of a risk. What if I, or you, hadn't been able to hold on as long as we did? I can't believe this was Khalia's doing. I won't. Too much could have gone wrong.'

'But it didn't.'

An impatient whistle interrupted their discussion. Kenzak had climbed to the top of the ridge from where he was waving like a maniac and pointing at the sky. It was clear why he was so worried. The clouds had congealed into a vast, towering wall of slate grey tinged with sickly yellow, and the wind was rising by the minute. Already the more distant mountain slopes were obscured from view. There was no more time for speculation. They had to hurry.

It soon became clear that Kenzak knew this land well. He led them unerringly through steep gullies and along narrow animal tracks that Mahleena and Edric didn't see until they were upon them. Before long the first snow began to fall, lightly at first – big soft flakes that should have been gentle on their skin but instead, driven by the rising gale, stung bitterly the exposed skin of their faces. All three pulled their furs up higher until just their eyes were showing and plunged their hands deep into the warm folds to keep them from freezing. The main body of the blizzard was drawing ever closer, blotting out behind the landmarks they had only shortly before passed by. They had no idea where Kenzak was taking them. They could only hope they would reach it in time. If they were caught out in the open when the storm's full fury hit, their chances of survival were negligible. Mahleena and Edric had encountered snow, fierce blizzards even, on many occasions during their trek. Nothing though had equalled the violence of the force that was now bearing down on them and gaining on them with every second that passed.

Half blinded by the driving snow, they were on top of it before they saw it – a village, tucked into the lee of a towering wall of rock. A few scrawny goats and cattle huddled miserably together in pens under rough lean-tos that afforded little shelter from the appalling conditions, their plaintive bleating and lowing mingling with the banshee screech of the ever-strengthening wind. Behind the enclosures, sturdy, low stone buildings merged into the cliff face and tumbled down the steep slopes at its base – a dozen, no maybe as many as twenty of them, built from the boulders and rocks that littered this terrain. Smoke curled from holes in their roofs in a welcome promise of warmth.

Buffeted now so violently by the weather that they could hardly keep upright, Kenzak led them to one of the farthermost houses. As they reached it, the door was pulled open from inside and a plump-cheeked woman, silhouetted in the welcoming glow of firelight, bustled them into its shelter and closed the door on the ice-bound hell that was breaking loose outside.

30.

It was not the home that Mahleena had envisaged for herself and Edric. Nevertheless these high mountains with their snow-bound winters and brief summers were where they remained until old age claimed them.

In the days that followed their rescue, it had not been their intention to make their life in these high valleys. Mahleena had found it impossible to abandon Khalia, however, even though she was irretrievably lost to them and so they stayed close to where she lay hidden, settling in the village that had welcomed them so warmly. They were happy, and their life there, though harsh and difficult in so many ways, was also magical. The villagers were kind and generous, and when the sun shone from skies of a deep unblemished blue, the beauty of the mountains and high valleys never ceased to stop them in their tracks. Even after years living in this land, they would still stand and marvel at the majesty and grandeur of their new home.

*   *   *   *   *

For several thousand more years, the snow and ice covered this most ancient of lands, one that had been born way back at the beginning of the world. Slowly however, the atmosphere warmed, and little by little the glaciers receded, the ice thawed and the once-permanent snows began to melt.

All this time, deep in the heart of the mountain, Khalia slept at the bottom of the crevasse on a bed of thick, soft snow. Her plunge into its black depths had been broken by a deep drift that had fallen in from the surface over time, which had cushioned her fall and saved her from destruction. In fact, there was not the slightest mark on her to indicate what had happened. She remained buried deep in its protective mantle, as she had done for millennia.

The base of the crevasse was formed from one of the channels in a system of ancient subterranean watercourses that had been carved out in warmer times by the rivers that had once surged through the bedrock. For a very long time those channels had been dry, the climate too cold for any water to flow. Now, however, Earth's surface was warming by the season and beneath the surface, everything was changing. Although this particular mountain range remained ice-bound and frozen solid, water from the snow and ice melt of distant regions was slowly trickling into its former pathways, finding its way once again into these underground channels, bringing back to life the rivers and streams that had once flowed there.

Though still barely above freezing, those few degrees of temperature were enough. In tiny increments, the snow beneath Khalia turned to liquid until she was no longer sleeping peacefully in the frozen, static embrace of the snow but swirling helpless and vulnerable in a stream of icy water. By some miracle the snow drift at the base of the crevasse had protected her from the initial plunge; now she was not so gently treated, nor so safely held. The current battered her relentlessly along the water-eroded tunnels until her once glassy surface was chipped and scuffed, the soft jade from which she had been created no match for the hard bedrock through which she was carried.

Until, for the first time in ten thousand years, Khalia emerged into daylight. Borne along by the spring melt-water that had provided the final thrust, she was carried out of the mountain's dark belly and into fresh air and sunshine, tumbling, more gently now, along the stony bed of a small river. As summer advanced, and the water's flow lessened, she settled amongst the other larger rocks and pebbles into the river bed. While the smaller stones still danced along in the current on their way downstream, she had come to rest, half buried, lost and forgotten. Her guardian was long gone. Unlike her brother and sister skulls, all of which were safely protected, the jade skull was in real danger of complete destruction at the whim of the elements that ruled this world.

GEMMA, 3

31.

Twenty five King Street was as forlorn and neglected as Paradise Avenue had been. The difference was that people still lived in King Street. The drab, uncared-for terraced houses – virtually all of them in dire need of a coat of fresh paint and a good dose of tlc – were only here and there interspersed with broken windows and boarded up doors. We parked the car down a side road in front of a row of derelict garages, not wanting to leave it standing right outside the house, and walked back up to King Street, hoping that when we returned, the car would still be in one piece.

Number twenty five was on the corner. It looked abandoned, its narrow front garden – if it could be called that – a meagre strip of straggly grass, a couple of dandelions, and a pile of empty beer cans. Could this really be it? I struggled to picture Callum living here.

We had no key, and a turn of the handle showed us we didn't need one when the front door opened with a reluctant creak. My nose wrinkled in protest as we stepped inside. The house was as smelly and dirty as Paradise Avenue had been, only here there were signs of recent occupation: a camp stove in the kitchen with a couple of almost clean pans on the burners, tins of soup and baked beans stacked up next to a half-eaten loaf and a jar of instant coffee. Confident we were in the right place, we headed upstairs.

Callum had been using the front bedroom, which was marginally the less squalid and damp of the two upstairs rooms. We found his sleeping bag laid out on the filthy floor next to a pile of reference books on ancient sites, and a notepad. There was no sign of his laptop or phone. Had he been carrying those when his kidnappers had pounced or had he hidden them in time? I dropped onto the sleeping bag, carefully avoiding the dirt-encrusted carpet, and flicked through the notepad. It contained only a half dozen or so pages of scribbled notes in Callum's untidy handwriting, nothing that stood out as important. I dropped it back onto the floor.

Joe was already searching the room for the envelope, rooting around in the few places that there were. Where had Callum put it? Together we turned the room upside down looking in every possible hiding place. Nothing. Despondent and frustrated, I slumped down onto the sleeping bag and scanned the small bare room for the umpteenth time.

Joe plonked himself down next to me, scowling. 'They've beaten us to it.'

Maybe …

'No, they haven't.' I sat up straighter, certain I was right. 'When we came in, the room was pretty tidy, the way Callum would have left it. If anyone had come in searching, they wouldn't have cared less about trashing it. They had him prisoner. They wouldn't have had to hide that they'd been here.' I gestured at the room. 'Look at what we've done to it, and we were being a bit careful.'

'Then it has to be here. In which case, where the fuck is it?'

'I have no idea. I give up. We've looked everywhere.'

We had been through the room a dozen times and more and found nothing. To be honest, there weren't many places to search. Other than Callum's belongings, the room only contained a couple of built-in cupboards and a pile of abandoned cardboard boxes, and to judge by the thick crust of grime that glued it to the skirting board, the carpet hadn't been lifted in decades, which ruled out a loose floorboard. I was exhausted and I was fed up, and in that moment all I longed to do was go home and forget all about it. Then I remembered Callum, lying battered and injured in his hospital bed. With the image came the realisation that, as much as I wanted it all to be over, it wasn't going to be. Not for a long time yet. I flopped back and stared at the leak-stained ceiling, searching for inspiration. *Something...* Oh, come on. There had to be a clue here somewhere. What were we missing?

'Joe, look.' The corner of the wall was nagging at my attention at the point where it met the bottom right hand edge of the door frame. Something wasn't quite right. I scrambled to my knees and, forgetting the filthy carpet, crawled across to take a closer look. Joe was right beside me. He could see it too now. The corner of the wall wasn't fixed properly; it didn't quite meet the wooden frame. I prodded the edge of the wall with my finger and it moved.

'Plasterboard. This room has been dry-lined at some point.' Joe plucked at the raw edge with a fingernail. It lifted slightly, then fell back. 'I need a knife. Something that I can slide in behind it.'

I raced down to the kitchen and found a dinner knife lying on the draining board. Holding it like a trophy I took it back to the bedroom where Joe was on his stomach, poking at the loose bit of wall.

'Work the knife in under the board to open it out a bit more,' he instructed.

It was fiddly, so close to the door frame. It took several attempts before I managed to slip the knife under the edge of the board and pull it forward far enough for Joe to get his fingertips in behind it.

'There's something there.' Had he found it? I leaned forward excitedly. 'Feels like paper. I think we've got it. Oh damn it, my fingers are too big. You try, Gemma. Your hands are smaller than mine.'

Carefully I swapped places with him, twisting so that I could wriggle my fingertips into the gap. Joe was right. They were brushing against some stiff, shiny-feeling paper. We'd found it. It wasn't going to come out without a fight though. Eventually, after a lot of wiggling and tugging, I got enough of a grip to edge it out far enough for its corner to show. I gripped tighter, not wanting to lose my hold on it, and drew the whole package out into the daylight. It was an A5 manila envelope with a small bulge in one corner.

We stared at it in silence. Was this small, innocuous-looking object the reason behind so much violence and menace? What could it contain that was so important? Whatever it was – whatever its contents, whatever its danger – it had pulled Joe and me into its clutches. Once again we had been caught up in Callum's secrets. This time, I wasn't sure we would be able to escape the consequences.

'Should we...?' Joe interrupted my brooding, his fingertips worrying at the sealed flap of the envelope.

I closed my hand over his, stopping him. 'He asked us not to. Let's tell him we've got it and go from there. We can always look at it later.'

Joe was beginning to argue when the sound of a powerful engine revving outside stopped him mid-sentence. It didn't sound like the kind of vehicle that would normally be seen in these poverty-wracked streets. The hairs on my neck prickled in warning. Joe leapt to his feet and peered cautiously through the dirt-filmed glass.

'We need to get out of here,' he hissed. 'Now. Whoever is in that car seems to be looking for a house, and I've a nasty suspicion it's this one. Come on.'

In a second I was on my feet and heading down the stairs with Joe hard on my heels.

'This way.' He grabbed my arm and dragged me through the kitchen and out into the backyard, where a wooden gate hung half off its hinges. We had scarcely raced through it and ducked out of sight into the dank, narrow alleyway beyond when we heard the front door creak open. It had been close, but we had got away with it – this time.

All we had to do now was return to Leeds, find a way to get Callum alone, give him the envelope, and find out what the hell was going on. I had the feeling that everything that had happened up until now would, in days to come, prove to be the easy part.

32.

At least, that was our plan as we set off up the M1 the following morning. Half an hour into our journey an angry phone call from D.I. Chamberlain turned the day upside down.

'Where is Callum Davis?'

'You know where he is. Leeds General Infirmary.'

'No, he's not. He disappeared from there early this morning. So I'll ask you again. Where is Callum Davis?'

I think my stunned silence was more convincing than any words could have been. 'What do you mean?' I stuttered out at last. 'How can he not be there?' Joe was glancing sideways at me in total confusion as he negotiated the busy motorway traffic.

'Where are you?'

'On the M1 on our way back to Leeds.'

'Come straight to the hospital. I want to talk to the pair of you. I want to know what you know.' He shut off the call abruptly.

'What was all that about?' Joe hadn't picked up on the other end of the conversation.

'That was Chamberlain. It's Callum. He's disappeared again.'

The seatbelt dug into my shoulder as Joe braked sharply and twisted to look at me. 'He's what? When? How?'

'He didn't say and he cut the call before I could ask. All I know is that he's waiting for us at the hospital and that he is not a happy man.'

*   *   *   *   *

We arrived on the ward to find it teeming with police officers. The medical staff were anxious and irritable, the police furious that they had let Callum slip away from right under their noses, and D.I. Chamberlain was nowhere to be seen. We plonked onto a couple of chairs in the corridor and waited. And waited.

From the snatches of conversation around us, we gleaned that the constable on guard outside Callum's door had left his post, for which he was now on report. Apparently there had been a bit of a commotion in the A & E waiting room, which was located only a short distance away, and he had dashed off to help believing Callum to be heavily sedated and unconscious and in any case too injured to be able to get out of bed, let alone walk out of the hospital. As, to be fair, had the entire medical team, along with everyone else, including Joe and I. Callum had been hoodwinking them all, it seemed, and by the time the police officer returned to his post, he had disappeared. From the CCTV footage of the corridors, it had been established that he had taken clothes and cash from an unlocked staff locker and slipped out through a service exit.

'Well at least we know he went of his own free will,' Joe muttered. 'What the hell is he playing at? He isn't in any state to be up and about. How far does he think he can get?

'Mrs Mason. Mr Cunningham.' The arrival of D.I. Chamberlain forestalled any probably useless conjecture. 'Come with me. I want to talk to you.'

Not unexpectedly, I suppose, we were prime candidates for the aiding and abetting of Callum's escape. I think our genuine astonishment and concern for him played a big part in eventually convincing the inspector that we had had nothing to do with it, helped in no small measure by the CCTV footage. Firstly, the hospital's cameras had picked up Callum shuffling painfully across the main car park to a bus stop and onto a number fifty two bus. Adding proof to our claims of innocence, the camera across the road from the hotel in Guildford where we had stayed the night confirmed our statement that we hadn't gone out between ten in the evening, when we arrived, until eleven that morning, when we had started the journey back to Leeds. Callum had made his escape at around five thirty am. Which put us in the clear. Sort of… That didn't spare us a lengthy barrage of questions, all of which we were – truthfully this time – unable to answer. Fortunately, the manila envelope we had brought with us was safely tucked away out of sight in my shoulder bag.

When at last we were allowed to go, we were once again both furious with Callum for landing us in it and deeply concerned for his wellbeing. He was seriously ill and in no condition to be wandering the streets.

'I have to say, though,' Joe turned to me, a wry smile lighting up his features, 'while I'm as mad as hell with Callum, I'm also quite impressed. I've always known he was a maverick and a risk taker. I'd never considered him an action hero as well. That escape was pretty Jason Bourne!'

In spite of my anxiety, I chuckled. 'It certainly was.' My lightened mood was only fleeting and it vanished as quickly as it had come.

'We have to remember that he's a hardened fugitive. He's been on the run for months,' I reminded Joe. 'I know that sounds dramatic but he must be if he's been living in places like King Street.' I shuddered. 'I can't begin to imagine what it's been like for him. Hiding out. Searching for answers. Constantly looking over his shoulder. Knowing he could be recognised at any moment and arrested, or worse.' I paused, the envelope in my shoulder bag growing heavier with every moment that passed. 'Why did he run, Joe? He must realise he'll have every police force in Britain hunting him down.'

'Maybe it was simply that he saw a chance and took it? There was only one result if he stayed – he would have been arrested and tried for murder. With the evidence that was planted, I doubt there's a jury in the country that would find him innocent. Callum may be on the run again but believe me, he'd rather that than a prison cell… Unless he really was on to something. Don't underestimate him, Gemma.'

'So what do we do?'

He leaned against the car. 'No idea. Head back to King Street? He might try to make his way back there.'

Yes, we were clutching at straws, and very flimsy straws at that. Nevertheless, King Street was where Callum had hidden the envelope and he didn't know yet that we'd found it. If its contents were his insurance policy, he'd be desperate to get hold of them. OK, so it was a crazy plan. At that point though we couldn't come up with a better one. Sitting around waiting for him to call wasn't an option as far as either of us was concerned. We needed to be doing *something*, however futile that something was.

So yet again we were in the car heading south on the M1 without a clue what we would do when we arrived. We agreed that we wouldn't hang around in the squat, in no small part because it was filthy and it stank. Our other concern was Callum's assailants and what would happen if they caught us there. No, we wouldn't wait inside. In the end, we decided to park a little way along the street and watch the building. At that point, I'll admit, we didn't even think consider how long we might have to sit it out.

33.

After only a couple of hours we realised the folly of our plan. You know how, on TV shows, the police stake out a building for hours? Well, it doesn't work in real life. Or perhaps just not the way we did it. We simply weren't used to it. Sitting in the car quickly became very uncomfortable, even in the spacious luxury of the Mercedes. We were soon hungry and thirsty, and on top of that we were getting more than a few suspicious glances from the residents. A high status car parked for so long in such a run-down area was bound to cause some curiosity, especially when its occupants didn't get out. We rapidly saw the flaws in our plan. We hadn't thought it through.

'This is ridiculous,' I burst out at last. 'Say that Callum does make it back here. It might not be for days. Weeks even.'

Joe leaned his head back onto the plump headrest and rubbed his eyes wearily. 'I've been thinking the same thing.' He grinned wryly at me. 'Not the best undercover agents in the world, are we?'

'More Johnny English than James Bond,' I agreed. 'Can't we leave him a note? Something cryptic that wouldn't incriminate us, saying that we've found the envelope and to call us?'

'I'll go. You stay here and keep watch.' He grabbed a black marker pen from the glove compartment. 'I'll only be a minute.'

I watched him disappear through the front door. One minute stretched to a good five before he reappeared in the doorway carrying two bulging carrier bags, which he dumped on the back seat.

'I thought I'd grab his notepad and reference books as well. We may find something useful that we overlooked last time.'

'What did you say?'

Joe turned the ignition and slipped the car into gear. *'Mission accomplished. Call.* I wrote it on the wall in six inch high letters, so he won't be able to miss it.' As the car pulled out into the street, he threw a glance at my bag. 'Regardless of Callum's orders, I think it's about time we headed back to Duncan's and took a look at what's in that envelope. He's still away.'

'Why not my house?'

'Because the last thing you want is to have these papers hanging around in your home. There's every chance that the break-in was someone going through it looking for evidence that you know more than you're letting on. There is no guarantee they won't come back again, especially after this business. Better safe than sorry.'

*   *   *   *   *

This was it, the moment Joe and I would find out exactly what it was that Callum had deemed so important that he had refused to reveal its whereabouts despite the brutal treatment he had endured.

My mouth was dry as I unsealed the envelope and tipped out its contents. A data-stick and half a dozen loose sheets of A4 fluttered down onto the floor.

'Is that it?' Joe sounded disappointed.

I shook the envelope. 'That's the lot.'

'It doesn't seem a very big reason for being beaten half to death.' He picked up one of the A4 sheets. 'Names, companies – all big multinationals by the look of it – countries. That's all is on this one.'

The others contained more of the same: lists of names, dates and cities. Dates of historical events and natural catastrophes. A photocopy of a world map. Nothing else. Nothing to link them or explain what they related to.

Joe scratched his head, puzzled. 'Is it me, or is there no sense in any of this?'

I was just as baffled. Maybe Callum understood it. To Joe and me, it was meaningless.

'What about this?' I picked up the data-stick.

'Let's see.' Joe plugged it into his laptop. 'Damn.'

'What?'

'He's passworded it.' We tried a few random guesses: Arizona2013, Crystal skulls01, CallumDavis65. Not surprisingly, none of them were right.

'This is ridiculous. We could be here for a month and still not get it.' Joe leaned back in the chair and stretched. 'Can I make a suggestion?' he ventured.

'Go ahead. I'm all out of bright ideas.'

'We put this somewhere safe for now. When – if – Callum calls, we can hand it over. If we haven't heard from him by the time Duncan gets back from Italy next week, I'll ask him to hack into it. It'll be child's play for him.'

It was a bitter disappointment but one that we could do nothing about. I watched as Joe prised up the loose floorboard in Duncan's kitchen and slid the envelope, its contents once more safely sealed inside, into the gap underneath.

'Do you think he's OK?' I was worried. 'He was so badly hurt.'

Joe's arms surrounded me in a reassuring hug. I leaned against him, grateful he was there. I don't know if I would have been able to deal with any of this if I didn't have Joe with me. He was my rock.

'Callum is an intelligent and resourceful man,' he stated firmly. 'If anyone can get through this, he can. I wouldn't be surprised if we hear from him within the next day or two.'

Only… we didn't.

KHALIA: The Jade Skull

Part V

PEL THE HERDSMAN

34.

He had been roaming these mountain slopes for weeks with the other men from his tribe, accompanying the herd while they grazed on the sweet rich grass of the upper valleys. Every year they made this journey throughout the sun months. As the days had lengthened and the air warmed, they had left the high plateau that was their home. Now that those days were growing noticeably shorter again, they were returning home. They were almost there. The moon had just touched its first quarter; by the time it reached its fullness they would be back with their families, preparing to barricade themselves against the harsh winter to come. They could not afford to delay their return. Once the weather broke it would be impossible to cross the final barrier of jagged unforgiving passes. To be stranded out here when the snows came would mean certain death.

It would be a difficult winter. It always was, but he was used to that as they all were. Born and raised in this starkly beautiful but harsh land they had never known anything else. His people had survived here for generations and understood its moods well. Before the first of the snows rolled in, they would dismantle their thick, hide dwellings and relocate to the caves in the cliffs that rose up to the east of the plateau where they would wait for the sun to return. Ever since his ancestors had arrived in this land, in a time lost in the mists of memory, they had spent the coldest months in those caves. Deep underground the temperature remained constant, and several subterranean springs provided them with ample water. They would be hungry come spring, both the people and their animals;

unless the warmth was very late in returning, however, all but the weakest would survive.

The men and their livestock had wandered far during the warmer summer months and their herd was healthy, fat and well-fed from the sweet, tender grass and fragrant meadow plants. It was time to return home. Only the menfolk made this trip. While they were away, the women and children would gather food from the land, look after the rough areas of carefully tended crops and dry the fish they had pulled from the streams. At this time of year the land was abundant in her gifts. Within weeks that generosity would be withdrawn. Their survival then would depend on the stores they had gathered in this time of plenty.

His thoughts drifted to his wife. She was strong and hard-working. A good wife. She had already given him three children – two sturdy sons, and a daughter who lit up his heart – and he had left her with another on the way. That one would have been born by now. Only briefly he wondered if it had been a boy or a girl before his thoughts returned to his woman. It had been a lonely summer without her warm body to sink into whenever he felt the desire. No matter. A long, dark winter lay ahead of them. There would be more than enough time to make up for his enforced abstinence. He grinned to himself. There would surely be another child growing in her womb by the time he left again the following spring.

* * * * *

The men had set up camp for the night and several of them were already swigging the coarse liquor they fermented from mountain herbs and wild honey, seeking in its dulling warmth the stupor that eased the harshness of this life. He did not touch it. He had seen what it did to those who became bewitched by the brew, as most of those who tried it were. They developed a thirst for its potent effects that they could never satisfy, no matter how much they poured down their throats. Quickly it turned their minds and ruined their bodies; those in its tightest grip stumbled shaking through the day, walking dead in a world of life. He left his companions to their oblivion and wandered off in search of solitude, a private place where he could dream of his wife and ease his hunger for her away from their mocking taunts.

All were affected by the same hunger – they had been away from their womenfolk for too long – but his rose up far more frequently and obviously. Maybe because he was the youngest, his heat not yet dulled by age, familiarity or, more likely, the liquor. Those who drank most, hardened least. Maybe that was why they drank, to relieve the torment of their unanswered desires. It was not a road he wished to take; when he got home, he wanted to be able to bed his wife so fully that she would not forget his fire during the next long summer absence. So, very often, as on this evening, he would take himself off alone, imagine her in his arms, and spill his juices onto the hard, unfeeling ground.

Today he paid no real attention to where he was going, which was nowhere in particular, taking in his surroundings just enough to be able to find his way back. He let his feet lead and, lost in pleasant thoughts of his wife, he wandered the mountainside following a narrow track, the faintest scar of an animal run, across the sloping ground. Downhill a steep grassy slope, dotted with a few scraggy stunted trees and shrubs, plunged down in a near vertical drop. On the uphill side, the ground rose almost as steeply until it flattened out into a plateau somewhere high above.

He scrambled through a rocky gap between two small outcrops that stood like gateposts to the valley beyond. Here the land lay in a shallow basin through which a small river bubbled and glittered in the late afternoon sunlight. A flower-filled meadow on the far side beckoned to him. It would be the perfect place to daydream and, in time, relieve his desire.

He gasped as the icy water clasped his ankles. The coldness of these waters took his breath away every time. The river was shallow and wide, not yet swollen by the autumn snow and rains, and ran gurgling and chuckling over its rocky bed as it swept in an easy curve through the centre of the basin. On this side, the inside of the bend, stretched a wide shallow beach, created from the stones and grit deposited by the river on its journey. The water deepened towards the far bank. He would have to take care. The jumble of sharp, uneven stones underfoot would test even his hardened soles.

He yelped in pain. He hadn't been careful enough. A clumsy step had brought his left foot down hard on a jagged edge. Involuntarily he glanced down to see what had cut into his skin. What was that? Right next to his foot a smooth dome-shaped stone roughly the size of his palm gleamed deep green, in striking contrast to the varying tones of grey and silver that surrounded it. It was an unusual stone, and looked totally out of place. His curiosity aroused, he bent to pick it up. To his surprise it wouldn't move, and he bent to look more closely. Although at first glance it appeared to be a shallow convex pebble, it was actually a much larger stone held firmly in place by those that surrounded it. His hardness and his hunger forgotten, he pulled and tugged at the rocks that held it prisoner. It was held more tightly than he anticipated and the frigid water robbed his fingers of any sensation, which made the task increasingly difficult. At last however, the smooth green pebble loosened and a moment later, it was free.

Lifting the stone for a closer look, he very nearly dropped it again in shock, the fragile grip of his frozen fingers barely holding on. He was looking into the vacant eye sockets of a skull, human in form, far from human in substance. This skull was carved of some deep green stone the colour of autumn moss, veined with paler streaks. It was a sad sight. The once-smooth sweep of the skull plates were deeply scratched and chipped, a thick crack ran along one side of the jaw bone, and a ragged chunk the size of his thumbnail had been broken out of the base of the skull at the back.

Still it captivated him. He stumbled awkwardly to the bank on deadened feet, as numb from the cold water as his fingers, and sank to the ground. For a long time he simply sat there, turning the skull over and over in his hands. What was it? Where had it come from? Did it belong to someone who would come looking for it and accuse him of stealing it? No. Reason denied the last. Buried as deeply as it had been in the river bed, the object must have been in the water for a very long time.

At last, as the shadows lengthened and the sun dropped towards the horizon, he lifted his eyes from his treasure. He would have to return to the camp. He could not risk being stranded out here when night fell. However warm the sun during the day, at this altitude the temperature dropped close to freezing after dusk even in the summer. He took off his tunic and wrapped it around the skull, shivering; the temperature was already falling. He pulled his cloak more tightly around his chilling torso so that it concealed the bundle beneath it and set out for the camp. He would not share his find with his companions. For reasons he could not explain, this was a discovery he felt he must keep to himself.

It was dark when he reached the camp, the quarter moon shedding little light. He gave thanks to the gods. In the darkness there was little chance his companions would notice the bundle he was carrying. They were still awake, drinking huddled around the welcoming glow of the campfire, and as he approached they greeted him with a chorus of ribald laughter. Only then did he realise that he had completely forgotten the reason he had left the camp. The once so urgent need had subsided completely with the discovery of his treasure. Ignoring the jeers of his companions, he wrapped his cloak and blanket tightly around himself to keep out the chill of the night air and quickly fell asleep to dream colourful dreams of strange flying craft and people with hair of white gold and violet eyes.

35.

'Take it away, Pel. It's not coming into my home.' His wife stood glaring at him, her feet firmly planted, hands on her ample hips. The gleam in her eyes challenged him to argue. He could not. He was dumbfounded. Never before had his wife, usually so placid and amiable, stood her ground against his wishes with such fierce determination.

'But, my wife…'

'No!' She shook her head so violently that the colourful scarf she wore slipped sideways. Her vehemence crumbled suddenly into desperation, her voice shaking with emotion. 'It is evil. An evil thing. It will possess us all. The children…' Tears welled in her eyes as she looked at them, no more than babies, playing happily on the sandy floor. She was pleading now. 'Please, my husband, think of the babies.'

The object he had found, the green skull, was not evil. He sensed that with every cell of his body. He could also sense the terror and aversion his wife was feeling as she gazed on it. If she felt so strongly – even if, as he believed, she was wrong – then he would not distress her further by ignoring those fears. And there was, he accepted, the possibility that he could be wrong, and that this object would bring ill fortune to them all. However small the risk, it was one he was not prepared to take. He would find another place to keep it, somewhere safe from the prying eyes and greedy envy of his neighbours.

'Very well, wife, I will take it away if it upsets you so much. Will you promise me though that you will speak of it to no-one?'

'I have no wish to speak of it at all.' Though her stance remained obstinate, gratitude softened her expression. 'You are a good man, my husband. Many would have insisted.'

He folded his treasure back into his tunic. 'I have no wish to distress you or bring fear into your life, beloved. Do not worry, I will go now and hide this where it will not be found. I will be back before nightfall.' He pressed his lips tenderly to her forehead and disappeared through the doorway.

He already knew where he would hide the skull. The previous winter he had wandered deep into the back caves, far further than he had ever gone before. There he had found a newly exposed passageway; a rock fall, so recent that the stone had not yet dulled, had taken away the side wall, revealing the tunnel. In his fascination for this dark, underground world, he had followed the shaft to its end. This was where he was heading now.

He carried with him a crude candle of animal fat held in a hollowed out stone. It was smoky and smelly but more reliable than the fire twigs he sometimes used. Two spare lamps were stuffed into his pocket. He peered through the dim light, certain he had gone the right way. The tunnel had to be near. Yes. There was the gaping fissure. The only way to reach it was by clambering up the precarious pile of fallen rock. He picked his way upwards cautiously – if he dislodged the unstable footing it would take him down as well – and crawled through the low opening. He was close to his goal now; reaching it however was far from easy. Narrow squeeze points came one after the other, so tight that he had to hold his breath and pull in his belly in order to pass through, twisting and contorting his body into shapes it was never designed to attain. Sudden drops and knife edge ledges lurked, waiting to steal his life if he missed a step. Each step of the way lit only by the flickering faint glow of his crude lamp.

The tunnel roof rose up above him. The walls opened out at each side. Lifting the weak light high, he gazed around with the same wonder that had enveloped him on his first visit. He could see more easily here in a chink of daylight that seeped in through a crack in the roof far above him where bats flapped disgruntled at his intrusion. It wasn't much, just enough to illuminate the cave in a dusky twilight.

He was standing on a ledge only a couple of paces wide and perhaps the height of a man above the cave floor. The cave wasn't large and was roughly rectangular in shape, far wider than it was deep, an irregular gallery with a soaring roof which, from the lowest point to the highest, disappearing into the gloom above, dripped icicles of creamy yellow stone. Some were tiny, barely the length of a finger. Others were so immense that their tips brushed the floor. In several places they formed massive columns covered in curious lumps and bulges. The same creamy stone flowed down the walls in frozen waterfalls that gleamed dully in the low light of his lamp. Other grotesque formations resembled nothing so much as the petrified guts spilling out of a slaughtered beast. Fans and pipes and ruffles, all more intricate and beautiful than anything that could be conceived by the mind of man, filled the space. He had seen similar elsewhere in this underground world. None had been as impressive, or in such number and variety, as they were here.

This was a fitting place for the skull. Here it would be safe from discovery. No-one else knew of this cave, and few in his clan would have either the curiosity or the desire to wander so far from the familiar and comfortable hallways of their winter shelter. He scrambled down from the ledge and carefully tucked the skull, still wrapped in his tunic, behind the knobby rounded lump of a stalagmite that thrust up from the edge of the main floor. Unless anyone looked closely the bundle was invisible, the pale brown of the tunic merging effectively with the surrounding stone.

He turned slowly, reluctant to leave. He had to; the villagers would be celebrating the safe return of the herdsmen and he could not stay longer without his absence being noticed and questions asked. With final glance and a silent promise to return as soon as he could, he hoisted himself onto the ledge and disappeared back into the tunnel.

* * * * *

Once more Khalia had left the sunlight and fresh air to rest in the black belly of the mountains. For five winters and five summers she remained there. During the summer she was always alone while he travelled with the herd far across the mountains until the days again grew short and the air chilled. Then, in those cold dark months, when the community took shelter in the caves, he came every day to sit with the skull and puzzle over what it was and who had carved her. Many times he fell asleep in the eternal twilight of the cave to dream of strange worlds and stranger beings, of gods who rode in the sky on chariots of light and produced magic with a wave of a hand.

* * * * *

True to her word, Pel's wife told no-one about the skull. She even kept her silence with the shaman, Tuczuk, to whom all such strange and magical finds should have been relinquished. If she felt guilty at keeping this secret, she consoled herself with the knowledge that she was keeping the promise she had made to her husband. She would not, could not, break her word to him, no matter what the reason. After all, she told herself, she had committed no crime. Nonetheless, she recognised that she was risking the deep disapproval of her clan and it weighed heavily upon her shoulders. The shaman was wise, learned in such matters. He would have pronounced the skull good or evil – a gift from the gods or the curse of demons. As long as Tuczuk remained in ignorance of the skull's existence, they would never know its true nature.

35.

The shaman, Tuczuk was puzzled. By the nature of his calling he was highly sensitive to changing energies and the existence of other, unseen, realms, and for some time now he had felt the presence of a new and powerful power source close by, one that was not of this world of mountains and bleak, barren plateaux. Something in this high and isolated world had changed. During that first winter, he had sensed only the faintest whisper of this new and unknown energy. With each that followed, the sensation had grown stronger and clearer. Try though as he might, however, he had never been able to trace its source. It frustrated him immensely.

* * * * *

Winter was always hard. There would be times when they were trapped in the sheltering caves for weeks on end while the weather raged and roared outside. Darkness, cold and, later, hunger assailed them and boredom was a constant companion for there was little to occupy mind or body. Many sought refuge in the rough herb liquor that gave some illusion of escape from the heavy pall that weighed on hearts and minds. As the days dragged past, voices would raise and tempers fray more readily. Irritations escalated rapidly to outright conflict that frequently erupted into violence. This was, inevitably, the time when the old and the sick found it too hard, or too dispiriting, to hold onto life and so moved on to the next world and their next adventure.

And yet, for the last few winters – Tuczuk couldn't pinpoint exactly when it had started, although he believed it was about the time he had sensed the change in energies – the despondency had not been so deep. Tempers did not snap so quickly or so often, and when they did the conflict was more easily resolved. He had even heard laughter rippling through the gloom from time to time.

There were other odd occurrences too. The food supplies were remaining in good condition for much longer and the people in much better health than was usual. His herbs and sacred healing rites, previously in high demand, were called upon less and less. And the winter death rates were falling noticeably. He had suspected as much for the last two or three years and put it down to natural fluctuations. This year however, he could not deny the truth; people had stopped dying. The previously high winter mortality rate had fallen to that of the kinder summer months. He had no explanation, other than a certainty that these miracles had to be coming from the energy source he could feel but not trace. What was it? He needed answers.

He had delayed long enough. The time had come. He would do what he needed to do to find those answers even if his action would put his life at risk. Lowering the heavy curtain that separated his small cell, a niche off the main cavern like so many others in this place, he closed himself off from the rest of the inhabitants. It was a signal to all that he was undertaking magical work. No-one would disturb him until he lifted the curtain once more. If he never did, they would simply leave him where he lay. The cave would become his tomb.

Lighting a small fire, Tuczuk brewed a pungent mix of the bitter herbs he gathered and dried from these mountain slopes during the summer months. He used this draught only rarely because it was potent and extremely dangerous; if he had made the smallest miscalculation in its preparation its effects would be fatal. But he needed to know, and this was the only way. The potion would transport him from this world into another, a nowhere world that contained everything and nothing, and where the answer to every question could be found. If he was allowed to leave and return here, to this cave, he would bring those answers back with him.

He raised the bowl to his lips and swallowed the still-warm liquid, gagging at the acrid taste. Heat poured down his gullet and into his stomach, spreading out into his veins like thorn-laden tendrils that ripped at his flesh as they crept through his body. He screamed at the agony. On and on it went until he was drowning in an ocean of unbearable pain. No more. Please. No more. He could not stand it.

Then it was gone, his body gone too. There was nothing left but this consciousness that he recognised as his mind, his thoughts, his soul even, drifting in an opalescent white. No sound. No scent. No taste. Nothing but this gentle, pulsing mist that enveloped him. And even that small part of him was fading. His awareness of himself, his mind, his thoughts – his consciousness – was dissolving into his surroundings, losing itself in the glowing white everything that was nothing yet was all there ever had been and all there ever would be. This was bliss. This was home. This was what he really was – ineffable, untouchable, unknowable. Infinite. He melted into the nothingness, his last fleeting thought that he wanted to stay there forever, cradled in its familiarity and surrounded by the purest love he had ever experienced. And with that thought, awareness of his human identity flooded back, dragging him unwillingly from his bliss.

'Not yet,' he was told. It was a feeling, not a voice. 'Not yet. It is not time.'

He did not resist. It would be of no use. It was this way each time that he travelled beyond the world. Each time he would be on the point of losing himself, desperate to merge with the opalescence. Each time, he was held back. It didn't matter. There would come a day when he would be allowed to stay.

'Show me,' he requested. Images, fleeting but clear, danced before him. A skull, carved of a deep green stone. The herdsman, Pel, finding the skull in the river and hiding it deep within the cave system where they sheltered. Soldiers – men in thick leather armour and helmets, carrying swords and other weapons. That was all, but it was enough. His questions had been answered. The skull was the source of their improved moods and health – and Pel knew where it was. The soldiers? That, the shaman believed, was to come; although he did not yet know the circumstances, or the significance of their arrival, a deep sense of dread warned him that it would not be good news.

He was falling, falling, hurtling down through empty space until, with a heavy thud, Tuczuk woke to find he was back lying on the floor of his cave cell, once more fully in his body, which felt as if it had been beaten by a hundred ironwood clubs. His stomach convulsed. He barely had time to turn over before he vomited violently. Again and again, his stomach spewed its contents until he was exhausted and empty, purged of the noxious cocktail he had so recently swallowed. So it was, every time. It would be several days before he regained enough strength to act on what he had learned. He lay back on his bed, exhausted, and slipped into unconsciousness.

36.

'Where is the green skull?'

Pel jumped at the unexpected sound echoing through the stalactite cave. He looked up, flustered. Although he could see no-one in the half-light, he had immediately recognised the voice. Tuczuk. The shaman must have followed him. But how could the old man have known about the skull. Unless… Could his wife have spoken of it? No. That would not be. She would sooner cut off her hand than betray her promise to him. Tuczuk would have his own ways – magical, mysterious ways – of uncovering secrets.

'Where is the green skull?' The question came again, commanding and forbidding defiance.

Pel hesitated, considering his options. There were none. The shaman knew about the skull. It would be useless to deny its existence.

'You should have brought it to me immediately.' Tuczuk's stooped frame was a dark silhouette on the ledge. 'It was not yours to keep. That is not the way.'

'I found it.' Pel wanted to argue, plead his case. Beg to be allowed to keep it, even as he recognised the futility of such a request. 'Why can't I keep it?' He sounded as petulant as a child and as defensive, fully aware that he had been wrong to disobey the shaman's authority.

'Give it to me.' There would be no further argument. Reluctantly, Pel retrieved the cloth-wrapped bundle from its hiding place and with a heavy heart handed it to the old man.

* * * * *

189

Tuczuk stared down at the skull in his hands. Where had it come from? Who had created it, this mysterious skull that looked so battered and worthless and yet held such power? He couldn't have let it go if he had wanted to; his palms were glued to the once-smooth contours. What felt like bolts of lightning surged one after the other into his hands, up his arms and into his chest causing his heart to pound wildly. He had lived a long life, with that whole lifetime's experience in the ways of magic. Never before though had he encountered anything to equal the treasure he now held. This skull was a truly extraordinary thing.

'I will take care of it now.' With those few words, he walked into the passageway and returned to his cell.

In the days that followed, the shaman was seen only rarely. He spent the hours shut away with the skull, using every skill he possessed to unravel its secrets. He had little success. The skull would not speak to him. Even another perilous journey into the veiled world brought no greater understanding. Eventually, he was forced to admit defeat. The origins and purpose of the green skull were not for him to know. He would have to be satisfied with his own insights and observations.

Several days later, his investigations exhausted, Tuczuk called the people together in the meeting place. Everyone was present, and a low hum of puzzled voices filled the high roofed cavern. Of them all, only two, Pel and his wife, guessed the reason for the shaman's summons.

Drawing on the showmanship he reserved for important ceremonies, Tuczuk had concealed the skull under a fine cloth and placed it in the centre of a circle of twelve small lamps. Now he was standing in front of the crowd with his arms raised to the sky.

'Behold, my friends,' he proclaimed in a tone heavy with dramatic tension, 'we have been graced by the gods. They have seen fit to bestow upon us a gift beyond value.'

With a flourish, he drew away the cloth to reveal the green skull. Gasps filled the chamber as it came into view, otherworldly and eerie in the dim, flickering light. From the back, a handful of villagers – one of them, he noticed, Pel's wife – turned and left, unwilling or perhaps too frightened, to remain in its presence. Most though were captivated by the treasure and agreed that it was indeed a sacred gift whose beneficial influence would bring increasing good health and fortune to everyone.

37.

Winter was nearly at its end. Soon it would be warm enough to return to their summer home on the plateau. Those days could not come soon enough. The winter they had just lived through had been long and hard, longer and harder than they had experienced in many years and even the skull's presence had been unable to spare them from the rigours of its harsh grip. To everyone's delight, however, in the past few days the sun's returned warmth had tingled their skin and awakened the sleeping world outside their winter refuge. Already, the tiniest of green buds were pushing out from the naked branches of those shrubs hardy enough to survive on these stark, high plateaus. Even though at night the temperatures still fell well below freezing, leaving behind a thick coating of crisp white frost as the sun rose, spirits were high and everyone was eager to leave the darkness of their underground refuge. The clear light and blue skies held a firm promise of easier days to come.

It was a promise that would have to wait. This morning the weather had closed in again, the way it so often did at this time of the year. While the sun would return, its journey would not be an easy one. It would have to defeat the sudden, unexpected snowstorms and roaring gales that challenged its growing strength in a last battle for supremacy.

Dark clouds had been building since just after daybreak, with a rising wind that carried the icy chill of a winter that was not yet conquered. Only a few men were still outside, making their way back from an early hunting trip. Their tiny figures could be seen scurrying across the plateau, heads down and shoulders hunched into the weather. They had turned for home the moment they had seen the first signs of the storm and they would reach shelter before its full fury hit.

* * * * *

Pel barely heard the warning shout over the howl of the wind. 'Soldiers. Coming this way.'

He rushed to the entrance and stared anxiously out across the flat plain. A large group of heavily armed men – seventy? eighty maybe? – was heading towards them, moving quickly in an attempt to outrun the blizzard roaring down on their heels. Voices muttered in growing consternation. Soldiers were never good news. They took what they wanted – food, shelter, sometimes women too – giving nothing in return, leaving those they had visited empty-bellied and empty-hearted. Pel's arm encircled his wife's waist, hoping to give her a reassurance that he was not feeling.

The soldiers charged into the cave with no regard for those gathered there, shaking snow from their tunics and demanding food and liquor. Ordering that precious livestock be slaughtered to provide meat. The villagers pleaded – with their animals gone, there would be none to provide milk in the spring or to breed the next generations. It was to no avail. These were rough, intimidating men, battle-hardened soldiers used to getting their own way. If they weren't given what they demanded, they would take it anyway. They wanted meat, and they would have it. The commanding officer stood before the frightened group, strutting like a peacock. Arrogance and disdain dripped from his lips as he addressed them.

'I am General Ho Sen Sha of the Emperor's elite guard, appointed by his Imperial Highness himself. These men are under my command. His Imperial Highness owns this land and owns you. As I act on his personal authority, you can consider that I also own you. Therefore you will do as I command. Defy me, and you defy your Emperor. The penalty for such treason is death. However,' he held up his hand as if he himself was that same glorious and all-shining Emperor, 'we are not animals.' This warning was addressed to several of his men who were eyeing up the younger women hungrily. 'Your women will not be touched. Show us the respect and honour that is our due and no-one will be harmed. When the weather breaks, we will be on our way and you can continue your lives. Should you oppose our presence, however,' his face hardened into flint, 'I will not hesitate to remind you who is your master here.'

38.

It happened the following day. Pel was playing with his children when he heard angry shouts coming from the main cavern. He abandoned the game and raced to see what was causing the commotion. At the cave entrance a small crowd was watching anxiously as General Ho Sen Sha confronted a cowering Tuczuk, who was clearly – and unsuccessfully – attempting to hide a rough bundle under his cloak. Pel's heart stopped. It was the skull.

'Show me,' the General demanded. Tuczuk didn't move. 'Show me!' the soldier repeated, losing patience. Still Tuczuk refused to obey.

Furious now, Ho Sen Sha stepped forward and wrested the shaman's hands from beneath his robes. His eyes narrowed in astonishment; the wrappings had slipped from the bundle revealing the deep green skull, which appeared sinister and menacing in the low light. Despite his surprise, he hesitated for only a moment before reaching for it.

'No!' Tuczuk clutched it tightly to his chest refusing to give it up. A ferocious backhand to his temple sent the old shaman sprawling to the ground, the skull tumbling from his hands and rolling across the floor. The shaman lay where he had fallen, dazed, blood pouring from a deep gash in his temple.

'Kill anyone who moves,' the General bellowed, stooping to scoop up the skull. He jerked his hand back as though stung. A powerful jolt of – what? An energy of some kind – had surged through his fingers and up his arm to his shoulder. More cautiously he reached for the skull a second time. The moment his flesh made contact with the cold stone his whole arm began to tingle and burn as if on fire. This time however, he did not let go. He stared at the skull curiously. What was this strange and macabre object? Where had it come from? In truth, it didn't matter. There was no doubt in his mind that it held a powerful magic and that its rightful place was with his master, the Emperor. He, General Ho Sen Sha of the Imperial Guard, would be well rewarded for his loyalty in bringing such a prize.

Guessing the General's intention, and without care for his own safety, Tuczuk pushed himself up from the floor and rushed at the soldier, snatching back the skull from the other man's grasp. He did not keep it for long. A flicker of movement, swift and silent. Lamplight flashing on metal. For the briefest of moments surprise flickered across the shaman's face before his legs gave way and he collapsed without a murmur onto the hard, cold floor.

The captain plucked the skull from his hands and handed it to one of his men. 'A gift for our Emperor. Take good care of it. Do not be tempted to trifle with it, for it carries powerful magic that will bring ill luck to those who are unworthy of its power.' The soldier looked at it fearfully, holding it at arms' length. Was this 'thing' about to turn into a demon and steal his soul?

* * * * *

Pel was the only one of the crowd whose attention was still on the General and the skull he had plundered. Every other villager was staring in silent horror at Tuczuk, who lay motionless on the ground. His eyes were open, pleading for the return of the skull, the light in them fading fast. His blood and his life were draining from his body, seeping down into the sand and dirt. He stretched out his hand in a final desperate plea, and his last breath rattled in his throat.

196

The crowd's horror turned to anger and then to blind rage. These soldiers had murdered their shaman and stolen their skull. The General, though arrogant, was no fool. He saw the rebellion growing. These people may not have had weapons, but they had courage. Fury was aflame in their bellies and their hearts and they were no longer afraid to act, no matter what the consequences. The soldiers maintained their dominance through intimidation and fear. When that fear vanished, so did their power. They could not threaten those who did not fear them.

'I warned you of the consequences of resistance,' he shouted, in a vain attempt to quell the flames. 'It need not have been this way. You will not deny the Emperor what is rightfully his.' His words were ignored. The crowd were already moving forward with murder in their eyes.

'Go,' he yelled to his men, who had by now retreated to the outer cave area. 'Go.' The soldiers fled.

The storm had passed and sunlight once more spilled over the land, glistening on the fresh snow. It was a stark contrast to the darkness and bloodshed within. The soldiers had no time to appreciate its beauty. They were running for their lives, knowing that the rage and hatred they had aroused were more powerful weapons than any sword.

Pel stood silently and watched the soldiers disappear into the distance with a heart filled with sorrow and regret. His wife had been right. The green skull had brought bad luck to their world and it was all his fault. He had found it and brought it here, and now Tuczuk lay dead. But Pel's heart ached most from knowing that the green skull had gone forever and that he would never see it again.

*   *   *   *   *

Tuczuk was filled with a peace unlike any he had ever felt. Once again he was floating in that beautiful soft white opalescence, only this time it felt gentler than usual, more protective, and drifting through it was the sweet scent of honeysuckle and jasmine. How strange that he had never noticed that before. This time he couldn't remember how he had got here. He couldn't remember anything. This glowing white world was all that existed. Perhaps it was all that had ever existed. He struggled to capture a memory and couldn't. There was nothing prior to this moment.

The mist was parting, opening before him. Far off in the distance, a dazzling light of blue and white and gold shone more brightly than the sun. Beckoning. Calling him forward. He drifted towards it, closer and closer, falling into its embrace. Floating effortlessly, the mist softly closing in behind. He was safe here. Safe and held and loved. He had never really known love. Here, though, now, in this place that was nowhere and everywhere, nothing and everything, he understood what it was. What it really was. It made him smile.

The light was directly in front of him now, not a beacon as he had first believed, but an open doorway, the light streaming through from the other side. He crossed the threshold and the light cocooned him, filling him, holding him safe.

'*Now* it is time,' it whispered. 'Welcome home.'

GEMMA, 4

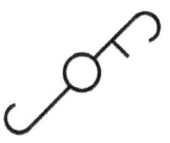

39.

The harsh ring of the phone jolted me out of a world of scented meadows and warm sunshine. Not properly awake, I fumbled to answer it with an unintelligible grunt.

'They've found Callum.' All sleep-induced dopeyness vanished with Joe's terse sentence. He sounded strained and unnatural. This wasn't going to be the good news I'd been hoping for.

'Is he OK?'

'He's dead, Gemma.'

No. It couldn't be. As the finality of Joe's words penetrated my mind, I had the strangest sensation that the world had stopped around me and that I was apart from it, enclosed in a bubble and unable to keep my hold on reality. Callum was dead. While I had left my infatuation with him behind on the arid sands of Arizona, the memory of our one torrid night under the desert stars was as vivid as if it had been yesterday. My face burned crimson as I remembered, and the tears fell for this brave, driven and oh so maddening man.

My heart was thudding against my ribcage so hard I thought it would burst out of my chest – alongside my sadness, a frightening certainty had settled over me in a thick, suffocating blanket. Whatever Callum had got mixed up in, it involved the blue skull, Gal-Athiel. Which meant I was mixed up in it too, and through his friendship with me, Joe. And Frankie and Davey, maybe even Ches Whitefeather too. They had all been on the Arizona expedition. An ominous shadow drifted through my world. The dark legacy of the Shadow Chasers was closing in.

'Gemma? Are you there?'

'How?' I managed at last, praying that Joe would tell me it had been an accident, or that it was a result of Callum's earlier injuries. Knowing, deep down, that he wouldn't.

Joe took a deep breath. 'He was found floating face down in a canal backwater in Birmingham. That's where I am now. I've been here since six o'clock this evening. After that business in Leeds I'm on the police records as a friend, so they brought me in to identify the body. I would have called you before but I haven't had a chance.' Even on the other end of the phone, I could tell that he was extremely upset and shaken.

'Oh Joe, I'm so sorry. Are you OK?'

'No, not really. It wasn't very pleasant. He'd been in the water several days...' His voice wavered as he broke off, shuddering at the memory of the grim task. It was a little while before he carried on. 'I told them I'd break the news to you. You told the hospital you were a close friend too. Remember?' I did remember, although that all seemed like a very long time ago now.

I was doing my best to keep my emotions from getting the better of me, and to haul my thoughts into some form of order. 'What do the police say?'

'Officially they are treating it as an accident but I get the feeling that off the record they're keeping an open mind and not ruling out foul play. They can't do much else, with all that's gone on.'

Tears welled up again, ready to spill down my face, and I swallowed hard to keep them back. 'Why the hell did he have to run out on the hospital, Joe? He was so ill and he was safe there. I don't understand what's going on.' I don't know if I'd ever felt so lost and bewildered as I did then.

'That makes two of us. Look, I'm heading back now. I'll come straight to you and tell you everything. What a bloody mess! Oh, and Gemma, you can bet you'll be getting a visit from the police sooner rather than later.'

'OK, Joe. I'll see you when you get here. Drive safe.' I hung up, lost in a tangle of grief, worry and unanswerable questions.

I lay back against the pillows. What were you up to, Callum? What had you found out that was significant enough to cost you your life? And what was going to happen next? My thoughts flew to the envelope hidden in Duncan's flat. Did it hold the key to all of this? Maybe we should just let it all go. Hand it over to D.I. Chamberlain and be done with it. I let my eyelids fall, although I knew I wouldn't get another wink of sleep that night. I was bone weary and yet again, I had had enough. I didn't want to be involved in this. I never had.

'But you are involved. It can be no other way.' A soft, sweet voice filled my bedroom. I recognised it immediately – it was Gal-Athiel, the blue skull, the Voice of the Mother. There was no mistaking the gentle soothing energy that enfolded me whenever her spirit was near. She had spoken to me first during my adventure in Arizona, when I had travelled with Callum and his team in search of her sanctuary. We had not found her, but she had found me. She had been silent for months.

'My dearest child, from the day the skulls came into your life and you accepted their invitation, you always knew, in some secret place deep within your soul, that this was the way it would go. That the road would not be an easy one. That it would demand of you more than you believed you were able to give. Even so, you said Yes. And you are still saying Yes. Make no mistake, there is

202

more, much more, to come, Little One. You, and those who walk with you, will be challenged again and again. Again and again, you will want to give up, yet you will not do so. Even now, when your head tells you No, your soul is saying Yes. You will find the courage to go on, and in doing so, you will prevail. Do not give up hope. Do not give up your quest. It is too important.' With her final words, a wave of warm reassurance washed through my body. Against all expectations, my eyelids grew heavy and my mind calmed. Within seconds I had fallen into a deep and restful sleep.

40.

I was already up and about when Joe pushed open the back door, walked into the kitchen and dropped onto a chair. He looked dreadful, exhausted and deeply upset. I shoved a mug of hot strong coffee into his hand and waited for him to speak.

'They found him yesterday morning,' he said eventually. 'A couple of council workers discovered the body. They'd gone to clean up the canal basin and saw it floating amongst the crap. You know, rusty shopping trolleys, old carrier bags, filthy oily water. That sort of thing. The police showed me a photo.' He looked up at me, his face grim. 'It was a bloody awful place to die, Gemma. A stinking forgotten backwater stuck in behind some derelict workshops where no-one ever goes. If those council guys hadn't been sent out to clear it out yesterday, he could have been there for who knows how long before he was found. Weeks. Months maybe.

'The police asked me shedloads of questions. Where he'd been since that woman was butchered in his hotel room. What he'd been doing. Who he'd spoken to. Whether he'd been in touch with us before that phone call when we found him "by the side of the road". For Christ's sake!' The tension finally exploded. 'I don't fucking know, do I? I wish I did. It might help me make some sense of it all. The tiny bits of information we have aren't going to lead them to his killers.' He was on his feet, stomping furiously up and down the kitchen as if doing so would erase the memory of Callum's bloated, decaying body and offer up the answers we both wanted so badly.

'So what happens next?'

'You tell me. Accidental or not, there wasn't a lot of sympathy around for Callum. Oh, the police'll do their job and investigate, but I got the clear impression that the overwhelming attitude is that he butchered that poor woman and deserves all he's got. One less criminal to deal with and a case they can wrap up. Let's face it, all the evidence points to him being guilty of that killing.'

'Except he's not…wasn't.'

'No, he wasn't.'

'So if we accept that he was murdered rather than it being an accident, the question is why and who did it.' I couldn't believe I was actually saying those words.

'Maybe whoever beat him to a pulp decided to get rid of him permanently. Perhaps he could identify them, or at least enough to make their lives difficult. If they'd planned on killing him when they had got the information they wanted, they might have been careless with their talk.

'It could be that they got it wrong, believing Callum knew more than he actually did. They wanted something they finally realised he didn't have. If that was the case, there'd be no point in grabbing him again. He'd be no use to them. So they set him up for an 'accident', tying up all the loose ends at once.'

'While they walk away scot free.'

'Yes. Bloody hell, what a mess.' Joe thumped his fist on the table in frustration.

'That doesn't explain the envelope,' I brooded. 'We know they – whoever they are – found out about King Street because they turned up there and almost caught us. Were they specifically after the contents of the envelope, or simply to turn the place over on the off-chance that they might find some lead to whatever they believed Callum was on to?'

'We'd better hope it's the second.' Joe ran his fingers wearily through his hair. 'If they know about the envelope, they're not going to stop until they find it. We'll have to be more careful than ever not to do or say anything that'll imply we're in any way involved.'

Only we were already involved, Joe and I, whether we liked it or not. We always had been. Gal-Athiel's words came back to me. *There is more, much more, to come.* What that 'more' was, we could only wait to find out.

KHALIA: The Jade Skull

Part VI

MADELEINE, 1
(China, 1893)

41.

Madeleine stirred. The gentle breeze drifting in through the open window tickled her skin with its perfumed breath, and through her closed eyelids sunlight danced a ballet of light and shade. For the first time in so long – months probably, though it felt like years – the thick suffocating fog that had enveloped her was gone. The pain and heartache still remained, only now it had dissolved into to a hollow, gaping pit within her breast as if someone, somehow, had torn out her heart and thrown it away. She didn't know if it would ever find its way back to her. She breathed deeply, eyes still tightly closed against the day, drawing the sunbeams and sweet fragrances down into her lungs and into her soul. She had been dead for too long. Today, she would begin to live again. She had promised.

Her hand closed around the crumpled scrap of paper. Paul's last will and testament. His dying wishes. Not for his estate or for his funeral but for her, Madeleine, his wife. She had found it the previous evening, a page torn from his journal, written in pencil, the handwriting faint and uneven. Paul must have been very ill when he had written it. But when? When could he have poured these words onto the page? She had barely left his side in all the time he was sick, and yet she hadn't seen him do it. And why had she only discovered it now, so many months after he had left her?

She had been curled up, weeping, hugging his greatcoat tightly as she had every night since his death, when she had noticed the corner of a small, tatty sheet of paper poking out of an inside pocket. Where had it come from? Why hadn't she seen it before? Her hands shaking, her vision blurred with tears, Madeleine had drawn it out and opened it. Reading the words written with such difficulty, her tears had fallen faster and harder. Only this time there had been a new quality to her tears. An unaccustomed sense of peace was stealing into her heart. For the first time since Paul's death, the grief was softening, becoming more bearable. She had fallen asleep sobbing her heartache into the darkness, clutching the tattered note in her fingers.

'My beloved Madeleine,

In the too short time we have been together, you have brought a meaning and a light to my life that, before I met you, I never believed I could experience. Mere words are not enough to tell you how I feel about you but they are all I have. You are my world, my sun, my moon and my stars. My night and my day. I love you more than you will ever know.

You are so strong and courageous, my darling. Your smile and your love for me is all that keeps me alive and the hope burning in me that we can overcome this and that I will be well again. These past weeks you have nursed me day and night with no thought for yourself. It hurts me so much to see the toll this is taking on you while I lie here, helpless to ease your burden.

I will not tell you this while I still live, my love, but I can no longer hold onto that hope. In my heart I know that I have precious little time left. This sickness that has claimed me will not let me go. And so I write you this letter as my dying wish, in the certainty that you will not find it until I am gone.

Let me go, Madeleine. Take our love and tuck it safely away in a corner of your heart, for it is eternal, then let me go. Live. Live each day as though it were your last, for

God knows it may be. You are a free spirit, wild and untameable, and for that I have always adored you. Never change, my darling. Never let that spirit be taken from you. Keep your hunger for life and adventure alive for as long as you breathe on this Earth. This is the last request I make to you, my beloved wife.

I know you will find it hard for I see, and am humbled beyond expression by, the depth of your love for me. It shatters my world to know I must leave that love behind. But you are strong and I know you will survive where I am not certain I could. You are too alive for it to be any other way. Grieve me as you must, my love, then set your grief aside and live your life to the fullest. Live it for me, as well as for yourself.

Know that I will always love and cherish you as deeply as I do now, no matter where this journey takes me next, and that I will always be at your side, watching over you. I love you, my darling.

Until we meet again, Goodbye.

Your ever devoted and adoring Paul'

This morning the words flooded back with crystal clarity, branded onto her memory by the fire of Paul's love for her. Lying motionless in the sunlight that streamed through the window and caressed her face, Madeleine vowed to do as he had asked. She would begin to live again. First, though, she had to lay to rest the ghosts that haunted her. As painful as it would be, she had to relive the nightmare of the past months. It was the only way she could set herself free from its shadows and move on.

*   *   *   *   *

For an hour, two hours and more, Madeleine lay on her bed remembering and letting go of memory by painful memory – that dreadful day Paul had fallen ill and the weeks that followed, trekking across the barren wilderness in search of help that did not appear, his condition worsening with every day that passed. It was strange, she considered in the midst of her remembering, how a landscape that in Paul's robust good health appeared so beautiful and alluring had suddenly turned so stark and menacing in the face of his sickness. Setting up camp when he became too weak to travel. Waking, bleary-eyed and with the last shred of hope gone to find themselves surrounded by soldiers in armour wielding swords and firearms. Another long and difficult journey, this time as captives, albeit well-treated ones, to arrive at last at this palace, Paul's health failing rapidly.

How long had he fought to hold on to life after they arrived here? One week? Two? Longer? Madeleine had no idea. Nothing had mattered to her but Paul, and she was losing him. He had grown weaker and sicker until the time came when he had no longer had the strength to fight. Silently he had slipped away from life and from her. In that moment a heavy, dark shroud of impenetrable grief had descended on Madeleine and had held her in its grip ever since. She had been treated well, given a light, airy room and a maidservant to tend to her needs. Of any more than that, she had been oblivious. She had been living in a world of pain and heartache, allowing it to consume her and rob her of her natural strength and resilience. No more. It was time to emerge from the twilight and reclaim her life.

* * * * *

At last it was done. Madeleine rose, noticing for the first time how weak and faint she was feeling, and crossed to the window. Below, the palace gardens were filled with a riot of colourful blooms that spilled over the borders and sent their cocktail of perfumes floating up to her balcony on the breeze. Here and there tranquil, still pools reflected a deep blue sky, soft green lawns beckoned and tinkling fountains sang. She breathed deeply, and in that moment she felt Paul's arms circling her waist and his lips nuzzling into the nape of her neck, the way they used to do.

'Stay strong, my darling,' she heard him whisper. 'Stay strong.' Her eyes filled with gentle tears that fell softly onto her cheek. She had vowed to step back into life, and she would, but the pain of his loss would be with her always.

'Mistress?' Madeleine's maid, Li-Mai, was looking at her wide-eyed. 'You are better?' Li-Mai's English, though hesitant, was surprisingly good.

'A little, thank you.'

'Good. Then I bring food. You eat now you are better. You do not eat for a long time.' She scurried off.

Madeleine moved to one of the large, gold-mounted mirrors that lined the far wall of her bedchamber, touching her face in dismay at the woman reflected back. The months of grief-filled, sleepless nights, scant appetite and almost complete self-neglect had taken their toll. Her face was drawn and pale, her eyes sunk into dark circles, skin as dry and papery as the dried honesty pods in her father's garden in England. Once lustrous hair fell in lank strands about too thin shoulders that matched a body much in need of proper nourishment. She put up a hand to brush a few stray strands from her forehead, scared at what she saw.

How had she let herself become like this? Paul would be distraught if he could see her now. In that moment, her promise became a rock-solid determination. She owed it to Paul, and she owed it to herself.

When Li-Mai returned shortly afterwards, Madeleine was dressed, her hair thoroughly brushed, with a spark in her eyes that hadn't been there for a very long time. Though it was only a tiny spark to be sure, the embers of her spirit had been rekindled. From that moment Madeleine grew stronger by the day, as if a force from outside herself was pushing her on. The spark grew brighter until it burst into flame, faint and wavering at first but never failing, burning ever brighter.

42.

As Madeleine emerged from the deadly tomb she had built around herself, she began to explore. The palace was a vast, sprawling, low-set stronghold nestling at the base of a range of low, rolling hills that swept up in the distance to form an imposing mountain range. Massive walls enclosed a seemingly endless expanse of gardens and meadows that clambered over the ridges and valleys surrounding the palace. A river meandered gently through the grounds, chuckling over tiny waterfalls, settling into still, glittering pools and feeding a small lake, in the centre of which stood the palace temple, accessible only by a delicate arched bridge. Charming, stumpy legged deer grazed its lawns. The whole landscape was beautifully tended, harmonious and tranquil. For Madeleine the gardens became a sanctuary where she could heal her shattered heart and regain her strength and zest for life.

From the window of the main gallery, she could see across the wide sun-drenched courtyard through the gates to the small town that clustered in the shadow of the palace walls. Although the ramshackle buildings were little more than rickety sheds, the streets appeared clean and free of the putrid waste she had seen in so many of the villages she had passed through on her travels with Paul. Li-Mai explained that the town existed only to serve the palace. All its inhabitants worked there, with the exception of a few more prosperous merchants whose homes were conspicuously grand against the rows of rough shacks. The servants were unpaid and penniless; nonetheless they were fed, housed and well-treated. Li-Mai considered the old Emperor to be a good and just man whose servants were a great deal more fortunate than most. Madeleine could not argue with that. She had been treated with nothing but kindness and generosity since her arrival at the palace.

Within the boundary of the palace walls, Madeleine was free to wander the grounds wherever she wished. She soon discovered however, that she would not be permitted to venture beyond. She had tried on several occasions; each time her way had been barred politely but firmly by the sentries at the gates. When she had asked about it, she had been told that she was not permitted to visit the town, for her own safety. The townsfolk would not welcome a stranger in their midst. It was an explanation she did not believe. Many of the servants – the townsfolk – were used to seeing her around the palace and she was far from being a stranger to them. No, that was just an excuse to placate her. The reality, Madeleine soon realised, was that she was a prisoner, even if the cage that held her was built of gold and roses.

While she had no desire to go into the town, she did deeply resent being prevented from doing so. She felt trapped. And the more she regained her strength and spirit, the more trapped she felt. Trapped, and desperately, achingly alone. She missed her home and family in a way she had never felt in all the time she had been travelling the empty plains of a far-off land with Paul. Here, though, now, with him gone, held captive in a strange land with strange people, a strange culture and a strange language, she was homesick and searingly lonely. The one saving grace was her maid, Li-Mai.

Now that Madeleine had climbed out of the deepest well of her grief, the two women quickly formed a close bond, in spite of the fact that they could not have been less alike in so many ways, both physically and in character.

Madeleine was tall, lithe – lanky, her brother had often teased her, in the way that brothers do – and athletic. A mane of fiery red hair and eyes of the deepest emerald green were a legacy of her father's Celtic heritage. She was not conventionally beautiful by any standards – her chin was a little too strong, her face a bit too angular and her features not as regular as they could have been. Nevertheless, men who she passed in the street would stop and stare after her captivated, although by what, they could not have explained. It was an indefinable quality of spirit that had for too long been submerged by heartache. It would not be held down for long. As Madeleine's strength returned, it re-emerged, feisty, fiery, independent and bold.

Li-Mai by contrast, was tiny, barely reaching to Madeleine's shoulder. She had been blessed with the delicate bone structure of her race, huge, almost jet-black almond eyes, and hair like polished satin, and raven black, that hung in a curtain to her waist when not pulled up in a top-knot and fastened with slender bamboo pins. Through a different accident of birth, she would have graced the arm of any prince or emperor as his consort. She was also submissive and obedient, a trait that Madeleine had observed in all the women she had encountered in this land. Even those of high status walked with their eyes cast down when in the presence of their menfolk. As a servant, Li-Mai had not even dared to meet Madeleine's gaze until the day that the young Englishwoman, finding Li-Mai's continual subservience embarrassing, had lifted the maid's chin until those coal dark eyes met her own emerald gaze.

'Li-Mai, you do not need to act this way with me. You are my friend and my equal. Do you understand? When we are alone, and when it is safe for you to do so,' Madeleine understood clearly the repercussions of a servant being judged to have dishonoured a guest, 'you must treat me as such. Not as your mistress.'

'Mistress, I cannot. You are a lady of rank and I am a servant.'

'There will be no argument, Li-Mai. If you do not do as I ask, then I will command it of you, and then you cannot refuse.' She smiled kindly at the young servant. 'Be my friend as well as my maid, Li-Mai. Please. I am in great need of a friend.'

After just a moment's hesitation, Li-Mai had nodded shyly and dipped her head in agreement. Her kind heart had ached for Madeleine in her grief and had been desperately worried in the weeks the Englishwoman had languished inconsolable. If Li-Mai could help her in any way then she would do so. She would do whatever it took to protect this exotic foreign woman who had suffered so much.

'Yes, Mistress. I will be your friend. I will always be here for you when you need me.'

43.

Madeleine soon discovered that the Emperor was fascinated by the western world. He spoke excellent English, a legacy from his father who, once and a long time ago, had been involved in some dealings with government representatives from England, France and Spain. Although that relationship had ended while his father still ruled, its consequences remained and the Emperor's fascination with everything European, and especially British, kept the English language alive amongst his court. As Madeleine's strength returned, he frequently requested her presence when they would talk at length about that strange and alien world so far and so different from his own kingdom, and she would share stories that he never tired of. To her surprise, Madeleine quickly picked up a good understanding of his language and before many months had passed their conversations, which included culture, customs and religious beliefs among many other topics, were carried out in a peculiar hybrid of the two.

She grew fond of the old Emperor. She could not begin to estimate his age, although he was clearly well past his physical prime. Within his frail, bent body however, he still carried the steel-hard authority that had kept him his throne through several attempts to overthrow him. She found him to be exactly as Li-Mai had described, a just and kindly man. He remained as solicitous as when she and Paul had first arrived and she did not hold back in expressing her gratitude for his kindness. Nevertheless, he pointedly ignored questions as to when she could leave and whether he could assist her in returning to England. When she pushed, he gave a myriad of reasons why she should or could not: there was rebellion, her life would be in danger, bandits were plundering the area. None of them rang true.

Madeleine was not prepared to spend the rest of her life trapped within this prison, which pressed in on her more and more with each day that passed, suffocating her within its silken walls. She would have to find a way to escape. When, she confided in Li-Mai, however, the young maidservant grew wide-eyed with fear.

'No, Mistress. You must not. You must not disobey the Emperor. He is very fond of you, it is true. That will not keep him from executing you if you try to escape. He will have no choice. He cannot be seen to be weak if he is to keep his throne.' Li-Mai was so distressed with genuine terror for Madeleine's safety that the Englishwoman let the matter drop. At least for a while. A captive she may be, but there were far worse cells than this in which she could be imprisoned, she reasoned, in an attempt to accept the situation. She would give it a little more time. An opportunity would present itself sooner or later. When it did, she would seize it and not look back.

* * * * *

Very quickly, Madeleine's desire for freedom turned into a life or death necessity. In the weeks since she had stepped back into life, she had blossomed. The haggard waif who had peered back at her from the mirror that morning had long gone. Now her eyes sparkled, her skin was firm and soft, and her hair once more gleamed lustrous and silken.

This newly restored radiance and vitality had not gone unnoticed. The women whispered about her in the privacy of their quarters, while the noblemen stared after her with undisguised lust. Many wished to possess her, for she was an exotic, golden creature, so different from their wives and concubines, though none dared act. She was under the Emperor's protection and for as long as he lived, no-one would touch her against her will. The second reason they kept a safe distance from Madeleine was Prince Ju-Lin, the Emperor's first-born son and heir. To a man they feared his anger and reprisals.

If Madeleine was oblivious to the heated stares of the courtiers, she was more than aware of the prince and his reputation. He was cruel, ambitious and arrogant, the opposite of his father and all that the wise old Emperor represented. Although handsome, Ju-Lin's good looks were not the kind that would last as he aged; already, in his late twenties, the tell-tale signs were appearing, his features thickening and coarsening. Madeleine had sensed him watching her and it frightened her. Instinctively, she recognised his barbarity, and took pains to avoid him whenever possible. It was impossible to do so completely.

The morning following her conversation with Li-Mai, he was lying in wait for her. Madeleine was returning to her room after an early audience with the Emperor, during which they had discussed at length the merits of several of Shakespeare's tragedies. She always enjoyed these conversations and she walked with a light step and a smile. It was as she passed through an ante-room, her thoughts lost in Shakespeare's sonnets, that he stepped out from behind a column and seized her arm in a steel-hard grip. The sneer on his face could not disguise the lust in his eyes.

In a low voice, so that those around could not hear, he hissed at her. 'You may have my father bewitched, harlot but you do not fool me. He cannot protect you forever, and when that day comes, I will be waiting for you. You will pay for your presence here.'

She would not let him see her fear. She must not. If he sensed weakness in her, he would have won. She wrenched her arm free of Ju-Lin's grip and glared at him. 'You will be waiting a very long time, Your Highness.'

She gathered her skirts and strode away with her head held high, hoping her legs would not give way until she had reached the safety of her chamber, where she threw herself onto her bed cursing with a skill that would have made a stevedore blush. Why had she listened to Li-Mai? Why was she not already half way across the mountains on her way to India? Because the urgency hadn't been there, she admitted. The palace, though a prison, was a comfortable one. What lay beyond its walls would be a great deal harder, infinitely more uncertain and, up until today, far more dangerous. Not any longer.

Her father had taught her to fight, and fight dirty, scorning every rule of fair play. 'Good manners be damned if you're fighting for your life,' he had told her. She would lash out like a cornered tigress if necessary. It would make little difference. She would not be able to fight off Ju-Lin for long. Staring up at the lavish gilded ceiling she saw none of its beauty; instead, her thoughts were filled with the fate that she was in no doubt awaited her if she remained. No, it would not happen. She would take her own life before she was forced to submit to the Prince's will.

'What are you thinking, woman?' Rousing from her dark thoughts, Madeleine shook herself angrily. 'You aren't going to kill yourself. You are going to get out of here. As soon as you possibly can.'

When Li-Mai returned to the chamber, Madeleine told her what had happened. The maid's eyes widened in alarm. In a voice trembling with anxiety she confirmed Madeleine's fears. 'You are right to be worried, Mistress. Ju-Lin despises you and all you represent.

'There is something more. I have heard talk that even as he hates you and all you are, he also desires you greatly. That you arouse in him a fire and a hunger that he has never felt before. Because of this he hates you even more fiercely. It fuels his determination to subjugate you to his will. To break you.'

She paused to steady her voice before she continued. 'It is said that he is determined to make you his concubine, with or without your consent. It must not happen, Mistress. He is a cruel and vicious lover. Many of those he has taken to his bed have taken their own lives to escape his attentions. You would eventually die at his hand through his perverted pleasures, as many others have done.' Her huge dark eyes stared up fearfully at the mistress, lashes wet with tears.

'For now, you are under our glorious Emperor's protection. While he lives, he will not allow Ju-Lin to touch you. I fear though that the Emperor's authority is fading. Ju-Lin is becoming bolder. He challenges his father's commands daily. If as yet he has not dared open defiance and disobedience, it is only a matter of time. Mistress, before I begged you not to escape, in order to save your life. Now, for the same reason, you must go.'

44.

Madeleine whooped in exhilaration as her horse carried her at breakneck speed across the flat, sun-drenched grasslands. The wind, warm on her skin, whipped her hair out in her wake like the fiery red tail of a comet. Joyful laughter bubbled up from deep within her belly and burst out into the sunlight. Over the sound of her own galloping hoof beats, she heard a second rhythmic drumming drawing ever closer. It didn't matter. She was almost there. He would never catch her now. With another elated whoop, this time of victory, she hurtled past the blasted tree stump and, in a display of outstanding horsemanship, wheeled her horse around to face her pursuer.

'You cheated!' Paul protested, panting, slowing his mount to pull up beside her. 'You started to race way before we got to the rock!'

Madeleine threw back her head to the shimmering deep blue sky overhead and let out a laugh that was filled with sunshine and happiness.

'Wasn't it you who told me never to play by anyone's rules but my own?' she teased, as out of breath as he was.

In a flash he had dismounted and reached up to throw an arm around her waist, pulling her from the saddle so that she slid into his embrace. She melted into him, surrendering completely to the lips that sought her own.

*   *   *   *   *

'Madeleine.' Why was he calling her name like that, as if he couldn't see her? She was here with him, wrapped in his arms. Only… she wasn't. Not any more. He was slipping away from her, fading into darkness.

'Madeleine.'

She reached out. Her hands grasped nothing but air.

'Paul?' Desperation sounded in her cry. She blinked as the hazy outlines of her room crystallised around her. 'Paul?'

No. Paul was dead. Paul had been dead for over six months. Tears pricked her eyes as she remembered. The dreams, ever present, were so bittersweet. Blissful when they came and she could hold him again, love him again. Painfully cruel when she woke to find herself alone.

She had promised to start living again and she was keeping that promise. Still though the dreams came. Still though she lived every day wishing it wasn't true. Knowing it was, for she had held him in her arms as he drew his last breath. Time had done little to heal the pain of this raw and ever-open wound. She doubted it ever would.

Only tonight it had been different. Someone else had called to her, filtering through her dreams, loud enough to wake her.

'Madeleine.' There. Again. Gentle but persistent. Refusing to be ignored. She rose and padded across to her maid's pallet. The young woman was in a deep sleep, snoring softly. It hadn't been Li-Mai.

'Hello?' Madeleine whispered warily. 'Is someone there?'

'Come.' One word. Repeating. 'Come. Come. Come.' It sounded like it was inside her skull and yet at the same time it was coming from outside of her, surrounding her, filling the air. Echoing seductively through the palace corridors. Enticing her to follow its call. Surely someone would hear and send the guards to investigate? No, beyond her door, everything was quiet. No-one and nothing moved.

'Li-Mai,' she called again softly. Li-Mai mumbled and turned over, sleeping soundly. Unusually so. She didn't wake even when Madeleine shook her shoulder.

'Come, Madeleine. Come.' The summons continued, a siren song compelling her to follow. Madeleine could not resist. She slipped her bare feet into soft felt slippers and drew a light silken robe over her chemise. It was mid-summer and the night balmy; she would not need more. The call whispered constantly, drawing her on through empty corridors and deserted chambers where the light of the full moon fell through ornately carved windows and doorways to cast intricate patterns on the floor.

Further and further into the heart of the palace stronghold she crept, into areas she had never seen before. Gradually the rooms and windows – and moonlight – petered out until only the corridor remained. Here the air smelled different. It felt different too. Flatter. Danker. Fear plucked at Madeleine's flesh. Was she entering the castle's forbidden sector? Shortly after her arrival she had been warned of the penalty for such a transgression. It was a fate she didn't wish to bring on herself. And yet, despite her misgivings and reluctance to continue, she was unable to resist the force that had drawn her from her bed and was calling her onwards.

Madeleine shivered and drew the thin robe more closely around her shoulders. In stark contrast to the warm night outside, these tunnels were cold. She slowed her steps to look more closely at her surroundings. These were not mere service passageways; the stonework was richly carved and the walls studded with alcoves that held statues and fountains. The walls, floor and ceiling were smooth and polished, lit by regularly spaced torches set in elaborate sconces. Her heart beat faster and harder. If this place was so brightly illuminated and well-cared for, it must mean it was used... and often. What if she was discovered here? She forced the thought – and the fear it gave rise to – away. She mustn't dwell on the risks.

Her fears were unrealised. Not one distant footstep or muted voice indicated the presence of another living soul. 'As silent as the grave,' she thought, then shivered again. 'Not a great comparison, Madeleine,' she chided.

'Come, Madeleine. Come.' The call resumed, urging her on. Grasping her courage in both hands, she followed it deeper and deeper into the underbelly of the palace.

45.

Madeleine paused. Ahead, a fan of light spilled out over the floor of the corridor. It didn't come from the torches; there were none in the vicinity and besides, they cast an altogether different kind of light to this flickering soft yellow glow that lapped at the stone through a half-open doorway. Instinctively, she knew that this was her destination.

She peered cautiously through the opening. Part of her knew that it would be empty; after all, would she have been summoned – and she had been summoned, of that she was now certain – all this way only to be caught now? The other, more down-to-earth and rational part of her was leaving nothing to chance. She must not be found in these corridors.

The room was empty. It was small compared to all the other halls and chambers of the palace, measuring barely ten paces or so across, and circular. Windowless, like the passageways that had led her here. Unlike those tunnels with their naked stone, every inch of these walls was hung with heavy satin drapes and richly embellished tapestries that fell from ceiling to floor in deep folds and spilled into pools of fabric over the ground. The centre of the floor was covered in thick furs, rugs, and plump, velvet cushions in the richest jewel-bright colours. Ribbons of crystal dripped from the ceiling, twinkling like raindrops in the light of a thousand slender candles held in gemstone-studded gold and silver sconces.

The rich luxury of the small room was completely unlike any other she had seen here. While the palace was filled with priceless treasures from every continent, the chambers and staterooms heavy with gold and precious stones, she had always found it too formal. Too stiff and uncomfortable. Here, in total contrast, the atmosphere overflowed with warmth and cosiness. It welcomed instead of holding at arm's length. She felt safe for the first time since Ju-Lin had threatened her. And yet... Alongside that unaccustomed feeling of security stood another, less welcome sensation. One of being watched.

Slowly Madeleine turned her head. Her hand flew to her mouth, stifling a cry. At the edge of the room, a low table of ebony inlaid with gold and ivory sat barely eight inches high. Lying on a soft cushion in the centre of the table top, and dominating the space, was an object unlike any she had ever seen. Unlike any she could ever have imagined existed. She found it grotesque; nonetheless it exerted such a powerful fascination that she was unable to tear her gaze from it. Was it *this* that had called her here tonight? Instinctively she knew it to be so.

She was no longer conscious of anything else in the room – the tapestries and silken drapes, the rugs, the candles. In the space of one brief glance, this object had become the sole focus of her attention. On a cushion of jet black velvet shot through with threads of the purest silver and gold that glittered in the flickering candlelight like stars in a midnight sky, lay a skull. Though battered and chipped now, it was obvious that it had been created by a craftsman of the very highest skill. It was life-size and highly detailed, the lines carved as accurately and intricately as Nature herself would have done. The ink black silk set off the rich, mossy green of the stone perfectly. Spellbound, hardly aware of her actions, Madeleine knelt in front of it, stretching out one trembling hand to brush its surface with her fingers.

A fierce jolt slammed through her body, knocking her backwards. She immediately recognised the sensation; she had just received an electric shock. Several years previously she had accompanied her father on a visit to one of his amateur scientist friends, who had been experimenting with electricity. There she had received a similar shock when she had accidentally brushed against a small steel cage. Amused, the scientist had explained to her that metal is a highly effective conductor of electricity. She had been fascinated by the phenomenon.

This object though was not made of metal. It was carved from stone. Jade, if she wasn't mistaken. Rich mossy green jade. And stone did not conduct electricity. She reached out again, tentatively, this time not quite touching the surface. It was definitely the source of the shock. Even at a distance the energy tingled and pulsed through her fingers. Curious and enthralled, Madeleine studied it closely, repelled yet at the same time strangely soothed.

Common sense was nudging a warning. The danger of discovery was increasing with every minute she spent in the room. She had to leave. It was no use. The skull had cast its spell. She couldn't leave, not yet. She curled up on the rug-strewn floor and let the energy pulse through her outstretched hand, up her arm and into her heart from where its warmth rippled out until her whole body quivered. A blanket of deep, reassuring peace – a feeling she hadn't experienced since the day Paul had fallen ill – settled over her, together with an understanding that no matter what happened, everything would be alright. She welcomed it in the same way that the parched earth welcomes rain. The voice had fallen silent. There was

229

nothing she had to do. Nothing else existed in that moment but this all-encompassing peace.

*   *   *   *   *

How long had she been lying there? Minutes? Hours? Madeleine couldn't guess. She couldn't stay there forever, no matter how much she wished it. The shuffle of soft footsteps on the stone corridor floor slowly penetrated the cocoon of serenity that held her. Someone was coming.

The spell was broken. Fighting down panic, Madeleine's gaze flashed around the room. She had to find another way out. She could not leave by the door; she would be clearly silhouetted in the lamplight. There was no other exit. The walls were solid stone. She would have to hide and pray that she would not be found. With scant seconds to spare, she darted behind one of the heavy drapes that lined the walls and attempted to disguise her outline in its folds. Surely whoever coming must hear her heart pounding. It was practically leaping from her chest. Hardly daring to breathe, she peeked through a tiny crack where the curtains met, only to pull her head back sharply.

The Emperor! Madeleine pressed back against the wall to stop her legs from giving way. His kindness and affection for her would not spare her if he discovered her here. The punishment demanded for trespassing in these forbidden areas was death, and he would not hesitate to mete out that punishment, whatever sorrow he might feel in doing so. To act in any other way would show weakness. With Ju-Lin seeking to take the throne, it would threaten his rule, if not his life too.

Through the narrow slit in the drapes, Madeleine watched the old man bow so low that his head reached his knees. Her eyes widened in surprise. This proud and powerful Emperor, sovereign of more than a million people, whose lands stretched beyond a month's ride in any direction, yielded to no-one. Yet here he was, standing acquiescent and humble before the skull. Did he consider its power to be even greater than his own? He bowed again and settled himself cross-legged on one of the plump cushions that filled the floor, his head still lowered in respect. Within moments the atmosphere in the room became charged, prickling in the way that electricity fills the air before a thunderstorm. He was communicating with the skull, she was certain of it. Did it call to the Emperor as it had called to her?

The cold of the walls was seeping into her flesh through the thin fabric of her robe. She breathed deeply, willing her body to relax. The slightest of movements could catch the Emperor's attention and give away her presence. She concentrated on the scene in the room. The old man seemed troubled, and she had the clear impression that he was asking the skull for guidance. But her focus could not stop the cold biting her skin. How long could she hold on before her teeth started chattering?

* * * * *

It was a long time later that the Emperor rose, bowed low a final time and left. Chilled to the bone, her limbs stiff with cold, Madeleine numbly fumbled her way out from behind the drapes. She must not linger here. It was too dangerous. Nonetheless, she could not stop herself kneeling one final time in front of the ebony table. Sharp curiosity, combined with a powerful desire to reach out to the skull once more, was too great to resist.

'You will return, little one. Many times.' Whispers in her mind. 'But you must leave now or you will be discovered. Go.'

This time Madeleine heeded the warning. She slipped back into the corridor and hurried back to her bedchamber. Although the sky was lightening in the pre-dawn, the palace, strangely, was still deserted. Normally at this time the slaves and servants were hard at work preparing for the day. This morning there was not a soul to be seen. Could the skull have had a hand in this?

'Oh, don't be ridiculous.' She scolded her fanciful imagination, wondering where the notion had come from. 'How could it?' Her rational mind was already questioning whether the past hours had been anything more than a flight of fantasy, a very down to earth experience made supernatural in a reaction to an emotion-charged dream. Except that it hadn't, had it? She could not deny what she had seen and felt. She must not.

Reaching the sanctuary of her room without incident, she closed the door softly and leaned against it. All was quiet. Li-Mai still slumbered peacefully, unaware of her mistress's lengthy absence. Madeleine ignored her bed. She would never be able to sleep after everything she had experienced in that small sumptuous room. Instead, she pulled a soft woollen wrap around her shoulders and leaned against the window mullion, filled with confusion. What was the skull? Where had it come from? Why had it called to her? And how? And had it really, as she had imagined, protected her as she wandered through the palace? Outside, dawn was breaking and the world awoke, the monochrome colours of night changing into the vivid palette of a sunlit day. The beauty of the moment was lost on Madeleine, wrapped up in her thoughts. She only stirred at Li-Mai's gentle query.

'Mistress, is everything well?'

Madeleine smiled her reassurance. This was her secret. She would speak of it to no-one, not even to Li-Mai who she trusted implicitly. Not yet. Not until she had found out more. Not until she had found out why.

46.

Over the next two weeks Madeleine returned to the little circular room every night, drawn by a force she couldn't explain or resist. Each time she was terrified that she would be caught and punished. Each time that fear was not enough to stop her going. Against all the odds she was never seen, and Li-Mai never woke, sleeping as deeply as if she had been drugged. Madeleine was bewildered. Usually the palace was buzzing with servants, guards and courtiers, yet in all her nocturnal wanderings she never met anyone. The suspicion that the skull was protecting her, born on their first encounter, would not go away. Why it would do so, Madeleine could not begin to guess.

There was something else, an unexpected and welcome shift in her situation. Ju-Lin had left the palace. She had learned from Li-Mai that a rebellion was building in the northern territories, the unrest arising apparently out of nowhere in a normally compliant population, and the Emperor had sent Ju-Lin to deal with the situation. It was likely he would be gone for some considerable time. Was it mere coincidence, Madeleine wondered. She couldn't let it go of the idea that this too might be the skull's handiwork.

She told herself that the reason didn't matter. All that was really important was that Ju-Lin and his threats had receded so that she could breathe more easily, at least for a while. Still the questions remained. Did the skull, that small object carved from inanimate stone, really exert some influence over what was happening in the palace? It seemed impossible, despite her experiences. And yet, hadn't the skull called to her and guided her through the maze of corridors? Madeleine fought to reject her suspicions, because to accept them would tear the foundations out from beneath everything she had ever been taught was true. It was a battle she was losing. The evidence was too great.

She could not deny that a tangible force emanated from the skull. It had hit her like an electric shock on that first occasion, and with each subsequent visit she was becoming increasingly sensitive to it. She felt it now as soon as she entered the room, shimmering on her skin and seeping into her flesh. It soothed her, gently healing the wounds of Paul's death. She never spoke to the skull. She simply sat on the floor in front of it, held by the plump, soft cushions, and allowed the peace and comfort that radiated from it to soak into her every cell of her body. Her soul, even. She rested peacefully, cocooned in a warm embrace of security and reassurance, just as she had on that first visit.

Every time Madeleine entered the skull's chamber, she was risking her life. On several occasions she had heard the Emperor's slow footsteps shuffling towards her down the corridor, sending her scurrying to hide behind the wall-hangings before he entered. Each time he came, she saw through the slit in the drapes that he carried a sad hollowness in his eyes and a deep frown that wrinkled his parchment brow.

* * * * *

The skull never set Madeleine free. It filled her thoughts during the day and silently called for her each night. She tried to shut it out and to concentrate on other things, always without success. Persistently, gently, it came back,

235

never threatening or forceful, simply a constant, steady presence that she could not ignore.

At some point over the course of those days and nights a realisation was born in Madeleine, slowly growing stronger and clearer until it settled into a certainty. In some way that was not yet evident, her destiny was irrevocably tied to that of this strange object. All she could do was wait to see what unfolded. In the meantime she would question Li-Mai about the skull in such a way that she would not betray her actions.

She asked one evening while Li-Mai was brushing her hair, as she did every night before Madeleine went to bed.

'Li-Mai, I have heard whispers of a great treasure hidden somewhere in this palace.' Madeleine kept her tone lightly curious, as if discussing a fairy tale. 'A treasure that only the Emperor has the right to look on. Have you heard these stories?'

Li-Mai froze mid-stroke, as if turned to stone. Her face was set into a wide-eyed mask of fear. 'You must not speak of it. It is forbidden.'

'Aha. So there *is* a treasure.'

'I cannot tell you. I will not. And you must say no more.'

'Why not? Please, Li-Mai. There is no-one else here. No-one will know.'

'If you are heard to speak of the treasure, you will forfeit your life. As will I.' The maid was clearly terrified.

Madeleine coaxed gently. She had to know. 'Please, Li-Mai. I love stories of secrets and treasures. Tell me what you know and I'll never mention it again. I promise.'

Li-Mai hesitated. 'You promise? If I tell you, you will never speak of it again? To anyone?'

'I promise.'

236

'I know only very little.' Li-Mai's faltering whisper showed her terror. 'No-one knows, except perhaps the Emperor himself. They are only stories. Legends of a great treasure that is as ancient as this world but not of it. It is said to have come to Earth from the heavens borne on a chariot of rainbow light and is the most powerful object to have ever existed. Whoever possesses it wields the power of the gods, and all will kneel before him. It was given to our Emperor's ancestor as the rightful king of the world, way back at the birth of time.'

'Do you know what it is, what it looks like?'

Li-Mai shook her head. 'The Emperor is the only man alive to have seen it. But it must be unusual, for it is said that only the wisest of men will recognise its true value because it resembles no other treasure ever known. There. I have told you all that I know. I will speak of it no more.'

She leaned forward and covered Madeleine's hand with her own, pressing it anxiously. 'Please, now that I have told you, you will keep your promise? You will not speak of it to anyone?'

'Yes, Li-Mai. I will keep my promise, no matter what happens. I will not mention it again. Don't worry. And thank you.'

Clearly still troubled, the servant girl rose and walked away to curl up on her bed. Madeleine stayed where she was for a very long time, thinking. Was it possible that the jade skull in the candlelit room was this magnificent secret treasure? Surely it had to be. Why else would the Emperor keep it hidden in the forbidden quarters and treat it with such reverence? The harder question, and the one she was refusing to face, was why it had chosen to speak to her. Madeleine couldn't even begin to guess. She only knew one thing – she couldn't keep away from it.

47.

Flickering candlelight filtered through Madeleine's closed eyelids in ever-changing patterns of colour. She was drifting in a state of semi-sleep, her thoughts floating back, as they so often did, to Paul and to the love they had shared. As always when she visited the skull, she enveloped in a cloak of serenity, a peace of mind and heart that she could not hold onto outside the confines of this room. Here, now, unlike in any other time or place, the cruel sword of inconsolable grief and heartache was absent. A soft smile of happy remembering played around her lips.

Footsteps, purposeful and angry, broke through into her dreams, jolting her unceremoniously back to the present. She scrambled to her feet and hurried to conceal herself behind the drapes as she had so many times before, her heart in her mouth. This was most definitely not the slow, weary footfall of the old king. So who was coming? The footsteps entered the room and stopped abruptly. She held her breath and pressed back even further into the cold rock of the wall.

'So this is where he hides you.' Ju-Lin! Madeleine barely stifled a cry of horror. What was he doing here? Why wasn't he in the northern territories as the Emperor had commanded? Her skin crawled at the memory of his barely concealed derision and threats.

Ju-Lin was still speaking. 'He will not have you for much longer, I guarantee it. My father is weak. He has grown soft with age. He seeks the love of his people rather than their fear and submission. Love!' He spat out the word in contempt and disgust. 'Only a weakling seeks love. And love in its turn makes a man weak. He puts in peril our throne and our empire in his quest for justice and goodness. Our enemies laugh at us even as they prepare to attack us.'

Madeleine could hear him pacing up and down in his fury. She was trembling from head to foot. This time she did not dare to put her eye to the crack between the drapes.

'You see,' Ju-Lin's voice was like flint, 'I will not permit it. I will not stand by and let my father throw away my birthright. Soon, very soon, Khalia, there will be a new Emperor. I will take his place on the throne. Then you will advise and guide me. Then you will help me to conquer every one of my enemies and take their gold and kingdoms for my own. Soon, Khalia, your power will be mine.' This was the first time Madeleine had heard the skull called by name.

At last she found the courage to risk a glance. The prince was standing ramrod straight in the centre of the room, his gaze fixed on the skull. The crawling sensation in her skin grew stronger. In profile, his cruelly handsome features, distorted by hate, could have been those of one of the carved stone demons that jutted from the palace ramparts. He glared at the skull for only a moment before he turned and strode from the chamber, wearing his hatred and fury like a cloak around his shoulders.

Pale and trembling, Madeleine pushed her way out from behind the curtains. Ju-Lin had just declared that he was going to seize the throne from his father. She had grown to know the old Emperor well – he would not give up his kingdom without a fight. The only way Ju-Lin would take it would be over his father's dead body. Literally. Shaking uncontrollably she stumbled back to her room, threw herself onto her bed and curled up into a ball under the covers. Would Ju-Lin really carry out his threat? Of course he would. He was ambitious, ruthless, and hungry for power. He had been deadly serious. She had to do something. The Emperor's life was in danger and she knew it. But what should she do? What *could* she do? If she warned the Emperor, she would be admitting that she had been in the skull room, and she would have signed her own death warrant. In any case, fond as he was of her, it was unlikely he would believe her. Although there was little love lost between father and son, the whole court also knew of the friction between herself and Ju-Lin. The Emperor would not take her word over the prince's. She would forfeit her life for nothing. There had to be another way.

At last she fell asleep, disturbed again and again by dreams of green leering skulls, treachery and murder, and of herself running and running, never able to escape her pursuers. When the early morning light woke her she lay exhausted, a fierce headache pounding at her temples. Within moments a familiar soothing warmth washed over her – the same warmth she experienced in the skull's chamber, buried deep in the bedrock below the palace so far from this room. The voice that had called to her that first night had returned, sounding softly within her head.

'You must leave here, my child. It is not safe for you to stay. Ju-Lin will succeed in his tyranny and when he does you will not be spared. On this occasion I can do nothing to prevent it. It must be.

'When you go, you must take me with you. I cannot fall into his hands. Do not delay. There is no time left. Ju-Lin's treachery is imminent.'

'The Emperor. I have to warn him…'

'No, Madeleine. It has to be this way. You wish to save him after his kindness to you. That is understandable. But you cannot. His destiny is set and nothing can change it. Yours is not. If you do not wish to suffer at Ju-Lin's hands, you must go.'

'How? I cannot leave the palace. The guards…'

'I will take care of that. Make the necessary preparations and come for me when I call.'

'How will I know…' It was too late. The voice had gone, leaving Madeleine more frightened and confused than ever. A moment later an even more gut-wrenching fear engulfed her – the fear of what her fate would be if these events did indeed come to pass, events that now seemed inevitable. She leapt out of bed and called for Li-Mai.

'I must leave. Ju-Lin.' She did not elaborate. There was no need. The threat of Ju-Lin's cruel lust was enough to galvanise both women into action.

'I will get you food,' Li-Mai promised. 'I will ask my friend who works in the kitchen.' She winked. 'He has an eye for me. He will not refuse.' She grew serious. 'I knew this day would come. I believed you safe while the Emperor was here. I was wrong. Ju-Lin grows bolder and less caring of his father's decrees by the day.'

Madeleine took the other woman's delicate hands in her own. 'Come with me, Li-Mai?' she asked earnestly.

The younger woman shook her head firmly. 'No. My place is here. I cannot come.'

'Ju-Lin will know that you have helped me. You will be punished cruelly. I can't let that happen.'

The maid would not change her mind. 'I cannot. Do not worry about me. I will be safe. I will find a way. Mistress, this is my home. I have no other and, whatever may befall this kingdom, I wish no other. But it is not yours. You must leave here before it is too late. Tonight, when the palace sleeps. Please the gods that you return safely to your family.'

She pressed a small carved ivory charm into Madeleine's palm. 'To keep you safe.'

Madeleine hugged her maid tightly, tears flowing. In the short time they had known each other, she had come to love Li-Mai dearly. 'You really won't come with me?'

Li-Mai looked fondly at the flame-haired woman who stood a head taller than she did, her own eyes wet with tears. 'That is not my destiny, mistress.'

'Sister, Li-Mai. Not mistress.'

'Sister,' she whispered. 'My love will go with you.'

48.

He came as dusk was falling, flinging open the heavy studded door to Madeleine's chamber with a crash that resounded through the stone. Madeleine leapt to her feet, overturning her chair, as Ju-Lin strode into the room. Though the look on his face terrified her, she would not let him see her fear.

Ignoring Madeleine for the moment, he turned to Li-Mai. 'Get out!' he hissed.

Bravely the young woman stood her ground. Afraid now for Li-Mai as well as herself, knowing that if her maid didn't obey Ju-Lin was likely to strike her dead without a second thought, Madeleine dismissed her with a faint nod. Reluctantly the maid slipped out of the room, fearing what might be in store for her beloved Madeleine, her sharp mind already busy looking for a way to save her from Ju-Lin's vicious hands.

Madeleine clenched her fists so tightly that her nails dug painfully into her palms. It was the only way she could hide their shaking. She squared her shoulders and confronted Ju-Lin angrily.

'How dare you burst into my chamber uninvited and unannounced?' she demanded icily.

'Your chamber but my palace, Englishwoman. My rules.' His words spat out with venom, filled with his hatred of her. She knew he could not bear her fiery spirit and bold manner, so unlike the meek, cowed women of the palace, and that he considered her shameless and despicable. And probably a spy into the bargain. At that moment, it wasn't his hatred which frightened her the most, however, it was the way he was looking at her, filled with white hot hunger – a rabid predator ready to tear its victim to shreds. She could no longer hide it.

He saw her fear and grinned, chilling Madeleine to the marrow. 'You act like a harlot with your bold gaze and your impertinence. Well, my precious white-skinned pearl, if you act like a harlot, you will be treated like one. By the time I have finished with you, you will never dare look a man in the eyes ever again.'

Ju-Lin had made his intentions crystal clear. Still, she would not cower or beg before this tyrant. 'Your father will not permit…' she began.

'My father is busy with matters of state. This is none of his business. You may have bewitched him with your guile. You cannot fool me.'

He had moved very close to Madeleine, pinning her against a stone pillar. His face, clammy-skinned, was right up against hers and she could smell the sweet odour of his breath. Some herb he smoked, Li-Mai had told her. He believed it gave him strength. From what Madeleine had seen, its main effect was to make him even more arrogant and cruel than usual and to take away any remaining shred of reason. She had seen him like this several times; fortunately for her, on those occasions it had been from a safe distance.

She gasped in pain. Quick as a flash, Ju-Lin had twisted one hand in her hair, wrenching her head back viciously. In the same moment his other hand ripped at her robe, exposing the creamy mounds of her breasts. Her hand flew up and slapped him, hard. He let go in surprise, not expecting her to fight back. Taking advantage of his surprise, she darted around the pillar and took refuge behind a stout table, grabbing a paperknife, the only weapon to hand. She had no doubt that this was a battle she could never win, but she would not go down without a fight.

Her actions had only enraged him further. He was faster than she had anticipated, much faster. Before she could react, he was once more upon her, slapping her so hard in return that her jaws and teeth rattled. Dazed, it took Madeleine a couple of seconds to recover her senses by which time he had twisted her arms excruciatingly up behind her back, holding them with one iron-strong hand. The other pressed the knife to her throat, pricking the skin so that she felt a thin trickle of blood, warm on her neck. Tears of pain filled her eyes. Through them she glared her defiance. A thin stream of saliva was dribbling down his chin and she felt him grow hard, pressing into her thigh. Her resistance was fuelling his excitement.

'Fight all you like, harlot,' he hissed. 'It makes the conquest all the more enjoyable.'

His cruel features disgusted her. Held tight in his grip, she was unable to turn her head away from that arrogant, mocking gaze. Drawing her head back as far as she could, Madeleine spat full in his face. Ju-Lin laughed, a harsh, chilling sound that matched the cruel amusement in his eyes. He didn't bother to wipe away the spittle from his cheek. Without saying a word, he threw her onto the floor and straddled her, pinning her wrists in a vice-like grip above her head and ripping what robe remained from her body so that she lay completely naked beneath him.

Oh God, no. This couldn't be happening. But it was, and there was nothing she could do to stop it. Despite his small stature, Ju-Lin was as strong as an ox. Her struggles were useless against his determination. What was worse, at each attempt to break free, she felt him grow against her belly. He wanted her to fight. It excited him.

'You see, harlot,' he whispered into her ear, 'I have total self-control. I can make this last as long as I wish. And I wish it to last a very, very long time.' He smiled down at her. 'I'm going to enjoy this.'

Madeleine screamed in pain. He had bitten hard into the soft tissue of her left breast. He raised his head and laughed again, a sound that chilled her bones.

'That's it, harlot. Scream. Scream loud and hard. You'll scream a lot tonight.' Again his teeth sunk into her flesh. Through her pain Madeleine felt his desire grow harder still. She nearly vomited, sickened by his blatant arousal in her suffering. Dear God, no. How long would she have to endure this torture? What other torments would he inflict before he was done? Satisfaction flared in Ju-Lin's eyes. His victim had recognised the inevitability of what was to follow.

'Highness.' The words reached her from a distant place. A place far beyond her fear and despair and pain.

'How dare you?' The weight on her body eased. Ju-Lin had leapt to his feet, whirling to face the intruder, his sword ready to strike, his rage at the interruption as hot as his hunger for this foreign whore. He would strike down the man where he stood. Steel sounded on steel as his blow was expertly parried. A moment later, recognising his opponent, he lowered his blade, though his anger had not diminished. Xiang-Chen, captain of the palace's elite guard, bowed low. If the captain had felt it necessary to interrupt the prince's fun it would be for a good reason.

'My apologies for interrupting, Highness. Your father demands your immediate presence. He sent me to fetch you, and commanded that I was not to return without you.'

'I am busy. Can you not see?'

'I'm sorry, your Highness, it is the Emperor's direct order.' Xiang-Chen kept his eyes averted from Madeleine's naked body sprawled on the floor. She grabbed her robe and covered herself the best she could in its tatters.

Ju-Lin nodded his acquiescence. If the Emperor had sent for him, he would not disobey. It would serve him better to pretend compliance. For now. The prince turned back to the white and shaking Madeleine. Kneeling at her side, he stroked her cheek in an obscenely gentle and affectionate gesture.

'Don't worry, harlot, I won't forget about you. You aren't going anywhere. You can't leave the palace, so there is no hurry. I will come back later to finish this.' With a bound, he was on his feet and disappearing down the corridor.

Moments later a pale and anxious Li-Mai hurried into the room and across to where Madeleine was sitting up shakily, livid bruises already showing on her injured flesh. Fortunately, Ju-Lin's teeth had barely broken the skin.

'Was I in time?' Li-Mai's voice trembled. Madeleine looked at her uncomprehending.

'Was I in time?' Li-Mai repeated, studying Madeleine's ashen face closely. 'He didn't...?' She let out a deep breath, relieved at what she saw there.

'N-no,' Madeleine stammered. 'He...he was summoned by the Emperor before...' She stopped, confused. 'What do you mean, were you in time? Was this of your doing?'

'I ran to the Emperor's second wife, Pai-qi. She is his favourite, and she hates Ju-Lin with a passion. Her sister was one of the concubines who died at his hand. When I told her what was happening she went straight to the

Emperor. He couldn't just burst in and stop Ju-Lin because it would have caused the prince to lose face, but he did come up with a very good reason to summon him away. The Emperor is very fond of you, I think,' she added shyly.

'Then you did save me and I can never repay you for that.' Madeleine's face darkened with worry. 'For how long, though? Ju-Lin has made it clear he hasn't finished with me. He'll be back as soon as the Emperor has spoken with him. It looks like it has only delayed the inevitable.'

For a brief moment she buried her face in her hands, despairing, before her fight returned. 'But it is a reprieve.' She hugged her friend. 'Thank you, Li-Mai.'

'You will have long enough, I think. The Emperor is no fool. He knows that his son will not be easily distracted from his goal so he has ordered him to return to the Northern provinces immediately on the grounds that the revolt is still a threat to the kingdom.'

Madeleine looked at the young Chinese woman in admiration. 'Li-Mai, you are amazing. I owe you my life, and for that I will never be able to repay you.'

'I need no payment other than your safety, my sister. I listen. I keep my head down. I learn. But enough talk of that. You must leave here. Tonight, after Ju-Lin and his troops have ridden out.'

'You must come too.'

Li-Mai shook her head sadly. 'No. I have told you this already. I will miss you very much, dearest Madeleine, but I will not come with you. This is my home.'

'Then you must find a very good reason to be elsewhere. There must be no way that you can be implicated in my disappearance or blamed for it in any way.'

49.

'It is time, Madeleine. Come.'

Khalia. Surely it couldn't be mere coincidence that the skull called to her now, in the hour she was preparing to run for her life? Of course it wasn't. In some inexplicable way, the skull was aware of everything that went on in the palace and – Madeleine suspected – influenced much of it, though she had no time to dwell on that thought for, in spite his father's orders, Ju-Lin could return at any moment to finish what he had started. She had to go.

She paused at the doorway of her bed chamber and peered into the hallway. At this late hour the palace was sleeping, its halls and staterooms empty. A heavy blanket of silence draped over the stone corridors; even the agonised cries of the tortured prisoners in the dungeons had stilled tonight. Madeleine prayed that the skull was working its magic once more, helping her to pass unnoticed through the maze of rooms and corridors. Nevertheless, she would have to remain on her guard. The slightest of sounds would echo, amplified over and over, through the stone, alerting the sentries to her presence. If they caught her in the forbidden zone Ju-Lin would take the greatest delight in meting out her punishment himself. In his hands it would be neither quick nor merciful.

She shuddered violently, her courage momentarily failing. The hideous screams of those who had displeased the Prince echoed throughout the entire vast palace complex day and night, a potent reminder of the wisdom of obedience. If she was caught with the skull… Madeleine pushed the grim picture from her mind. She had no choice but to run. Ju-Lin had clearly and mercilessly shown her his intentions if she stayed.

Madeleine longed for the riding breeches she had worn constantly on her adventures with Paul, but they had been burned long ago, too torn and filthy to be saved. Instead she had dressed in a thick travelling skirt and blouse, all that remained of her own clothing, and she wore the gold locket Paul had given her on their wedding day around her neck. His pocket watch was tucked safely in her chemise.

She looked around the room for the final time, then bent to pick up the two bundles that lay on the floor at her feet. They were small, far too small for the journey she faced, but they had to be enough. She couldn't carry more. Stuffed into the larger of the bags were her warm travelling cape, Paul's hunting knife and ivory handled pistol, his greatcoat, food and water. Li-Mai had worked miracles in the last few hours, bringing enough supplies to keep Madeleine going for a week or more. In the second bag, along with more food, she had stuffed her boots. Too heavy and noisy to wear moving through the palace, she would have need of them later.

She thought of Li-Mai with a heavy heart, afraid for the young servant girl. Despite Madeleine's continuing attempts to persuade her otherwise, Li-Mai was adamant that she would not leave the palace. Hoisting the bags onto her shoulder, Madeleine sent up a prayer that she would be safe.

She was ready. Or, to be more truthful, she was as ready as she was ever going to be. It was time to go.

50.

Flitting like a phantom through the dark halls and corridors. Madeleine's soft felt slippers made no sound on the cool, grey flagstones. She headed first for the small side room where she had found an empty chest that would conceal her belongings until she had fetched the skull. Pale moonlight filtered intermittently through the latticework shutters, just enough to find her way. Holding her breath she lifted the lid, praying it wouldn't creak and give her away. It was on her side. Not a squeak betrayed her.

The late summer air was hot and sultry. Even so, Madeleine found herself shivering uncontrollably as she entered the passageway that led to Khalia's room. These corridors were heavy with menace tonight, soaked through with the unnerving stillness that precedes a violent storm. She recalled the skull's words: *Ju-Lin will succeed in his tyranny. The day of his treachery is imminent.* Was this then the tempest brewing? She quickened her pace as much as she dared, pausing at every corner to check that her path was clear. She saw no-one – no guards and no servants. Only the ghosts walked these flagstones tonight.

* * * * *

Madeleine came to an abrupt halt. Flickering lamplight was spilling through the part-open doorway to the skull's room, only thirty paces from where she stood. Voices, burning with anger and challenge, echoed through the passageway. Although she could not make out the words, it was clear that a furious and bitter argument was taking place between the Emperor and – her blood ran cold – Ju-Lin. Under her breath, Madeleine swore so colourfully that

Paul would have been proud of her. She had, perhaps rashly, assumed that no-one would be here. After all, hadn't Khalia called her? Had she been led into a trap?

'No, Madeleine.' Reassurance enveloped her. 'All is well. But they must not find you. Hide yourself. Quickly.'

A shadow fell across the pool of lamplight. They were leaving. They would run straight into her. In their present rage, either would likely strike her dead on the spot. Desperately, Madeleine looked around for somewhere to hide. There. Only a few paces away a large statue of a water-bearer stood proud of a shallow alcove. It was poor cover but it was all she had. Hastily she squeezed herself into the tiny gap between the statue and the wall, huddling as low as she could.

The voices grew louder, still raging, the quarrel unabated. The two men had come out into the passageway. Madeleine held her breath. Each step brought them closer to her until she could see them clearly in the torchlight, and hear every word. Surely they had to notice her cowering in the shadows? They were too engrossed in their conflict however, completely oblivious to anything else.

'How dare you enter the sacred room without my permission?' The Emperor could not contain his fury.

'It is my birthright. I have the right to come here whenever I choose.' Ju-Lin oozed arrogance and contempt.

'Only the Emperor has that right, and I would remind you that you are not Emperor yet. Until that day comes – if it comes – you will not enter this room again, Ju-Lin. Do you understand me?'

'Do not underestimate me, beloved father. That day may come sooner than you believe. The warlords tire of your soft ways, as do I.' Menace darkened the prince's words.

'You will not threaten me, Ju-Lin.' The Emperor was cold and controlled. 'Though you are my son, I will not hesitate to execute you for treason if you give me cause. I am Emperor. My word is law. You would do well to remember that.'

Sadness now replaced anger. 'I prayed that you would leave this arrogance and cruelty behind as you grew in wisdom. I was wrong. You will never be the worthy and merciful ruler that I hoped, in spite of all the evidence, you would become. Tonight everything has become clear. My decision is made. I revoke your right to inherit the throne, Ju-Lin. You will never become Emperor.'

'You can't do that! It is my birthright.'

'I can and I have. You have had every opportunity to prove yourself a worthy heir. You have taken none. I will not change my mind.'

'We shall see, father. We shall see.' White with rage, his footsteps ringing harshly on the flagstones, Ju-Lin stalked away.

Only a few paces from Madeleine, the old Emperor finally let his emotions show. For a brief moment he crumpled and it appeared that he might collapse from the strain. But the man who had ruled a million people for over sixty years was made of sterner stuff; with a deep, resonant sigh he straightened, lifting his head and squaring his shoulders. He was the Emperor. He would not let weakness rob him of his power.

Madeleine felt a wave of affection for the old man. Even when weighed down with affairs of state, he had always treated her with a respect and kindness that few others in his court afforded her. She had often noticed how the character and actions of his eldest son troubled him, filling him with anxiety for the future of his people after his death. Until tonight, however, she had not understood the gravity of those concerns.

Ju-Lin would not sit idly by and let the throne slip through his fingers. She felt a sudden rush of fear for the old man and she had to quash the desire to rush from her hiding place and warn him. The Emperor was intelligent and wise. He would already have considered the dangers of his actions. Moreover, Khalia had warned her that she must not. So Madeleine held her breath and pressed further back against the wall as he passed by, so close that she could have reached out a hand and touched him. Then he was gone, disappearing into the shadows.

* * * * *

Madeleine waited for a long time before moving from her hiding place, afraid that one or the other would return. When she was as certain as she could be that they would not, she wriggled out and darted into the room. Khalia was lying on her velvet cushion, illuminated by the flickering light of the candles that surrounded it. Hurriedly, Madeleine picked up the skull, surprised by its weight, and carefully placed it in the heavy brocade bag she had brought for the purpose. Then she moved to the door, checked that the way was clear, and slipped back out into the passageway. Her feet flying, she raced back through the labyrinth of passages and hallways towards the ante-room.

She was almost there when she spotted a dark heap lying on the floor up ahead, barely visible in the gloom of the corridor. She skidded to a halt. What was it? The heap groaned faintly and rolled onto its back, causing a jewel to flash for a moment in a shaft of moonlight. Madeleine skidded to a halt. The royal seal. It was the Emperor. He groaned again. Ignoring the danger she was putting herself in, she ran to him.

A dark wet stain was spreading across the Emperor's silken tunic, soaking it and pooling down onto the floor. He grasped at his belly, pain etched in his face, from which the colour drained as rapidly as the blood drained from his body.

'Madeleine?' The old man's eyes opened wide in surprise. He groaned in the agony of his butchered belly, and a trickle of dark liquid seeped from his lips and trickled down his jaw.

'Who did this?' Knowing the answer even as she asked the question, her tears falling.

'Ju-Lin.' The pain in the Emperor's face came as much from the betrayal of his own kin as from his injuries. He fought to stay conscious. 'My son. My murderer.' A single teardrop fell from the corner of his eye and his head slumped. He had drawn his last breath.

Ju-Lin had taken control! Panic rose up in Madeleine, threatening to overwhelm her. She had to leave. Now. With the Emperor dead… And she was carrying the jade skull…

51.

Silent in her slippers, Madeleine raced to the chest and dragged out her packs, pushing the brocade bag that held Khalia to the bottom of the smaller one. A narrow and rarely used door led from this side room to the working area of the palace complex where the laundry, livestock and other services were situated. It was the best chance she had of leaving unseen. She had discovered it not long after she had arrived here. When Paul was still alive, she thought sadly. She shook herself fiercely and hoisted both bundles onto her back. There was no time for memories now. They could come later, when she was a very long way from here.

She still had one last obstacle to overcome before she would be free of the palace – the building and its grounds were surrounded on every side by a massive stone wall, easily as tall as three men and wide enough for a sentries' walkway to have been built on the top. The only way in or out was through the one heavily guarded gate that lay directly in line with the main palace entrance on the other side of a wide, empty courtyard. Everyone and everything that entered or left the palace complex had to go through that gate.

It was a huge problem and one for which she had no solution. Firstly, she had to reach the gate unseen, then she had to pass through it, right under the noses of the elite troops who guarded it. This time, for the first time, she had no choice but to place all her trust in Khalia.

The skull didn't let her down. A bank of clouds had drawn in from the north, hiding the moon and plunging the square into darkness. Nothing could be seen beyond the pools of light cast by the torches that burned at the gate throughout the hours of darkness. Madeleine studied the gatehouse apprehensively, still with no idea of how she would get through, knowing only that she must. She was virtually invisible as she darted across the open expanse and huddled into the cover of the wall. Nothing moved. There was no warning shout. She crept closer, keeping out of the bright circles of flaming torchlight, her feet in the felt slippers making no sound.

It was unnaturally quiet. Not a cough or a grunt broke the night's silence. She peered more closely. The gatehouse was deserted; not one sentry was at his post. That was impossible. The gate was always guarded day and night. If she had held on to any lingering doubts over Khalia's ability to influence events, the abandoned sentry post finally laid them to rest, and she wondered how far that influence might stretch. Her spirits lifted and the challenge that lay ahead for the first time appeared just a little less daunting. Maybe she would come through this alive after all.

'Thank you, Khalia,' she breathed.

There was no time to dwell on her good fortune. She had to be long gone by the time the guards returned. Hugging the stonework, she crept through the gate, still half expecting to hear a harsh challenge or feel a rough hand seize her shoulder. There was nothing. In less than a minute she was outside the palace walls for the first time in so many long months.

The moon broke briefly through the clouds, illuminating for only a few short seconds before vanishing again the ramshackle huts and dirt streets of the town that were separated from the palace walls by a stretch of rough open ground. Hidden by the darkness, Madeleine picked up her skirts and raced across this no-mans-land to the nearest building, a rough hut, where she crouched low against its flimsy wall breathing hard, from fear more than exertion. She may be out of the palace but she was still in mortal danger.

Suddenly all hell broke loose in the palace. Earsplitting shouts and shrieks were soon followed by loud wailing. The murdered Emperor must have been found. Half dazed with sleep, the townspeople came out of their homes to see what the uproar was all about and milled around as confused and bewildered as lost sheep, all eyes on the royal residence where every window now blazed with light. Through the gateway that she had passed through only a couple of minutes earlier, torches flared and soldiers leapt into action, preparing to hunt down the assassin.

Madeleine drew back into the shadows. With what seemed like the whole town awake she could no longer simply walk out through the empty streets as she had intended. Her flaming hair, pale skin and tall stature would stand out like a beacon amongst the slight, dark-haired, olive skinned population. Madeleine pulled out her cloak. If she wrapped it tightly around her body and drew it up over her head as far as it would go, it would just about hide both her clothes and her hair, and its dark brown colouring would blend into the night. It was a poor disguise but it was all she had. She fought down an overwhelming urge to run. She mustn't do anything that would draw attention.

She peered around the corner of the hut. No-one was looking in her direction. They were all transfixed by the frantic activity taking place within the palace walls. She hunched down into a slouching walk to conceal her height

– just in case someone did glance her way – and crept unnoticed from her hiding place. Moving from the cover of one house to another with a slow, unhurried step that demanded all of her willpower, she wove her way through the clutter of huts until she was free of the town and out in the open countryside.

* * * * *

Then she did run, flying across the ground as if her heels had wings. The thin felt slippers she still wore offered her feet no protection against the hard stones that littered her path and their hard edges cut cruelly through the thin soles. Time and time again she stumbled and tripped but she dared not stop. Not yet. Not until she had put a much greater distance between herself and the palace, and the now even greater dangers that awaited her there.

Madeleine ran until she could run no more. She had crossed the wide valley floor and was clambering the smooth easy slopes of the low hills on the far side when her legs and her lungs gave out and she sank to the ground, her chest heaving. She wanted to keep going. She had to keep going. There was no way of knowing how long it would be before Ju-Lin discovered that the skull – and she – was missing. But she couldn't, she was spent. She was also deeply frustrated and angry at herself for not having the stamina to continue. Once, not so long ago, she had been strong and fit, able to ride at full gallop for hours without fading. Now she was already exhausted. She had grown soft during her months of inactivity in the palace, her muscles unused and weak. This journey was going to be much harder than she had anticipated, and she had been anticipating it as virtually suicidal as it was, even with Khalia at her side. Well, she thought wryly, if she could stay ahead of Ju-Lin and his thugs, and if she could avoid starvation, or being eaten by the wolves and bears that roamed these barren lands, or freezing to death in the high mountains, that strength and stamina would return. It was a big 'If'.

For a few fleeting seconds, despair swamped her. It was madness to think that she could survive this. Had she been wrong to even try? In front of her, far in the distance, soaring mountain summits were giant looming shadows in the night sky. Her heart sank a little further. What else could she have done though? With a grim determination she pushed away her doubts. This had been the only possible course of action. She would go on, for as long as she could walk. Far better to die a free woman in these hills than to fall into the prince's merciless hands. First though, she would have to rest. Just for a few minutes.

While she waited for the heaviness to leave her legs and their strength to return, she stared out across the valley plain. In the town, a sea of lights flickered in the pre-dawn darkness and the muffled echoes of shouts and screams carried through the still night air to where she rested. Please God, keep Li-Mai safe, she prayed. There was nothing Madeleine could do now to help her. She had to keep moving, save herself. Ju-Lin's men could even now be crossing the valley, invisible against the night, drawing ever closer to where she rested.

She rummaged in her bag for her boots. Though they were old and well-worn from her travels with Paul, they were comfortable and sturdy and would last for many miles to come. Ignoring the pain from her bruised and cut feet, she pulled them on. As she stuffed the felt slippers back in their place, her hand brushed something hard and cool. It was Paul's pistol, with two bullets in the breech. If the worst happened and Ju-Lin found her, she would use the pistol and die by her own hand before he could capture her. Her fingers touched the gold locket she wore around her neck. The locket Paul had given her.

'Courage, Maddy.' She could hear his beloved voice as his dear face swam through her mind and then faded. 'Courage, my darling.'

52.

Madeleine studied the sky, taking her bearings. During her travels with Paul across the deserted plains of Russia he had taught her to navigate by the stars, just for fun. Little had either of them foreseen the day those lessons would be called on to save her life. Though the navigation would be extremely vague, because she really had no idea of where she was to begin with, it would guide her in approximately the right direction. Paul had been taken ill somewhere on the plains of Mongolia and they had headed roughly south from there. As his illness had grown worse she had been too busy caring for him to take any real note of where they were going, and after the Emperor's troops had found them and escorted them to the palace, any vestiges of her sense of direction had evaporated completely. Her plan was to head west, for that was where England lay.

She laughed out loud even as she thought it, though there was no humour in the sound. England! The idea that she would ever make it back was ludicrous, an impossible dream. No, Madeleine was certain she would never see her home again. This journey would cost her her life – maybe tomorrow, maybe not for a month or more, but at some point it would happen. It made no difference, there was no turning back. She had made her decision the moment she had lifted the skull from its cushion. Whatever lay ahead could never be as bad as the fate that waited for her behind the palace walls.

She got to her feet, her leg muscles protesting, and turned towards the west. More mountains loomed ominously in the distance, an intimidating barrier silhouetted against the lightening sky. Dawn was almost upon the world. Madeleine shrugged her packs more firmly onto her shoulders, picked up the brocade bag and set out on her long, lonely trek carrying with her the ever-present threat of Ju-Lin.

To her astonishment, there was no sign of any pursuit. Not that day, nor the next, nor the next. Why weren't his men scouring the area? Could he be dead? No. She was convinced that Ju-Lin remained very much alive. She must not allow herself to become complacent. He would come, she was certain. Even if, by some miracle, he decided she was not worth his trouble, he would never allow Khalia to be taken from him. Oh yes, he would come.

* * * * *

The weather remained kind, the unseasonable warm spell continuing. The days were hot and sunny, the nights mild enough that her cloak kept her warm. The early autumn harvest was plentiful and she feasted daily on a rich supply of fruits and berries that weighed down every branch, saving the limited reserves she carried – at least, those that would keep without spoiling – for the days when nature would not be so generous. This good weather would not last and soon the first icy blasts of a proper autumn would herald arrival of harsher days. For the moment, however, the fates were smiling on her.

Madeleine's feet did not fare so well. Unused to the non-stop trudging over unforgiving terrain, they suffered badly. She bandaged them with strips of fabric torn from her underskirt but it did little to help, and within only a few days she reached the point where she no longer removed her boots as she slept. It was simply too painful to pull them back on again in the morning. Still she carried on, stumbling constantly with the pain that accompanied every step, until it became impossible for her to do so. It was too much to bear. Madeleine sank down on the bank of a shallow river and pulled off her boots, which were soaked and dark with her blood. Her tortured feet were a mass of raw, bleeding, angry flesh. Tears of pain and frustration spilled down her face. Surely this wasn't to be the end? Not here, not like this. If Ju-Lin's soldiers came across her now they would seize her where she had fallen, helpless. Even if he didn't, how long could she survive in this wilderness, crippled like as she was? What was the use? Despair rose up, drawing her into its grasp.

'No!' The simple word, uttered aloud, bounced around the hillsides. She would not give up. She would find a way to go on.

Awkwardly she pushed herself onto all fours and shuffled forward to the river bank. One yard, two, until she knelt in the shallows. The cold took her breath away. The water was glacial, melt-water that ran down from the high mountain peaks that stayed snowbound all year round, and it snatched the breath from her lungs. She gritted her teeth and pushed herself upright to stand ankle deep in the current, sobbing in agony as the icy water swirled around her burning, raw, blistered feet like a white hot cloak, forcing herself to endure as it enveloped them in its healing embrace. It was only when the pain subsided into a numbness that dulled every sensation that she hobbled back to the bank and fell to the ground.

'Madeleine. Look for the star flower. Look for the yellow star flower with leaves like a sword. It will heal your wounds.' The words fell into her head, soft like fresh spring water. 'The yellow star flower, Madeleine. It is close at hand.'

Khalia was speaking to her. She shook her head to clear the fog that was creeping into every corner of her mind. Yellow star flower – what was that? Over there. Could that be it? A hundred paces or so downstream a mound of gold splashed the coarse dark green of the undergrowth. A hundred paces! The condition her feet were in, it would feel like a mile. Well, she would crawl if she had to. Khalia had given her a lifeline and she would not waste it.

Madeleine concentrated only on the yellow blooms that winked gaily at her in the sunlight. Putting one foot in front of the other, she moved step by gruelling, faltering step, each one feeling as if knife blades were piercing the soles of her feet and driving up into her legs. She forced her mind from the pain, refusing to consider failure. Closer and closer she tottered, until the moment that her strength gave out and she fell heavily to the stony soil. Only inches from her face, little gold daisies danced in the breeze. She had made it. She reached out her hand and clasped the rough wiry stem.

'Take the whole stem, Madeleine. All of it. Flowers, stalk and leaves. Pound them to a pulp, press the pulp onto your skin and bind it well in place. Then rest. Tomorrow, your feet will be healed.'

So Khalia knew of the healing properties of plants. All at once, Madeleine found it all just too absurd and bizarre. She began to giggle, and once she started she couldn't stop. She squawked until her belly ached and she could no longer breathe. Exhaustion, pain and fear had combined to drag her to the edge of hysteria.

'Madeleine. Madeleine. Madeleine…' The sound was soft, low and melodic, repeating her name over and over. Khalia was calling to her, dragging her back from the brink of the abyss. Gradually Madeleine's giggles subsided and her breathing slowed.

'The flowers, Madeleine. Remember the flowers.'

She grasped a large handful of the stems, placed them on a flat rock that she brushed clean of sand and earth, and started to pound them with a smaller stone. Soon the vivid yellow flowers and moss dark leaves had turned into a fibrous sludge that stank of damp cellars and stale cabbage. Madeleine wrinkled her nose with distaste. The sludge smelled revolting and looked just as bad. Was she really going to smear it onto the open wounds of her skin? What else could she do?

She ripped two more strips from the hem of her skirt. With only a brief hesitation, she scooped up the unpleasant gloop and smoothed it onto the damaged skin. In moments the rank paste had a miraculous effect, cooling and soothing the damaged skin, the pain easing rapidly. Hurriedly she treated the other foot and bound them both securely in the fabric strips.

'Now rest.' The whisper came, as soft as the breeze in the grass that surrounded her. The world grew hazy and within seconds, Madeleine was in a deep sleep.

53.

Madeleine drew the cloak tighter around her shoulders and opened her eyes. A wind had struck up overnight and its cold fingers were reaching through her cloak to pinch at her skin. That's what had woken her. She had slept as if drugged and this morning she was filled with renewed strength and determination. Next to her the star flowers gleamed golden in the grey light. Her feet! To her amazement the pain had gone. Cautiously she stood. Still she felt no pain. Discomfort lingered, yes, but nothing like the agony of before. After taking a few tentative steps, relief swept through her. She would be able to go on – not at full pace maybe but well enough.

She looked anxiously at the sky. Over the mountain peaks, heavy clouds held the menace of a rapidly approaching storm. She had to find shelter. Madeleine stuffed a good-sized clump of the star flowers into her bag and pulled on her boots, wincing a little as she did so. Walking would be uncomfortable, but she could do it. Grabbing a stale cake from her supplies for breakfast she set off as fast as she was able. Behind her, the land was still deserted. Every time she looked back, which she did a hundred or more times a day, she feared seeing Ju-Lin's men in pursuit. This morning, as every morning so far, not a soul was in sight. She couldn't believe that he had given up on her. He would hunt her down for no other reason than because she had defied him and fled. If he believed she was in possession of the skull, that hunt would be relentless.

The storm rumbled its threat ever closer. The sky was as dark as dusk now, the wind gusting so strongly that at times it almost knocked Madeleine off her feet. Where on these barren grass and rock covered hillsides would she find the shelter she so desperately needed? There were no trees, no overhanging cliffs, no caves of any kind. She trudged on, and the rain came, at first in sparse drops that hit the dry soil like mini explosions, falling more heavily with every minute that passed. Madeleine pulled on Paul's greatcoat. It wouldn't keep her dry for long. If she didn't find a refuge soon she would be soaked to the skin and dangerously cold in minutes.

What was that up ahead, just off to her right? Madeleine peered through the gloom. It appeared to be a small mound of stones. More in desperation than any real hope, she headed towards it, a grin breaking over her face as she drew close. Once more, fortune – or maybe it was Khalia – had blessed her. This wasn't a tumbled heap of rocks. She was looking at a tiny hut, open at the front, that stood no more than four feet tall and wide and half that deep, and was constructed from close-fitting boulders with a rough stone roof. A shrine of some kind, she guessed, for in the centre the remains of flowers lay on a flat stone slab. Although it would be cramped and uncomfortable, the rear was to the prevailing weather and, with the greatcoat covering the entrance, it would offer at least some element of protection against the fury unfolding around her. She curled herself tightly against the back wall and fixed Paul's greatcoat across the entrance by pushing it into gaps between the stones above the doorway. It wasn't perfect, but it would have to do.

The storm raged for hours while Madeleine blinked in the glare of lightning bolts that danced around the mountain peaks and ducked at deafening thunder crashes that shook the little shrine hard enough to rattle its stones.

Through it all, the sturdy little structure stood firm, as it had for years.

54.

When Madeleine emerged from her shelter in the late afternoon, the world had changed. The lingering embrace of summer had at last yielded to the first kiss of winter. There was an icy chill in the air that hadn't been there before, and a keen breeze carried the promise of snow. She was trembling, as much from apprehension at what she would find as from the cold. Apprehension turned to despair when she reached the river. The deluge had swollen the level to many times its previous depth and the mud-brown waters roiled and churned as they spread out beyond their banks, tossing branches and tree trunks that had been ripped from the soil by its powerful current. It was impossible to cross. She would drown within seconds if she tried. She couldn't head downstream – she would be heading back in the direction she had come – so her only option was to follow it up towards the mountains and the perils they posed in the encroaching winter. Firmly pushing her fear aside, she turned upstream to face whatever awaited her there.

That night, for the first time, the temperature dropped to below freezing. Madeleine huddled miserably in the lee of a small rocky outcrop, bundled up tightly in her cloak and wrapped in Paul's greatcoat while the chill seeped into her bones. Despite her fatigue, sleep would not come. She was too cold and too uncomfortable. Moreover, she was unable to shake off the troubling feeling that she was being watched. She had no proof, only a crawling sensation at the back of her neck. In the weak starlight, she could see nothing and the only sounds were the scratchings and snufflings of small mammals and birds in their nocturnal search for food. Still the feeling would not go away.

Scolding herself for such an overactive imagination, she pulled Paul's coat more tightly around herself, comforted by his familiar and dearly loved scent. At last fitful, restless sleep overcame her and she woke as dawn was breaking to find a light dusting of snow covering both the ground and her. Stiff with cold, she struggled to her feet and carried on because there was nothing else that she could do.

Madeleine was frozen and running out of food. Surely her situation couldn't get any worse? The question was answered in the early afternoon when she paused for a brief rest in the warm afternoon sun while its rays eased the stubborn chill from her bones. She was lying on a slope of coarse grass that stretched upwards towards the higher mountain peaks with the sunlight playing on her face and for a brief moment she allowed herself to relax. Her peace did not last.

A sharp flash of light pierced her closed eyelids, then another. She leapt up, scanning the mountain slopes. In the distance, she could see movement, followed by another series of flashes. She strained her eyes to see more clearly. Oh God, no. Around a dozen men in dark tunics and trousers, highlighted through with the crimson slash of the sashes wrapped around their waists, were scrambling down the boulder strewn slopes. These were Ju-lin's men. She recognised their uniform.

Madeleine grabbed her pack and ran, paying no attention to where she was going, her only thought to get away from the advancing soldiers. They were moving much more quickly than she was; with every glance she threw over her shoulder, they had gained ground. A shout went up. They had seen her. Their pace increased so that they were now covering the distance that separated her from them at a terrifying speed. She turned and fled, panic giving wings to her heels. It was useless to attempt to outrun them, she couldn't, but she had to try. Stumbling and tripping over tree roots and rocks, somehow keeping her feet, Madeleine hurtled across the ground. They couldn't catch her. They mustn't.

It was higher here, the air thinner. Madeleine's lungs burned as they sought the precious oxygen. It was so hard to breathe, and she was already weak from hunger the rigours of the past days. Still she plunged on in a futile quest for an escape that she could not attain. Her headlong flight came to an abrupt end when her foot caught on a boulder and she crashed painfully to her knees. As she scrambled to her feet, a challenge from only a few paces distant stopped her in her tracks. She turned slowly. Three of Ju-Lin's men stood facing her, their swords raised and a murderous look on their faces. She was going to die here on this barren, windswept hillside. There was no-one here to defend her and nothing that she could do. She had no strength left to fight. Her hand gripped Paul's pistol. She would not go with them alive but please God she did not want to die.

A wave of uncontrollable dizziness overwhelmed her. The sparse oxygen, combined with the exertion of her flight and the adrenalin that surged through her body, had taken its toll. She fought against the encroaching fog as the world closed in around her. She had to fire. Put a bullet in her temple. But her arm was too heavy. It would not answer her command.

The soldiers moved in slowly, deliberately. There was no rush. She posed no threat. They were enjoying the fear that swamped her as she stood there helpless, her strength gone, unable to react. She was watching her fate unfold in slow motion, awaiting the inevitable. The world around her had stopped. This time, surely, even Khalia could do nothing help her.

A bloodcurdling howl split the air. It came from somewhere high above, from behind a rocky outcrop that jutted out over their heads. It was joined by another, and then another, until a hideous chorus filled the mountainside. Madeleine's blood ran cold at the unearthly noise. The soldiers too were staring around searching for its source, fear etched into their faces. Moments later, as if to a given signal, the clamour died away and silence settled once more.

Ju-Lin's men turned their attention back to Madeleine. As soon as they did, however, the howling started up again. Louder this time, and closer. More chilling than ever.

'Yeren.' The shrill fear-filled whisper reached Madeleine. 'Yeren.'

The colour had drained from her pursuers' faces. What did *Yeren* mean? The soldiers knew what was making that sound, and it terrified them. Whatever it was, it was clearly not good. The remaining men, following up at the rear, had now stopped too and were standing with swords and pistols drawn, alert and ready to fight this unseen danger.

Their commanding officer, who Madeleine recognised as the Captain of Ju-Lin's personal guard, was not so easily unnerved. His gaze remained fixed on her. He motioned towards her with his sword, hissing an order. Its meaning was unmistakeable: Seize her.

With the first step his men took, however, the howling started up again, this time only yards away. The men faltered.

'Seize her,' the Captain repeated coldly, pointing his pistol at the nearest soldier's belly.

Another wave of dizziness and nausea swept through Madeleine. She battled to hold on to the last vestiges of consciousness as darkness enveloped her. She would not let them take her without a fight. But the darkness was too strong. She slumped to the ground, barely conscious.

Later, she could not have said if what followed was a nightmare or a nightmarish reality. From a long way away, through the shadows that filled her mind, she heard a frightful chorus of screeches and screams, accompanied by monstrous howls and the sounds of battle. The screams came from Ju-lin's men. The howls, on the other hand, didn't sound human. Madeleine fought to open her eyes.

For the fleeting moment that she succeeded, she wished she hadn't. She was in the middle of a nightmare of the worst kind. Giants, dressed in long white furs streaked red with blood, battled with the soldiers who fought back fiercely with swords and pikes. And yet... And yet. Even in that brief instant, Madeleine had the clear impression that the giants were not slaughtering the men indiscriminately, attempting instead to chase them off. But the blood... It was confusing and frightening. Madeleine didn't want to know. She allowed herself to slip gently into the warm darkness of unconsciousness until blackness consumed her completely and she lay senseless on the ground.

55.

Madeleine snuggled down. She was warm and cosy, so warm and oh so cosy. More than she had been in days. If only it hadn't been for that horrible dream... Her sleepiness evaporated as memory flooded back, hazy and incomplete. Ju-Lin's men. They had found her. There had been shouting, and the noise of battle. And there had been giants...

She lay completely still, holding her breath. Listening. Keeping her eyes tightly closed, she took stock of her situation. Her hands and feet were unbound, which surely meant she had not been taken prisoner. If she had been captured, she would be in chains. The only sounds she could hear were birdsong and the soft sigh of the wind that brushed its cool breath across her face. There were no voices, no sense of anyone – or anything – else nearby. She held on to the peace, eyes still closed though softer, more relaxed now, not wanting to break the spell. What, though, was that god-awful smell?

She could tell from the air on her face that it was a very cold morning and yet she was blissfully warm, which puzzled her. At last Madeleine blinked her eyes open to the dark grey rock of the bluff that rose above her to the clear, pale blue sky of early morning, a sky dotted with candytuft clouds like she would find in a children's picture book. Beyond the bluff the mountains rose up, white-peaked with the eternal snows of their altitude. She was still on the lower slopes where she had tripped and fallen.

She was completely alone. What had happened to the soldiers? She hadn't dreamed them. They had been within yards of her and she had been completely at their mercy, so where were they? An alarming possibility stirred in

275

Madeleine. What if everything she believed was a dream hadn't been a hallucination born of exhaustion, hunger and a rarified atmosphere after all? What if those creatures had been real? The battle real? Unwilling to believe an unbelievable truth Madeleine attempted to come up with a more logical explanation.

Maybe they had been bears – polar bears from the Arctic, like the ones she had seen in Regents Park zoo. They had stood seven, eight, or more feet tall on their hind legs, and snarled and growled like beasts from hell. And maybe she had survived the attack because they hadn't noticed her, their attention captured solely by the soldiers who were running and shouting. If Ju-Lin's men had been attacked by huge white bears, distant cousins perhaps of that Arctic species, had any of them survived? She did not want to look, fearing the grim scene she may find.

Moreover, although Madeleine desperately wanted to believe in her theory, she knew her desire to make logical sense of what had occurred was hiding the truth. These giants had not been indiscriminate hunters. In that brief lucid second when she had opened her eyes, she had realised that they were not attacking the soldiers, merely driving them off. Steeling herself, Madeleine turned her head to the side to count the bodies, at which point all her determined reasoning vanished. For on the ground beside her, within arm's reach, a rough wooden platter was piled high with meat – roasted meat. No matter how she looked at it, bears simply did not roast their meat. Neither did they serve it on a plate, however crude that plate may be. She was in no doubt that the meat was for her; the overriding question was – who had left it?

Once again she had the strong and unsettling sensation that she was being watched. From her prone position she scoured the rocks and scrub. She could see no-one, nothing stirred in the still air, and yet the feeling remained, as strongly as the smell, which was a disagreeable combination of old goat and something else pungent and unsavoury that she did not recognise. She pushed herself to a sitting position and immediately saw both why she was feeling so snug and cosy – even in the sub-zero temperatures – and the source of the stench. She was wrapped from head to toe in a thick black fur. Actually more than one, crudely stitched together with some kind of leather strip.

Her blood ran cold. Someone had been here, wrapped her in the fur and left the meat. She was certain that whoever it had been was watching her still. The hairs rose on the back of her neck and goosebumps prickled her skin. She pushed down her anxiety and forced herself to consider the situation rationally. Whoever – whatever! – had done this could mean her no harm or she would already be dead. She had been an easy target, unconscious and defenceless. Instead 'they' had wrapped her in fur to keep her warm – no doubt saving her life by doing so – and brought her food. She didn't understand what was going on and she didn't want to. Her only wish was to get out of these mountains and to a place of safety. What she would do then, what would happen to the skull, she neither knew nor cared.

* * * * *

With each day that passed the temperature dropped further, bringing frequent flurries of snow that dusted the ground with white. Madeleine's hands and feet were permanently numb with cold. Still she went on, carrying the fur sleeping bag on her back. Though it was heavy and

277

awkward, she never once considered leaving it behind, for without it she would have died of cold in her sleep.

The watchers never left her and soon she grew to welcome their constant if unseen presence. They were taking care of her, keeping her alive. Every morning when she woke, she found roasted meat and dried berries piled on the ground at her side. The supplies she had brought from the palace were virtually exhausted and without these gifts she would not have had the energy to get up on her feet and carry on.

Even so, she was weakening. Exhaustion, cold and altitude were ruthless enemies that robbed her of both her strength and of the will to continue. As the days passed, her mind began to wander. More and more she could no longer be certain of what was real and what she was imagining. Low growls and grunts merged with old nursery rhymes from her childhood. Paul's darling face morphed into Ju-Lin's thick, cruel features and back, then to a pair of unusual soft sapphire blue eyes framed in a mask of white hair.

She was no longer really aware of walking. She stumbled along blindly, automatically putting one foot in front of the other, because that was what she had to do. Somehow she avoided the obstacles and dangers in her path – until the moment, late one afternoon, when she didn't. Her foot caught on a protruding stone, she tripped, and plunged headlong down the mountainside. A hammer blow resounded through her skull as her head hit a rock, and she felt herself falling, falling, into nothingness.

She drifted in a soft, silvery cloud, sometimes floating almost to the surface where she hovered on the borderline of consciousness, only to sink back down into its soothing depths. She was vaguely aware of strong, roughly calloused hands lifting her gently, carrying her, and of strange shapes and smells and sounds that stayed tantalisingly out of reach. She was wrapped in softness, furs, warmth. From time to time, a bowl was held to her lips and warm, salty liquid, like soup, trickled down her throat. Being set carefully down on a rough bed. Rocking, as if she was on a ship at sea. Floating back down into nothingness once more.

In this hazy, nowhere world, she dreamed such strange dreams of a face that she recognised, only she couldn't remember from where. A dream of soft sky-blue eyes peering anxiously at her through a mask of thick, white fur. Gentle eyes. Kind eyes. Smiling eyes. So real for a moment, before it too dissolved into the cloud.

Her eyelids flickered. She was rising upwards, out of the comforting safety of the darkness towards the light. She wasn't sure she wanted to go. It felt so safe here. Why couldn't she stay wrapped in this blanket of serenity? Try as she might to hold onto it though, that place was falling away, the light growing brighter and brighter through her eyelids, drawing her back to the world.

56.

'What the devil..? Good God.' A very masculine, very English voice penetrated the thick fog in Madeleine's head. 'How in the name of blazes did you get here?'

Her eyelids fluttered and opened, blinking in the bright sunshine meeting eyes of the deepest brown, darkened still further at this moment by concern and utter bewilderment, that stared down at her.

She was too tired to answer, already slipping back towards unconsciousness. As the world drifted away again she felt strong arms lift her onto a horse, holding her firmly so that she wouldn't fall. What seemed like only minutes later those same arms were lifting her down, carrying her indoors. She had a hazy impression of a simple stone building and a fire burning in a crude hearth, surrounding her in a cheerful warmth that she welcomed after the icy chill outside. It was the last thing she remembered before she fell back into the abyss.

When at last Madeleine woke she felt almost herself again. The deadening exhaustion that had been with her for so long had evaporated, leaving only a leaden weariness in her limbs, and all the hardships she had lived through had faded into a half-forgotten memory. She luxuriated in the warmth of her bed and the softness of its covers. At any other time, it would not have been anything special, simply furs and blankets thrown onto a rough wooden base. After the rigours of her recent experiences, however, the bed felt as good as any she had slept in.

Her rescuer was sitting by the fire, tending to the crackling logs. Noticing that Madeleine was awake, he rose and walked across to her. In that moment Madeleine became painfully aware that beneath the heavy covers she was completely naked. When had that happened? She had no recollection. This man must have… Horrified, she grabbed the covers tightly up under her chin.

'Where are my clothes?' she demanded, all gratitude towards him completely forgotten.

'They were filthy, soaked through and in tatters. If I hadn't got you out of them, you would have pneumonia by now.' Madeleine's eyes glittered dangerously.

'Look, it was take them off you and give you a fighting chance, or leave you in them, in which case you'd more than likely be half way to dead by now.' Madeleine still glowered.

He sighed. 'There is no question that you are a lovely woman, but believe it or not I don't get my thrills from undressing unconscious young ladies. I prefer my women wide awake.'

For a split second Madeleine's temper threatened to erupt at his bluntness. Just as quickly it receded again and the absurdity of the whole situation hit her with the force of an express train. She began to giggle, releasing the tension of weeks.

'I'm sorry,' she spluttered at last, 'I'm attacking you when I should be thanking you for saving my life.' One pale bare arm snaked out from beneath the covers. 'I'm Madeleine Parker.'

'Andrew Mountjoy.' His handshake was strong and confident. 'Don't thank me. Thank the mountain people. It was they who saved your life. They led me to you.'

'The mountain people? I didn't see anyone.' Or had she…? Playing on the edges of her mind was a mask of white fur and blue, blue eyes.

'They rarely allow themselves to be seen. Legend tells that they been in these mountains since the beginning of time. The locals tribes call them Yeti or Migoi. There are many people, particularly amongst western scholars and scientists, who don't believe they really exist. They are wrong.'

'You've seen them?'

'No, but I've heard their calls and I've seen their tracks, and I've spoken to enough local people who have encountered them.'

'You said they led you to me.'

'They did. I heard them calling two days ago, just before sunrise. They sounded very close. When I went outside to investigate, I found a gold locket and a hunting knife lying on the snow.'

The locket. Paul's locket. Madeleine's hand flew to her throat. 'Where is it?' she asked urgently.

'On the table.' He paused. 'Who is Paul?'

She looked at him sharply.

'You talked in your sleep. You called out 'Paul' several times.'

'My husband. He gave me the locket on our wedding day.'

'Where is he? Was he with you? Is he still out there?'

Tears dampened Madeleine's lashes. 'No. He fell ill, and died several months ago. That locket is almost all I have left of him.'

Andrew pressed the gold heart into her hand where it lay small and cold on her palm. She smiled her thanks as she refastened it around her neck.

Andrew was continuing his tale. 'I couldn't see the mountain people but I heard them alright. There was such an urgency in that sound, and they kept on and on. Calling and calling. Next to the locket and knife three sticks were laid out like an arrow. I guessed they wanted me to follow it so I grabbed my coat and rifle and I set out. All the way, they had left marks – scratches on rocks or in the bark of trees, a small pile of stones, more stick arrows. I rode for a good couple of hours. You can perhaps imagine my astonishment when I saw this bundle wrapped in furs and covered in a dark grey greatcoat, lying in the shelter of a cove of rocks next to the embers of a small fire. Even more so when I saw it was a woman. You. Anyway, I put you on my horse and brought you back here.'

'Here?'

'My hut.'

It was all so fantastic. Madeleine tried to get her head around what Andrew was telling her but it was all too much to take in. Sleep began to overwhelm her once more. Andrew noticed immediately and went across to the hearth where he spooned some thick soup into a bowl, a steady arm supporting her shoulders as she ate. She had no sooner finished the last drop than she fell into a deep sleep again, a sleep that was once more filled with strange faces, white fur masks and deep blue eyes, and pungent animal smells.

57

Madeleine slept for a very long time. When at last she woke, the dreams had settled into a certainty that the faces she had believed to be hallucinations were, indeed, the mountain people Andrew had spoken of. Was it possible that Khalia had called on them to take her to Andrew? While it seemed a crazy idea, so did the mere notion of a race of human-like, though not human, beings – 'Yeti', Andrew had called them – living in these high valleys, who no outsider had ever seen. Except that she had seen them, if only in half-conscious glimpses. They had watched over her and had brought her safely to this hut and to Andrew, against all the odds. Madeleine couldn't help wondering what would happen once she had done as the skull had asked and taken it to safety.

Khalia – where was she? Her heart missed a beat. How could she have forgotten about it until now? Had the skull been left behind out in the mountains? Madeleine threw her legs over the side of the bed, only then remembering her nakedness. She clutched the furs to her and looked around properly for the first time. The fire still burned strongly in the hearth and the tiny, one-roomed hut was cosier than should have been expected, in stark contrast to the snow falling heavily outside. She was alone. Andrew had to be outside somewhere. A pile of blankets in the corner next to the fire showed where he had been sleeping. He had given up his bed to her. Wrapping a couple of the furs covers tightly around her naked body, she clambered off the ramshackle cot.

This was more than a temporary shelter. It was well, if basically, equipped with cooking pots and pans, canned food and essential furniture. A rough wooden table and two equally rustic-looking chairs stood against the end wall next to some wooden planks balanced on stones that served as a dresser and washstand. The brocade bag was nowhere to be seen.

She whirled around as the door opened to a blast of icy air and a flurry of giant snowflakes. Andrew hurried in, shaking the snow from his hair, a bundle of firewood in his arms. He was clearly surprised to see Madeleine up and about. Equally startled, she pulled the furs tighter.

'Hello.' His chestnut brown eyes were smiling at her. 'Sleeping Beauty is awake. Welcome back. Are you feeling better?'

'Yes.' It was true. She felt better than she had done since before she had fled the palace.

'Good.' He studied her face carefully. 'You look better.' He grew serious. 'It's nothing short of a miracle that you still have all your fingers and toes. It was bitterly cold out there even wrapped up and looked after as you were. You were blue when I brought you in. Your feet and hands should have been destroyed by frostbite. I don't know how but except for some superficial ice-burn, they are fine.'

Madeleine examined her hands. He was right. Other than a little redness at the tips and an accompanying tenderness, they looked healthy.

'Where are my clothes?' she asked. 'I want to get up.'

'I burned them.' He laughed out loud at her shocked expression. 'They were past all hope of wearing. Your boots were the only thing I kept. Here.' He had moved to a small metal trunk and pulled out trousers, socks, a shirt and a heavy wool sweater. 'They'll be too big but they'll have to do. I'll just go and feed the horses.' He disappeared back out into the blizzard.

As he had predicted, the clothes swamped her. Still, with a bit of judicious tucking and folding, and using a length of rope as a belt to hold the trousers up, they would look do. She was once more free to move about. A rap at the door warned her of Andrew's return.

'Come in. I'm decent.'

His face creased into a grin as he saw her, clearly finding her new look amusing. Catching her reflection in his shaving mirror, she understood why. She looked just like a little girl playing dress up. Likewise, his grin turned him from the somewhat stern and serious man into a mischievous boy. The transformation immediately put Madeleine more at ease.

'Good.' He turned to ladle a thick brown stew into two bowls from a pot that was bubbling above the fire. Despite its unappetising appearance it smelled – and as Madeleine discovered a few seconds later – tasted wonderful. She cleared three bowlfuls before laying down her spoon with a satisfied sigh.

'I don't think I've ever eaten anything better than that,' she declared.

58.

'Tell me, what on earth are you doing out here in the middle of nowhere? I know you said your husband had died, but if I understand you correctly that was nearly a year ago. Which leaves a lot of blanks.'

Trying to piece together the events in some form of coherent order, Madeleine related her story, from the time she and Paul had left England.

'He was so handsome and dashing.' She was no longer in the hut; she was back with Paul, laughing with him, kissing him, surrounded by the endless plains of the Steppes. 'He was exciting and I loved him more than the world. I still do. And for some strange reason, he loved me too.'

Sitting across from this compelling woman, watching the passion burn in those incredible eyes, Andrew could see exactly why Paul had fallen in love with her. Her husband had been captivated by her light and spirit, as so many men had been. Madeleine was so alive. So comfortable in her skin. So unaffected. He shook himself out of his trance.

'Do you miss him?' He could have slapped himself. What a ridiculously stupid thing to say. Of course she missed him. The pain of her loss was etched into every contour of her face. She didn't treat it as a stupid question though.

'Yes,' she replied softly. 'I always will. When Paul died, a part of me died with him.' A smile played around Madeleine's lips as she remembered. 'You know, I was everything a decent, eligible young woman was not. I hated needlework and small talk, and I couldn't understand why my governess scolded me when I ran or climbed trees when my brothers were praised for doing so. Paul once told me that was one of the reasons he fell in love with me. He had found someone who would share his love of adventure and not fall in a dead faint if she tripped and tore her stockings.

'So when we got married we decided that our honeymoon would be the adventure of our lifetime – an expedition across Europe and into the heart of Russia. Those first months were so wonderful, on our own with just the endless horizon and the sky. Then, when we were nearly a year into our trip, Paul fell ill.' Grief clouded Madeleine's features.

'We were in the middle of this vast empty plain, weeks from any settlement, with nothing but flat grasslands for as far as we could see. And not a soul anywhere. Not even the nomadic peoples travelled through there – or at least, they didn't in all the time we were there. Paul grew weaker and weaker, and I had to nurse him day and night. We pushed on in the hope of coming across a town, or a doctor, or *someone* who could help us. When he became too ill to travel, we stopped and set up a permanent camp. I was terrified of losing him, more even than of being left out there on my own, I think. I lost track of time. It could have been days, weeks or even months. No, not months. At least, I don't think so…Anyway, that's when the soldiers found us and took us to the palace. I don't know why, because I didn't think we were anywhere near the Chinese border but to be honest, by then I had no idea where we were.

'The Emperor was very kind and even sent his own physician to tend to Paul, but it was no use. Paul got sicker and weaker, and only two, maybe three weeks later, he died.' Tears glistened on her lashes.

'And you?'

'To tell you the truth, for several months I really didn't care what happened to me. I was so lost in my grief that I wasn't really aware of anything else. I had become ill too, from exhaustion, lack of food and worry over Paul. Losing him just about finished me. When I finally pulled myself out of it, I came to realise that I would never be allowed to leave the palace. Although I was never called a prisoner, it was clear that was how it was. I still don't know why.

'It wasn't unpleasant, far from it. At least not until much later. The old Emperor was kind and treated me well.'

'What happened?'

'His son, Ju-Lin. He was as unlike his father as it was possible to be. He was a cruel, ruthless tyrant and he hated me from the beginning. Just after Paul and I arrived, I overheard him tell his father we were spies and should be put to death. He was speaking in English. I think he wanted me to hear so that I would be afraid. It was more than that though. Once I was better I began noticing the way he was looking at me, and it scared me. My maid warned me that he intended to take me as his concubine and crush my spirit. I was determined that I would never let that happen. The day he tried to rape me – he didn't,' she added hastily, catching Andrew's horror-struck expression, 'he was interrupted – that was the moment I knew I had to find a way to escape. It would only be a brief reprieve. I had no doubt Ju-Lin would return at the earliest opportunity to finish what he had started.

'I was almost out of the palace when I stumbled over the Emperor's body. Ju-Lin had murdered him. From then

289

on there was no going back. With the Emperor dead there was no-one to protect me from his son.'

What she didn't tell Andrew about however, was the skull and the role it had played. Or that she was carrying it. If she still was…

'The bag?' she asked anxiously. 'The brocade bag. Where is it?'

'Under the bed.'

'Did you look in it?'

'No. How odd,' he puzzled. 'I don't know why I didn't. It would have made sense. I might have found out who you were. It simply didn't cross my mind.' He let go of the thought and returned to Madeleine's story. 'Where was it, the palace?'

'I don't know. China somewhere. That's all I can tell you. Paul was so ill. I wasn't thinking about anything but him.'

'What can you tell me about it? The people? The geography?'

Madeleine related what she had seen. When she had finished, she leaned back against the wall. 'I can't think of anything else.'

'From your description of the landscape and the culture, my guess would be that it was somewhere in the central region,' Andrew mused. He was frowning. 'I don't see how you could have been though. It would be impossible to cover that distance in such a short time. You left the palace in early autumn, you say?' Madeleine nodded. 'So we'll assume somewhere around mid-September. It's only the third of November now and you're in Nepal. No, it's impossible. I must have it wrong. You can't have been where I thought you were.'

He was thinking hard. 'If this Ju-Lin's troops caught up with you in the mountains... That could have been the Hengduan range. Which still doesn't explain the time factor...' He gave his head a shake to clear away his confusion. 'What happened then?'

'It was all over. I didn't stand a chance. I'd tripped and was flat on my face on the ground with the soldiers only yards away. Right at the moment the captain ordered them to grab me, a frightful howling started up. It was a sound like nothing I'd ever heard before or want to hear again. The soldiers were scared – no, more than scared, they were terrified, and so was I. That was when I fainted. When I woke up it was all quiet again. There was no sign of Ju-Lin's men, and I was wrapped in those smelly furs with a pile of food beside me. Anyway, I carried on until I managed to trip and knock myself out.' She felt around her scalp, wincing as her fingers pressed on a still tender spot.

'After that it's all a blur. Strange sounds and smells and faces covered in long white hair.' She paused. 'They must have been the mountain people you were telling me about. They brought me here, to you. Why? Who are you, Andrew?'

'I'm an anthropologist. I've spent the past five summers in these foothills researching the local tribes and their legends, including that of Yeti, the mountain people. I don't know why they brought you to me. Possibly because I was here and can take you with me to safety when I leave. I'm heading down into India in a couple of days, before winter sets in properly and I can't get out. In fact, if it hadn't been for your unexpected arrival, I would have already gone. You were fortunate, Madeleine. A day later and I wouldn't have been here to find you.'

Surely the mountain people hadn't carried her halfway across China just to bring her to someone who could escort her safely home to England when they could have found a much closer refuge for her in one of British enclaves that was dotted across the country. No, they – or more likely Khalia – had another reason for choosing Andrew. She already suspected that he wasn't telling her the full truth, for in addition to the hunting rifle that lay against the wall, she had spotted a decidedly military looking sabre and pistol poking out from under his makeshift bed. It wasn't the kind of weapons she expected an anthropologist to carry. He didn't look much like a scholar either. He was maybe thirty years old or so, only a few years older than she was, and beneath his thick jacket, unbuttoned in the warmth of the hut, his body was fit and strong. He looked much more a soldier than a man of learning. There was more going on here than Andrew was saying. Didn't the same apply to her as well though? Wasn't she keeping secrets too? She said nothing.

'When do we leave?' Madeleine wanted nothing more than to return to the safe familiarity of her father's home in England.

'Not until this snow eases. It won't last long. It's just a taste of what will hit this place later in the season, although it wouldn't be wise to set out until it stops. A couple of extra days to regain your strength won't hurt you either. It'll be a tough trek down across the border.'

59.

The hut was in semi-darkness, lit only by the fire and the moonlight that filtered in through the single window. Madeleine listened intently. Outside Andrew's horse and the two mules were shuffling and stomping restlessly. Something had spooked them, maybe a bear, or a wolf. Was that what had woken her? The dull clatter of a dislodged rock broke jarringly into the quiet of the night. She sat up, now fully alert. Not something. Someone. On the far side of the hut, Andrew was already on his feet, his sword in one hand, pistol in the other. He pressed a finger to his lips, warning her to silence.

A shadow passed by the window, blocking the moonlight for just a split second. Without a sound, Madeleine slid from the bed and across to where Andrew waited and listened. Winking at his raised eyebrow and surprised expression, she picked up the rifle from against the wall, examined it expertly and cocked it, ready to fire.

He leaned forward, pressing his lips against her ear. 'Bandits,' he whispered.

Or Ju-Lin. Whichever it was, the purpose would be the same: to rob, kidnap or, most likely, kill them both. Adrenalin surged into Madeleine's bloodstream, her nerves on a knife edge, as she waited for the attack to come. Her father had schooled her intensively in shooting and fencing, firmly believing that women should be able to defend themselves effectively, and she was an expert shot and swordswoman. Never until this moment though had she had to face using those skills in a situation where she would be forced to maim or kill in order to save her life, and she felt sick to the stomach. Well, there was no time for such niceties now. They would have to wait. She forced down the bile rising in her throat and squared her shoulders, ready for what would follow.

The attack, which came only moments later, was two-pronged. Three men burst in through the door brandishing short swords and pistols; simultaneously, a fourth dove expertly through the small window opening. Not allowing herself time to think about what she was about to do, Madeleine aimed the rifle at him and squeezed the trigger. His scream was cut short by the bullet that tore into his belly and out through his spine. He was dead before he hit the floor, blood gushing from his ruptured intestines. Madeleine felt the vomit rising into her throat. Swallowing hard, she turned towards the doorway.

Andrew had downed one of the assailants with his first shot. With his second however, the barrel of his revolver had jammed and he was now trying to hold off the two remaining men in the narrow doorway with his sword, keeping them too busy to have time to aim their firearms. Madeleine lifted the rifle to fire again, only for it to be swept out of her grip. The blow barely missed slicing off the fingers of her left hand.

Andrew was an expert swordsman but so were the men he faced. Feinting, parrying, thrusting, he couldn't find an opening, and it was two against one. The rifle lay crooked and useless on the floor, its barrel wrecked by the power of the sword blow, and Paul's pistol was stuffed in Madeleine's bag, out of reach. By the time she found, primed and loaded it, they would both be dead.

With a howl of pain, the jammed gun in Andrew's hand clattered to the floor. An on-target slash had hit home and his left arm was now hanging uselessly at his side, blood streaming from a deep gash just above the elbow. His hand no longer had the strength to hold onto, let alone fire, the gun. Against two skilled and uninjured opponents the eventual outcome would be inevitable. Andrew didn't stand a chance.

Madeleine leapt forward, her feet slipping and slithering on the blood-soaked floor. She could feel the sticky wetness, chilled by the stone, soak through her breeches as she slid through it, her fingers scrabbling for the revolver. The remaining chambers were still loaded. Frantically she cocked and re-cocked the mechanism, working the barrel to free it until, after what seemed like hours but was in reality only seconds, she at last felt it move.

One of Andrew's assailants realised what she was doing and, leaving his companion to finish off Andrew, turned his attention to Madeleine. He was a fraction of a second too late. The vicious curved blade was already raised in preparation for bringing it down to cleave her skull in two when she fired. His features dissolved in a sickening spray of blood, bone and flesh that hit Madeleine full in the face. This time she could not hold back. She bent and vomited until her stomach was empty.

Her hand shook as she lifted the revolver again, unwilling to relive the nightmare, knowing she had to if they were to come through this alive. Cocked it again. The sharp sound reached the final assailant who turned and saw the gun aimed squarely at his chest. He had no back-up, his companions were all dead. Staring down certain death, he switched target and lunged at Madeleine, his sword outstretched, leaving himself wide open. With a grunt, Andrew thrust his own sword deep into the man's belly, pushing upwards so that it emerged by his shoulder blade. The assassin clutched at the hilt of the blade embedded in his flesh as if to pull it free, his features a mask of surprise mingled with disbelief. Seconds later his final breath rattled up from his lungs and he slid to the floor with a thud.

Madeleine felt the dizziness claiming her. She was hot, light-headed. Darkness was closing in…

'Madeleine, help me.' Andrew's urgent plea dragged her back from the brink. She hurried to where he sprawled across the chair, blood streaming down his arm, his face ashen, ready to pass out himself.

She tore at what was left of his sleeve to reach the wound. It was deep, to the bone, and several inches long. Andrew had been lucky not to lose his arm to the blow. He still might, she thought grimly, if not worse. Blood was spurting profusely. If she couldn't stop the flow, Andrew would soon be dead. She grabbed one of his shirts, folded it in a thick pad and pressed it onto the gash, telling him to hold it in place with his good arm while she rummaged in her bag for the few remaining strips of fabric she had torn from her dress. With them, she bound the pad tightly to his arm, hoping it would be enough, afraid it wouldn't, and half carried, half dragged him to the bed where she piled the covers on top of him. He was already losing consciousness. His breathing was frighteningly shallow, his skin the colour of putty. He had lost a lot of blood, perhaps too much already, and he was in deep shock. In his favour, he was strong, young and otherwise healthy. All she could do now was wait and pray.

Madeleine left Andrew to sleep. Others things needed her attention. Within a few short ghastly minutes her home for the past few days had turned into a blood-soaked slaughterhouse. A grim task lay ahead. She would not stay in this hut with these mangled corpses and, as there was nowhere else for he to go, she would have to move them out. Surveying the scene, nausea once more overwhelmed her. She steadied herself and gathered up her courage.

It was hard, exhausting, stomach-sickening work. Inch by muscle-torturing inch she dragged the bodies out of the shack and into the small goat pen then soaked up the pools of blood with a blanket and dumped it outside the door. Finally she scrubbed the floors and walls as clean as she could. Although the sickly sweet odour of death still filled the little building it was now – just about – bearable. It had to be. They were going nowhere until – unless – Andrew recovered.

Madeleine was afraid of falling asleep, fearful that others would come and kill them while she slept, yet she could not resist. Her body was demanding rest, the chance to recover from the aftermath of the flood of adrenalin that had poured through her body during the attack. It would not be denied.

60.

When Madeleine opened her eyes, chinks of bright light were patterning the floor. The sun had to be high in the sky. Her head was resting on Andrew's chest, which rose and fell rhythmically. He had regained some colour and, although the dressing on his arm was caked in dried blood, no fresh seeped through. That was a good sign. It meant the bleeding had stopped. Although she was no nurse, it seemed to her that it had done so surprisingly quickly for a wound of such severity. She felt a sudden blast of hope that he would be alright.

He hadn't woken and lay like a dead man, which he very nearly had been. Now though, he slept peacefully, his breathing deep and regular, while his body healed and repaired itself. It was Madeleine's turn to nurse the man who had so recently saved her life. Gently, not wishing to disturb the wound but needing to dress it, she peeled away the strips of hard, stained fabric and, even more carefully, the pad they held in place. The blade that had sliced through Andrew's arm had been as sharp as a surgeon's scalpel; although the wound was a livid red where the flesh had been brutalised, it looked clean and healthy. It badly needed stitching but there was neither needle nor thread in the hut. Madeleine also knew enough to understand that, clean as the wound looked, infection would be the greatest threat to his life now that the blood loss had ceased.

Of course. The star flowers. They had worked miracles on her injured feet, why wouldn't they do the same for Andrew's arm? She scrabbled in her bag and pulled out a few twisted stalks and some ragged, dried-out flower heads and leaves, all that was left of the huge bunch she had collected.

'Please let it work,' she whispered. This time, because they were so desiccated, she ground them to a powder rather than a pulp, and went outside for water.

While she had slept the snow had returned and gone again, and she stepped out into a clear, sun-bright day. The ground was covered in a thick, soft duvet of snow and the world was breathtakingly lovely in its pure white robes. For a moment its dazzling beauty stopped Madeleine in her tracks and she gazed around, lost for words, transported to a fairy-tale world of icing sugar and crystals. There was no sound, every movement muffled by the snow, and no sign of life other than a pair of eagles that circled and soared in the still, calm air.

A gentle whinnying and restless stomping nearby drew her from the dream; Andrew's horse and the pack mules wanted feeding. In the next moment, her gaze fell on the blood-stained blanket by the door. In this silent serenity it looked out of place, an unwelcome gate-crasher at a party. For a short time she had forgotten that the horrors of the previous night had ever happened. The blanket was a grim reminder that it had. The illusion was well and truly over.

Madeleine's stomach twisted. How long would it be before more men came? She pushed down her fears and tended first to the horses, then scooped up a handful of the fresh snow and returned inside to dress Andrew's injured arm.

'You handle a gun pretty well for a woman.' His voice made her jump. She had been busy with the dressing and hadn't noticed him wake.

'You handle a sword remarkably well for an anthropologist,' she replied, not looking up from her task.

He didn't answer, changing the subject instead. 'We have to leave. We're not safe here. If they came, more will follow.'

'Were they Ju-Lin's men?'

'No, I don't think so. You're too far from the palace for him to reach you here.'

'Bandits then.'

Andrew shook his head. 'Bandits wouldn't be that well trained or that well-armed. Those are quality weapons.' He indicated the swords and guns piled by the fire.

'Then who?'

'I don't know.'

'But you suspect…'

'This country has its fair share of secret societies, ancient cults and superstitions, Madeleine. More than you might imagine. Before I came here I was extremely sceptical that they actually existed. It didn't take me long to find out how wrong I was. These groups are real and active. This is an ancient land of isolated peoples and deep spirituality. Along with that come powerful, deep-rooted beliefs. Did you notice that the men who attacked us all had a small tattoo shaped like a wheel on the lower right hand side of their throat?' He shrugged, baffled. 'Though why they attacked us is beyond me. There is no rational reason, unless they thought we were someone else.'

He lay back, exhausted by the effort, leaving Madeleine's mind a whirl of guilt and fear. Had they been after the skull? But no-one knew she had it. Not even Andrew. And although Ju-Lin might suspect, Andrew believed he was too far away to be a threat to her here. Unless the new Emperor had used his influence to reach beyond the borders of his kingdom.

'The one thing I am certain of is that they'll come back. If I'm right – and I'm sure I am – and they belong to some mysterious cult, they'll be dedicated fanatics. If they are after something, they won't stop until they get it. And they won't worry about who they kill on the way. We have to leave. Quickly.'

'You aren't well enough to travel.'

'I have to be. The alternative is to wait here to die. We can't withstand another attack. With my arm like this, I couldn't hold off even one man. When the first party doesn't return, they'll know we've fought back. They'll come in greater numbers next time. We won't stand a chance.'

'Where will we go?'

'The route I had planned. We'll head south and cross the border into India, then make for one of the garrison hill-stations. From there, we'll travel on down to Calcutta and find passage on a ship sailing for England.'

Andrew swayed violently as he pushed himself upright, brushing off brusquely the hand Madeleine put out steady him. He started to grab some essential items, all the while letting out a non-stop string of curses at his injured, useless arm.

'Be careful,' Madeleine scolded. 'You'll start it bleeding again, banging it around like that.' She tore a strip of fabric from one of the bedcovers and fashioned a sling. Ignoring his scowls, she trussed up his injured arm and set about helping him to pack what they would need. Andrew's injury was a bigger handicap than he wished to accept; much to his chagrin, he was forced to leave it to Madeleine to load up a mule and saddle his horse while he stood and watch, pale and unsteady on his feet.

'Are you sure you are well enough?' she risked asking.

'I have to be,' he muttered, struggling up on to the horse. He held out his good hand. 'Come on. We'll have to ride two up.'

'What's wrong with the other mule?'

'No saddle.'

Madeleine threw back her head and laughed. It was an unexpectedly joyful sound after their recent ordeal. She led the animal from its shelter, folded the last remaining blanket into a thin pad and threw it over the mule's back. Shoving her arms through the handles of the brocade bag containing Khalia so that it sat on her shoulders like a back pack, she vaulted onto the mule's back.

'Who needs a saddle?' she grinned.

If the mule looked surprised at its unexpected passenger, Andrew looked no less so. 'Well, blow me. You're full of surprises.' He couldn't hide the admiration in his voice.

Touching his heels to his horse's flanks, he led the way down the rough trail. Madeleine followed, leading the pack mule and watching Andrew carefully. He was swaying precariously in the saddle and she wondered if he would be strong enough for the journey that lay ahead.

* * * * *

They were closer to human habitation than she had believed. Two days steady riding brought them to a small village tucked into the hillside where they were greeted warmly; that warmth increased tenfold when Andrew addressed the villagers in their own dialect. It surprised Madeleine, though perhaps it shouldn't have done, she conceded. By his own admission, he had spent a lot of time in these mountains.

302

They were standing in the middle of a group of curious villagers when the crowd parted and an old woman with no teeth and hardly any hair tottered up to Andrew She was tiny, standing no taller than his belt. She studied him carefully for several minutes with unexpectedly bright, intelligent eyes and then nodded. Her arm shot out and, before Andrew could stop her, one bony finger stabbed hard at his injured arm. He gasped and staggered forward at the sudden harsh assault. Madeleine stepped forward angrily, only to be halted in her tracks by a piercing stare from the old hag, who immediately turned her attention back to Andrew. She nodded again as if satisfied, and gestured for his to go with her.

'Andrew?'

'It's alright, Madeleine. She's the village healer.' The woman was waiting at the entrance to a small building, gesturing impatiently. 'I'll see you later.' He ducked into the doorway after her.

Madeleine was given food and shown to a room in one of the villager's homes, where a thick mattress of animal skins filled the floor. After two full days of riding and two very cold, uncomfortable nights sleeping on the hard rough ground protected only by the thin canvas of Andrew's tent, Madeleine was asleep as soon as she lay down, waking only when the sunlight tickled her eyelids. It was a few seconds before she remembered where she was. Andrew! Where was Andrew? Welcome reassurance came only a couple of minutes later when she heard him whistling cheerfully outside. There was a light knock and his head appeared around the doorway. Although he still looked pale, he seemed stronger.

'Are you alright? What happened?'

'Potions and magic and spells. Oh, and she stitched this up too.' He indicated his arm, which was neatly bandaged, then grimaced. 'With a needle the size of a tent peg, I swear. It's never going to look pretty, but at least it'll heal now and I'll keep my arm. Come on.'

'Where are we going?'

'India. I've found a guide who'll take us to the nearest border garrison. He says it's only a few days' trek from here. We'll leave as soon as you are ready.'

Madeleine was already on her feet. Within minutes, they were heading out of the village along a well-worn trail. At long last, Madeleine was going home.

GEMMA, 5

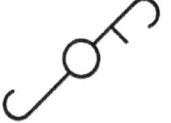

61.

Only two minutes earlier Duncan had walked into his home after a couple of days away. Now he was staring at Joe in astonishment as his friend knelt down on the kitchen floor, tugged up a floorboard and fumbled underneath.

'What the…?'

'It's a long story.' Joe grimaced. 'The short version is that Callum is dead. He's been murdered.'

Duncan stared at us, horrified. 'Murdered? When? How?'

'He was kidnapped and beaten half to death.' I picked up the story. 'Joe and I found him and took him to hospital. Before we left him, he asked us to go to his squat to find that envelope,' I nodded at the brown rectangle Joe was holding, 'and hold onto it for him. When we took it back to him at the hospital, we discovered that, despite his injuries, he'd run off.'

'Sneaked out of the place right under the noses of the police.' Joe put in, not without admiration for his friend's heroics. 'Next thing I knew, I was being asked to go to Birmingham to identify his body. It'd been fished out of a canal.' He shuddered at the memory. 'Anyway, we had to hide this somewhere, and under your kitchen floor seemed as good a place as any.' Joe didn't mention the safety deposit box key that was also concealed there.

'What is it?'

'Not much really.' Joe handed him the envelope. 'We took a look at it before we stashed it. There are a few sheets of A4 containing lists of names, nationalities, dates and global events, some of them ticked, some crossed out and others with a question mark beside them. A few of them we recognise, most we don't. Google hasn't been much help either. And there's a photocopy of a world map marked with sticky blue dots.'

'Do you know what it means?'

'No, and Callum didn't tell us. He couldn't. There was a police guard with us in the room and on top of that he was drugged to the eyeballs. I'm amazed that he managed to say as much as he did. Actually, he told us *not* to look at it, but when he disappeared from the hospital…'

Duncan led us into his living room, scanning the sheets of paper.

'Oh, and there's that…' I pointed to the data-stick he had just pulled from the envelope.

'What's on it?'

'That's the problem. Callum password protected it and we haven't been able to get in. We were hoping you might be able to.'

Duncan peered at the small slice of plastic in his hand and nodded. 'I've got to head out for a couple of meetings shortly. I'll take a look at it later this evening when I get in. I doubt it'll be too difficult.' He glanced again at the scribbled notes.

'Like Joe said, we can recognise half a dozen or so of the names on the notepaper. The ones that are on the news regularly because he or she is the CEO of some huge corporation or the leader of such and such a country. We don't know many of them though.'

'If you were to talk to my conspiracy theory friends, Gemma, they would tell you that these faces are the real power behind the major corporations and governments of the world. Most are anonymous, known to virtually no-one outside their inner circles, and they want it to stay that way because they wield immense amounts of power, invisibly pulling the strings.' Duncan frowned. 'If Callum was digging too close for comfort it could explain what happened to him. These people have way too much to lose to be squeamish about covering their tracks.

'Whoever got to him must have suspected he was on to something. If he was, I expect we'll find the meaty stuff on here.' He waved the little black stick cheerfully. I had a hunch that nothing made Duncan happier than when he was busy prying into secrets others would prefer kept hidden.

His mood changed and he looked at us hard. 'Make no mistake, these people are dangerous. They don't mess around. Whatever Callum was digging into got him killed. If we start meddling, it could get you ... us... killed too. Now I'm willing to take that chance. If I can expose the darker side of Earth's civilisation, I will. But before I open this can of worms,' he brandished the little rectangle of black plastic, 'you need to be sure that you do as well. So I'm asking you now – are you sure you want to do this?'

No, of course I wasn't. A big part of me wanted to let it all go and return to my writing and the quiet life I used to lead. Only I would never be able to, would I? This had all gone too far. Besides, there was that other part of me that was pushing for answers and for justice for Callum.

'No harm in finding out what's on there.' Joe had beaten me to it. 'When we know that, we can decide what to do next.'

'OK' Duncan's ear to ear grin gave away his delight. 'Just wanted to give you the chance to say No.'

'We're heading back to Gemma's. Will you call us as soon as you find out anything?'

'Of course.' Duncan tucked the data-stick into his jacket pocket and glanced at his watch. 'I'm late. I've got to run. I'll ring you when I've got into the files.' With a brief wave of his hand, he was gone.

62.

The hairs on the back of my neck prickled a warning. 'Someone's been here...' I was standing with one foot inside the hallway of my cottage, my hand still on the keys that nestled in the front door lock.

'How can you tell?' I had stopped so suddenly that Joe only just avoided crashing into me.

'I just know. I can feel it.'

Joe didn't doubt me for a moment. 'OK, let's go carefully. They may still be here.'

We checked every room; the house was empty. Nothing was missing, nothing was out of place. There was no indication at all of anything untoward or that anyone had been in there while I had been away. All my senses screamed otherwise.

'What do you want to do? Call the police?' Joe was checking the window latches.

'And tell them what? There's no sign at all of a break-in. Nothing appears to have been stolen or even touched. There's not one bit of evidence to back me up. I'm sure they would be very sympathetic, reassure me that it was perfectly natural that I should have freak-out moments now and again following the trauma of the previous burglary, and assume that's all it is.' I plonked onto the sofa. '*Is* that what it is? Am I imagining it?'

Dear Joe. He was, as always, blunt and honest. 'It's possible. But no, I don't think so for one minute. Your reaction was too immediate and too strong. You felt something was wrong the second you walked through the door. After this business with Callum, I'm dismissing nothing as mere imagination.'

If he meant to reassure me, that was where he got it badly wrong. My thoughts leapt to the data-stick that had, until an hour ago, been tucked securely under the floorboard in Duncan's kitchen along with the key to the safety deposit box holding the golden symbol that had cost Olina Gjerde and who knew how many others before her, their lives. Was the same organisation that murdered Callum responsible for beating Olina and her colleague to death in their laboratory in Trøndheim? Or were we facing the possibility that several groups were involved, each with their own agenda? And which of those groups had broken into my home?

'I'm glad I listened to you and didn't bring the envelope here. If they'd found it... When will Duncan get round to taking a look at it, do you think?'

'He said he'd work on it later this evening. If we don't hear from him tonight, I'll call him in the morning to see how he's got on. He'll have no problem breaking through Callum's password.' Abruptly, he fell quiet.

'What is it? What are you thinking?'

'About you being out here all on your own. It worries me. I know, I know – you love it here, and you love your solitude. But with that first very obvious burglary and now this...'

I wasn't going to admit that the secluded position of my home had been playing on my mind too, not quite yet. It had though. Before that first break-in I had always felt completely safe and at ease here. Now I had become ridiculously nervous, worrying at every bump and noise in the night. While it was a perfectly normal psychological reaction, it wasn't one I enjoyed. No matter that my rational brain told me over and over that those noises were part and parcel of living in any old building, my imagination constantly persuaded me otherwise. In the words of the best horror movies, out here there was no-one to hear me scream. While my landlord had been very understanding and generous, and was going to install a burglar alarm linked to the police station, it had not yet happened and wouldn't for at least another month or two. In the meantime, I was feeling vulnerable.

'I do get the jitters sometimes.' The words came out before I could stop them. Once I'd spoken them, I was relieved I had confessed. 'After today I'll be even more on edge. This is the second time someone has broken in. Both times, fortunately, I've not been here. Maybe it's deliberate and the house is being watched until I go out,' – which was in itself a highly unpleasant scenario – 'but it could also be sheer good luck. I don't want it to be third time unlucky.' Suddenly goosebumps ran over my skin. Someone had walked over my grave. My thoughts flew to Callum and the fate that had befallen him.

'What would you say to me moving in here for a while?' Before I could get a word out, Joe was already raising a hand to stall my objection. 'Just until the alarm is fitted. It would be reassurance for you and it would help me out too. I was only meant to be staying at Duncan's for a couple of weeks and it's been a good few months now. He hasn't said anything but…' Joe was watching carefully for my reaction, aware of how much I love and need my space and solitude.

He knew me too well! Maybe that's why I didn't immediately dismiss his suggestion. In fact, the more I considered it, the more appealing it sounded. I liked having Joe around – I liked it a lot – and we got on so well. It would be easy, having him stay here, and I would feel a lot safer. I always did when he was around; he had been there for me so many times over the past year or so. In any case, I told myself, the spare room was effectively his anyway because he already stayed over several nights a month. I made my mind up.

'I'd appreciate that, Joe. Much as I like to act all brave and independent, I've really not slept well since I came back. I've been too on edge, seeing spooks everywhere. It'll be good to have you here. You need to be patient with me though. I've been living on my own for a while and it'll take a bit of time to get used to having someone share my living space again.'

He grinned. 'Don't worry, we'll work it out. You won't know I'm here.'

That I doubted.

63.

As it happened events took a very different turn from the one Joe and I anticipated. Joe was woken just after midnight by a call from an extremely shaken Duncan, and banged on my door to wake me so that I could listen in on the speakerphone.

'I've lost it.' Duncan sounded odd.

'Lost what?' I was still shaking the fog of sleep from my brain.

'The data-stick.'

'Lost it? How?' Joe's incredulity was in the stratosphere.

'No. Lost isn't the right word. It was stolen. Ten minutes ago. Two men broke into my flat.' Duncan was gabbling his words, still shocked by the experience.

'Slow down, Duncan. Tell us what happened.'

I heard him draw in a deep breath to steady himself, and when he spoke again he sounded more composed. 'I got back from my meeting at around ten o'clock. Fixed some supper. Answered a few emails. Then I remembered the data-stick so I settled down to see what I could do. I don't know how long I'd been working on it – it hadn't been very long, because I hadn't got past Callum's password – when there was a knock on my door. Which was a bit odd at that time of night but I thought it might have been one of my neighbours, so I opened it.' We heard him swallow hard.

'Two men were standing there pointing guns at my chest. They pushed me back into the hallway and followed me in. Didn't say a word. Knew exactly what they wanted. One headed straight for my laptop and pulled out the stick, and grabbed the envelope off the desk. I wasn't going to argue with them. Then they turned and left, closing the door.'

'Are you hurt?'

'No. Rattled as hell as you can imagine but otherwise I'm OK.' His composure cracked. 'Christ almighty! They might have killed me.' There was a short silence before he carried on, more puzzled than agitated now. 'It's weird though…' He tailed off again.

'What's weird?'

'Looking back on it – now that they aren't standing there with their guns pointing at my guts – I'm not so sure any more that they would have actually shot me. The more I think about it, the more I wonder if those guns were simply to frighten me sufficiently that I wouldn't put up a fight.' Another pause. 'Couldn't say why I think that. I don't know where the idea came from. It's just a gut feeling. In any case, it worked. Like taking candy from a baby.'

'Have you called the police…? What?' Joe had just shot me a glance that said 'get real'.

'I'd rather not have the Old Bill poking around my flat, Gemma. There are a few things here that I might not have come by through – er – official channels. In any case, what would I tell them was stolen? Notes written by a man who had not only escaped from their custody after being kidnapped and beaten up only to turn up dead a short while later, but who was also a prime suspect for a particularly nasty murder? I'd be in the police station for a week and so would you. And that's before they started asking me about all the other stuff they'd find here.'

'Sorry, Duncan. I wasn't thinking.' I'd completely forgotten about Duncan's considerably less than legal moonlighting activities. So much had happened recently that I was beginning to lose the plot. Literally.

'I'm really sorry too, Gemma. I know how important that envelope was to you.'

'It wasn't your fault, mate. Go get yourself a stiff drink and take it easy. I'll give you a ring tomorrow.' Joe hung up, frowning. 'Bugger! At least Duncan's OK. After what happened to Callum, he got away lightly.'

'So, what do we do now?'

'What can we do?' Joe sounded dejected. I suspected he had secretly been looking forward to a bit of cloak and dagger investigation. 'We've lost the only lead we had. That envelope held the key to whatever Callum was on to. How the hell did anyone know Duncan had it?'

'Joe, what if it wasn't Callum's killers? The men who turned up at Duncan's. Maybe someone else wanted the contents of that envelope.'

He looked at me sceptically. 'Who?'

'Oh, I don't know.' I was fumbling in the dark, sharing my thoughts out loud to try and make sense of them. 'Look, the thugs who grabbed Callum have no qualms about using violence whether they need to or not. We've seen that. The men who went to Duncan's acted very differently, from what he said. Calm and workmanlike. Not in the same vein at all.'

'You could be right, Gemma. If you are, the whole situation becomes a lot more worrying and a lot more confusing. The big question still stands though – how did *anyone* know about the envelope? No-one knew we had it. We've told no one about it. So how did they trace it to Duncan?'

KHALIA: The Jade Skull

Part VII

MADELEINE, 2
(South of France, 1894)

64.

Madeleine drew back the heavy curtains, blinking fiercely in the sudden onslaught of dazzling sunlight. Far away over the rooftops, a deep cobalt Mediterranean sea glittered as if dusted with the splinters of a shattered mirror. Distant shouts and crashes echoed through the still morning air – the clamour of a busy port going about its business. Their ship had docked the previous evening in rough seas and driving rain; this morning the storm had blown itself out and she woke to a different world. She gazed out to the sparkling horizon and smiled. Marseilles. They had made it. They were back in Europe. Not yet England, it was true, but close enough to feel she was home.

While they had been waiting to leave Calcutta, Andrew had received a telegram that changed his plans. Instead of travelling to straight to England, he would head for France for an important meeting with a colleague in Marseilles. Madeleine could have waited for a ship sailing directly for Liverpool as they had originally planned. As soon as she had discovered that Andrew was going to the South of France, however, she had been seized with a powerful compulsion to accompany him. Maybe it was because her grandmother's family were from Avignon, not too far from the famous port. That was where she had received her name; her grandmother had been Madeleine too. The flame red hair and green eyes, on the other hand, were the unmistakeable heritage of her father's Scottish roots.

Whether it was the family links, or whether some other force entirely was influencing her, the compulsion to travel to France had been irresistible. The deciding factor had been that the ship for England did not sail until the following Saturday, over a week away, while that bound for France left the next day. She hadn't wanted to stay in that wretched land one moment longer than necessary. There were too many hideous memories – Paul's illness, the palace. Ju-Lin. Despite the thousand miles between Calcutta and the Emperor's palace, she had still looked over her shoulder a hundred, two hundred times a day, fearing he would have somehow caught up with her. Moreover, even with the detour to Marseilles, she would arrive back in England with barely a couple of days delay. Though she had a deep longing to see her home again, having been away for so long, those few days would make little difference.

* * * * *

The previous evening Andrew had informed her that his meeting was scheduled for ten o'clock the following morning and would last for several hours at least. She badly needed exercise and to find her legs again after weeks of inactivity on board ship so, with the day to herself, she decided to get out and explore, taking care to keep well away from the dock area and waterfront which, as in all ports, was where the less savoury aspects of life were to be found. They had seen the prostitutes and rum-soaked seamen staggering into the dark, menacing alleyways as the carriage drove her and Andrew from the ship to their hotel the previous evening.

She asked the hotel to hire her a cab and trustworthy driver and after lunch she ventured out of the city, east along the coast. Soon the stinking waters and narrow, grimy crime-filled streets of the port were behind them. The sun shone from a sky of the deepest blue and

319

Madeleine was captivated by the magical landscape of steep rugged cliffs and inaccessible rocky coves where glass-clear waters of soft, enticing turquoise lapped gently against the shore. A light scent filled the air, drifting from the shrubs that blossomed freely all year round in this temperate climate. Above, in the infinite sphere of the sky, seabirds shrieked and wheeled in thermal currents created by the cliffs and jagged stone spires that thrust up from the ground, eternal sentinels for the land beyond.

Madeleine called to the driver to stop. Stepping onto the soft green grass, she took a deep, deep breath. The clear air was heavy with the scent of lavender, thyme and rosemary, and for the first time since Paul had become so very ill, she began to feel truly free of the horror of the past long months and of the threat of Ju-Lin's revenge. She filled her lungs with the herb sweet air and found a patch of shaded ground, soft with fallen needles, where she rested with her back against the trunk of a tall pine. She spread out her shawl and leaned back, closing her eyes and letting the warm rays of the sun bathe her face. At last Madeleine was able to relax in a way she had not experienced for so long, her mind clear of all worries.

'Madame.' The cab driver's voice interrupted her peace. 'Il se fait tard. Il faut rentrer.' It took Madeleine a few moments to pick up the meaning of his words, heavily accented with the twang of his patois. *'It's getting late. We must go back now.'* She nodded, climbing reluctantly into the carriage.

The sun had set by the time she arrived back at the hotel. As Andrew had not yet returned she dined in her room and retired early, enjoying the luxurious comforts of the expensive hotel suite. She fell asleep wrapped in the soft embrace of the plump eiderdown and dreaming colourful dreams of sparkling blue sea, craggy cliffs and rocky coves, all bathed in the sweet scent of the Mediterranean countryside. And of wandering the ruins of a long-abandoned castle, or maybe it was a monastery, carrying the green skull in her outstretched hands.

She woke early, rested but troubled. Why had Khalia come into her dreams? The remaining images she could understand after her daytime excursion, but not the skull. She had hardly given it a thought since they had left the hut in the mountains. Although she had been carrying it in her luggage all this time, she had paid so little attention to it that she had virtually forgotten its existence. Not once, since she had left the palace, had she felt the energy that had filled her in the small, circular room.

She had begun to believe she had imagined at all, deceived by her grief and need for comfort. In the safe surroundings of her hotel room, Madeleine laughed at her fancies. Now she was back in a safe land her experiences had taken on the feel of a distant dream – or, more accurately, a nightmare. But nonetheless as imaginary as the fantasies that had come to her in the night. They had been hallucinations, no more, no less. The skull was nothing more than a macabre ancient relic. There was no message, no mission, no hidden meaning. Stone was just stone, no matter what its form. It could not speak, or communicate in any other way. It had no consciousness, no energy, no power. And yet… She had to hold it again. She had to know.

Madeleine rummaged in her trunk. She hadn't even looked at the skull since they had left India, and Khalia was still wrapped securely in the thick woollen shawl she had used to protect it during the voyage. Resting it on her lap – she had forgotten how heavy it was – she let her gaze fall on its sweeping curves. It really was an amazing object. Even her untrained eye could tell that the rich mossy green jade from which it was carved was of a very high quality, in spite of all the chips and scratches. Brushing the crown gently with her fingertips, her doubts melted away in an instant. The skull had come alive in her hands; she could feel its energy vibrating powerfully through her body.

She blinked in surprise. A halo of pearly light had appeared at the crown, growing brighter, expanding until it enveloped the skull. The stone was warm in her hands and a deep vibration, a slow steady pulse, moved through her body until she was aware of nothing else but its heartbeat, matching her own. She was being drawn into the depths of the skull's empty eye sockets. The room no longer existed. The bed no longer existed. Madeleine was back on the cliff top. But it was not the place she had visited the previous day. This was somewhere she had never seen before.

Yes she had. She had been there in her dreams. That night. It was the same ruins, the same rocky promontory jutting out into the sea far below. She had been holding the skull in her hands then too. Looking for….what?

'You must hide me.' It was a command, not a request. 'Those who sought me then hunt me still. Hide me in a place where they cannot find me. There is such a place very near.'

'Where is it? How do I find it? Where do I look?' She felt crazy, speaking to this voice in her head. If anyone heard, she would end her days locked up in an asylum.

'I have shown it to you. Follow where you have been led. Seek it out and hide me there. Hide me well. But take care. Let no-one suspect what you do.'

The voice fell silent and the room came back into focus. In that moment a cloud passed across the sun, plunging the world into shadow. Madeleine shivered. If that was an omen, it was not a good one. She dropped the skull onto the bed as if it was a hot coal.

A light rap on the door interrupted her turbulent confusion. It was Andrew.

'Good morning, Madeleine. I'm sorry, I can't accompany you out and about today. I have yet more meetings to attend. Will you be alright on your own again?'

Madeleine threw a glance at the bed. From the doorway the skull was invisible, tucked into the folds of the bedspread. She turned back to Andrew and nodded.

'Don't worry, I'll be perfectly fine. I'll enjoy a little more exploring.'

Bidding him a good day, she turned her attention back to the skull. It was lying inert and lifeless, showing no indication that it was anything other than a simple curiosity. Carefully Madeleine rewrapped it and stowed it back in the trunk. Leaning back against her headboard, she considered Khalia's message.

The place she had seen in the vision, the place she had *been* in her dream, was so like that which she had visited only the previous day that it had to be on the same stretch of coastline. Very well, she would continue to explore the area until she found it. Even as she contemplated the action, reason argued with her. It was crazy. A whim. Irrational behaviour brought on in a late reaction to the traumatic events she had lived through in China. To do this, just because a bit of stone told her to – it was fantastical nonsense. It made no sense at all. And yet, she would do it. Because underneath all the doubts and logical thinking, some deeper instinct recognised that Khalia was the reason she was safely back in Europe. The skull had saved her life many times. Coincidences had been too fantastic, serendipities too many, for it to have been otherwise. Besides, she reasoned, it would hardly be an unpleasant task. Exploring this beautiful coastline would always be more a delight than a chore.

65.

That day and for the four days following, Madeleine toured the area, sometimes on horseback, sometimes hiring a carriage. She lunched in quaint cafes, or took a simple picnic. Working from the vision in her dream she asked at the hotel lobby about the ruins of any castles in the locality, claiming a keen interest in history and archaeology, and she included that information when planning her excursions. On the third day, heeding Khalia's warning to deflect any possible suspicion, she ventured inland, away from the coastline. It felt unnecessary, she had no reason to suspect that she was in danger, but she wasn't prepared to take any chances. The memory of her experience in China was too vivid.

They were a delightful few days. The weather was on her side, the capricious Mediterranean winter settling down into a sunny, if cool spell, and Madeleine was happier than she had been at any time since Paul had fallen ill. By the evening of the fourth day, however, she was starting to feel a little anxious. She had still not stumbled on the ruins, and in only a few days she would be leaving for England. If she was to hide Khalia here, on this wild coastline, she was running out of time.

It was on the fifth day that she found it. It was a Sunday and for once Andrew had accompanied her, free of commitment for the day. In his company, she ventured some way further along the coast than she'd previously explored, and towards noon, they emerged from a thick forest of pines that reached to the cliff edge and tumbled over it, covering the steep slopes down to the shoreline. They came out of the shadows into the bright sunlight of midday to be met by a jumbled mass of stone that stretched up the hillside where it rose up into crumbling grey walls and towers. Below the ruins, a grassy sward sloped downwards, ending in a sheer drop to the sea, which gently caressed the base of the cliff far below. It was exactly as Khalia had shown her.

Behind and to the landward side the forest closed in around them. This must once have been a magnificent structure; now it was just a crumbling shell, overgrown, tumbledown and forgotten. No sense of its former identity remained. Here and there, what was left of the walls piled up in massive heaps, layering upwards. Further along, towards the cliff, the walls appeared to grow out of the rocky outcrop on which they had been built.

The hair on Madeleine's neck prickled and she shuddered violently. In spite of the sunshine and blue skies, this hillside was overwhelmingly oppressive and disturbing. Now she had found it, all she wanted was to run away. A lingering chill of sorrow, death and suffering pervaded every inch of the ruins, unsoftened by the daylight. Terrible things, unspeakable things, had happened here. She turned and looked out to sea, wanting to break the spell that had trapped her so uncomfortably.

Beyond the cliffs lay different world. Brilliant sunshine caught the ripples of a sapphire blue sea, turning them into glittering diamond points that dazzled the vision. The calm waters were sprinkled with pleasure boats and yachts carrying wealthy tourists who had travelled south to escape the damp grey of a northern European winter. On either side, forests of deep green pine stretched down the vertiginous slopes of the shoreline, cut through here and there by perilously uncertain cart tracks.

'Are you alright?' Paul had come up behind her.

She shivered again. 'No, not really. I don't like this place. Where are we?'

'I think we're about here,' he pointed to a spot on the map, 'I was certain of it but now I'm not so sure. I should be right, only there aren't any ruins showing on here.'

'That's odd. I trust your judgement over the map any time. It must be wrong.' She had total faith in Andrew's navigation skills. Her skin prickled again, more urgently this time. 'Come on. Let's get out of here. This place is giving me a bad feeling.'

'I'm with you there.' Andrew needed no persuasion.

Walking back to the horses, Madeleine threw a glance over her shoulder at the decaying castle. She was going to have to come back here, and next time she would be coming alone. It was not an excursion she was looking forward to. There were only three days left until she boarded the ship to England. She prayed Andrew would be busy with meetings and unable to join her on at least one of those days. She could not refuse his company without difficult – and untruthful – explanations. She wasn't even sure she could lie to Andrew after all he had done for her. And it would have to be sooner rather than later. She wanted the whole affair to be over and done with so that she could return home to her family unburdened. Despite her apprehension, however, not once did it occur to Madeleine to refuse to do as Khalia had asked.

* * * * *

Fortune – or was it Khalia? – continued to bless Madeleine. When they returned to the hotel that evening, they found a message waiting for Andrew. His business contact needed to see him the following day.

'It'll probably be another long drawn out affair,' he apologised. 'I won't be able to come out with you tomorrow after all. Do you mind?'

'Of course not.' Madeleine smiled her understanding while her heart thudded against her ribcage. This was it then. Tomorrow she would return to the ruins with the skull. A creeping chill set the hairs on her neck on end and crawled down her spine. She shuddered involuntarily. Andrew noticed.

'Is everything alright?'

She hurried to reassure him. 'Of course. As my grandmother used to say, someone must have just walked over my grave.'

It was a phrase she regretted as soon as she had uttered it for she had suddenly had the uncomfortable feeling that she was being spied on. Casually she turned her head, glancing around. The hotel's dining room was full of guests busily eating, talking and laughing. No-one was out of place, nothing out of the ordinary caught her attention; nevertheless, the feeling would not go away.

Even after Madeleine returned to her room she couldn't shake off the sensation. Someone had been watching her. Though she had seen nothing suspicious, the conviction remained firm. She couldn't begin to guess who would be interested in her here, so far from the exotic world of the Emperor's palace. No-one here could possible know about the skull. Khalia's words came back: *They seek me still.* Who were they? The question rolled over and over – how could *they* know the skull was here? And, assuming they did know, when would they act? Because she was certain that they would. She would have to take steps to ensure she wasn't being followed before she went anywhere near the ruins.

Madeleine headed for the hotel lobby and booked her usual carriage for the following day, explaining at length that she was heading out to explore countryside in the direction of the picturesque town of Marignane. If anyone was listening, or made enquiries, they would be sent in completely the wrong direction. A few additional whispered instructions to the concierge, and her plan was set.

66.

Madeleine woke full of anxiety and foreboding, pulling back the curtains to a low, grey overcast sky that carried an intermittent drizzle. The weather had caught her mood.

'Let's get this over with,' she told herself sternly. Passing over her prettier dresses – they were too light, neither warm enough for the damp weather nor hardwearing enough for the task that lay ahead – she settled on a practical skirt and jacket in a deep, almost pewter grey, thin woollen fabric, and pulled on her old boots. They were still serviceable, comfortable and sturdy enough to stand up to the potential rigours of the day.

She placed the skull, still wrapped in the shawl, in her satchel, and added a sheaf of good quality sketching paper held inside a thin leather wallet and a packet of charcoal sticks, ensuring that a good part of the wallet protruded from the bag. To all intents and purposes Madeleine was an amateur artist heading out to sketch the local beauty spots. The cab was waiting for her outside the hotel.

'I've changed my mind,' Madeleine told the driver quietly as he helped her in. 'I'd like to head west along the coast road.' He nodded and, with a light flick of the reins, set out along the route that would lead Madeleine to the fulfilment of her mission.

It was still early, and once out of the bustling port the roads were quiet. Madeleine glanced behind frequently to check whether she was being followed; there was never anyone in sight. At the next village, she hailed the driver.

'Drop me here, please, then drive on to the next town. Stay there until you come back here to pick me up at three o'clock this afternoon when I shall return to the hotel. Tell no-one of this change in my plans. You will be paid well for your discretion.'

The driver looked at her, hesitating. He was an honest man and had serious doubts at the wisdom of leaving this captivating woman alone at the roadside.

She smiled her most bewitching smile. 'Please, m'sieur. It is a matter of the heart. I cannot explain more but will you not help a woman who wishes to steal a few hours of happiness with the man who holds her love?'

As she suspected, his Latin spirit was unable to resist her tale of forbidden love. 'Ah oui. L'amour. C'est la perle la plus précieuse du monde. Oui, madame. I will do as you ask. I will keep your secret.'

'Be back here at three o'clock exactly. Don't be late.' She pushed a handful of coins into his palm. 'Enjoy a good lunch and don't drink too much. I'll be waiting for you. And please,' her emerald gaze held him spellbound, 'promise me that you will not tell a soul. My future happiness depends on it.'

'You have my word, madame.' The carriage moved away, leaving Madeleine alone by the side of the track. Impatiently she shook off the fear that settled in her belly. This was no time to waver. By tonight it would all be over and she would be free.

* * * * *

She drew her horse to a stop and slid easily from its back. She had picked up the horse, complete with side-saddle, from a local farm as the concierge had arranged. If anyone came along asking questions there would be nothing to indicate that she was anything other than a respectable English widow venturing out to explore the beauty of the landscape. As usual, however, she was not prepared to ride any distance in such an uncomfortable way and now she was riding bareback again. Once safely away from the village and the curious stares of its inhabitants she had removed the saddle and stowed it safely in the undergrowth, marking its location with a large white rock. Gripping the animal's naked flanks with her thighs, her heels had urged it onwards. With her skirts billowing around her knees and her hair streaming out behind her in the breeze, she had raced across fields and hillsides, through woods and valleys. Despite the unknown dangers that might lie ahead, joy had filled her heart and she had laughed in delight at the wild picture she offered to the rare farmworkers she encountered. Yet again, freedom had embraced her.

She had reached her destination all too soon. The weather had not improved, and if this place had given her the chills in the sunlight, it was infinitely less welcoming in the grey gloom of an overcast day. Abandoned, overgrown, left to rot. Madeleine's bright mood evaporated in an instant. She had slowed to a walk as she came out of the forest onto the grassy expanse and now stood silent and subdued, contemplating the task that lay ahead. Well, delaying would not make the task easier.

'Let's get on with it,' she muttered. Leaving her horse nibbling at the short grass, she strode purposefully towards the nearest of the tumbledown walls.

A jumble of broken rock littered the ground and brambles and straggly trees had grown up in every free space, thickly covering the walls and heaps of shattered stone. Where on earth was she going to find a hiding place amongst all of this? A hole in the wall? Too obvious. Besides, any further collapse could expose it completely. A secret chamber? Too improbable, and just how would she find it anyway? A cave? There were none. The rocky outcrop on which this structure had been built rose solid and unbroken to the sky. Madeleine pushed deeper into the ruins, far beyond where she and Andrew had explored the previous day. It was slow progress. It would be only too easy to turn an ankle on the uneven ground or lose her footing as she clambered over the fallen stonework.

She passed through what had once been an elaborately carved doorway, now nothing more than a crumbling skeleton, and into an open courtyard. Thorn bushes and fragrant shrubs thrust up through ancient paving that was broken and littered with dead leaves and branches. On two of its sides, the walls had crumbled away; the third remained intact, a two-storey cloister whose rear wall was solid bedrock. From the first floor the dead eyes of empty windows stared darkly down like portals to another world. Madeleine couldn't shake off the uneasy impression that they were following her.

She was getting close to her goal. It was a conviction that had come from nowhere and wouldn't leave. Fighting an urge to flee that grew stronger with every minute that passed she picked her way across to the cloister and, with only the slightest hesitation, ducked inside. It was gloomy and uninviting. The dull light of the day barely touched this place.

The long, narrow hallway ran for perhaps forty feet in length and a little less than half that wide. Nothing remained to give a clue as to its former purpose. Madeleine walked slowly, staying in the low light that filtered in from outside, wondering who had lived here and why they had left. She stopped and peered through the gloom where, around a dozen paces ahead in the far rear corner of the hall, a darker shadow stood out against the deep grey of the floor. Scrabbling in her bag, suddenly uncomfortably conscious of the skull it held, she pulled out a candle.

'Is this it, Khalia?' she whispered. 'Is this where I am to leave you?' There was no reply.

A yawning hole several feet across emerged in the candlelight, the faint, flickering glow revealing a narrow stone stairway that spiralled down into the earth. Madeleine's heart sank even further and fear tightened its grip. She took a deep, steadying breath and grasped her courage in both hands. She hadn't come this far to abandon her mission now.

The stairs, hewn from the living stone of the land, twisted down and down. Only a few feet from the top the dressed stone walls of the upper section changed to bedrock. The staircase descended for about fifty steps, opening out into a small room in the centre of which a second sinister circular cavity yawned, this one smaller, only three feet or so in diameter. The room itself appeared to be a natural cave that at some point in its history had been enlarged, and ledges cut into the walls. The central aperture, however, looked entirely man-made, its position and form too regular and too precise to be natural.

Madeleine knelt cautiously at the rim. No stairs led down into this shaft. It was deep, the bottom engulfed in blackness. She picked up a large pebble from the floor and tossed it in. One. Two. Three. Four. She counted to eight before it hit the bottom with a faint dull thud. It had landed on something soft – sand or earth maybe. It had certainly not been the sharp clatter of stone on stone or the splash of water. Perhaps it was an old well, the water that once flowed there long vanished. Really though, it didn't matter. Madeleine could tell by the fluttering in her belly that this was the hiding place she had been searching for.

The candle in her hand sputtered, threatening to go out. No. Not here. Not now. The thought that she might be left in total darkness in this underground cell was terrifying. Quickly she pulled all the candles from the bag – she had brought a dozen – lit them, and jammed them around the room.

She was to hide the skull at the bottom of this shaft. The question was how to get it there safely. She could not simply drop Khalia into the hole. It was too deep. Even with the soft layer at the bottom, the skull would to shatter as it landed. She tipped out the contents of her satchel: Khalia, still wrapped in the thick woollen shawl; the sketch pad and charcoals; a flask of water, some cheese and half a baguette… and a roll of thin twine. Would it be strong enough to take Khalia's weight? It would have to be. She had no other solution. Working quickly, she tied the twine firmly around the shawl and its precious contents.

'Goodbye, Khalia,' she murmured. Tears streamed down her face as she lowered the bundle over the edge. It was quickly swallowed up by the darkness.

The drop went on forever. At least, it felt like it, with the thin twine cutting painfully into her fingers. There was barely three feet to spare when the weight eased. The skull had reached the bottom. Her job was over. She had done as Khalia had asked and hidden her safely. Only… suddenly Madeleine didn't want to let it go. She didn't have to. She was still holding the end of the twine and could easily pull the skull back up again. Khalia had been her constant companion through so many arduous months, had saved her life – and her sanity – on so many occasions. How could she leave it here and walk away?

'Release the twine, Madeleine. Let me go.' Khalia's gentle voice echoed softly, filling Madeleine's mind so that there was no room for other thought. 'Let me go, Madeleine. Let me go.' With a sob, Madeleine opened her hands and let the line fall into the shaft, staring after it into the blackness.

She was wrenched roughly from her desolation. One of the candles spluttered and went out; the others would soon follow. If she didn't hurry, she would be left down here without light. She took a final, sorrowful look at the hole in the floor. It was done, and it couldn't be undone. She had repaid her debt and fulfilled the skull's request. All at once, she felt lighter. With Khalia hidden beyond any chance of discovery, any threat to herself must now have also been removed. She would be safe now too.

* * * * *

The carriage was already waiting at their rendezvous. The driver took in Madeleine's tousled appearance and said nothing, simply smiled knowingly. She didn't care. Let him think what he would; it gave weight to the story she had told him. She sank back into the seat and half dozed throughout the drive back to the hotel.

Her new-found peace of mind didn't last long. No sooner had she stepped down from the carriage at the hotel entrance than the sensation that she was being watched returned, more strongly than ever. This time she did not attempt to hide her actions. She spun rapidly round, scanning the street. There. Movement. Although she could not be certain – he had vanished so quickly – she thought she spotted a stocky, dark-skinned and dark-haired man dart out of sight into an alleyway. The unease that had so recently evaporated wrapped itself back around Madeleine like a shroud.

She forced her lips into a relaxed smile and waved a cheery 'Bonsoir' to the concierge as she entered the hotel. She had to keep acting the part of the innocent tourist.

'Bonsoir, madame. You had a good day sketching?'

'Yes, thank you Albert. In spite of the grey skies this morning. It is a beautiful place.'

Once in her room she locked and bolted the door and threw herself onto the bed, thinking hard. She had been suspicious before. Now she was certain. Someone was spying on her. Maybe it was time to tell Andrew the truth. If she was wrong, and it was just her imagination, there would be little harm done now that Khalia was safely hidden where she would not be found. If she was right, however, as her travelling companion it was likely that he would be pulled into the mess. Whoever was watching her would believe he was her accomplice... She had to warn him.

67.

The opportunity came when she joined Andrew for dinner in the hotel dining room that evening. He was unusually quiet, and when at last he did speak, she very nearly choked on her bouillabaisse.

'I'm being followed.'

'Are you sure?' she managed to sputter at last.

'Completely. I've suspected it for a couple of days but didn't want to worry you until I was certain. This morning I knew I wasn't imagining it.'

'Who is it?'

'That I don't know. I only caught a silhouette against the light. He vanished into an alleyway as I turned around. Not quickly enough though.' He paused for a moment as if considering whether he should continue, then made up his mind. 'I believe there's a connection to the attack on the hut.'

Seeing Madeleine's puzzlement, he explained. 'Before we left the hut, I took a good look at the bodies. You remember that I told you about the tattoo at the base of the throat? Well, in addition to that, each wore a thin plaited thong of black, red and white silk that incorporated a small embossed gold stud woven into in the strands around the left wrist.'

'What's the significance of that?'

'Both the tattoo and the bracelet are the signature of an ancient organisation that has long passed into legend. I've been researching it for years and travelled all over the world searching for traces of it. It's grown to be something of an obsession with me, and it was one of the reasons I was in the mountains. I was following up clues to

338

rumoured ancient strongholds. The cult was widely believed to have died out centuries ago and I had no reason to believe otherwise. Until I saw those bodies, I honestly didn't think it still existed.'

'Does it have a name?'

'Yes, rather a grand one. They call themselves "The Warriors of the Golden Kingdom." The story tells that they have been around for thousands of years, descendants of a powerful and evil force that overthrew the benevolent ruling council of their country. Their ultimate aim was to take control of the entire planet. Only to succeed they had to take possession of thirteen mystical and sacred objects of immense power that contained the life-force and wisdom of the universe. They failed. Somehow the guardians of these treasures were forewarned and spirited them away before the raid. Neither the guardians nor the treasures were ever seen again.

'Within a few years, a series of earthquakes ripped the continent in two. Eventually it slipped beneath the sea and disappeared, whereupon the Warriors scattered to every corner of the globe. Ever since, it is said, they have been searching for those thirteen sacred objects, believing that when they are reunited, the Warriors will fulfil the destiny that is rightly theirs. Legends tell that they have come very close on several occasions, only for the prize to slip through their fingers. There is also an even more fanciful element to the legend that claims that the objects themselves have ensured that this is so.'

He glanced up at Madeleine. 'While I have seen enough strange things in the course of my work to recognise that there is much more to this world than our rational minds can make sense of, I admit to being highly sceptical about that part.'

Madeleine's mind was in a whirl. It all made sense, only… She needed time to collect her thoughts and cover her confusion. 'Are you really an anthropologist?'

Andrew looked at her in surprise. 'Yes. Why? Did you think I was lying?'

She flushed with embarrassment. 'Perhaps. The way you fought and handled your weapons was more like a soldier than a scholar.' She took in the strong physique that his jacket could not disguise. 'You're hardly the fusty old professor.'

He grinned. 'In my field, doing what I do, I have to keep myself fit and, to put it bluntly, battle ready. I spend a lot of time wandering around pretty inhospitable territory and the natives don't always welcome me with open arms.' He steered the conversation back to the Warriors and the attack on the hut.

'Ever since we docked I've been digging for any vital details I may have missed. I was convinced that the cult was extinct. The attack on us appears to prove otherwise. It may be that those men actually were descendants of the original Warriors, although given that the legend talks of them rising up in the 'time before time' it seems highly improbable. It's more likely that at some point in the much more recent past a shrewd bandit chief decided to revive the legend and bring the Warriors back to life, using their reputation to increase his power. Whatever the truth, it seems that the Warriors of the Golden Kingdom are, in some form, very much alive and kicking, at least in the borders and foothills of the Himalayas.'

'How in heaven's name would they have followed us from China to here?'

'I don't know. The original warriors wouldn't have had any problem doing so. Apparently they were spread all over the world, so keeping track of our movements would have been easy for them. On the other hand, I doubt any recent incarnation would be so international. The question that really bothers me is, why us? Did they believe I was on to something? If so, they couldn't be more wrong. I was – am – getting nowhere. Every lead has come to a dead end. No-one I've spoken to, whether in India, China or anywhere else, has admitting knowing anything about them. I can't imagine why they would have followed me back to Europe. What do they think I know?' He drew his hand wearily across his forehead. 'I'm all out of ideas,' he admitted.

Madeleine came to a decision. 'I'm sure someone was watching me too. When I got back to the hotel earlier.' She was hesitant, still unsure how much to tell Andrew.

He looked at her sharply. 'Did you get a good look at him?'

'No. Like you, only a momentary glimpse. Long enough to see that he wasn't Chinese or anything like that. He was quite short and stocky. Swarthy. Like the dockhands.'

She finally voiced the question that had been pressing to be asked. 'These sacred objects, what were they?' Instinctively she already knew. Her mind flew to the green jade skull, lying in blackness at the bottom of a narrow shaft in the bowels of an ancient ruin.

Andrew shrugged. 'That's the biggest mystery of all. The legend doesn't tell us. It refers to them frequently as 'the sacred objects' and 'the sacred gifts' and at one point, in one of the versions I've researched, I found the phrase 'gazing into the eyes of the cosmos'. No more than that. I have a few theories on what it means, but that's all.

'I'm inclined to believe that this legend is the same as every other legend that has even existed; there is a grain of truth in it somewhere. Maybe a secret society called the Warriors of the Golden Kingdom *did* exist centuries ago, and maybe the current group have modelled themselves on that. Over the years, just like a game of Chinese Whispers, a simple, probably unremarkable reality has been built upon and embellished to make it more exciting, until the version we get today bears almost no resemblance to the original.'

'You don't think the story is true, then?'

'No, I don't. Look, there are smatterings of truth in every good tale. That's why those stories draw us in. The rest though is pure fiction, as in this case. The land the Warriors are said to have taken by force doesn't exist and it never has, except in fable. Its name is Atlantis. Which doesn't give any answers as to why we were attacked, or why we are being watched.'

He mistook her deep thought for fear. 'Don't worry, Madeleine. It isn't you they are concerned about, it's me. There is no reason to believe you are in any danger. Once they realise I know nothing of importance, I expect they'll leave me alone.'

'But what if the story is true, Andrew? What if these objects *do* exist and the Warriors are still hunting them down?'

'I told you…' The haunted expression on Madeleine's face brought him up sharply. 'What is it, Madeleine? What's wrong?'

'They aren't after you. They are after me.' She blurted out, no longer in any doubt. The Warriors wanted the skull and they would stop at nothing to get it.

'Why would they be after you?' He gripped her wrist across the table. 'What aren't you telling me, Madeleine?'

She swallowed, remembering her promise to Khalia. Only now the situation had changed. Khalia was safely hidden and couldn't be retrieved; by keeping quiet, she was putting Andrew's life in danger once again. He had a right to know.

'I took something with me when I fled the palace. It was the reason Ju-Lin murdered his father. It... it sounds crazy, but it *asked* me to rescue it. To take it away and hide it somewhere safe, where it wouldn't be found.'

'What was it?' The word came out in a strangled whisper.

'A skull. Not a real one,' she added hastily. 'One made of green jade. I kept it wrapped in a shawl in that ratty old brocade bag I wouldn't let out of my sight. The question is, how did the Warriors know I had it?'

'The question is, why didn't you tell me you had it?' Andrew was barely holding back his anger.

'Because the skull told me not to. I'm sorry, Andrew. I made a promise. I really didn't believe it would put you in danger. I couldn't see how the attack in the hut could have anything to do with it.'

Andrew was stunned. 'I knew you were keeping something from me. I thought you might have taken gold or precious stones. But a jade skull...' In the face of his curiosity and professional interest his anger was dissolving rapidly. He drifted in thought for a few minutes.

'Of course! Yes, it makes perfect sense.' He looked up, excitement lighting up his features. 'I've read the transcript of an ancient text dating from Egypt's Old Kingdom. It speaks of thirteen heads of power, each possessing a different quality and relating to a different

343

field. It was discovered in the basement library of an old scholar in Cairo about twenty years ago. Three years ago, the house burned to the ground. The library, and the transcript along with it, was destroyed. It was my sheer good fortune to have been able to view it before its destruction.

'Now that I think about it, and after what you've just told me, it wouldn't surprise me if this Ju-Lin chap *is* involved in this somehow. He could have learned of the Warriors' search, put two and two together and made a deal to hand the skull over to them when he came to the throne. You know – if I get this for you, you give me even more power and wealth type pact. Because if the legends are true, if the Warriors could unite all thirteen objects – skulls? – they would be unstoppable. Ju-Lin's current supremacy would count for nothing. Joining with them would be his insurance policy of even better things to come.'

'It would explain why he was so desperate to get rid of the Emperor,' Madeleine mused. 'I heard the old man say that he would never hand over the skull over before his death, if ever. Not long afterwards – on the night I ran away – he disinherited Ju-Lin completely.'

'You really must have thrown the cat amongst the pigeons when you took off with it. Ju-Lin wouldn't have been able to follow you beyond the borders of his kingdom. Luckily for him, the Warriors have no such limitations. They'll track you until they can get it back.' He glanced at her sharply. 'Where is it now?'

'Hidden where it will never be found, I hope.'

'Where?'

'I can't tell you, Andrew. Really, I can't. I won't. It may sound like I've gone mad but I gave the skull my word that I would never reveal its hiding place to anyone. Not even you, and I trust you completely. Please, don't ask me again.'

Andrew looked as if he was going to argue, then thought better of it. 'Perhaps you're right. Maybe it is better that I don't know. As much as I want nothing more than to get my hands on that skull, I do recognise the danger in bringing it back out into the world. And not just because of the Warriors. If this is one of the thirteen sacred treasures, then it's concrete proof of the truth of an ancient legend. I'm not sure that the world we live in is ready to deal with the implications of the legend becoming reality. I wonder if it ever will be. It would turn history – and religion – upside down. The repercussions could be devastating. No, perhaps it's best to let the legend remain just that – a legend.

'I'd like to take you to see an old friend and colleague of mine, a Monsieur Descrinault. He knows all there is to know about the legend of Atlantis and the Warriors of the Golden Kingdom. That's where I've been for the last few days – discussing theories with him and digging into his research. What you've just told me changes everything. I want him to hear your story in your own words.'

When Madeleine nodded her agreement, Andrew excused himself and headed for the hotel lobby to send a message to M. Descrinault. The reply, received less than an hour later, was an invitation for the two of them to lunch with him the following day.

Later, when Madeleine rose to retire to her room. Andrew's hand on her arm held her back. 'Keep your doors and windows locked,' he warned. 'Don't let anyone in. I don't honestly think you'll be in any danger while you're in the hotel. It would be too risky, and they don't need to take unnecessary chances. But better safe than sorry. When we leave for M. Descrinault's tomorrow, make it look as if you are carrying the skull in your bag.'

He became deadly serious. 'These people don't mess around, Madeleine. They are not nice to know. If they believe you have hidden the skull somewhere they will try to find out where and they won't be squeamish in forcing you to tell them by any means necessary…'

Icy fingers gripped her spine. She understood his meaning only too well.

68.

At exactly ten to eleven the next morning, they left the hotel. A familiar prickle stood the fine hairs at the base of Madeleine's neck on end; without looking, she could sense they were being watched. Andrew nodded imperceptibly. He had noticed it as well. He gave her hand a reassuring squeeze as he helped her up into the carriage.

It was only a short ride to M. Descrinault's home and they arrived in plenty of time. When they rang the doorbell, however, his flustered housekeeper informed them that he wasn't there.

'He sends his deepest apologies,' she told them, 'but he was summoned to an urgent meeting at the university only half an hour ago. To do with his work, I think.' She knew Andrew from his frequent recent visits. 'I don't know more, other than that he was very angry and upset when he left the house. He asked if you would meet him there, M. Mountjoy. He said he would be grateful for a friend at his shoulder.'

Madeleine and Andrew climbed back into the cab, which was still standing at the kerb, and set out for the university. Andrew was silent, lost in thought, and Madeleine had no wish to disturb him so she sat back and watched the city pass by.

They arrived to find that the meeting was already underway and a doorman barring their way, apologetic but firm. Andrew could enter. Madeleine would not be allowed to do so.

'Women,' the doorman explained, 'are not permitted to attend these academic meetings.'

Despite their explanations and efforts he would not yield, always courteous, always unmoving. 'Monsieur Mountjoy, le docteur Descrineaux awaits you in the lecture hall. I regret that the lady must wait here.'

She turned to Andrew. 'Your friend needs your support. Go on. I'll return to the hotel.'

Andrew looked worried. 'Why not wait for me here?'

'Because you may be a very long time and I have no desire to sit around in these gloomy halls for hours.'

'Be careful, Madeleine.' He sounded extremely concerned for her safety, and equally certain she would not be swayed from her decision. 'Keep your wits about you. I'll call on you when I return.' With that, the doorman ushered him into the meeting room, leaving Madeleine staring at the polished wood of a closed door.

Slowly she turned and walked back into the daylight. It was another glorious day. Settling into a cab with the autumn sunlight gently bathing her face as it carried her through the wide light-drenched boulevards and parklands of the city's most fashionable and prosperous quarters, her thoughts wandered through the series of crazy and unimaginable events that had overtaken her in the last few months. Could it all really be over at last?

A sudden jolt jarred her roughly back into the present. The cab had come to a sudden halt, its passage blocked by a large crowd that filled the street.

'What's happening?' she called.

'I will find out, Madame. One moment.' The driver quickly returned. 'It is an accident. A horse was startled by a loud noise and it bolted with its carriage. It crashed into coal cart and overturned. It is not pleasant, Madame, and I think it will be a while before the way is clear.'

'Is there another route?'

'Yes, but it means a very long detour. This carriage won't be able to negotiate the side streets here. They are too narrow.'

Madeleine considered her position. She didn't want to wait around in the cab for the street to be cleared. Who knew how long that might take? Nor was the prospect of a long carriage drive over rough streets particularly enticing.

'How far on foot to the Hotel Millefiore?' she called.

'About twenty minutes along the main thoroughfares. Shorter if you take the alleyways, though I would not advise it.'

Surely she would be safe enough in these open, sun-drenched streets filled with wealthy Marseillais shopping and socialising. She made up her mind.

'Thank you. I shall walk from here and enjoy the fresh air and exercise.'

'You are sure, Madame?'

'Quite sure, thank you.'

The directions the cab driver gave her were simple, and despite a nagging doubt over the wisdom of her decision, Madeleine set off with a lightness in her step. Since leaving the hotel there had been no indication that they had been followed, no hint of danger. It would be pleasant to wander through the town on such a fine day. Little by little, her lingering anxiety evaporated in the sunshine and gentle breeze.

She skirted the site of the accident. Through the gathered crowd she could just see a woman and two men lying on the cobbles, surrounded by those who had rushed to help. Nearby lay the body of a horse, unmoving, one leg twisted awkwardly under its body. She turned her gaze away, not wishing to spoil the good mood that was taking her over.

She had not walked more than a few hundred yards, however, when an all-too-familiar sensation prickled at the nape of her neck. She spun around, her heart thumping; no-one suspicious stood out among the passers-by who strolled along this boulevard. Was her imagination working overtime, or was her sixth sense warning her of a very real danger? She picked up her pace a little, reproaching herself for having abandoned the relative safety of the cab. She had to get back to the hotel where she could wait for Andrew behind her locked and bolted door.

It was lunchtime and the avenues were busy. Everywhere she looked people were heading out to eat in the numerous small restaurants that lined these streets, or pausing to browse the windows of the upmarket stores that interspersed them. After several surreptitious glances behind, or in the mirror of a store front window, Madeleine's nerves calmed. No shadows stepped hastily into doorways. No-one turned too quickly to study a window display or menu.

Only seconds later she realised that she had let down her guard too soon. A little more than twenty-five yards in front of her a man stood motionless in the centre of the pavement. He was short, dark and stocky – the man she had caught a glimpse of outside the hotel? – and he was looking straight at her. Not blinking. No expression. Just staring at her. Holding her gaze with an arrogance and inevitability that chilled her to the bone. Then he smiled, and the chill turned to ice. There was no warmth, no amusement in that smile, simply the satisfaction of a spider who has its prey trapped firmly in its web. The blood drained from her face and she swayed for a moment, her heart beating an unwelcome tattoo against her ribs, before she regained her self-control. She spun around, ready to run. It was no use. A second man, this one with Asian features, waited there effectively blocking any escape in that direction.

Desperately Madeleine searched the avenue for a way out. There. To her left, and only a pace or two further on, a narrow opening between two buildings beckoned. She had no idea where it led, only that it was away from her enemies. Lifting her skirts, she darted into the gap, running as fast as she could through the maze of narrow, twisting alleyways. She only slowed, gasping for breath, when she could run no further. No footsteps echoed behind her. Had she shaken off her pursuers?

The street, if it could merit the name, was dark and dingy. More of a narrow corridor between adjacent buildings than even an alleyway, the light did not reach down here. Nor, by the stench, did any cleansing breeze. As in so many cities, this was the underbelly that existed just beyond the glitz and wealth of the avenues, boulevards and fountain-embellished squares. The smell of the sea pervaded everywhere; not the fresh, invigorating scent of the open ocean, but the rank fish and oil odour of the quayside, mingling with that of the effluent and rotting rubbish that was piled up against the filthy walls.

Madeleine felt curious, suspicious yet invisible eyes peering at her through the grime-thick windows and crumbling doorways. She was completely out of place here in her fashionable butter yellow dress dotted with embroidered blue forget-me-knots – an intruder, trespassing in an alien world. Yet despite feeling uncomfortable and unwelcome, it wasn't these surroundings that frightened her. That fear was reserved for the two men who had chased her into this labyrinth.

Again she looked behind. Again, there was no sign of pursuit. She could only hope that she had lost them in the tangle of passageways and alleys. All she had to do now was find her way back to the main thoroughfare, and from there to the hotel and the sanctuary of her room.

69.

Madeleine barely felt the slender blade pierce her skin and slide upwards through her ribs to her heart. Only at that final moment did she become aware of a split second of burning pain that burst into her consciousness and vanished just as quickly as she plunged into black oblivion. Someone screamed as the young woman slumped lifeless to the filthy ground, the slim ivory hilt of the knife embedded in her back incongruous and obscene in the sunlit afternoon, a crimson stain already spreading over the bodice of her light cotton dress.

The two men who had been following her melted away. No-one had paid any attention to them; they had been indistinguishable from the other sailors and dockworkers who frequented the area. And no-one had seen them go. It was as if they had never existed. With them they took the heavy, well-worn, brocade bag Madeleine had been carrying. No-one had noticed that either, or that in the moment that the young woman fell, one of these men had skilfully scooped it from her already lifeless fingers in a sleight of hand that would have delighted the most adept and experienced of pickpockets.

A crowd was gathering around Madeleine's body, lying lifeless in the squalor of the gutter. Two street whores – their faces haggard and world-weary beneath the paint – knelt at her side. Hearts, hardened by the brutality of life in this underworld, softened as they tried to help this beautiful young woman who had been attacked in front of their eyes. It was too late. Their efforts were in vain. Nothing could be done. Nothing could ever have been done. The assault had been skilful and polished, and its outcome had never been in any doubt. Madeleine had been dead from the moment the knife entered her body.

The growing mass of onlookers were strangely quiet, stunned by what had just taken place, for while violent death was nothing unusual on these streets, murder here was invariably the result of a fight or argument. It rarely came in such a stealthy way or to such a well-born victim. This silent, invisible assassination was something else, unsettling in its clinical execution. As unusual as its victim. The woman on the ground was not from these ghettos. She was a stranger: young, well-dressed and soft-skinned with hair like beaten copper. Who was she and what had she been doing roaming these alleyways? Strong hands gently lifted Madeleine's body and carried it into a house to await the arrival of the authorities.

GEMMA, 6

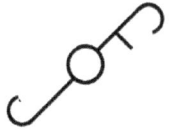

70.

Joe squeezed my hand. 'Are you OK?'

I pulled a face. 'I can think of a lot of better ways of spending a sunny afternoon than at a crematorium, if that's what you mean. But yes,' I squeezed his hand back, 'I'm OK. Thank you.'

We were in Callum's home town of Newbury for his funeral. It was a lovely late summer afternoon but I couldn't appreciate the beauty of the day. The warm sun and clear blue skies were so out of step with the horrific events that had brought us here. Resolutely I hauled my thoughts away from those events and back to the present.

'Gemma.' A very American voice was calling to me. Frankie! I spun around, searching for her. She was waving at me from across the car park. Her long legs covered the space between us in seconds and I hugged her tightly.

'Oh, Gemma. It's so good to see you. I only wish the circumstances were different.' Tears sparkled on her lashes. 'Callum was often a first class pain in the butt but I was still fond of him.'

She let me go and thrust out her hand to Joe. 'Hi, you must be Joe. Good to meet you.' I smiled in spite of myself. Joe had been rendered speechless, dazzled by Frankie's film star looks.

'Davey's here somewhere...' She looked around for him. 'Over there. Talking to the short, bald guy.' Davey flung his hand up in greeting. 'We flew in from Colorado last night. We've been working on some First Nations sites out there that are throwing out a lot of unusual finds.' She changed the subject. 'Had Callum found what happened to Jack?'

Jack's disappearance during our Arizona expedition remained a mystery to everyone except me. And much as I wanted to, I couldn't tell what I knew. Not yet.

'No. We're pretty sure he was murdered because he had got too close to something, if he hadn't already found it, only we have no idea what it was because he wouldn't tell us. Now we'll never know. As usual, he was playing his cards really close. Whatever he found died with him.'

I thought of the envelope we had found in King Street. Would its contents have taken us closer to finding an answer? There was no point in dwelling on that or in telling Frankie about it. It was gone, and that was the end of it.

'That's a pity. It might have laid a few mysteries to rest. I do have something important to tell you though. I bumped into Ches Whitecloud a couple of weeks ago when I was down in Sedona. You remember him?'

How could I forget Ches, our native American guide in Arizona? I had always been convinced that he too knew more about Jack's disappearance than he was letting on.

'He gave me an intriguing message,' she continued. 'Said it was for all of us but I think it was mostly for you. You'll see why when you hear it. I was going to email it, then all this business with Callum blew up so I decided to wait until I saw you.'

'What was it?'

'Hold on. I wrote it down.' She fumbled in her bag. 'Here it is.' She pulled out a well-worn notebook and began to read. '*The thirteen sacred voices are preparing to return. They are ready to be heard by the world.*'

Thirteen sacred voices? Was Ches talking about the thirteen Skulls of the Light? A powerful electric tingle ran up and down my spine. Yes. That's exactly what he meant.

Frankie winked. She understood. So did Joe, standing beside me. I could feel him tense with excitement.

'There's more. Listen. *The Voices will choose their new guardians, as they have throughout time, and will reveal themselves only to those guardians who will hold them in secrecy and safekeeping until the hour comes when they emerge once more into the world.*

'*This hour may be many years in the future, or it may be tomorrow. Everything depends on how humankind assumes its responsibility. In the meantime, with their guardians, the Voices will be working to build a new Atlantis on Earth, bringing in lasting era of peace and harmony where profit and power give way to the wellbeing of humankind and the natural world, and where co-operation and compassion take the place of competition and self-interest.*'

'The prophecy of Atlantis.' Joe was all but bouncing up and down, the solemnity of the occasion momentarily forgotten.

I had no chance to reply. The hearse bearing Callum's coffin had just pulled up, reminding us why we were there. Our excitement faded as quickly as it had arisen and we filed silently behind the dark wood box into the chapel room. It was a small turn-out. Other than Frankie and Davey, Joe and I, I saw DI Chamberlain with a female colleague – to be expected, I suppose – and a handful of academic friends. All of them mavericks in their own fields, so Frankie whispered in my ear, who weren't afraid to be associated with Callum's controversial and often outspoken theories. Sitting apart from everyone else, and standing out like the proverbial sore thumb, was a tall, considerably overweight man with blond hair and a receding hairline. He wore round, wire-rimmed spectacles and a dark grey suit that had seen better days. I didn't see him speak to anyone, and he didn't appear to know any of the other mourners.

It was a short service, and sad in so many ways. Frankie gave a short and heartfelt eulogy. The second, from one of the academics, was much less warm and personal. Callum, it seemed, had no close family and few close friends. As I watched the coffin disappear behind the curtains, I was carried back to that night in the Arizona desert. This afternoon, for the first time, it felt distant and unreal. I was remembering another Callum and another, very different Gemma, in another time and place. So much had happened since then. Grief flooded me and the tears flowed. For Callum, yes, and a life cut short, but also for that innocent, naïve woman who events had stolen from me in the months since then.

I was glad to get back outside, away from the stifling heat of the chapel. Breathing in the fresh air, once more the contradictions hit me. The day was filled with sunlight, and heavy with the fragrance of the roses, honeysuckle and lavender that bloomed in profusion in the crematorium's gardens. Meanwhile, inside, only a few yards from where we stood, the flames were already devouring Callum's broken body.

'Gemma?' Frankie's west coast drawl broke through my melancholy. 'Davey and I have to go. You will let us know if you find out anything?'

'You're leaving already?' I had been looking forward to catching up on news with her and Davey, and introducing them properly to Joe.

'Sadly, yes. I'm really sorry, Gemma. We'd love to stay but we have to be back in the States tomorrow for an important conference in Utah.'

I hugged her warmly, Davey too. It was good to see them again, even for such a brief time and in such unpleasant circumstances. 'I'll keep you posted,' I promised.

'Take note of the message, Gemma. It's really important for you.' Frankie climbed into the taxi after Davey, waving goodbye as the car disappeared out of the gate.

Joe's arm encircled my shoulders. 'It's been one hell of a day. How about lunch? A very late lunch,' he suggested. The clock on a nearby church tower was showing nearly four o'clock.

'Yes please.' I wasn't ready to head home just yet. I needed to time breathe and take on board the full significance of Ches' message. Besides, I was ravenous, not having eaten since breakfast.

'Come on, then.' He gave my shoulders a squeeze. 'There's a lovely little pub a little way up the road that does great food all day.'

* * * * *

'What's that?' I was hanging my jacket over the back of a chair when Joe noticed a small square of yellow notepaper flutter from it to the floor. He picked it up. 'It's addressed to you.'

I took it from him, puzzled. 'Where did that come from? I'm certain there was nothing in my pockets this morning.' The paper carried several lines of neat handwriting. I read them out loud: *'Dear Mrs Mason. I have read your books with great interest and understand the truth behind the fiction. I have discovered the black skull's location. Please call me as soon as you have read this. I am nearby.'* A mobile phone number followed.

360

I let the note drop from my fingers. Joe was staring at me in disbelief.

'Do you think it's for real?' he forced out at last.

'Only one way to find out, I suppose.' I pulled out my phone and tapped in the numbers. It connected but there was no answer. 'Great. Just what I need right now. Someone trying to be funny.' I picked up my drink.

'I'm not so sure.' Joe was peering over my shoulder with an odd expression. 'Look.'

I turned, curious. Making his way towards us through the tables was the plump, blond-haired man who had been at Callum's funeral.

'Pieter de Broek,' he announced by way of introduction, keeping his voice low and staring around anxiously. He stuck out his hand to shake mine. 'I'm very pleased to meet you, Mrs Mason. I find your books inspiring and extremely interesting. Particularly knowing what I know.'

'You've found the black skull?' Excitement, mingled with a considerable level of incredulity, hijacked all thought of good manners.

'Not exactly. However, I am certain that I have pinpointed its whereabouts.' He glanced around constantly, like an antelope keeping watch for a predator that would strike out of nowhere even though, this late in the afternoon, there were few other customers in the pub.

'Where is it?' My mouth was dry. The intensity in Pieter's words eliminated any suspicion that he was duping us. If nothing else, he believed totally in his claim.

'I can't talk now, not here. It's too public.' I stared at the empty tables. 'Take my word for it, Mrs Mason. They have eyes and ears everywhere as your friend Callum found out to his cost. I have your number,' he nodded at

361

the phone in his hand. 'I will call you tomorrow with a safer place to meet.' With that, he turned on his heels and hurried out of the bar, leaving Joe and I staring open-mouthed in his wake.

'If he *has* found it...' Joe began.

'If.' I was determined to stay sceptical until Pieter de Broek convinced me otherwise. Still, I couldn't stop a wide grin from pinning itself onto my face. 'But if he *has*...'

It was some time before Joe and I stopped speculating long enough to return to the car and start the journey home. Ches Whitecloud's message had, for now at least, been completely forgotten.

71.

'We're being tailed.' Joe was staring hard in the rear view mirror. 'They've been with us for around twenty miles. Gemma! Don't...'

His warning came too late. My instinctive reaction had been to twist around and peer back down the road. Fortunately dusk was falling, the light fading, so it was unlikely that whoever might have been following us would have seen me looking.

I turned back, doubtful. 'Are you sure? There are at least four cars right behind us and a whole stream of them a bit further back again.'

'I'm sure. The dark-coloured Range Rover two back. It came up behind us at the traffic lights in Faringdon and it's been with us ever since.'

'That doesn't mean anything. This is the A4. It's always busy, especially this time on a Friday evening. What makes you think it's interested in us?'

Joe gave a brief shake of his head, his eyes flashing to the mirror once more. 'Gut instinct?' I was still dubious. 'Trust me on this, Gemma. What you say makes sense, but I've got a hard knot in the pit of my stomach that tells me otherwise. Besides,' he hesitated, as if uncertain whether to go on, 'that Range Rover is exactly like the one that pulled up outside the house in King Street.'

The blood drained from my face. 'Are you sure?'

'Totally sure? No. Sure enough to be worried? Yes.'

It couldn't be the same one. Joe had to be mistaken. As much as I trusted his instincts, it seemed just too unlikely. How could they be following us? They couldn't have seen us. Hadn't known we were there. What's more, Joe and I had gone out of our way to do nothing to raise suspicion since we had returned home.

On the other hand, someone had found out that Duncan was in possession of Callum's envelope and its contents, and had taken it from him by force. Reluctantly I forced myself to consider the possibility that Joe was right. It wasn't reassuring. If this really was the Range Rover that he had seen in Guildford, then we were being tailed by the same men who had beaten Callum to death and dropped him in the canal.

I glanced across at Joe. 'What now?'

'Let's see if I'm right.'

'What do you mean? What are you going to do?'

By way of response he swung the steering wheel hard to the left. The tyres squealed as the big car shot into a side road without signalling. I could hear the furious horn and protesting brakes of the van behind us as its driver slowed sharply to avoid the unexpected manoeuvre.

'We'll take a detour through the back lanes. If he is following us, it'll soon become obvious. I've no intention of heading home until we've lost him.'

To my dismay, within a few seconds our tail reappeared in the mirror.

Joe grimaced. 'Looks like I was right. You do not know how much I wish I wasn't!'

At the next junction we turned left again into a single track road. The Range Rover was still with us, now only about twenty metres or so back. It had had no choice but to close up considerably to avoid losing sight of us on these winding roads. For several miles we twisted and turned through the narrow lanes, taking junctions and crossroads without warning. Fortunately we met very little other traffic. The big 4 x 4 was still with us, sticking even closer now. I turned and peered hard at its windscreen but its powerful headlights, which had been switched on to full beam in the falling light, shielded any view of the driver and any passengers. Why was he still with us? It was obvious we had been on to him, ever since we had turned off the A4.

'What the hell do they want?' I was thinking out loud, not really expecting Joe to answer.

'I haven't a clue. To be honest I don't want to find out. If he's still following us, this isn't some cloak and dagger surveillance. He doesn't care that we've seen him, and that scares me.' The powerful V12 engine growled as Joe stepped on the accelerator.

'What are you doing?'

'Losing them if I can. Or at least, getting them to show their hand. I'm fed up with this.'

'Joe…' He wasn't listening. The engine roared as he dropped a gear and the Mercedes surged forward. I gripped the seat, my heart in my mouth. Up until now, we had been travelling at a fast but just about manageable speed for these roads, merely monitoring the Range Rover behind us. Now Joe was throwing all caution to the wind. I fully expected us to slam into an oncoming vehicle every time we hurtled around a bend. Joe drove skilfully but he was no expert. With a sinking heart, I realised that the driver of the Range Rover was. Effortlessly it was gaining on us. We had called our pursuer's bluff and, it seemed, had lost.

'Hang on,' he muttered.

'What?' A split second later I was flung violently forward, saved from smashing my face into the dashboard only by the seatbelt. My teeth rattled in my head. 'What the…?'

365

The tyres beneath us screeched like raging banshees as the car skidded across the road, Joe fighting to regain control.

'The bastards rammed us.' His knuckles were white on the wheel, his eyes darting between the rear view mirror and the road ahead. 'Hold tight. They're coming back for another go.' I braced myself.

For a second time, the Range Rover's front bars collided with the Merc's back end. Joe spun the wheel desperately, trying to keep the car out of the ditch and the thick hedge that lined the lane. This time, I shrieked out loud. I am a forty nine year old author, divorcee and mother, not Lara Croft, and I was terrified.

An equally frightened yell from Joe echoed my own. Closely followed by a 'Fucking maniacs,' uttered through his clenched teeth. 'They want to run us off the road.'

I glanced back. The 4 x 4 was lining up for another run. 'Joe…' I could hear the panic building in my voice.

'I know. Hold on.'

As if I wasn't already! The car leaped forward like a rocket. Fear, adrenalin and his natural survival instincts had annihilated the last remnants of Joe's caution and honed his reactions scalpel sharp. We hurtled around each bend, avoiding disaster more by blind luck than his driving skills. From what little I saw! Most of the time I had my eyes clamped shut as I fought to keep down the dinner that was highly likely to come back up from the constant wild swerving and lurching. Joe was driving like a man possessed. More than that, he was driving for our lives.

'Joe. Crossroads!' I had blinked open my eyelids for a second just as the warning sign flashed past. 'We're coming up to a main r…'

My shout came too late. We were on the junction and across it before he could touch the brakes. Not that it would have made much difference. The speed we were travelling, we would never have stopped in time. It was nothing short of a miracle that we made it unscathed through the stream of vehicles crossing our path, but make it across we did and into the minor road opposite, the rear of the car fishtailing madly as we plunged through the traffic. Joe had his foot pressed to the floor, aware that if he slowed we would slam into the fast-moving stream of cars and lorries. Aware too of the vehicle right on our tail. His knuckles were clenched in a death grip on the wheel, his face a mask to match.

I know it's a cliché to say that time stood still, but that is exactly what happened. It felt like an age passed. In reality, it could only have been a second or two. Behind us, tortured brakes shrieked and wailed as too much was asked of them too quickly. Suddenly their gut-wrenching howl was cut off, overtaken by a thunderous crash and the ghastly scream of tearing, dragging metal.

Joe did slow then, the horror that had unfolded in his mirror pulling his foot from the accelerator and draining any remaining colour from his skin.

'Oh my God,' he whispered. His eyes were blank, empty.

I turned to look back. 'Oh God, no,' I echoed. A forty foot articulated lorry was sprawled at an angle across the main road, its trailer jack-knifed. Wedged under the trailer, barely recognisable, was the Range Rover, crumpled and crushed into a mass of mangled, distorted wreckage. Brakes squealed and metal banged still as approaching traffic screeched to a halt.

I dragged my gaze away from the carnage to stare unseeing at the road ahead, swallowing down the nausea that threatened to spill out over Duncan's plush carpets and soft leather seats. This was a dream. A bloody awful one, but a dream nonetheless. It had to be. I would wake up in a minute and see the morning sunlight filtering in through my bedroom window. Except that this wasn't a dream and I wasn't going to wake up from it. This was brutally, sickeningly real.

'We have to get out of here,' Joe muttered, stamping down hard on the accelerator.

We fled. Our only thought in that moment was to leave the carnage behind. To get as far away as possible as quickly as possible.

It was another ten miles before Joe pulled off the road into a deserted picnic area and killed the engine. Silence settled around us. Neither of us spoke. We had no words. Joe's hands were still in a death grip on the steering wheel, his whole body trembling violently as he finally allowed reaction to claim him. I was in no better state, shaking so much my teeth rattled. Our faces, reflected in the windscreen, were grotesque – expressionless, colourless death masks with hollow, blank eyes.

After a very long time, Joe opened the car door and walked slowly to the edge of the woods that surrounded the car park. He stared blindly into the darkness.

'I killed him,' he whispered. 'I killed him.' He sank to his knees, a rasping sob escaping his lips. I heard a second, louder and harsher. It was a moment or two before I realised that this one had come from me.

All the pent up tension, fear and adrenalin released itself in a flood of unstoppable, necessary tears. I knelt beside Joe, put my arms around his neck and held him tightly as he wept, seeking to comfort him and needing in return the reassurance of his closeness, to know that I was safe. To know that he was safe – Joe, my rock, my safe harbour. By some miracle we had cheated death, perhaps by mere inches, and it was all because of me. Because of the skulls and all that came with them and because, in agreeing to tell their stories, I had also agreed, however tacitly, to take on this madness. What had started out as an innocent writing process was rapidly turning into a horror story worthy of Stephen King.

Once more, Gal-Athiel's message drifted into my thoughts. *'You, and those who walk with you, will be challenged again and again. Again and again, you will want to give up, yet you will not do so. Even now, when your head tells you No, your soul is saying Yes. You will find the courage to go on, and in doing so, you will prevail.'*

She was wrong. I had no courage left. I'd had enough. I wanted to get off this crazy ride into hell. Only I couldn't. It was going too fast.

GEMMA
Postscript

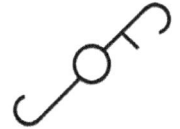

72.

I knew this place. I had been here before, only then it had been a clear, bright day. The sun-drenched paths of white marble chippings had glistened in the light, and the hum of insects had filled the warm, still air as they moved busily through the profusion of colourful flowers that perfumed these gardens, each bloom glowing as if lit up from inside.

This time, by contrast, a steady rain plastered the hair to my scalp and trickled down my neck. Under the wet, leaden skies the paths were soil-splashed and puddled, the gardens empty of bees and butterflies. Previously vibrant blooms hung waterlogged and drooping to the ground. The only sound was the relentless patter of raindrops. Even the fountains were quiet.

I was back in the gardens of the Pyramid Temple. I was back in Atlantis. Why had I been brought here? The other times – it had happened twice now – I had stayed for only a very short while before I woke up in my own bed. Would it be the same today?

I glanced down at my body. Just as on the previous two occasions, while on the inside I was definitely Gemma, outwardly I most certainly was not. Beneath a light, oiled cloak that was no doubt designed to keep me dry in this downpour – and failing completely – I wore an ankle-length white robe edged with blue and gold. Slender, delicate feet, totally unlike my 'real' size sevens, were pushed into sodden sandals. Equally slender hands with long graceful fingers held the waterproof cloak tightly closed. No, this slim, almost fragile, woman was *not* the one reflected back to me in the mirror every morning.

'Haanu.' I jumped at the sound of a male voice and turning, I saw a tall, stooped man with a bald head. I recognised him immediately; I had seen him enough times in the skull visions. This was Omar, the Temple's High Priest. He was watching me with concern.

'Haanu, are you unwell?'

'N-no…No, Omar. I am very well, thank you.' I prayed I was addressing him correctly, anxious not to arouse his curiosity or worse, suspicion.

He peered closely at me for a minute or so, then nodded as if satisfied. 'Where is Regus?'

'Who?'

Another puzzled stare. 'Regus. Your husband.'

'My apologies, Omar. My thoughts were a long way away. Um…' I was stalling, buying time to think. 'I don't know. He must have been delayed.' I was trembling from a combination of fear and incredulity – I was actually having a conversation with one of the characters from my stories. I was either dreaming, going mad… or there was something far weirder going on with the skulls than I could ever have imagined.

'These are difficult times, Haanu, but we must stay focussed on the task that lies ahead of us. We cannot allow ourselves to be distracted by our fears.'

'Here he comes.' A second man, smaller and younger than Omar, stepped into view from behind the High Priest, waving his hand in the direction of the pathway where a figure I assumed to be Regus had just walked through the gate.

Joe. It was Joe. Only…. how could I even think that? The man walking towards us was nothing like him. This man was tall – around six feet six I'd guess, against Joe's five feet ten – and much broader in the shoulders, with a thick mane of dark chestnut hair that fell several inches below his collar and a neatly trimmed full beard and moustache to match. Joe's hair was sandy blond and he'd been clean-shaven all the time I'd known him. And yet it *was* Joe. Memories buried deep within me recognised him and suddenly, I understood. Just as I wasn't in the body I knew so well, nor was Joe. This was a different time and a different place.

I'd seen this chestnut-haired man here before. The last time. He had walked with me through these courtyards and gardens. I hadn't seen his face on that visit, although I remembered that for a split second I had thought I'd seen Joe in him, so fleetingly that I'd immediately dismissed it as imagination. This time I couldn't. Every time I looked at him there was Joe looking back at me through those coal-dark eyes. More disconcerting still, with every glance a powerful wave of love pulsed through me.

'You are late, Regus. We do not have much time.' Omar's reprimand brought me back down to earth.

'I am sorry, Omar. I was delayed and could not get away without causing suspicion. Hello, my love.' This to me as he kissed me fully on the lips. If his arm hadn't been holding me tightly around my waist, I would have found myself sitting on the floor because the surge of love intensified so strongly that my knees buckled. He looked at me anxiously. 'Are you unwell, beloved?'

I shook my head vehemently. 'I am absolutely fine.'

'Regus, Haanu, please.' Omar was hovering impatiently. I attempted to ignore Regus' arm, which was still around my waist, and the sensations it was creating in my body, to concentrate on what the tall priest was saying.

'Our time is short. The Shadow Chasers are preparing to make their move.'

'Is there nothing we can do to stop it?' The small man, who I thought I remembered was called Oolan, wrung his hands in despair.

'Nothing. It is too late. I hoped our words of warning would be heard but they have fallen on deaf ears. The people will not stand against this dark tide. Their belief in the inevitability of what is to come is too strong, and they are too afraid.'

'Then it will be as it was foretold.' Regus' grip on my waist tightened as he spoke.

'It will, although it has come upon us earlier than expected. We cannot fight without the support of the people. We cannot win this war. We can however win the most crucial battle, the battle for the Skulls of Light. Our energies must now be directed in ensuring the Shadow Chasers do not succeed in that ambition. If we can do nothing else, we must ensure the safety of the Skulls. You are all fully conversant with the plan.' I tried hard to look as if I knew exactly what he was talking about.

'Are the replicas ready?' Regus had let me go and was pacing up and down, stone crunching under his feet.

'Ready enough,' Oolan put in. 'They have to be. We have run out of time.'

Omar's expression was grave. 'I do not need to tell you how important this is to the future of this world. No-one must discover what we are doing.

'I will go to the Skull Chamber tonight and speak with the Skulls, requesting the names of their chosen guardians. That responsibility is out of our hands, I am happy to say. The Skulls will choose wisely. Two days from now, we will summon those new guardians and tell them of their mission. Within five days, the Skulls will be gone and all that will be left for us to do is pray.' He turned on his heels and disappeared around the corner, Oolan following closely behind.

'This is it, my love. This…' Regus gestured to the sloping form of the Pyramid Temple that rose up on the far side of the gardens. 'It is over. Our fate is set.'

His arms went around me, drawing me close to his chest. I could smell his masculinity through his wet tunic; his familiar and oh so comforting scent set my belly on fire. He kissed me, full and hard, and the deep love I was already feeling for him exploded into an emotion beyond anything I have ever felt before. I kissed him back, passionately, not wanting to let him go, not wanting those hungry lips ever to leave mine.

All at once I was no longer kissing a tall, chestnut-haired man with coal black eyes. It was Joe's arms holding me, Joe's lips moving against mine – and I didn't want him to stop. In that moment I understood. Regus *was* Joe…. or Joe was Regus, just as I was Haanu. Or had been, back then.

* * * * *

I opened my eyes. I was back in my bed, soaked in sweat despite the chill of the night, feeling extremely confused and disoriented. A full moon was shining in through the window, striking the light-catcher hanging there so that it sparkled like a giant star against the night sky.

'At last,' it seemed to be saying to me. 'We thought you would never wake up and remember.'

TO BE CONTINUED…

Thank you for reading Khalia's Tomb.
If you enjoyed it, I would very much appreciate it if you
would take a moment to leave a review at your favourite
online retailer. Thank you again.

D.K. Henderson

OTHER BOOKS IN THE SKULL CHRONICLES SERIES

LOST LEGACY
(Book I)

A beautiful young woman is entombed alive as a sacrifice to angry gods...

A young priest embarks upon a desperate flight across a hostile landscape deep in the heart of Atlantis...

In the possession of each, a sacred crystal skull.

England, 2012. With her life falling apart around her, Gemma Mason's sleep is increasingly disturbed by vivid dreams of crystal skulls, extraterrestrial beings and the ancient temples of Atlantis. Dreams that contain vital messages for us at this point in our history. As they unfold, Gemma realises she has been chosen to share a secret that will have repercussions for the whole of humankind.

Reluctantly she accepts her destiny and finds herself plunged into the forgotten history of an unknown world where myth and legend suddenly become irrefutably real. It is a journey that calls into question everything Gemma has ever believed to be true and demands that she faces her own deepest fears. For she is being asked to share with the world the shocking secret of our hidden past, a secret that will change forever the way we look at ourselves and our place in the universe. But are we ready to hear such a truth?

Travelling from the dense humidity of the rainforest to the desert lands of North America, from frozen Arctic wastelands to the cities and mountain ranges of Atlantis, Lost Legacy weaves past and present together seamlessly in a rollercoaster ride of emotion and adventure.

What readers say…

'An intriguing, nail biting, gripping, intricately woven, magnetic page turning read … Love, Love, Love this!!'

'Wow! From the moment I started reading this book through to the very last page I was completely immersed! I was in this story - I could see the people, feel their energy, anxiety, tension and happiness.'

'If you like adrenalin pumping action and stories that leave you guessing what the next page will reveal, this is the book for you. It made me laugh, it made me cry and it made my heart pound with anticipation and excitement from start to finish.'

'This book was recommended to me and is not the sort of thing I would normally read, but wow! I couldn't put it down!'

THE RED SKULL OF ALDEBARAN
(Book II)

The adventure continues…

Gor-Kual: the red skull whose origins lie on the distant star worlds of Aldebaran…

Gemma Mason: an ordinary Englishwoman, chosen by these ancient sacred skulls to be their mouthpiece, sharing their stories through her writing…

In this fast-paced sequel to Lost Legacy, the story of Gor-Kual unfolds, from the barren plateau of an ancient land to the fabled continent of Atlantis and, ultimately, the empty deserts of North Africa: a story of loss, heartbreak, courage, sacrifice and love, all to protect this most powerful and sacred of objects.

Meanwhile, in 2013, Gemma is undertaking a quest of her own, travelling to the deserts of the south west USA with a group of maverick archaeologists in search of the blue skull Gal-Athiel, whose story was told in Lost Legacy. As her own journey of self-discovery unfolds further, Gemma is forced once more to step beyond the boundaries of her fears. What will she find there?

What readers say…

'Even better than the first one.'…'I couldn't put it down'…'Excellent read.'

DAUGHTER OF THE GODS
(Book III)

The game turns deadly

Maat-su, daughter of the gods. Object of beauty and power brought to Earth to watch over the human race. Lusted after for tens of thousands of years by those who sought to use her for their own dark purposes.

Maat-su, the lapis lazuli skull, created on a world far from our own. Present at the birth of the first great civilisation of Atlantis, rescued at its fall and carried half way across the world to guide the emergence of a second. One whose legacy strikes wonder into hearts even today.

Far in the future, in 2013, Gemma Mason returns home to England after an abortive expedition through the deserts of Arizona in search of the blue obsidian skull, Gal-Athiel. Wanting only to return to her quiet life, Gemma soon realises this is not to be. After a series of murders, break-ins, and a disturbing encounter with a sinister stranger it becomes clear that someone else is looking for the skulls. Someone who is prepared to stop at nothing.

Will Gemma be their next target?

What readers say…

'Absolutely enthralling. I was completely absorbed by the story of the crystal skulls and the journey they took with

OTHER BOOKS BY THIS AUTHOR

FORGOTTEN WINGS
(Dawn Henderson)

Is your life filled with Life? Or do you feel that somehow you're missing the point but don't quite know why?

We are all born with glorious powerful wings that will carry us through life joyfully and effortlessly if we let them. But all too often we forget their existence and they lie dormant and unused.

In Forgotten Wings, Dawn Henderson offers us 10 simple keys to remembering our wings and opening up to the magical and limitless potential of life. Knowledge that seems new but is as old as existence.

Through the insights, wisdom and reawakened knowing she has received on her own on-going voyage of spiritual discovery, Dawn reminds us of who we truly are and why we have chosen to play this game of life. Guiding us gently by the hand, Dawn shows us how, by changing the way we perceive these 10 key areas, we can reawaken our wings and open them once again to the light.

'Uplifting & inspirational'...'An amazingly beautiful book'...'Wonderful self-help book'

'Keep a copy by your bed and take nightly doses to keep you sane' Kindred Spirit review (5 stars)

'This book is truly worth reading amongst all the books on the bookshelves out there'

ABOUT D.K. HENDERSON

D.K. Henderson lives in the beautiful county of Wiltshire, surrounded by its mysterious ancient landscape and stone monuments, which are an important source of inspiration for her writing.

She writes several occasional blogs and is passionate about spiritual development and the metaphysical side of life.

Please contact the author through her website at
www.dkhenderson.com

BLOGS:
www.soulwhispering.wordpress.com
www.thenakedheartblog.wordpress.com
www.thebigadventureblog.wordpress.com

WEBSITE:
www.dkhenderson.com

FACEBOOK:
www.facebook.com/DKHendersonAuthor

TWITTER
@DK_Henderson

GOODREADS
www.goodreads.com/author/show/6476514.D_K_Henderson

Printed in Great Britain
by Amazon

82917618R10222